Secrecy
Wars

Secrecy Wars

National Security, Privacy, and the Public's Right to Know

PHILIP H. MELANSON

Foreword by
Anthony Summers

BRASSEY'S, INC.
Washington, D.C.

Library of Congress Cataloging-in-Publication Data

Melanson, Philip H.
    Secrecy wars : national security, privacy, and the public's right to
know / Philip H. Melanson ; forword by Anthony Summers.—1st ed.
        p. cm.
    Includes bibliographical references.
    ISBN 1-57488-324-0 (alk. paper)
        1. Executive privilege (Government information)—United
States. 2. Official secrets—United States. 3. Security classification
(Government documents)—United States. 4. Freedom of informa-
tion—United States. 5. Government information—United States.
I. Title.

    JK468.S4 M45 2001
    323.44'8'09773—dc21

                                                        2001035332

ISBN 1–57488–324–0 (alk. paper)

Printed in the United States of America on acid-free paper that meets
the American National Standards Institute Z39-48 Standard.

Brassey's, Inc.
22841 Quicksilver Drive
Dulles, Virginia 20166

First Edition

10 9 8 7 6 5 4 3 2 1

To the thousands of dedicated government employees who competently and honestly try to balance legitimate secrecy with the public's right to know.

———

To the thousands of requesters whose dedicated pursuit of the freedom of information has enriched us all.

CONTENTS

LIST OF ACTS

with Dates Enacted

Freedom of Information Act (FOIA)	1966
Privacy Act	1974
CIA Information Act	1984
FOI Reform Act	1986
JFK Records Act	1992
Electronic FOI Improvements Act	1996

LIST OF ABBREVIATIONS
AND ACRONYMS

ACLU   American Civil Liberties Union

ARRB   Assassination Records Review Board (re JFK assassination)

CARS   Center for Atomic Radiation Studies

CIA   Central Intelligence Agency

COPA   Coalition on Political Assassinations

CORE   Congress of Racial Equality

FBI   Federal Bureau of Investigation

FOIA   Freedom of Information Act

GSA   General Services Administration

HSCA   House Select Committee on Assassinations

INS   Immigration and Naturalization Service

LEIU   Law Enforcement Intelligence Unit

NRO   National Reconnaissance Office

NSA   National Security Agency

OCID   Organized Crime Intelligence Division

FOREWORD

One afternoon some years ago, the telephone brought me intriguing and exciting news. My Washington attorney was calling to report that, before Marilyn Monroe's death in 1962, she had been the subject of an FBI "security" investigation. Later, at a special verbal briefing by FBI officials, my attorney learned that censored documents in the actress's file reflected contacts with President Kennedy's brother Robert just weeks before her death.

The younger Kennedy had apparently taken part in a luncheon discussion with Monroe about nuclear testing, at a time when the atom bomb was the most sensitive international issue of the day. The Cuban Missile Crisis, the moment the world came closest to nuclear war, was to occur just three months later. Since much of the Monroe security file is still withheld, we do not yet know its full significance. We would not know of its existence at all, though, were it not for the Freedom of Information Act.

Nobody knows more about this important law, known to those who use it as "the FOIA," than James Lesar, the attorney who got me—and thus hundreds of thousands of readers—tantalizingly close to that state secret about the Kennedys and Marilyn Monroe. Lesar, a FOIA specialist whose career is described in these pages, considers the act "perhaps the most important innovation in democratic theory since the Constitution." Professor Philip Melanson, this book's author, agrees. He has, moreover, pulled off what some might think impossible: the trick of making the nature and history of a little-understood law comprehensible and interesting.

The U.S. government is believed to be withholding some twenty-five million documents. If we define these as "secrets," some six million new ones are generated each year—most of them by the CIA, the Department of Defense, the FBI, and the State Department.

As in many European countries, secrecy in the United States was long an unassailable bastion of officialdom. With the passing of the Freedom of Information Act in 1966, however, the notion that the public has a "right to know" gained legal muscle. "No one," President Johnson declared that year, "should be able to put up curtains of secrecy around decisions that can be revealed without injury to the public interest."

Right! Yet FOIA has had a rough ride since then. Key agencies such as the CIA and the FBI have not taken kindly to the idea that files long inviolable should be open to the citizenry. Responsibly, Melanson lays out the arguments they make for continuing to withhold information. As one who has long done battle on the subject, he also tells the inside story of what has become a protracted paper war.

As Melanson puts it, and as I can confirm, the CIA has been the "stingiest," using every possible legal maneuver—and some not so legal—to keep its secrets, however ancient, just that—secret. The FBI, which under J. Edgar Hoover had abused civil liberties and snooped on politicians, has also doggedly sought ways to resist the FOIA.

The process of obtaining documents has become a duel, a potentially costly marathon. The filing systems of the intelligence agencies, for obvious reasons, are a labyrinth. Officials are not about to hand FOIA applicants the key. The expense of extracting information, the act says, should be reasonable. In reality, the cost can be high, the damage to applicants' pockets varying according to whether they are ordinary citizens, lawyers or historians, scientists or journalists. Long struggles ensue over whether agencies should waive fees, which they must do if the releases requested add to public understanding of government activity.

Another countertactic is foot dragging, often disastrous for authors and journalists. On paper, the act requires expeditious processing of requests. I have waited for documents, however, for more than six years.

That is longer than most authors can devote to the writing of a non-fiction book, as the agencies well know. It is now commonplace for releases to arrive long after a publication deadline. Speeding up the process involves recourse to the courts, itself time-consuming and scarily expensive.

When releases do arrive, it is also commonplace to discover that they have been massively censored by those Melanson calls the "secret keepers." These are the agency employees charged with deciding what should remain withheld even if a document is—in theory at least—made public. Primary justifying reasons for such withholdings are "privacy"—a provision designed to protect living individuals—and "national security." As I have discovered on numerous occasions, the latter pretext is widely abused. Whole pages are sometimes "released" with barely a word surviving below the letterhead. Proving abuse, again, usually involves costly litigation.

It turns out on occasion that agencies have done to documents what dictators have notoriously done to people. They have "disappeared" them, preempting FOIA suits simply by ordering that sensitive material be destroyed. When such destruction is discovered, the classic explanation is to claim it was "routine." Such was the case with Defense Department records potentially crucial to resolving one of the past century's greatest controversies. Subject: alleged presidential assassin Lee Harvey Oswald.

Melanson's book, although designed to illuminate a subject that many would think arcane, contains hidden treasure on this and other puzzles: the killings of Robert F. Kennedy and Dr. Martin Luther King, Jr.; the deliberate exposure of U.S. troops to atomic radiation; illegal or unacceptable spying on citizens and organizations by the CIA and the FBI; and insights into the lives of celebrities, from FBI Director Hoover to Beatle John Lennon.

Exotica aside, no thinking person can come away from this book without being struck by the essential truth at its core. Knowledge and understanding of the past is vital equipment for a society as it moves into its future. Transparency in government defines true democracy.

Anthony Summers
Ireland

PREFACE

The genesis of this book is my nearly three decades of involvement in obtaining documents from government (150,000 pages reside in my two offices and university archives). It is also rooted in the frequent, consistent questions I have been asked over the years by widely varying audiences. Whether my topic was Secret Service protection of the president, Central Intelligence Agency (CIA) covert operations, or the assassination of Dr. Martin Luther King, Jr., the questions were the same. Although the audiences varied from a political science seminar of twelve, to a national radio or television audience of tens of thousands, to retired military officers, to celebrants of African culture, and to grade school students, they would invariably ask: How can you get documents? How many secrets do they keep? Are there files on us? How does the law (Freedom of Information Act) work?

In my professional roles as author/researcher/professor/activist, almost everyone I encounter is not only familiar with the Freedom of Information Act (FOIA) and the Privacy Act (and governmental secrecy versus the public's right to know), they are actively involved with some facet of it. This is not the case with the vast majority of the American population, and it was not the case with me for some time. While everyone is aware that government keeps secrets (partly because we get such a heavy cultural dose of the world of espionage), few understand the complexities of the secrecy system and the conflicts that surround it.

There is an aura of mystery concerning classified files and how they might be released.

When the revolutionary Freedom of Information Act was passed in 1966, I was a senior political science major at the University of Connecticut. It was just another footnote on the political horizon, dutifully noted as part of my homework. It had no personal connection. When the Privacy Act of 1974 became law, I was teaching an upper-level political science class in which information policy was a topic. I had more than a passing interest.

My first FOIA request was in 1972. I asked the CIA for documents on the downing of its U-2 spy plane in the Soviet Union on May 1, 1960. "No releasable documents" were found. My curiosity had been piqued. Did I ask the right question? Was my request letter competent? Didn't they at least have some newspaper clippings to give me at ten cents a page? Were they supposed to tell me the number of pages they found and the reason(s) for not releasing them?

In the ensuing decades I would deal with such questions many, many times (with numerous federal agencies). I dealt most frequently with the CIA, Federal Bureau of Investigation (FBI), Secret Service, Nuclear Regulatory Commission, and Department of Defense (in that order). More than 100 requests and 150,000 pages later, I have learned a great deal about the secrecy process. My knowledge comes as much from the experts I have been privileged to work with—lawyers, academics, journalists, political activists—as from my personal experiences.

In offering what is hopefully a vivid portrait of the conflict between governmental secrecy and the public's right to know, this work does not claim to provide a definitive history or a reference-volume coverage of laws and policies regarding public disclosure. It is a highlight film of a complex legal/administrative/political game. It is intended to inform and to spark thought and interest. It is based on experience, observation, research, and analysis. The work is also a political view of the process from the perspective of a political scientist. Lawyers, bureaucrats, and journalists have different lenses through which to examine and interpret this arena.

Our collective understanding can benefit from varied perspectives on this shrouded dimension of our political life: one take is not enough to grasp all the problems and prospects.

Philip H. Melanson
Marion, Massachusetts
May 23, 2001

ACKNOWLEDGMENTS

My largest debt is to my wife, Judith, who edited, typed, and encouraged me on this project from start to finish, and without whom it would not be finished. My sons, Brett and Jess, were sources of encouragement, as was Judith's family.

The dedicated lawyers who have generously given their time and expertise to help me navigate the secrecy system in one corridor or another have my sincere gratitude: Jim Lesar, Dan Alcorn, Marilyn Barrett, Larry Teeter, and Dan Bernstein. Various kinds of assistance in obtaining files or reading documents were provided on numerous occasions by the following organizations (in order of their frequency): the Coalition on Political Assassinations, Assassination Archives and Research Center, National Archives, Center for National Security Studies, FOIA Inc., Assassination Records Review Board, University of Southern California Doheny Archive, and the southern California chapter of the American Civil Liberties Union.

The Robert F. Kennedy Assassination Archive at the University of Massachusetts-Dartmouth continues its special role of help and support for my work, going back to the now-retired Helen Koss and including archivist Judy Farrar and Patricia Sikora. My research assistant Kelly Syer gave valuable feedback on the early draft. My friend and colleague Clyde W. Barrow took his scarce time to help me rewrite the proposal and has helped keep me motivated. Political science department secretary Lisa Porto typed the proposal and most of the extensive correspondence. Congressman Barney Frank of Massachusetts supported some of my disclosure issues when others would not take a stand regarding FBI resistance.

I cannot thank individually the many dozens of people from all walks of life whom I have been privileged to work with on public disclosure in various venues. But I do want to single out the late Greg Stone and Floyd Nelson, as well as Paul Schrade, for their years of effort that culminated in the release of the Robert F. Kennedy assassination files. Also, John Judge (with his unwavering commitment to disclosure) was helpful and insightful, as was Bill Kelly.

Some important role models include the following people. Washington attorney Jim Lesar has persisted for decades as a tireless champion of the public's right to know and has single-handedly made a huge difference in the secrecy process. Sandra Marlow, as a citizen activist in the atomic veterans movement, taught me tenacity in the pursuit of information. Professor Peter Dale Scott's expertise at reading documents and understanding everything from their core meaning to their marginalia has been an inspiration, as has Tony Summers' ability to link politics and personalities to files, be it J. Edgar Hoover, Marilyn Monroe, Richard Nixon, or the anti-Castro Cubans.

The retired Helen Neer and her staff at the FBI reading room were very helpful during my peak years of documentary research in the 1980s. Four information and privacy coordinators dealt with my requests very extensively, and we exchanged numerous, often lengthy, correspondence concerning the various phases of my requests: James K. Hall and Emil P. Moschella of the FBI, and John E. Bacon and Larry R. Strawderman at the CIA. Their courteous professionalism made the conflicts easier to process even if the results were often disappointing.

I thank those who broke the standard rules of the game to leak me information, sometimes at considerable risk (real or imagined). While their agendas were usually different from mine and their actions were sometimes at odds with my moral compass, they all enlightened me even from their dark niches in the covert system.

My agent, Frank Weimann, has continued his support of and faith in my work through some rough times. His honesty and energy have benefited me greatly. Much thanks to Don McKeon of Brassey's for taking this project on and following it through so effectively, and to Don Jacobs for his editorial guidance.

INTRODUCTION

Secrecy and Democracy

I know no safe depository of the ultimate powers of society but the people themselves, and if we think them not enlightened enough to exercise their control with a wholesome direction, the remedy is not to take it from them but to inform their discretion.

—Thomas Jefferson

I t is generally, if not universally, agreed that a democratic political system requires an *adequate* and *effective* level of public information. The question has always been: What is this level? Democracy requires an informed citizenry, a free press, the public's right to know, and institutional checks and balances. These ideals cannot be achieved without a free flow of information. But how much—some, all, whatever leaders decide? Information *is* power. Without it, the public, the press, and Congress are powerless.

How can citizens render informed opinions on defense and foreign policy if military operations are covert and diplomatic negotiations are secret? How can Congress control military spending if billions of dollars are spent for weapons so secret that their function, design, and specific costs are withheld by the Pentagon (the so-called "black budget")? How does the press report on the environmental hazards of weapons plants when the relevant data is "Top Secret"? How can a person correct a false, malicious entry in their FBI file if they are not aware that the file exists?

1

No government, no matter how totalitarian, can keep everything secret from its people, although many have tried. The repressive communist regimes of China and the former Soviet Union have come as close as possible. No democracy tells its citizens everything. Where is the United States on this continuum? The People's Republic of China is near one end; Sweden (generally acknowledged to have the most open government) is at or near the opposite end. The United States is somewhere between the middle and the open end—more open than our sister democracy, the United Kingdom. The British Official Secrets Act is, without a doubt, more restrictive.*

Our position on the continuum is in constant flux. The balance between governmental secrecy and the public's right to know is not a fixed point established by the founding fathers. It is constantly evolving— and not always in the direction of greater freedom. As we shall see, there have been dramatic shifts from the 1960s to the present, in both directions.

Our secrecy system is vast and complex. It affects virtually every facet of politics and public policy—and of our lives. The U.S. government creates an estimated six million secrets a year. These range from single pages to massive files. In fiscal year 1996 alone, classification "actions" increased by 2.2 million.[1] The super-secret National Security Agency stores its hard copies of satellite-intercepted messages in half a million cubic feet of building space. Military records starting at World War II consume twenty-seven acres of underground storage at a site in Maryland.[2] The secret makers, those who can classify a document top secret with the hit of a stamp, are estimated at more than a half million.[3] In vaults at the CIA, State Department, Justice Department, Pentagon, and other agencies, there are a staggering four to five *billion* secrets (one and a half billion were created before 1970). If all of the classified documents were stacked in a pile, they would be three times as tall as one of the most prominent symbols of freedom—the Washington Monument. There are more than 200 statutes that affect governmental secrecy.

---

*The British model had been proposed for adoption in the United States. This option will be discussed in chapter 8.

Agencies process nearly 500,000 Freedom of Information Act requests a year, at a cost of $200 million.

The secrecy system is out of control. Its growth seems unstoppable. Periodically, "sunset laws" are proposed to curb it. Under such laws, after a fixed number of years (twenty or twenty-five), documents would automatically be declassified unless their secrecy was renewed. All such proposals have been defeated as too risky. Presidential orders for periodic declassification have, without exception, been met with delay and resistance by federal agencies. The administrative burdens of declassifying are alleged to be overwhelming. Within the bureaucracy the urge not to process documents for release remains strong. Secrets continue to pile up in volumes that could bury entire city blocks in the nation's capital.

Prior to passage of the Freedom of Information Act of 1966, the public had no effective legal right to request information about its government. Before the Privacy Act of 1974, there was no specific legal right to request information about yourself.* These revolutionary advances in the public's right to know are themselves in a state of continual evolution, shifting on their own continua as they are strengthened and weakened by congressional revisions, court decisions, and presidential orders.

At any given point in time, the quantity of information made public by our government is shaped by numerous factors and entities. The Supreme Court and federal courts play a major role. In case after case, they decide if the "public interest" in disclosure outweighs agency claims of secrecy, thus broadening or narrowing the Freedom of Information and Privacy statutes. Judges sit in chambers reading top-secret CIA documents to decide the fate of their secrecy or disclosure.

Presidents create executive orders defining the policies and standards for the secrecy system. In 1983 President Ronald Reagan issued Executive Order 12333, arguably the most restrictive pro-secrecy directive in the last three decades. Within the broad government-wide

---

*The Freedom of Information Act was signed by President Johnson in 1966 and became effective in 1967. The Privacy Act was signed by President Ford in 1974 and was operative in 1975. While some works refer to these statutes by their operational dates, most (including this one) cite them by the years that they were signed into law.

system of statutes and presidential requirements, agencies have their own processes and policies for classifying and releasing documents. The information cultures and secrecy systems of the CIA and the National Archives are worlds apart, despite their existence within the same federal structure of laws and guidelines. Congress, the courts, the president, and governmental agencies all have a profound impact on the key variables of the secrecy system:

- *Classification:* What are the standards? When is a document stamped "classified," "secret," or "top secret"?
- *Declassification:* How are billions of backlogged secrets dealt with? What are the criteria and schedules for release?
- *Legal punishments:* What are the penalties for leaking secrets to the press or public? Are they severe, wide ranging?
- *Legal access:* What are the statutes that allow entrée to the secrecy system?
- *Recall:* If agencies perceive that they have mistakenly released documents that may cause harm, what are the laws allowing for their recall and the legal penalties for noncompliance?
- *Cost:* Is the price of requesting and obtaining information affordable or prohibitive and for whom (law firms, corporations, college students)?
- *Destruction/preservation:* If agencies discard the junk but keep "historically valuable" material, at what pace should this be done, and what is the definition of "value"? (It takes resources both to preserve and to destroy files.)

The impact of where the balance lies is profound. A functioning democratic political system requires congressional and presidential oversight of the agencies; checks and balances among the legislative, executive, and judicial branches; knowledgeable voters; and a watchdog media. The criminal justice system depends upon information. Lawyers are estimated to be among the most frequent users of the Freedom of Information Act, whether their clients are corporations facing antitrust suits or accused individuals fighting for their freedom. The quality of the legal process has been enhanced by the access of both defense and prosecution to government files.[4]

History also benefits. If history is not what happened but what the surviving evidence says happened, then disclosure of government records is vital to our understanding of the past and is a guidepost for the future. Change the available evidence and history is changed. Documents on the Japanese attack at Pearl Harbor, U.S. nuclear testing in the 1950s, the Vietnam War, the U.S. government's experimental testing of human subjects, and the covert operations of U.S. intelligence agencies at home and abroad can prove extremely enlightening. Access to these records provides a clearer picture of how decisions were made and how they affected the successes and failures of these events. If records are destroyed or are accessible to only a select elite of former officials, then our history becomes "official history." We are left with government reports, government-commissioned histories, and self-serving memoirs—with no informed, independent analysis.

Secrecy shapes the direction of scientific research. It also affects the return on the scarce dollars we spend for it. Military and intelligence agencies duplicate the same expensive studies in a wide variety of fields and fail to share the data. Scientific research is enhanced by the free flow of information; secrecy cuts it off. The result is a paralyzing waste of brainpower. Classified research is not a small, esoteric portion of U.S. scientific inquiry: approximately seventy-five cents of every federal research dollar goes toward national-defense-related projects.

The space program did provide a number of technological discoveries that were applied to civilian life—including a powdered orange drink (Tang). In contrast, thousands of discoveries in chemistry, biology, computer science, and human and animal behavior that would be extremely valuable in the search for medical cures, environmental preservation, and new technologies have never been effectively mined or utilized. They are classified beyond the reach of civilian researchers. While no responsible observer would argue for the release of formulas for nerve gas and biological weapons, one can only imagine the related discoveries about the human central nervous system produced by defense researchers over the decades (discoveries relevant to a host of health and safety problems).

Undeniably, there are legitimate secrets to be kept. But there is no agreement on which ones or how many. There is a consensus for withholding information on such matters as the locations of nuclear missiles, the identities of undercover drug-enforcement agents, or commercial processes (for example, a manufacturer's formula for hair restoration). More typically, however, the definition of legitimate secrecy is a subject of ideological debate and clashing priorities (national security versus the public's right to know).

This is further complicated by the Machiavellian dimension of the politics of information. Organizations have a proprietary interest in the knowledge that they possess, even within the planning process of domestic policy agencies. As Guy Benvenisti puts it in *The Politics of Expertise:*

> Contrary to conventional wisdom, the secrecy that prevails in any bureaucracy, instead of being a deterrent, is an asset of planning. Given enough time, planners acquire information that they can exchange for different kinds of favors. Moreover, their access to facts and figures differentiates them politically from other contenders surrounding the Prince.[5]

Reporter Evan Thomas put it more succinctly: "Bureaucrats like secrets. They will go to absurd lengths to keep secrets from other bureaucrats."[6]

Nonlegitimate secrets abound. Agencies sometimes withhold information in order to cover up their mistakes or scandals. The following chapters are replete with examples. The problem in a democracy is that it is very difficult to distinguish a legitimate secret from a nonlegitimate one if you do not know the substance of the secret (or even of its existence), that is, if you are on the outside peering in through the veil of secrecy.

Governments also lie—even democratic ones. Is this justified? If so, under what circumstances? How often can a government deceive its people before it is no longer a healthy democracy?

After the Cuban Missile Crisis of 1963, Arthur Sylvester, Assistant Secretary of Defense for Public Affairs, made himself an instant historical footnote by asserting, "It is inherent in government's right, if necessary, to lie to save itself when it is going up into nuclear war *[sic]*."[7] As

Victor Zora observed in the *Washington Post* in 1965, the reality is that "the intelligence agencies of the democratic countries suffer from the grave disadvantage that in attempting to deceive the adversary they must also deceive their own public."[8]

Another threat to democracy involves violations of rights to privacy created by new technologies. While traditional privacy issues still exist, such as invasions into people's houses by law enforcement and the regulation of sexual practices, the capacity for illegal surveillance has increased exponentially in the last decade. The United States has a spy satellite system capable of monitoring and recording millions of phone calls here and in Europe. This mountain of data is processed and utilized within a highly secret technological maze that is understood by only a handful of technicians and policymakers. We have official assurances that the privacy of ordinary citizens is not threatened.

In what has been termed "the cult of secrecy," secrecy is seen as absolutely necessary, if not inherently desirable, and generally more precious than the public's right to know. A frustrated Senator J. William Fulbright, chair of the Senate Foreign Relations Committee, complained in 1971 that "secrecy . . . has become a god in this country, and those people who have secrets travel in a kind of fraternity . . . and they will not speak to anyone else."[9] His senate colleague John Stennis had a more accommodating view:

> You have to make up your mind that you are going to have an intelligence agency and protect it as such, and shut your eyes some and take what is coming.[10]

The antidemocratic manipulations of secrecy are not the product of fertile political imaginations: they are very real. "National security" has been misappropriated to hide illegal arms sales, drug trafficking, and covert operations not approved by Congress and/or the president. Secrecy has been distorted by the FBI to hide its surveillance of political leaders and celebrities whose rights to privacy were violated by the Bureau. The public policy debate regarding Vietnam was distorted by governmental secrecy and the manipulation of information. Innocent citizens have had their lives ruined by mistaken or malicious reports about them, which they never knew existed, much less were able to rebut. These personally damaging reports were hidden by false or over-zealous applications of "privacy" or "national security."

The ability of U.S. democracy to deal effectively with these issues is impaired by the superficial treatment often accorded them. My own dis-cipline is no exception. Political science textbooks for both introductory and upper-level students tend to neglect the importance and complexity of governmental secrecy. Many offer simplistic, sometimes pious, gener-alizations as to how well things are working.

One introductory text has only one-half page on the topic, under the heading "Bureaucratic Secrecy." It contends that "electoral pressures have sharply curtailed the amount of secrecy in American government."[11] The authors then quote a prominent political scientist who observes that "secrecy has less legitimacy as a governmental practice in the United States than any other advanced industrial society with the possible exception of Sweden."[12] The textbook reassures introductory students: "Secrecy is hard for agencies to preserve, even when it is both permitted and essential." No wonder the issues are so little understood: they are sometimes not even recognized. Many of the cases in the pages to come will severely challenge such optimistic views.

At the opposite extreme, we find equally simplistic assessments. The dark end of the spectrum holds that the government, the intelligence agencies, or the military-industrial complex are so omnipotent and ruth-less that the freedom-of-information process is little more than a civic farce. It also claims that nothing, or very little, that matters to govern-ment is ever released. This pessimistic extreme can also be put to rest. Significant disclosures *do* come from the most secretive of agencies, such as the CIA. This information has sometimes had a significant, positive impact on our public policy (as well as on the accountability of the agen-cies themselves).

Secrecy Wars is an analysis of the ongoing battle between secret keepers and those seeking access; between those who value national security or privacy more than the public right to know and those who hold the opposite position; between agencies seeking to shield them-selves from the burdens and consequences of the disclosure process and citizens who demand greater accountability. Whether as combatants,

CHAPTER 1

Your Right to Know

The assumption behind the [Freedom of Information] Act is that taxpayers support the development of information and thus have a right to it. More importantly, the act is built on the belief that control over bureaucracy and government, essential to democracy, is impossible without information about what government is doing.[1]

—Joseph Cayer and Louis F. Weschler,
Public Administration, 1988

Secret keeping in the United States has been present since the nation's inception. The Constitutional Convention was held behind closed doors. President George Washington refused to provide Congress with the documents used in the negotiation of Secretary of State John Jay's Treaty with Great Britain. More than a century and a half later, President Franklin D. Roosevelt issued the executive orders creating the modern secrecy system.[2] He also enhanced the political surveillance function of the FBI. After Hitler invaded Poland, Roosevelt instructed Director J. Edgar Hoover to publicly announce that the Bureau would surveil communists, Nazis, and other extremists. This measure was designed to calm the citizenry and frighten "extremists."[3]

Since World War II, however, the size and complexity of the secrecy system have grown exponentially. As far back as 1964, Secretary of Defense Robert S. McNamara revealed to the Senate Foreign Relations Committee that the top-secret clearance for access to information was already obsolete, as indicated by his testimony:

Secretary McNamara: Clearance is above Top Secret for the particular information involved in this situation.

Senator Albert Gore, Sr.: . . . would you please clear up the exact identity of this clearance status that is something superior to Top Secret . . .? I would like to be informed. I never heard of this kind. I thought Top Secret was Top Secret.

Secretary McNamara: . . . Mr. Chairman, may I try to answer it. . . . There are a host of different clearances. I would guess I have perhaps twenty-five. There are certain clearances to which only a handful of people in the government is exposed. There are others with broader coverage, and overlapping coverage, and it is not really a question of degree of clearance. It is a question of need to know, and need to know clearances apply to certain forms of data. . . . There is another clearance, Q clearance, which relates to certain categories of information.

There is another clearance which is the special intelligence clearance we are talking about, that relates to intercept information, and it is this latter clearance in particular that is at issue here, and the staff members of this committee have not been cleared for that kind of information. . . . I do not want to get into a further discussion until the room is cleared of those not authorized to handle it.[4]

The "public's right to know" has always existed as an ideal within our democratic system. Defining this right has been a constant and uneven evolution. In 1966 a revolutionary event occurred: the passage of the Freedom of Information Act (FOIA). In the nearly two centuries that preceded it, there was no effective legal right for citizens to obtain information from their government. People could sue the government to compel release of information about them, but only within the narrow legal venue of proving that government was acting maliciously against them. No legally defined right existed to obtain information about government itself: how it operated, what it had done, and how it had made a decision. Whether it was a citizen, a news organization, or a corporation, information could be requested, but government could—and usually did—refuse. No legal recourse existed for such denials.

There were laws granting limited access to certain records. Some information did flow to the public. FOIA, however, created a process by which citizens were entitled to information unless government could prove otherwise. The public's right to know is shaped by many factors as described in the introduction (the political climate, federal policies, court decision, agency behavior, executive orders, and so on). As powerful as these influences are, FOIA is the centerpiece of public disclosure. It is the focus of the political struggle over conflicting priorities and ideologies.

While requests for documents are made singularly by individuals or organizations, the process has a cumulative, societal impact. A journalist obtains data on overspending by the Pentagon. Through the resulting newspaper article, the president, Congress, and the public are informed. A historian writes a book based on military and intelligence files, providing valuable insights on Vietnam policies to be read by the public and policymakers alike. A vetting of past CIA covert activities informs the public and Congress concerning what the nation's ethical and policy positions were, and ought to be. In short, FOIA made government more open and subject to scrutiny than at any time in our history. Some releases of information have little or no impact on the political system and its issues and policies; others have a momentous impact. But the cumulative effect is collective and system-wide.

As with all revolutions, an intense struggle occurred at its inception, the outcomes uncertain both before and after passage of the law. From 1966 to the present, the political conflicts have been a constant element: expand FOIA, kill it, keep the status quo. Not only was the basic concept of legally defined citizen access revolutionary, but so also was the ultimate design of the statute. On the one hand, it was not intended to be a carte blanche entrée to the secrecy system: government could still withhold documents and was given nine legal justifications for so doing. On the other hand, FOIA was not a narrowly defined, esoteric access that few could use or that applied to only a small segment of the secrecy system. Its goals were lofty. As President Lyndon Johnson stated when signing the bill:

> This legislation springs from one of our most essential principles: A democracy works best when the people have all the information that the security of the nation permits. No one should be able to put up curtains of secrecy around decisions that can be revealed without injury to the public interest.[5]

The government "records" to which the law applied were broadly defined. Individuals asking for information were not required to explain their reason(s) or intended use. Requesters did not have to be U.S. citizens. The law provided that "any person" (or organization) could make a request with the same legal rights as anyone else. This is still the case despite strong criticism and opposition over the decades. A countering argument has been that foreign nationals could use *our* law to obtain information from *our* government. These individuals included communists, terrorists, and other enemies or political opponents of the United States. And the rub was that we subsidized this nefarious access to our secrecy system, spending tax dollars to find and deliver the data. In other words, patriotism, jingoism, and anticommunism were galvanized by the law's provision of access to noncitizens.

As part of the political compromise that is typical of landmark legislation, there were exceptions to the law. Those agencies that opposed its passage (and virtually all did) would continue to try to avoid it by having themselves exempted from its purview. Most agencies failed. The CIA would partially succeed in 1984 and the FBI would be partially successful in 1995. Records included and excluded under FOIA are as follows:

Governmental Entities
Whose Records Are Subject to FOIA

- All "agencies," "departments," "regulatory commissions," "government controlled corporations," and "other establishments" within the executive branch.
- Cabinet offices (such as the departments of Defense, Justice, Treasury, and State). This includes the agencies housed within the Justice Department: FBI, Immigration and Naturalization Service, and the Bureau of Prisons.
- Independent regulatory commissions, such as the Federal Communications Commission, the Nuclear Regulatory Commission, and the Consumer Product Safety Commission.
- Presidential commissions. These exist for a fixed term and are usually created to study problems and recommend policies regarding such matters as airline safety and CIA domestic spying (perhaps the

most famous is the Warren Commission, created by President Johnson in 1964 to investigate the assassination of President Kennedy).
- The Executive Office of the President. The White House bureaucracy that works directly for the president, including the Office of Management and Budget, the National Security Council, and the Council of Economic Advisors.

Governmental Entities
Whose Records Are Excluded from FOIA

- The United States Congress
- The federal courts
- The president and his immediate staff (chief of staff, press secretary, national security advisor)
- Private corporations
- Organizations that receive federal funding but are not controlled or administered by the government (the American Red Cross, the Corporation for Public Broadcasting)
- State and local governments[6]

The debate over FOIA's passage was intense partly because the political system was entering uncharted territory. Agencies put forth an apocalyptic scenario of the consequences. Criminals would use the law to evade FBI capture. Soviet spies would pillage CIA secrets. The State Department would be unable to conduct sensitive negotiations with foreign countries. Tax cheaters would flaunt the Internal Revenue Service. Trade secrets for everything from bubble gum to birth control pills would be ripped off from the Federal Trade Commission. Military personnel would be at greater risk in times of conflict. U.S. agents would be assassinated when their covers were blown. No one would dare be an informant for a federal agency. The costs of implementation in terms of human resources (then referred to as manpower) and dollars would break the bureaucracy. Organized crime would run amok while FBI employees labored over frivolous requests. Government would cease to function effectively, paralyzed by a deluge of invasive demands for information.

The other side of the debate conjured up an impressive litany of democratic ideals: the public's right to know, governmental accountability, effective checks and balances, a more informed citizenry. It also asserted that the law's safeguards would protect government functions. Agencies still controlled their secrets: they could refuse requests using one of the nine exemptions. Outsiders would never see a secret unless the agency released it or a court compelled its disclosure after determining that there was no harm. The costs in resources would be well worth it, creating a revitalized democracy. Because of the increased scrutiny, agencies would become more efficient and more responsive to Congress and the public. Everyone would win. Moreover, it was time for this change after 190 years of keeping the public estranged from its own government. The secrecy cloak had too often been abused to cover up malfeasance and stupidity.

After the bill was passed, both sides nervously assessed the outcome. Apart from the hyperbole about democratic ideals on the one hand and bureaucratic disaster on the other, no one really knew exactly what the impact would be. The first few years of FOIA produced middle-of-the-road results. Government did not grind to a snail's pace. Criminals and terrorists did not reign. Bureaucracy and democracy were not radically transformed for the better. Agencies and requesters alike floundered in the act's vague definitions and unclear procedures. Secret keepers and pro-disclosure interests competed for advantage in fleshing out the new process. By and large, the agencies resisted the law—some mildly, others fiercely. In 1966 and 1967, the FBI exerted maximum pressure on the Justice Department for a complete exemption of its files.

Significant information *was* released. The public, Congress, and the media gained more insight into government operations than ever before. Media reports citing "documents obtained through the Freedom of Information Act" became increasingly common. But the law remained a relatively elite, if not arcane, tool used predominantly by four groups: citizens curious about their own files, reporters working a story, academics conducting research, and lawyers working a case.

One prominent media spin was that Congress had created a windfall for the legal profession—an extremely useful tool provided free or with a taxpayer subsidy (this was in an era in which lawyers were not the target of negative stereotypes that sought to portray them as a societal scourge). As a *Washington Post* article assessing FOIA's debut described:

> The boxes [29 boxes at the Federal Trade Commission] were in response to a single Freedom of Information Act request from a lawyer on a fishing expedition, a symbol of a law that has not worked out exactly as planned. . . . "Everybody over there [lawyers requesting data from the Food and Drug Administration] is on a big fishing expedition for new information on pharmaceuticals," says one freedom of information specialist with a big law firm.[7]

By the early 1970s it had become clear that FOIA was not working as Congress had intended and supporters had hoped. Bad press was the least of its problems. Some agencies were conducting administrative guerrilla warfare against it. The Congress, energized by Watergate, by executive branch deceptions about Vietnam, and by revelations of disturbing (if not illegal) activities by intelligence and law enforcement agencies, was ready to strengthen the act. In 1974, to save the law from becoming a hollow symbol of public disclosure, Congress took action.

Agencies had been subverting the process by taking months, or indefinite periods, to respond to requests. They often charged a dollar per page for copying documents when the going rate was a few cents. Congress's ire was piqued by the discovery that some agencies kept files on its members.

Colorful New York Congresswoman Bella Abzug, wearing her signature wide-brimmed hat, read excerpts from her CIA file into the congressional record. She had obtained it using FOIA. It went back twenty-two years to her days as a lawyer and political activist.[8] Congressman Charles Porter of Oregon found that the CIA had a file on him as well. He was given seventeen documents under FOIA. One included a report on his attendance at a meeting of the Congress of Racial Equality (a civil rights group). An irate Porter responded: "What the hell does that have to do with the CIA? They're treating me like a security risk."[9]

Congress strengthened the act. Agencies must reply to requesters within ten working days. Copying costs were to be at normal commercial rates. Agencies were required to devote resources to administering the law and to report annually to Congress on their FOIA activities and compliance. Perhaps most significant, the federal courts were written into the law as the arbiters of the disclosure process. President Gerald Ford vetoed the changes; Congress overrode him with a two-thirds majority. The reforms were law.

The inclusion of the courts was a major change. Requesters now had a specifically defined, legal right to appeal an agency's rejection. Congress put the burden of proof squarely on the agency to show that the withholding was justified. In essence, Congress was bringing the court system to bear on the bureaucracy, to enforce the public disclosure process. This would have a profound and lasting impact on the secrecy system and on the public's access to it.

Congress's specific inclusion of the courts stemmed in major part from a confrontation with the Nixon administration (for which Congress had developed a deep distrust, culminating in presidential impeachment hearings and Nixon's resignation in August 9, 1974). In 1971 the administration approved underground nuclear tests in Alaska. Experts gave conflicting assessments of the environmental risks. The National Security Agency (NSA) compiled a report on the safety issues, but it was classified. Congress was refused access.

In federal district court, the NSA's refusal was upheld, simply on the basis of the agency claiming "national security." A federal appeals court partially overturned the decision and ordered the release of pages not related to national security (the appeals court had actually seen the report; the lower court had not). The government appealed to the Supreme Court and won: the high court ruled that the appeals court had erred in ordering the release of any of the report. In its sweeping opinion, the Supreme Court stated that courts do not have the authority to review information classified by government. Courts could only review the agency's compliance with the procedure for disclosure, not the substance of what was withheld.

Essentially, FOIA was eviscerated. Agencies could now refuse disclosure and no court could stop them, provided the procedures of the law were followed. Congress responded to the high court's decision by giving the courts a substantive as well as procedural role in monitoring FOIA. In addition to interpretations of legal precedent and practice, judges were now empowered to read documents and decide if their release would threaten "national security," or whether the public's right to know was overriding.

Time magazine glowingly reported that the 1974 reforms were working and that FOIA requests had drastically increased throughout the federal government; the FBI was experiencing a "sixteenfold increase": "As a result [of the reform]," said *Time,* "officials are speedily granting many of the requests for information, a mass of formerly withheld material is being turned over to academic researchers, reporters, and other citizens."[10]

This perceived renaissance in the public's right to know would be relatively short-lived. The setting in which all political issues exist changes over time; interest group alignments and political values shift. In the late 1970s and early 1980s, the ideological climate changed, and the political pendulum began to swing toward secrecy. Congressional distrust of the presidency and of intelligence and law enforcement agencies had diminished. Key congressional liberals who had championed accountability and disclosure, like Idaho Senator Frank Church, had retired or been defeated. A "conservative revolution" held sway in Washington—pro-defense, pro-intelligence, pro–law enforcement. Ronald Wilson Reagan was president.

Media criticism of FOIA escalated. A quintessential example is the 1980 *Reader's Digest* article written by author John Barron, who had written a book on the Soviet KGB: "Congress passed the Freedom of Information and Privacy Acts with the best of intentions, but criminals and spies have perverted that intent to hobble the work of our law-enforcement agencies." A series of anecdotal horror stories alleged that criminals, terrorists, and spies were using the public disclosure laws to undermine our government: "A laughing Soviet KGB officer told a confidant (actually a U.S. spy) that the Russians systematically exploit such laws to extract information. . . ."[11]

If this was so, it was the fault of the secret keepers for not effectively administering the withholding process. It was not the fault of the law or a consequence of who decided to use it. The insider nature of Barron's piece was revealed by his claim that "some 500 persons affiliated with the Communist Party last year demanded information from FBI files." This is an interesting assertion since requesters are not required to state their purpose or affiliations. Did the Bureau run a records check on the names of those seeking information?

In the early 1980s, the Reagan administration launched a full-scale assault on FOIA. Executive Order 12356 ended the thirty- to fifty-year limit on classification. No longer did agencies have to show *identifiable* damage resulting from release, as President Carter had required. Documents could now be classified in perpetuity, so long as required by national security considerations. Government could reclassify previously released documents at its discretion. Secret keepers were ordered to classify material at the highest possible level, reversing the order of President Carter that it be at the lowest level possible.

President Reagan proposed to Congress a series of FOIA reforms that were not passed: allowing agencies eighteen months to respond to requests, limiting requests to one per year per person, increasing fees ten times over. Law enforcement agencies, led by the FBI, stepped up the pressure for broadening their exemptions from FOIA, claiming that their effectiveness was being severely handicapped. In 1983 the Senate Judiciary Committee approved a compromise bill (S774) that would have drastically altered FOIA's timetables, fees, and scope to the detriment of the requester. That bill did not pass. In 1986 Congress did pass the FOI Reform Act, which made it considerably more difficult for requesters to qualify for fee waivers of the costs of finding and copying documents.* In the opposite direction, Congress expanded FOIA to include electronic records, which was a major pro-disclosure change. Overall, FOIA had been considerably weakened by this onslaught compared with its invigoration by Congress's 1974 changes. But it had escaped the extreme measures proposed by its most strident opponents, such as Republican Senator Orrin Hatch—measures designed to severely narrow and weaken it.

The political ebb and flow of the public's right to know, and of its legal centerpiece, continue with each new presidency. A highlight of the efforts of George H. W. Bush's administration to reduce available information

---

*The FOI Reform Act is described in chapter 2.

concerning government was a proposed "ethics bill." It sought to make it a crime to reveal nonsecrets. In 1989, one month after President Bush signed a proclamation celebrating "Freedom of Information Day," this proposed law was sent to Congress. The law made it a criminal offense to reveal *non*classified information that *"would* [emphasis added] be damaging to the interests of government" (such as insider information on trade negotiations with foreign countries). Restrictions applied even after a person had left federal employment. This open-ended gag order would preclude the disclosure of millions of pages of documents releasable under FOIA.[12] It would also make it very difficult for former policymakers to write memoirs about their government experiences. The bill did not pass.

The Clinton administration sought to roll back some of the restrictions created by its predecessors. In contrast to President Reagan's executive orders, Clinton issued order 12958 which made older secrets more accessible.* Any classified document twenty-five years old or older was to be automatically declassified within five years, unless it fell into a narrowly defined category that justified continued secrecy.[13] These categories included protection of informants, data "assisting in the development of weapons of mass destruction," or information that would "clearly and demonstrably damage national security." The latter was a reversal of the Reagan standard for withholding, which was that documents were withheld if they *could* cause damage. Clinton Deputy Secretary of Defense John Hamre openly expressed his opposition to secrecy reforms that sought to broaden access: "The 'public interest' in the content of the information should not be a consideration," he asserted.[14]

The positive outcome of the Clinton reform was that more of these decades-old secrets were released between 1995 and 1997 than in all of the previous sixteen years.[15] But most agencies strongly opposed Clinton's declassification order and did not meet its timetable. They were hundreds of millions of pages behind in the mandated, five-year disclosure

---

*During FOIA hearings before Congress in 1966, it was revealed that information regarding the strategic uses of mules by the Union Army during the Civil War still bore its classification stamp.

plan. In 1999 Clinton extended his year 2000 deadline eighteen months. In 1997 the Republican-controlled House of Representatives passed a bill slashing the funding for declassification of intelligence agency documents by 50 percent.

Still, impressive disclosures were accomplished. The CIA alone released one million pages in 1998, two million in 1999, and a whopping five million in 2000. Agency Director George J. Tenet called the latter "the largest release of formerly classified CIA documents ever." The material included intelligence reports from 1947 to the 1970s, which chronicle world events as well as the creation and emerging mission of the Agency.[16] By August of 2000 an estimated 600 million pages had been released. But the process was further slowed by Congress's fears that nuclear secrets might slip out. A specific agency review for nuclear secrets was mandated. In the case of 4,500 documents on foreign policy held by the JFK presidential library, the CIA came to Boston in 1998 and took the documents (now on disks) back to Washington, D.C., for page-by-page scanning for nuclear secrets. The agency then returned them, and they were finally released in August 2000. JFK library archivist Maura Porter told the press, "It's sort of a long process."[17]

In 1995 President Clinton also created a separate disclosure process for national security records. Instead of requesting documents under FOIA, people could now opt for "mandatory classification review." A panel composed of representatives from various agencies would review the classification of the requested documents and decide whether they should be made public. In September of 2000, the panel reported to the president that, for the fourth straight year, it had reversed a majority of agency classification decisions and ordered release in 174 of 218 cases of agency withholding. As promising as this sounds, the new option has not fundamentally altered the balance between secrecy and disclosure. It has been little used compared with FOIA. Moreover, requesters opting for the mandatory-review process give up their FOIA rights for the particular request. The Reporters' Committee for Freedom of the Press advises: "You should probably choose to file a FOIA request rather than seek declassification review if you have a large, open-ended request that covers many classified and unclassified documents."[18]

In another area of FOIA policy, Clinton would sorely disappoint pro-disclosure advocates, despite their five years of concerted lobbying of the administration. President Carter had issued an executive order requiring that the public interest in releasing documents be balanced against the potential harm it might cause. President Ronald Reagan eliminated this balance test by *his* executive order. Instead of restoring the Carter principle as advocates had urged, President Clinton's order made the balance test optional. Professor Jon Wiener, a historian who is heavily involved with FOIA, observed that Clinton had "made the balance test useless" by giving the agencies the option of not using it.[19]

In 1996 Congress passed the Electronic FOI Improvement Act. This increased the availability of some information. Many documents that would previously have been available in agency "reading rooms" (to which requesters would have to travel to research released files) were now required to be made available electronically.

The second revolutionary statute for the public's right to know is the Privacy Act of 1974. Congress passed it in a context of distrust of law enforcement and intelligence agencies which had been engendered by FBI and CIA spying on antiwar groups, celebrities, and even congresspersons; the indiscriminate interagency circulation of dossiers on individuals; and the Nixon "enemies list" (political foes to be targeted by government agencies by instruction of the White House). The Vietnam-Watergate era produced the first law whose primary goal was granting citizens access to their own files.*

Previously people had no effective legal right to obtain their files. A person had to be involved in a criminal case or a civil suit against the government (or some other specific, legal circumstance) in order to gain access. Now citizens could simply ask, whatever their situation or motivation. The Privacy Act even provides a process, imperfect as it is, for individuals to attempt to correct errors in their file.

Unlike FOIA, there is no charge for a records search, although there can be fees for copying. There is no deadline requiring the agency to respond. The Office of Management and Budget directed that agencies

---

*The Privacy Act will be discussed in more detail in chapter 3.

"should" respond within ten working days, with access to the files within thirty working days. Needless to say, long delays constitute a major impediment to requesters. The "should" is much weaker than FOIA's *shall,* and even in the latter case delays are endemic.

The Privacy Act is clearly intended to protect citizens from unwarranted snooping and political harassment by government agencies. It forbids the creation of a file concerning "how any individual exercises rights guaranteed under the first amendment." Lawful political expression and activities cannot legally be the subject of a file on an individual. Both the FBI and CIA had created thousands of such files on the famous and not famous alike.

This act further provides legal recourse if people discover that an agency has improperly kept gathered information on them—information that had "an adverse effect on the individual." Such alleged victims are specifically granted the right to sue with the possibility of recovering monetary damages.

The debate over the Privacy Act was also intense, but less so than with FOIA. It was politically a more difficult argument for agencies to make. Keeping secrets on citizens has an Orwellian, "big brother" dimension that invokes fears of totalitarianism. Absent was the powerful, national security justification regarding the protection of weapons, spies, and soldiers. Law enforcement agencies argued that the proposed law would drastically impede their ability to pursue criminals.

The Privacy Act forbids the indiscriminate or speculative circulation of dossiers. During the Nixon administration, agencies traded files like collectors trade baseball cards: 100 dangerous people in Secret Service files for 100 tax cheaters from the Internal Revenue Service. The act requires that there be a definable law enforcement purpose for circulating a person's files.

A primary opponent of the Privacy Act's restrictions has been the Secret Service. It has complained to Congress, and the Treasury Department within which it exists, that the flow of intelligence data has drastically declined. Other agencies (federal, state, and local) on which the Service depends for information on potentially dangerous persons have allegedly been hesitant to forward information as they did in the past. They fear lawsuits from some of the people suspected of being a threat to the president or other protectees. The Secret Service also claims that potential informants are afraid to name would-be assassins for fear the person in question will get their name when a file is released. Under the privacy law, this should never happen because confidential sources are protected. Nonetheless, the Service claimed that, by 1983, "protective intelligence" data on threatening people had declined a staggering 40 percent.[20]

Political contests concerning which records should be legally exempt from FOIA have been constant from its creation to the present. The foremost protagonists have been the FBI and CIA. In 1984, on the political wave of the Reagan administration's efforts to narrow FOIA, the CIA was finally successful.

In an amendment to the National Security Act (entitled the CIA Information Act), Congress excluded the CIA's "operational files" from FOIA. The debate centered on the meaning of the term. How broad was the exemption? Would this super-secret organization be beyond the public's right to know, beyond accountability? Specifically, operational files included foreign intelligence, counterintelligence, the work of informants, technical/scientific methods of gathering foreign intelligence, and relationships with foreign governments. Congress precluded the CIA from withholding documents that pertained to requesters personally, even if the documents qualified as operational files. Congress was attempting to grant the agency relief from FOIA without exempting it from the Privacy Act. Also, records relating to oversight functions of Congress, the CIA Inspector General, or any executive watchdog entity could not be withheld under the new dispensation. In this way, Congress was seeking to prevent the Agency from covering up violations (of its charter or the law) that might be discovered by outside monitors.

The specified categories of legitimate secrecy under "operational files" have a distinctly foreign thrust. But the inclusion of "counterintelligence" and "informants" would conceivably cover many domestic projects and activities as well. Although the CIA's 1947 charter forbids domestic spying, the Agency has always justified its activities within the United States as a legitimate extension of its foreign mission. For example, the CIA conducted extensive surveillance of antiwar and civil rights groups during the 1960s and 1970s via projects such as CHAOS and MERRI-MAC. The main justification for the surveillance (and sometimes infiltration) of such groups as the Women's Strike for Peace, the Congress of Racial Equality, the Student Nonviolent Coordinating Committee, and the Friends Service Committee was the alleged foreign communist influence on them. The fear among many critics is that certain "operational files" categories will allow the Agency to hide the very kind of domestic spying activities that oversight bodies have attempted to curtail.

Special legislation can also supercede FOIA for disclosure as well as for blanket withholding. In 1998 Congress passed the Nazi War Crimes Disclosure Act which mandated the release of federal documents pertaining to this rubric. In 1999 President Clinton appointed a commission to oversee the release of U.S. intelligence files on World War II war crimes of both the Nazis and the Japanese. Still, the commission's legal mandate and its power over the disclosure process remained murky at best. One journalist termed the disclosure "cumbersome and sometimes confused."[21] While the initial legislation gave the citizen panel the authority to override agency withholding, the bill that funded the commission through 2003 contained no such provision. However, the latter bill did expand the commission's purview to include Japanese war crimes. The opinions of commissioners and congressmen varied as to how much power the panel would be able to exercise regarding agency claims for continued secrecy.

This arena is controversial because of the role of U.S. intelligence in protecting, even hiding, Nazis charged with war crimes. The CIA was especially active in relocating and sheltering German intelligence operatives who were perceived as useful assets in Cold War spying against the Soviet Union. As one commissioner put it: "The real winners of the Cold War were Nazi war criminals."[22] The morality of this policy had been a subject of intense debate for decades. German spymaster Richard Gehlen's apparat of four thousand operatives was adopted first by U.S. Army Intelligence and then by the CIA. One of the commission's primary goals is to determine how many members of Gehlen's network were alleged war criminals. Needless to say, the agency fought for decades to keep all of this information sealed.

Despite the intense political conflict and an uncertain mandate, significant progress was made. Three million pages relating to Nazi war crimes were released between 1999 and 2001. In April 2001 there was a milestone CIA disclosure: twenty "name files," the dossiers on major Nazi figures. The release was a major step in clarifying the historical record. The files confirmed the status of at least six Nazis who avoided international justice by providing intelligence to the allies. For example, Emil Augsburg had worked at the Wannsee Institute, a Nazi think tank that mapped out the extermination of six million Jews. Augsburg was a member of the Gehlen network. Upon release of his dossier, an ex-CIA officer commented: "He should have been a war criminal but he was not . . . brought to trial. He met all the criteria."[23] Among the files was that of Klaus Barbie, the infamous "butcher of Lyons," who oversaw the deportation, torture, and extermination of French Jews. His status as a CIA asset was not revealed until 1983 when he was caught hiding in Bolivia.

On the lighter side, in bringing the historical record into focus, the public learned some colorful new details about Adolf Hitler:[24]

- The quintessential fascist was so enamored of American college football marching songs that his "sieg heil" salute was "a direct copy of the technique used by football cheerleaders."
- An informant's report asserted that in 1937 a German doctor had concluded that Hitler was "a border case between genius and insanity" who could become "the craziest criminal the world ever saw."
- In response to criticism in the 1920s that his strangely cropped mustache was ugly, he allegedly retorted: "Do not worry about my mustache. If it is not the fashion now it will be later because I wear it."
- Hitler reportedly had a phobia about being seen naked, would never walk straight across a room (only diagonally), and favored Gypsy music (although he would murder a half million Gypsies). He also had a sophisticated mechanical knowledge of automobiles, but did not know how to drive.

Commissioner and former Congresswoman Elizabeth Holtzman observed that this disclosure is "an important beginning because it is not common for the CIA to release this sort of material."[25]

Sometimes, exemptions of large categories of records from FOIA can be created by the record keepers themselves, without special legislation or even congressional approval. In 1984 I initiated a FOIA request to the Gerald Ford Presidential Library in Ann Arbor, Michigan. I sought records from the Rockefeller Commission, appointed by President Ford to probe "CIA activities within the United States." The commission's 1975 report was backed by thousands of pages of documents that Ford had taken with him when he left office. Yet Library Director Donald W. Wilson refused my request, claiming that the Rockefeller Commission files were part of President Ford's papers and "did not originate as federal records." Thus, Wilson asserted, FOIA did not apply.

These commission files dealt with many sensitive and controversial subjects, including possible CIA involvement in the assassination of President Kennedy and domestic spying activities of a questionable, if not illegal, nature. While considerable withholding would be expected for reasons such as national security and privacy, in this case, the entire record was being placed outside the public disclosure process by the decision of a single administrator. Moreover, although the files may not have "originated" as federal records, they were not a private project of President Ford's nor were they personal papers (as were his notes, letters, and some memos).

The Rockefeller Commission was appointed by a sitting president to investigate major issues of law and policy regarding a federal agency, all at taxpayers' expense. Wilson's decision created an onerous precedent for public disclosure. I could not assemble the resources or expertise to mount a legal challenge in federal court. Commission records were sealed in the Ford library, controlled by its staff.

Since then, some of the Rockefeller Commission documents and transcripts were released by the JFK Assassination Records Review Board, as mandated by the JFK Records Act of 1992. They can be viewed at the National Archives or at the Ford Library. However, the only documents made public were those dealing with the JFK assassination and anti-Castro activity. The bulk of the records, which deal with the CIA's domestic spying and other covert operations, remain sealed as of this writing.

In a paradoxical case of the politics of disclosure, President Clinton's 1995 executive order requiring declassification of older records contained a hidden exception. It was unknown to the public or press—a secret, backroom deal for a public disclosure reform. The FBI was relieved of compliance with the president's order.[26] This blanket exemption was not unearthed until three years after Clinton signed it. It was discovered by Washington attorney James H. Lesar in June of 1998. He was suing the Bureau for release of the files on three women who had been active in left-wing causes during the 1930s. The *Washington Post* followed up and used FOIA to obtain the actual two-page memo that sealed the secret deal.

The CIA had lobbied vigorously against this executive order, but the Bureau successfully pleaded its case to the White House. It alleged that its 6.5 million cubic feet of older records (twenty-five years old or more) would be a bureaucratic nightmare to process. The sheer volume made the tasks impossible. Moreover, the Bureau asserted, old files on bank robbers were mixed in with those on foreign spies; classified and unclassified documents were jumbled together in one massive mountain of paper. Sorting out sensitive, national security items would be an impossible burden, and so on.

Stephen Garfinkel, Clinton's Director of the Office of Information and Security Oversight, told the *Washington Post* that the executive order was ready to be signed six months before it was, but "it took the last six months to negotiate with Justice [Department] over the provisions of the order and the impact on the FBI."[27] Leaving no doubt about the political nature of this process, White House Press Secretary Michael McCurry revealed that the FBI "had a chop" on Clinton's order, meaning that the Bureau's opposition could have scuttled it.

"It sounds like a real coup," an anonymous FBI agent told the *Post*. Attorney Lesar, who discovered the deal, had a different take: "It is preposterous. This covers hundreds of millions of pages having nothing to do with national security at all. It's [the exemption] every piece of paper they've got, except maybe payroll records." For its older records, the Bureau had won a stunning political victory, placing them beyond public disclosure.

The courts have greatly influenced the scope of the public's right to know since Congress legislated them into the process in 1974. Judicial decisions are supposed to be based on legal precedent and constitutional/legal interpretation. Yet both the impact and context of these decisions are undeniably political. Federal and Supreme Court judges read top secret documents in chambers and significantly influence the scope of the public's right to know. Consider the importance of these judicial decisions during the last two decades:

- One struck down the FBI's use of the Privacy Act as a justification for withholding its entire central records system from disclosure under FOIA.
- The Nuclear Regulatory Commission must disclose "classified" information because it was previously disclosed to the public (once any public entity is given the data, an agency cannot withhold this information from other requesters).
- FOIA withholding exemption number two, "internal agency rules," could not be used by the air force to refuse release of information concerning ethical violations at its academy.
- An agency has no legal obligation to segregate and disclose nonclassified portions of documents that are classified (subsequently, Congress amended FOIA so that this *was* required).
- Law enforcement documents do not lose their exemption from release simply because they are mixed in with files that do not have a law enforcement purpose.

One similarity between the legal process and the political process is that neither evolves solely in one direction. The judicial pendulum also swings both ways, although it is slower and more incremental.

The legal revolution in the public's right to know that was precipitated by the passage of the Freedom of Information and Privacy Acts has been successful. It has enhanced the effectiveness of public policy, governmental accountability, and the quality of democracy. At the same time, the secrecy system has not only survived but expanded. Limitations on public access remain formidable. Is there *sufficient* public information? *Excessive* secrecy? The debate, and the political contest, will continue in the new millennium of U.S. democracy.

CHAPTER 2

The User-Unfriendly Law

The Freedom of Information Act provides a procedure for
extracting documents and records from agencies. . . .

—James E. Anderson, *Public Policymaking*, 2000

A procedure is indeed provided. The problems for anyone using
FOIA are twofold: the procedures are weighted toward the discretion of government and not toward the requester, and procedures are
often ignored or manipulated by agencies. There are many who would
disagree with this assessment. The Reporters Committee for Freedom
of the Press asserts in its "How To" booklet, "The possibilities of the act
are endless. All that is required is that you use it."[1]

Both positions are correct. The procedure for requesting information
is quite simple and straightforward to execute. No scholarly or legal
expertise is needed. In millions of instances, requesters will obtain the
desired data (or at least some of it) via a user-friendly legal process. But
there exists a broad range of agencies, requesters, topics, and political
contexts regarding Freedom of Information Act (FOIA) requests. Some
will collide with the legal/administrative defense mechanisms of the
secrecy system. Some will be settled not simply by the provisions of the
statute but by legal or political conflict with the agency.

As with court cases and with campaigns for or against government policies, FOIA requests differ greatly in their political context and impact. Some do not present a political threat to an agency, nor do they challenge an agency's secrecy system. They are not entangled in related secrets involving national security or covert operations. Most requests are in subject areas devoid of political sensitivity or issues of cover-up, for example:

- A high school student obtains documents from the National Oceanic and Atmospheric Administration on hurricane projections in the North Atlantic. The request is granted swiftly and at no cost.
- A lawyer in a patent infringement suit brought against a pharmaceutical company obtains thousands of pages from the Food and Drug Administration, after the agency has deleted everything relating to "trade secrets."
- A reporter from *Crops Gazette* gains easy access to voluminous files at the Department of Agriculture relating to soybean production.

In contrast, requesters dealing with the more highly trained secret keepers at the more politically charged agencies will have a far different experience when seeking information on such controversial subjects as:

- CIA records on its MK/ULTRA project involving mind-control experiments (using LSD and hypnosis) on unwitting human subjects.
- FBI surveillance of Dr. Martin Luther King, Jr., during his civil rights and antiwar activities.
- Data from the Nuclear Regulatory Commission relating to the safety of U.S. troops who were purposefully exposed to atomic radiation during nuclear testing.
- Secret Service "improvements" on homes owned by presidents, and paid for by taxpayers, to enhance the "security" of the grounds and dwelling.

In such cases, following FOIA's simple steps can be time-consuming, financially draining, frustrating, and ultimately unsuccessful. In conflict-ridden, potentially explosive turf, secret keepers may use every stage of the process to create a new challenge for the requester. They will do so not only legally but sometimes illegally. The success or failure of the request will depend not only on the strength of the law but also on the expertise, resources, and tenacity available to the requester. Should an agency refuse, the requester faces the daunting prospect of entering federal court, where the agency's lawyer is paid for by the taxpayers and the plaintiff's is not.

What follows is a step-by-step look at using FOIA and the problems and pitfalls that can be encountered. This chapter deals with requests for information about topics other than one's self. (Chapter 3 will examine the Privacy Act and the procedures for obtaining one's own personal records from the government.)

The good news about starting out is that anyone can use the law— "any person." As previously mentioned, this includes not only U.S. citizens but also foreign nationals (a point of political contention since the act's inception). There is no minimum age: any grade school student with a science project can participate. As previously mentioned, requests can be made in the name of a group or organization as well as an individual. The legal steps are the same regardless of the requester. That said, the law is not administered in a political vacuum. The bureaucrats who process these millions of letters must surely take note of their origins:

- Ms. Mary Arrington, Frederick Douglas High School, Silver Spring, Maryland
- John Legalese, Corporation Counsel, CBS News
- Center for National Security Studies, Washington, D.C.
- Mr. Clyde Alcot, Administrative Assistant to Senator Daniel P. Moynihan
- Common Cause
- Ms. Ethel Marlor, the *Plattsburg Eagle,* Plattsburg, N.Y.

The initial request is mostly uncomplicated. As the Reporters Committee booklet instructs, "A simple letter is all you need."[2] The prototype is one page (a sample letter is in appendix B). It cites the statute, states a willingness to pay fees, asks for a waiver of fees (if applicable, as will be discussed shortly), requests quick processing under the "expedited review" procedure, and looks forward to a reply within twenty working days (as required by the act). It is mailed to the Freedom of

Information Office of the particular agency. The addresses are easily obtained from the *Federal Register* or from the pamphlets or websites of several organizations.

It is not necessary to have a return receipt to establish the date of your request, but many sources recommend it. You do not have to certify your identity as you do when requesting your own records under the Privacy Act. This legal boilerplate is easy to follow. The crux of the letter, however, and the likely field of battle, should there be one, is the substantive request for information. It can be simple and straightforward and can receive a response in kind. The law specifies that you "reasonably describe" what you want, for example:

- Documents and data relating to federal aid to California from the National Highway Trust Fund, 1999–2000.
- FBI files relating to the apprehension and killing of bank robber John Dillinger.

If the request is too broad, an overwhelming and unaffordable volume of material may be reported out. A student of mine once requested the FBI's "file" on the assassination of President Kennedy (she had not consulted me beforehand). The Bureau dutifully responded with several categories of files—JFK/Dallas, Jack Ruby, Lee Harvey Oswald, and so on—each containing many thousands of pages.

If the request is too narrow, you may miss some or all of the data. Agencies are not required, nor will they volunteer, to presume which files you must really want. They give you only what you ask for, at most. One author was interested in FBI files on Marilyn Monroe as a biographical source. He mistakenly limited his request to the actress's death, thereby excluding the Bureau's surveillance of her activities and liaisons. It is too expensive to go on a fishing expedition for files. Agencies charge for searching. They are legally required to publish their fee schedules and their FOIA rules and regulations in the *Federal Register.* Since 1993 they have also been required to disseminate this information online as well.

In addition to the request's substantive description of the material, there is the matter of where to find it. Federal agencies do not operate like libraries or archives—user-friendly facilities where the staff may be dedicated to helping you find what you need. Agencies are legally required to "search" for records relating directly to your request. But they will do so only within the confines of a legally "adequate" search, not within the scholarly or journalistic paradigm of leaving no stone unturned in the pursuit of information. This is true even with domestic, civilian agencies that have no law enforcement, military, or intelligence functions.

When requesters are dealing with the FBI, CIA, National Security Agency, or Army Intelligence, however, it is an entirely different venue. A mindset of secrecy pervades some agencies. Secrets are entwined with other secrets. Arcane filing systems are designed to reflect complex missions. They are also designed to baffle foreign rivals and to compartmentalize the knowledge afforded their own employees. These information systems are designed to be user-*un*friendly. There are cryptonyms, numerical codes, intricate cross-references, and transposed names (first name and surname backward). Such systems exist within complex organizational setups that are themselves a secret.

One is reminded of the "clandestine mentality" portrayed by Marchetti and Marks in *The CIA and the Cult of Intelligence* (New York: Dell, 1974). The vignettes provided by the authors include the CIA's use of certifiably blind sandwich vendors as a method of preserving office security. There was also the Agency's refusal to provide the air-conditioning contractor with the plans for the new headquarters building in Langley, Virginia. This resulted in erroneous estimates that made the new offices sweatboxes during the humid summer weather. The CIA published a secret orientation manual for employees entitled *What's Where?* This is an appropriate term for complicated, controversial FOIA requests: you actually need to tell the agency what's where, or as close to it as possible. This hide-and-seek paper chase takes many forms. In 1982 I requested files from the U.S. Secret Service concerning the attempted assassination of President Ronald Reagan by John W. Hinckley in 1981 (I was writing a book on this agency). My request was reasonably thorough, although not expert, and included information on: President Reagan, Hinckley, protective intelligence (a Secret Service term), records of liaisons between the Service and the FBI, and with the Washington, D.C., Police Department; records relating to protection both before and after the shooting—the president at George Washington Hospital, the would-be assassin at the D.C. jail, and after-action reports (which I did not expect to obtain).

To my chagrin, I was offered fewer than 500 pages. This may seem like plenty of documents to keep an author writing, but something was wrong: the attempted assassination of a president (and a near-fatal one, at that) is not a 500-page event. After consulting with three expert sources (two authors and an attorney), the simple problem and solution became clear. Since the event had occurred in the nation's capital, the primary case file resided not in Secret Service headquarters, but with the Washington, D.C., field office across town. This made sense, sort of. At least there was nothing nefarious in the Service's response. I had asked for the headquarters file—my mistake.

This ended my academic naiveté in assuming that the headquarters of law enforcement and intelligence agencies were central repositories for all records, like some sort of archive. It is common, even typical, for such agencies to have different files on the same subject in field offices and headquarters. A competent request must ask for both. Otherwise, the requester loses the game of *what's where*.

In 1975 Washington attorney Bernard Fensterwald, Jr., made a FOIA request for the FBI's files on the 1968 assassination of Senator Robert F. Kennedy. Although the case seemed open and shut, serious and unresolved issues remained.[3] These included the most important one of all: did convicted assassin Sirhan Sirhan's gun actually kill Kennedy, as opposed to the other two, highly suspicious guns present at the Ambassador Hotel crime scene? There was no ballistics match to Sirhan's gun. There were also the usual questions of conspiracy: whether Sirhan had accomplices or was encouraged or manipulated by others. The Bureau had been called in by President Lyndon Johnson to investigate the third major assassination case of the decade (President Kennedy in 1963, Dr. King just two months prior to Robert Kennedy).

In response to Fensterwald's request, the Bureau released more than 3,000 pages. The major revelation was the documents and photographs that seemed to acknowledge the presence of second-gun bullets at the crime scene.

A decade later my colleague Greg Stone and I were ready to ask the

FBI anew. Three thousand pages seemed a very sparse record for such a major national event. Our request had the distinct advantage of using the previously released Fensterwald documents as clues for what might be found. In addition, we had the benefit of the formidable expertise of our attorneys, James H. Lesar and Lawrence Teeter. We also polled five people with expertise regarding Bureau files—two authors and three professors.

The result was a five-page, single-spaced request letter. Many of the strange acronyms and rubrics were foreign to the two signatories (Stone and Melanson), but very effective.

The core of the request letter read:

> Our clients request a complete and thorough search of all filing systems and locations for all Los Angeles Field Division and FBI Headquarters records maintained by the Federal Bureau of Investigation pertaining to the assassination of Senator Robert F. Kennedy and all investigative activities related thereto, including, but not limited to, files and documents captioned in, or whose captions include the names of Sirhan Bishara Sirhan or Robert Francis Kennedy (insofar as related to his assassination or the investigation thereof), or logical variants thereof, in the title. This request specifically includes "main" files and "see" references, including, but not limited to, numbered and lettered subfiles, 1A envelopes, enclosures behind files (EBFs), Bulky Exhibits, control files, ticklers, agent interview notes, abstracts, index cards and "JUNE" files. We ask that all records be produced with administrative markings and that all reports include the administrative pages.

Thanks to Fensterwald's release, we were now privy to the Bureau's code name for its case file—KENSALT. Kennedy had survived for slightly more than twenty-four hours after he was shot. When the FBI opened its investigation he had been *assaulted,* not assassinated. The file bore this original designation even though the outcome had changed. Whereas we would previously have requested files based on our own guesses about the rubrics for the case, we now had the Bureau's main one.

The result was spectacular. This was the same file we had sought a decade earlier. There were no official developments in the case in the intervening years. All of the documents released to us in 1985–86 had been in Bureau files when Fensterwald made his request. Most had resided there since the original investigation. Now, thanks to the collective wisdom of our request, the FBI's "search" produced a tenfold increase—more than 32,000 pages.

The phrasing of the request is a primary factor in the agency's search for documents. The law requires an "adequate" search. If requesters believe that the search was deficient, they may appeal within the agency. If still not satisfied, they can go into federal court to attempt to compel a more thorough search. The requesters may suspect that the agency did not look hard enough, but proving it from the outside is very difficult. The agency can cite chapter and verse concerning its filing system, codes, and computer programs. Requesters are usually guessing, or, at best, extrapolating from other releases. It is an uneven competition.

In two instances, I was convinced that the CIA had not adequately searched for the records I requested. In both cases my appeal was rejected. I lacked the resources and commitment to go to court. In 1984 I requested the Agency's file on Dr. Martin Luther King, Jr. With the help of Boston attorney Dan Bernstein, I crafted a multifaceted letter that included Dr. King's organizational affiliations, CIA field offices, and code names from previously released documents dealing with the Agency's monitoring of the Civil Rights Movement. This was a controversial subject. The CIA's 1947 charter forbade domestic spying. Yet the Agency had targeted black political groups for decades, believing (without substantiation) that many of them were communist-influenced if not controlled. I was suspicious that a leader of Dr. King's stature who was at the epicenter of the civil rights and antiwar movements (which the agency regarded with extreme suspicion, if not paranoia) would be the subject of a mere 134 pages of documents found in the agency's search. Moreover, my release failed to include twelve pages that had been previously released to Professor David Garrow and were cited in his book *The FBI and Martin Luther King, Jr.*

I wrote the CIA and confronted it concerning their missing documents. My response came in a March 23, 1984, letter from Information and Privacy Coordinator Larry R. Strawderman:

> Upon receipt of your recent letter, we immediately queried our system again, but were not able to locate the missing documents. We are

attempting to do so by retrieving the original FOIA cases on which the releases were based. Failing this we will then initiate new documents searches.

We regret that we are unable to provide you copies of the seven documents you mention at this time. We will be back in touch with you when we have completed our efforts.

Both the old and the "new" searches failed to produce the missing items. Nor were any additional documents released beyond the 134 pages.

In December of 1990, I met a retired CIA man whose bona fides had been established by *60 Minutes* (for a segment that did not air). A mutual acquaintance had set up the "interview." This high-ranking field agent had participated in the domestic surveillance of Dr. King (in concert with the FBI, but also independent of it). As I awaited our meeting in the lobby of a downtown Washington, D.C., hotel (per his instructions), I sensed that he was observing me from afar. During our encounter, as is usual with intelligence types, I was more the interviewee than the interviewer.

He had first-hand knowledge of an incursion into Dr. King's Miami hotel room, which had produced several of the most controversial documents among the 134-page release. Items included handwritten messages and King's credit card slips. I showed my source the file I had been given. He shook his head as he skimmed the documents. "It's too bad they lied to you," he said ruefully. "I personally filed more cables [on Dr. King] than they gave you. . . . In fact, . . . there aren't *any* cables here. Where are the cables?" he asked rhetorically. Then he leaned back in his chair and laughed heartily, briefly exposing the large pistol holstered under his suit coat. "They *didn't* lie," he exclaimed with some relief. "You didn't ask for the right files."

The criticism made me bristle since I had no way of knowing what to ask for. "We filed the King stuff in the Western Hemisphere file—Castro, Cuba, assassinations. That way, no one could ever get at it—national security."

Although this was a low point in my sense of efficacy regarding the FOIA process, I dutifully—perhaps compulsively—queried the CIA again, asking it to look in the "Western Hemisphere file" for records on Dr. King. Allegedly, none were found.

In 1987, as part of the general effort to obtain release of all files relating to the assassination of Robert Kennedy, I made a request to the CIA on behalf of the RFK Assassination Archive that had been established at my university (University of Massachusetts-Dartmouth). The letter contained the appropriate geographic references and relevant buzzwords from other CIA releases. I also added a heavy dose of convicted assassin Sirhan Sirhan's middle-eastern background. He had grown up in Jerusalem, and the Palestinian-Israeli conflict allegedly provided his motive for killing Kennedy, who was a strong supporter of Israel.

The "search" failed to produce a single document—not even a newspaper clipping. I was told: "This agency has no file on the domestic assassination of Senator Robert Kennedy." Domestic or not, this response was not credible. The possibility of an international terrorist conspiracy had been very prominent in the first two weeks of the case, even though it would eventually be discounted. Sirhan had received support, even kudos, from Arab interests within the United States and abroad. It is unfathomable that the CIA did not create a file on a major domestic political event that might well have international dimensions. But there was allegedly nothing—not even a broadside from one of the several terrorist groups that falsely claimed "credit" for the assassination.

Although I was certain that the search had been inadequate, I was not about to enter the federal judiciary system in hopes of compelling the Agency to discover some press clippings from a Beirut newspaper. My lawyers worked pro bono, but they had no inclination to tilt at windmills or engage in wild-goose chases.

The Freedom of Information Act is cast broadly in terms of what can be accessed. It pertains to all "records" held or controlled by the federal bureaucracy. At times, agencies have attempted to narrow the definition of what constitutes a record, seeking to exclude electronic communications and to limit searches to hard copy. But the law has been held to apply to a wide variety of sources beyond official documents: letters, audiotapes, computer tapes, photographs. Anything that can be duplicated is considered to be within the act's purview. The Italian rifle belonging to Lee Harvey Oswald that allegedly killed President Kennedy cannot be reproduced; therefore, it is not a record. The courts have ruled that the message slips and appointment calendars of bureaucrats are also fair game, so long as they were created for official rather than purely personal purposes (shopping lists of FBI agents are out of bounds).[4]

The law does not require agencies to answer questions about documents posed by requesters. You must answer them as best you can from whatever information is disclosed. Agencies are not required to "create" records. You are entitled to the data in whatever form it is possessed. Agencies need not collate, tally, organize, or reorganize for you. This is to preclude federal bureaucrats from doing research for requesters (whether they are law firms or high school students).

In 1982 I requested CIA files on training and assistance provided to local police departments (the substantive results of this request are described in chapter 7, "Leaks from the Vault"). The Agency responded that it had no such file. I was aware from congressional hearings and media reports that assistance did exist. Citing these sources in hopes of jogging the Agency's memory, I asked again. I was informed by the Information and Privacy Coordinator that "this Agency is not required to create a record pursuant to your request."

I suspected that a game was afoot. As would later emerge from released documents, the CIA's official position was that its assistance to city police departments was such a minimal, sporadic activity that no file was kept. I decided to launch a flurry of requests, city by city. This was successful in producing 362 pages of previously unreleased documents pertaining to Agency liaisons with various police forces, even though an umbrella file supposedly did not exist. This *noncreated* record constituted a major exposé of the Agency's covert links to urban police.[5]

As with all administrative-legal processes, time and money are major factors in shaping the public's right to know. The law mandates that the agency respond within twenty working days—not simply acknowledging the request, but granting or rejecting it. This is required unless there are "unusual circumstances" that justify further delay, circumstances defined in detail by the statute.

The deadline is rarely adhered to. Delay continues to be one of the main impediments for requesters, as it has been since FOIA became operational. Some agencies take longer than others due to the volume of requests and the pace of their process. The CIA, FBI, and State Department are notorious in this regard. The FBI has at times claimed a backlog not of six weeks or months, but six years. This destroys any timeliness or current relevance of the information for any journalist, author, lawyer, or college student.

The courts have generally taken a laissez-faire approach with regard to these violations. The requester must prove that the agency is acting in bad faith: that it doesn't really have a backlog and is acting arbitrarily and unreasonably toward this particular request. This is a huge burden of proof for someone outside the agency.

Speed in processing is primarily determined by resources. How many employees are assigned? What technical facilities are committed? Whether the logjams in the flow of public information are natural phenomena or are, as some suspect, artificially enhanced by the secret keepers, the only solution is additional agency resources. These could be internal (shifted over from within the organization), or external (an appropriation by Congress earmarked for FOIA). Neither option is popular in an era of tight budgets and opposition to bureaucratic expansion. As with every aspect of the FOIA process, there are two sides: (1) given the importance of the public's right to know, our system should encourage or force agencies to provide what is needed to reduce the backlog; (2) wouldn't we rather have more FBI agents tracking terrorists and solving crimes than employees working to provide information services for curious civilians?

Congress perceived that interminable delays were undermining the very essence of FOIA. Seeking to provide relief, in 1996 it passed the Electronic Freedom of Information Improvement Act.[6] The new law created an "expedited review" for requesters who can successfully make a case that there are compelling circumstances for speedy processing. Requesters must "certify" or warrant to the agency that the circumstances they cite are true. In reality, however, such circumstances are defined by the new law in ways that severely limit their application. Few requesters can certify that there exists a life-threatening situation or that the physical safety or protection of another person demands prompt action. If the requester is a person "primarily engaged in disseminating information" (a reporter, for example) *and* the request is a matter of "compelling need," then the law requires that expedited review be granted. However, the agency is the one who decides.

The congressional reform also set up a two-track process by which agencies *can* separate simple and complex requests and deal with them within two separate processes. In addition, Congress raised the standard by which agencies could justify delays with claims of "exceptional circumstances." No longer is a routine backlog considered a sufficient reason. Yet, with all these attempts at reform, Congress's new law doubled the required agency response time—from ten to twenty working days. Despite the well-intentioned changes, long delays still undermine the basic goals of FOIA.

Next comes money. FOIA never intended to provide free goods and services to information wonks. The question has always been: what is a reasonable cost, a cost that relieves the burden on the federal budget but does not render the price of public information prohibitive? And to whom is it "prohibitive": law firms, secondary school students? The answers are still being debated.

Agency fees are required by law to be "reasonable" and "direct." "Reasonable," like beauty, is in the eye of the checkbook holder. "Direct" means that only the costs of searching can be charged. It precludes fees for the process of deciding which documents to withhold or which passages to delete. Such costs would definitely be prohibitive for most requesters. Commercial requesters, as defined by the agency, must pay all costs, including those incurred in withholding and deletion.

The dollar amounts vary wildly throughout government (each agency must publish its fee schedule). Search fees range from $10 to $55 an hour, depending upon the human-resources price tag of the workers who do the looking. The salary/benefits tab for a search conducted by CIA employees is likely to be much higher than that for the Department of the Interior. The files of defense, intelligence, and law enforcement agencies tend to be more complex to search. Sheer volume is a factor: some agency's holdings are in the tens of millions of documents; some, hundreds of millions. Computer time varies greatly and can approach $300 per hour. Copying released pages can be as inexpensive as below ten cents or as costly as thirty-five cents per page; the latter is the norm.

There are no discounts for deletions. This author has paid twenty cents per page for dozens of CIA documents that are totally blank.

For the average requester, the investment can be risky—a kind of paper-chase lottery. Many agencies require the money up front: any projected cost over $25 must be paid before the search begins. You pay even if no documents are found, or if they are found but the agency refuses to release them. In the FOIA letter, requesters are advised to set a ceiling on how much they are willing to pay, and to ask to be informed when the limit is reached. There is no such thing as a good credit rating: despite dozens of full and prompt payments, the CIA always asks me for money up front.

The FOI Reform Act of 1986 addressed the issue of cost. Commercial users pay full freight but many others get a break. Requesters affiliated with educational and scientific institutions (and requests from such institutions themselves) as well as requesters from the news media are not charged search fees, and the first 100 pages are free. All other requesters are entitled to two hours of free searching and 100 pages. In millions of cases, this means that cost is not a problem. But for those who fall outside the definitions of financial relief, the cost can be prohibitive.

Many requesters do not have the luxury of a scientific, educational, or media affiliation—many authors, lawyers, political activists, and concerned citizens. For them, search fees beyond the first two hours can be far more than they are willing or able to pay. While 100 free pages may sound generous, it depends on the situation. For untold numbers of researchers and authors, their topics of interest may involve files containing thousands of pages: problems of nuclear safety, environmental pollution, high-profile criminal cases, CIA domestic spying, historical events. For these requesters, there is help in the form of "reading rooms" and potential salvation in the form of "fee waivers."

Agencies are required to have reading rooms where the public can peruse files. Requesters usually must set up in advance the agency's procurement of the files they wish to inspect. Readers can tab documents for copying, write a check, and wait for them to arrive by mail. This is obviously much more cost-efficient than paying for piles of unseen documents, many of which may be uninformative or heavily deleted. This does not absolve readers of search costs; however, you can read documents that have been previously released and pay no search fee.

The hitch is that reading rooms are generally located at or near agency headquarters. There are no branch facilities near your hometown as is often the case with lending libraries. Transportation, food, and lodging can be prohibitive on their own, depending on the requester's geographic and financial situation.

During the 1980s, I made extensive use of the reading rooms at the CIA, FBI, and Secret Service. I read thousands of pages and copied hundreds, on topics ranging from surveillance of atomic veterans' groups to assassination attempts on U.S. leaders. This provided yet another rich experience in the diversity of agency information cultures.

The FBI reading room had the friendly ambiance of a research library. Access was by appointment; it was an eight-to-four operation. The only delay was in waiting for an armed special agent to escort me from the front desk, across the courtyard of the Hoover Building, and through the corridors leading to the room. Sometimes the wait was a half-hour. But it seemed eminently reasonable that people could not wander inside FBI headquarters unescorted. The reader could look forward to hours of uninterrupted research under the oversight of a helpful staff of clerks and supervisors. Readers can actually browse without direct supervision.

The Bureau's reading room publishes a catalog of files that can be read there. The topic list of more than 100 subjects also indicates the number of released pages. The broad range of subjects, as described by the FBI, varies greatly in terms of numbers of documents: Alphonse Capone, 2,032; Chappaquiddick, 87; John Dillinger gang, 36,795; Errol Flynn, 391; John F. Kennedy Assassination, 220,436; Kent State shooting, 8,445; Watergate, 16,277; Unidentified Flying Objects, 1,694; Elvis A. Presley, 807; Communist Party U.S.A., 30,776; Samuel M. Giancana, 2,780; Patty Hearst Kidnapping, 37,120.

At the CIA's small, windowless back room in an office building in Rosslyn, Virginia, it was totally different. The Agency seemed almost a parody of itself. This facility for *public* disclosure was unmarked for the public. The office building's directory had no reference to the Agency or its reading room. I had been instructed by letter to go to the front window on the second floor and ask for a Mr. Harrington, who would turn out to be my provider of documents and ever-watchful supervisor. The woman at the window did not respond directly to what I thought was a very logical question: "Is this the CIA reading room?" Instead, she asked who I was supposed to meet.

Mr. Harrington collected me and led me through a large office where dozens of female secretaries typed and filed. At the other end was the reading room furnished with a table, four chairs, and file cabinets. Harrington would sit with me continually while I read; only he could access the file cabinets and retrieve documents. (During this time, he read a paperback: *The Man Who Kept the Secrets: Richard Helms and the CIA.*) My host explained that, "due to budget pressures," this was a shared space. It served simultaneously as an interview room for prospective clerical hirees. Should the latter function materialize, the reader's time would be cut short, and he or she would have to leave. Having flown down from Boston with an inflexible seventy-two-hour window of opportunity to conduct my research, this was not welcome news. Sure enough, on day three I was evicted in late morning. The rest of the day was lost. Files went unread and uncopied.

In the most recent development, the Electronic FOI Improvements Act of 1996 required agencies to begin to make some released documents even more accessible than in reading rooms. Data released after November of 1996 is supposed to be made available electronically. For these documents, the reader's investments of time and money are greatly reduced. In addition, this reform requires that agencies inventory those FOIA requests that have covered the same subject, or that are likely to be frequently requested in the future. The agency responses to such requests are also to be made available online, simplifying and speeding up the disclosure of these select documents.

Any requester may ask for a waiver or reduction of fees (under the original act). The agency "shall" grant a waiver if the request meets the standards established by the 1986 Reform Act: "disclosure of the information is in the public interest because it is likely to contribute significantly to public understanding of the operations or activities of government and is not primarily in the commercial interest of the requester." For the author, the "reform" was a great leap backward. Previously, a requester need only show that the information was not for personal use but would be publicly disseminated (accessible to the public and not locked away in a basement). Publishing books and articles met this standard by definition. While publication of the data, in whole or in part, still helps to make the case for a fee waiver, it is by no means as strong an argument as it used to be. Now, the topic must relate to broadening the understanding of how government works. While I would argue that most of what I have written in the last three decades meets this standard, not every information officer would necessarily agree.

In 1987 there was another setback for the flow of public information. The Justice Department issued a lengthy and complex memorandum stating the criteria for granting waivers. In essence, this further restricted them. The department ruled that a waiver should be granted if one of six criteria are met. These were even more specifically linked to noncommercial public understanding of how government works.[7] Agencies have tremendous latitude in interpreting these vague-but-restrictive standards. For example: How encompassing is the definition of "government operations and activities"? What sort of information enhances public understanding, and when is this "significant"? What is a "limited commercial interest" (the majority of the book's royalties go to charity?)? How is the "public interest" in disclosure defined when it is compared with the requester's "commercial interest"?

The Reporters Committee for Freedom of the Press informs us that requesters "seeking relatively modest numbers of documents are more likely to be granted fee waivers than those whose requests encompass thousands of pages." It advises requesters to "narrow your request as much as possible" so that you will not "unduly" burden the agency.[8] This makes sense from the stark perspective of cost cutting. But it can be argued that many of the most significant illuminations of how government works comprise thousands of pages precisely because they involve weighty and complex matters. The present waiver policy discourages and often precludes pursuit of such subjects.

Even when the criteria were clearer and more favorable to requesters, agencies sometimes ignored them. This was the case in the 1985 request for the FBI's Robert F. Kennedy assassination file. The letter, on behalf of the RFK Archive at my university (with researcher Greg Stone and myself as corequesters), made it clear that this facility was housed in a public institution that offered complete public access. This was the perfect case for a waiver, based on "public dissemination."

It seemed like a fait acompli until the Bureau refused to decide on the granting of a waiver. Weeks dragged into months. The disclosure process was on hold. Stone and I consulted our attorneys, Lesar and Teeter. Both were certain that, legally, the waiver had to be granted. But when? As Lesar put it, "This is what the Bureau does when it knows it has to grant a waiver." Advice of counsel was that, while we would win in federal court, the ensuing delay would seriously inhibit the disclosure process in the RFK case. It would take months to get into court, longer to get a decision and obtain Bureau compliance. We would not see a single document for perhaps six months to a year. It was Lesar who suggested political action.

As a student of the political process, I was not averse to this idea. Massachusetts Congressman Barney Frank, then an upcoming member of the House, was perfect for the task (except that I didn't know him and had had no contact with his office). The University of Massachusetts-Dartmouth and its RFK Archive were in his district (due to the weird gerrymandering by the Democrats in the State House in Boston). Frank also had a plum appointment to the House Judiciary Committee, which oversaw the FBI's budget and practices.

My colleague Jenny Stone of the University archive (no relation to corequester Greg) got us a meeting with the congressman. I had expected the TV Barney Frank, the affable, laser-witted debater with the twinkle of humor in his eye. The in-person version was strikingly different—brusque bordering on impolite, cigar-chomping, humorlessly acerbic about the public disclosure process, and in a huge rush. When the meeting was over, I needed a reality check with my colleague: "We *did* get a letter?" I asked her. The answer was affirmative.

The congressman's letter went out within two weeks. It was forceful: "This matter deserves the prompt attention of the FBI and I urge you to make it a priority." The Bureau granted a fee waiver two weeks after that. We had saved months of delay. The clear intent of FOIA had been met, but only because of political pressure.

At any stage, requesters can initiate a formal appeal with the agency to overturn a denial of a waiver, withholding of documents, a faulty search, or illegal delays. The boilerplate appeal letter is short and simple. It is addressed to the person at the very top of the agency—the secretary of state, the attorney general. A decision is required within twenty working days. You need not write an extensive brief or argue the legal merits of your case in order to obtain a review. The agency is mandated to examine your original request by virtue of your appeal letter. But laying out some supporting points surely cannot hurt.

Appeals have worked for untold thousands of requesters. Sometimes the problem is a simple matter of an error made in processing the original request or a misinterpretation of its meaning. Personally, however, I have not shared in this experience. My twenty-seven appeals to the FBI, CIA, Nuclear Regulatory Commission, Department of Justice, Army Intelligence, and Secret Service have all been denied. There were no political magic wands to reverse the outcomes.

Agencies may withhold or delete files, documents, paragraphs, sentences, or words. Any such withholding must be justified by one or more of the nine exemptions provided by FOIA. Withholding of information is not legally required. The exemptions allow the agency to keep secrets but do not mandate that they do so. It is up to the discretion of agency personnel.

Professor Athan Theoharis, who uses FOIA extensively in his research, describes his 1980 experience in requesting the "office file" of FBI Director J. Edgar Hoover:

> This file consists of 164 folders numbering approximately eighteen thousand pages; when it was released to me in 1983, I received approximately six thousand pages, many of which were heavily redacted.* The FBI withheld in entirety some of the 164 folders, including one captioned "White House Security Survey." This folder totaled 431 pages and had been withheld on grounds that the information was either national security classified, would reveal FBI sources and methods, would violate personal privacy rights . . .[9]

The following discussion of these exemptions is illustrative, not exhaustive. The legal-administrative definitions and precedents for each one are extensive and often complex. This is especially true of the

---

*"Redacted" is a buzzword commonly used by agencies to mean deleted or censored or blacked out.

most controversial and frequently used exemptions—national security, privacy, and law enforcement. Each of these is a battleground for disclosure versus secrecy. Each has its own shifting boundaries. A full exposition of the intricacies would require a treatment that is much closer to an administrative law text than this work desires to be.

Five of the nine exemptions are quite specialized and are not relevant to the vast majority of requests:

Internal Agency Rules: Relating solely to the agency's internal personnel practices and rules, and its so-called "housekeeping" records.

Trade Secrets: Commercial or financial data that is confidential and valuable—product formulas, client lists, or other secrets that competitors could use to the disadvantage of a commercial entity.

Internal Agency Memoranda: Memos or letters that are interagency or intraagency; private, confidential communications among bureaucrats that would not be accessible to any outsider during a civil suit against the agency.

Bank Reports: Prepared by government to assess the performance and financial stability of banks and other federally regulated financial organizations (trust companies, investment banking firms); audits or reports that might erode public confidence in specific banks or the federal system of which they are part.

Oil and Gas Well Data: Geological data (test results, maps) showing the location of wells owned by private companies; this prevents competitors and speculators from knowing the most prized industry secrets.

The remaining four exemptions are relevant to a wider range of requests. "Statutory Exemptions" are records that have been placed outside the disclosure process by the passage of legislation. As described in the previous chapter, this is an arena of political contest. Many agencies desire to get out from under FOIA, partially or entirely. Advocates of the public's right to know vehemently oppose such exemptions as placing agencies above the law and beyond public accountability. Unlike the other exemptions, secret keepers are legally required to withhold documents falling into this category. The question is, what falls in? The inventory of records placed beyond the reach of public disclosure is long. Here are some key examples:

- Data submitted to the Consumer Product Safety Commission by private companies, if it is deemed "not accurate."
- CIA "operational files" relating to foreign intelligence gathering, counterintelligence, espionage technology, investigations on informants, as well as other subjects[10]
- National Security Agency personnel records showing the number of employees and their names, titles, and salaries

In seeking to invoke this "statutory exemption," federal agencies have cited more than 100 laws that bear upon the exclusion of particular documents.[11]

The exemption for "Law Enforcement Records" has been increasingly used in the 1980s and 1990s. Its simple purpose is to prevent FOIA from exposing information on criminal investigations or prosecutions that would aid criminal elements or impede law enforcement. Obviously, this is a huge category of material. In some terrorist cases, the FBI would regard every jot of information as privileged. The act specifies that the exemption includes protection of witnesses and confidential sources, information that could prejudice a fair trial, data on how law enforcement catches criminals, and anything that would jeopardize someone's safety (no matter what their role or relevance to a case).

Over the life of FOIA, law enforcement agencies have lobbied for increased exemptions. The prestigious, powerful FBI has led the way. In 1986 Congress broadened the exemption by establishing a new standard for withholding. No longer do federal crime fighters have to prove that negative consequences *would* occur upon release: they need only establish that harm "could reasonably be expected" to occur. The law enforcement exemption is heavily used by agencies, especially the FBI.

The two most frequently used exemptions are national security and privacy. From the passage of FOIA until the present, national security has ranked first. Increasingly, privacy has become a much-used exemption. These two are also the most administratively and legally complicated. Agencies may withhold anything that would "damage" national security. Since neither *damage* nor *national security* have strict definitions, these are points of interpretation and of political/legal contest. National security records have been defined to include military strategy; weapons operation, design, and deployment; intelligence sources and methods; information regarding foreign policy and diplomacy; sensitive scientific, technological, and economic data; the safety and operation of nuclear plants and projects; and anything revealing vulnerabilities of weapons or facilities.

The national security exemption is legally tied to the executive orders of the president, which set forth criteria and policies. Naturally, each administration has its own perspective, sometimes overlapping with its predecessors; sometimes sharply diverging. President Reagan's order 12333 and President Clinton's 12958 reflect very different priorities, yet both maintained the essential power of the national security exemption. Reagan's was pro-secrecy; Clinton's, more pro-disclosure (especially regarding older records). In fact, as discussed in the previous chapter, Clinton created a parallel disclosure process to FOIA. Requesters could ask for "mandatory declassification" of national security documents rather than initiate a request for release using FOIA. This clearly demonstrates the power of the president in defining the rules of disclosure in matters of "national security."

The privacy exemption seeks to protect individuals from harm or intrusion resulting from the release of government records about them— personnel and medical records, law enforcement and intelligence files. The agency must weigh the balance: the public interest in accessing the information versus the protection of the individual. If someone agrees to the release of his or her own file, government cannot withhold it based on protecting the rights of that person. The exemption applies only to individuals, not organizations. As with national security, the key terms are vague, priorities are conflicting, and the case law and administrative regulations are voluminous. During the 1990s, Congress and the Supreme Court dueled over FOIA's protection of privacy rights—the court expanding the exemption, Congress seeking to narrow it.[12]

The boundaries are murky and shifting. Do federal agents' privacy rights outweigh the disclosure of their work in law enforcement investigations? Are records regarding the exposure of military personnel to atomic radiation a confidential matter or a matter of public health and safety? Where is the line between public and private in scandal-ridden agencies being scrutinized by the media? Are the names of authors whose work and books were subsidized by the CIA exempt because of their privacy, or does the reading public have a right to know which books the Agency was behind? Many such questions are addressed by the Privacy Act of 1974 (as discussed in chapter 3). But these are also the kinds of issues that are involved in the FOIA exemption for "privacy."

Two external remedies are available to requesters who believe that an agency has violated their right to access—the courts and administrative sanctions against federal employees. However, neither provides effective redress. The requester's disadvantaged status vis-à-vis the bureaucracy still exists (although the courts sometimes rule in favor of the requester).

FOIA provides that federal employees who "arbitrarily" or "capriciously" withhold information can be subject to disciplinary action by the Office of the Special Counsel of the Merit System Protection Board. The possible penalties are a written reprimand, a fine, or loss of employment. This provision was never anything more than a symbolic gesture by Congress, as evidenced by the fact that no federal employee has ever been sanctioned.

The number of secret keepers who could be proved to have acted arbitrarily or capriciously is very small. It is not necessarily capricious to decide that the release of documents could jeopardize national security or that the requester's purpose is too commercial to deserve a fee waiver. Such judgments may be shortsighted or mistaken, but it takes a higher threshold of proof to show that the employee was arbitrary or capricious.

In addition, even if the sanctions were levied frequently enough to get the attention of secret keepers, the powerful pull of the opposing risks would still exist. If an employee releases sensitive information, the risks can be much more daunting than if they do not. Not only might there be sanctions from peers and superiors on the job but, in some circumstances, harm could result (especially in matters related to national defense, foreign policy, spying, and law enforcement). "Harm," in the calculations of secret keepers, could range from blowing agents' covers, to fueling the agency's critics, to politically embarrassing the organization and its higher-ups. Strong motivations exist for employees to err on the side of secrecy, FOIA's toothless sanctions notwithstanding.

The courts (Supreme and Federal District) are often touted as the ultimate guardians of the public's right to know, the enforcer of agency conduct in the disclosure process. It is true that the courts can review and interpret the secrecy laws and regulate how they are administered by agencies. But the court's role as legal arbiter of the FOIA process does not make the law user-friendly. Moreover, most requesters would be more disadvantaged in relation to the agency in the courtroom than in the FOIA process, through no ill intent on the part of judges.

Any requester can file a FOIA lawsuit in the federal district court nearest their home or in the nation's capital. The filing costs are relatively inexpensive. If you hire an attorney and win your case, the act allows judges to award you attorney's fees. This is only if your side has "substantially prevailed" in showing that the government improperly denied your request. This recouping of expenses is by no means guaranteed, even if you win. The burden of proof is on government to prove that its decision was reasonable. It must provide specific justification relating to the information that is being contested: it cannot merely argue platitudes or broad generalities such as "national security."

In some court cases, agencies have made arguments that are contradicted by their own practices. One vivid example concerns the CIA's assertions to federal courts that its monumental backlog is the cause of delays in responding to requesters and that it must withhold every item relating to "sources and methods" (that nothing could be "selected out" for disclosure). In contrast, it found exceptions to both of these positions when dealing with one of its own.

Former CIA Director Robert Gates published his memoir in 1996. It was based largely on classified information. He writes that all of the documents he quoted or summarized were officially cleared for his use, as required by his terms of employment with the agency. Gates thanks his former colleagues for their "cooperation and promptness, particularly in light of the massive number of classified documents and Agency activities that I describe."[13]

These descriptions included verbatim quotes from presidential "daily briefs," National Intelligence Estimates, and intelligence "alerts." In this same era, scholars at the National Security Archive (a private facility in Washington, D.C.) were informed that no presidential daily briefs could be disclosed. Gates also describes numerous covert operations. In this case, the CIA has proved that speedy disclosure of selected secrets from the 1990s *can* be processed, if only for an agency insider to allow him to tell the story from primary sources withheld from independent scholars.

Recent legislation has done away with automatically expedited judicial review in FOIA cases (and other types of cases as well). While it is no longer legally mandated that FOIA cases be "expedited," plaintiffs can argue to the court that the information is needed in timely fashion, without prolonged judicial delay. If "good cause" is demonstrated, the calendar can be sped up. If not, the crowded docket and delays could void the timeliness and effective use of the information.

In some cases, government will capitulate at the mere filing of a lawsuit—to avoid investing time and money, to avoid a legal setback that might be precedent-setting. It depends on how important the secrecy is to the agency: How sensitive or controversial is the material? What are the implications for future requests? What are the political ramifications of disclosure (with the press, the public, other agencies, or Congress)? Plaintiffs, like government, must calculate just how important the legal contest is to them. How much time and money should be invested, given the envisioned consequences of a disclosure?

If it is a simple case without complex agendas involving other secrets, cover-ups, political fallout, or major legal-administrative precedents, requesters can effectively represent themselves. They may draw upon the free expertise offered by several organizations; they invest little time or money, and they may prevail. In contrast, if the outcome is perceived by the agency as high stakes, a victory for the requester is very unlikely without legal expertise. The resources of time and money will escalate accordingly. If you are fortunate enough to have competent, pro bono counsel, this helps enormously. But this, too, is a very scarce resource. Such lawyers must select their involvements carefully, measuring the possible gains from their investment (by whatever goals or priorities they adopt). All of the plaintiff's resources are scarce in one way or another. The government's are too; but, in a very real sense, somewhat less so. Agency lawyers already work for the agencies and are paid by the taxpayers. Agency experts are readily available and in place to testify. For example, agency employees can testify in great detail about the records system and the search process. To prove that the search was inadequate, the plaintiff must find and import experts who know the agency's information system.

Political scientists Morris P. Fiorina and Paul E. Peterson state that government "must bear the burden of proof when arguing its case before the judge."[14] While this is true, government has a powerful advantage. They know the secrets they are trying to preserve. Plaintiffs do not. Under what is called a "Vaughn motion," requesters may petition the court to require the agency to provide an index of the contested documents. This would list each document or segment being withheld and provide a specific justification for each. The Vaughn motion form letter is short and simple (see appendix C). A prototype can be obtained from "how to" booklets. But there is a catch-22 to Vaughn motions. The court may defer considering the motion until the government has seen and responded to the complaint. Thus plaintiffs may not be in possession of the index when they prepare the statement of their case.

At no stage short of legal victory do plaintiffs see the substance of the secrets they are pursuing. Requesters or their lawyers may argue their way out of this secrecy vacuum, but it is not easy to do. This is especially true when national security, spying, or law enforcement functions are involved. Unlike domestic secrets that are unconnected to these areas, the negative consequences of release (real or invented) are much more easily argued by government and much more difficult to refute without substantive knowledge. The legal playing field is *not* level.

The judge may see the secrets in chambers, absent the plaintiff. Federal judges in Washington, D.C., surely have more experience with agency documents than any of their counterparts in other districts. Even so, they are not expert in matters of espionage or antiterrorism. The secret keepers do have this expertise available to use in their defense. This does not mean that federal judges dare not reject government arguments. It means that they, too, are relative strangers in the wilderness of secrets, where they must distinguish the real risks from the smoke screens created by agency lawyers. This problem of substantive expertise is a fact of judicial life in many areas of litigation: environmental science, medical ethics, and antitrust suits. The difference is in the discovery process. Requesters do not have access to the primary "evidence" in the government's case—the documents. The battle of dueling experts, so common in our courtroom dramas, is not as equitable when one side has a secrecy cloak at their disposal.

Moreover, there is no jury of the requester's peers. These cases are decided by judges. Attorneys present many of the arguments on paper, rather than in impassioned legal orations. There are no potentially sympathetic jurors who might have survived jury selection even though they themselves had used FOIA, no citizen deliberation concerning whether the public interest outweighs the government's claims. It is a difficult process, as I experienced firsthand in 1989.

The Freedom of Information Act provides mandatory procedures, appeals, external monitoring, and broad definitions of "records" and of who can be a requester. Its application is easily understood and fairly simple to execute. It is not necessary to have a law degree or extensive expertise about the topic of the request. Free help is available—from form letters to hotline advice.[15] Millions of requests have produced the sought-after information without administrative or legal resistance from the agencies.

In the high-stakes arenas where disclosure issues are complex and politically sensitive, it is an entirely different game. Elevated levels of skill, resources, and commitment are needed for requesters to be successful. Each stage of the act becomes not a gateway but a hurdle. An agency will often delay, refuse access, and sometimes dissemble to preserve its precious secrets. The failure of journalists, lawmakers, and academic experts to acknowledge this situation, and to attempt to remedy it, has left the public disclosure process seriously flawed. Limited and uncontroversial requests will fare well. Giant corporations, prestigious law firms, and the *Washington Post* are poised to contest the government effectively with skills and resources waiting. Tens of thousands of requests fall in between the simple and the politically complicated. Many of these are of crucial importance for the public's right to know.

CHAPTER 3

Documents About You

If there had been a Mr. Hoover in the first half of the first century A.D., can you imagine what he would have put into his files about a certain troublemaker from Nazareth, his moral attitudes and the people he consorted with?

—*New York Times* reader's letter, 1970[1]

M ost of us are curious about what *they* might have on us. Everyone who ever sought or held federal employment, served in the armed forces, paid income taxes, or has been in the social security system has a file. But what about law enforcement or intelligence files—the FBI, CIA? Many people assume that if you are a law-abiding citizen having no shady involvements with criminals, terrorists, or spies, you will have no file. Others believe that if you write a letter to the editor asking who killed President Kennedy, the CIA will open a file on you. The reality is more complicated.

Beyond the ordinary files resulting from our interactions with federal agencies and programs, the scope of law enforcement and intelligence interest (or surveillance) surprises a lot of people. When agencies go after spies, terrorists, and organized crime figures, tens of thousands of "ordinary" citizens are caught in the data net. The legitimate reason is that investigators do not know, at the start, precisely who should be targeted as appropriate subjects who are involved in a case, or have knowledge of it. The nonlegitimate reason is that federal agencies have

manifested a nearly insatiable appetite for compiling dossiers—based
on speculation, miscalculation, or worse. At times, the surveillance of
U.S. citizens by its government has been unconstitutional and/or illegal.

Between 1956 and 1971, the FBI conducted COINTELPRO, a project
designed to monitor, infiltrate, and disrupt dissident political groups
deemed to be suspicious or threatening to national security. Records
indicate that there were 2,679 "action proposals" against various groups,
and 2,340 of them were implemented.[2] More than 700 of these were
designed to cause disruption within or between groups. The Bureau's
tactics included sending fictitious letters in hope of creating feuds,
forging membership cards and signatures, disseminating defamatory
or threatening information, spreading false rumors, and using agents
provocateurs to insight violence. There were also campaigns to discredit
certain groups in the perception of the media, the circulation of criminal records of group members, and the initiation of hostile actions
toward target groups by Bureau-friendly organizations (such as the
American Legion or Catholic War Veterans). Thousands of informants
reported on hundreds of organizations, including black-nationalist
"hate" groups, white "hate" groups, leftist college groups, the Women's
Strike for Peace, and the Southern Christian Leadership Conference.
Whether the entity was violent or nonviolent, if it was politically to the
left and focused on civil rights, opposition to the Vietnam War, or economic reform, COINTELPRO was there. If you were not a member of
such a group but an informant linked you up, you, too, were in the
Bureau's net.

As Frank Donner describes in *The Age of Surveillance:*

> [T]he FBI's investigation of individuals absorbs most of the time and
> energy of its field agents. The subjects of individual investigative files
> released under the FOIA are not only members past and present, of
> Marxist or violence-prone ("extremist") groups but thousands of indi-
> viduals targeted solely because of their involvement in controversial
> causes and dissident organizations. These records reflect common pat-
> terns: intensive investigation, highly detailed accounts of subject's
> political and private life, a negative bias that finds clues to subversion
> in everything the subject does, a high factual error quotient, endless
> repetition. . . .[3]

The CIA, whose 1947 charter forbids domestic spying, generated thousands of files on U.S. citizens. Its mail-opening project (HTLINGUAL) ran for two decades (1952–72). More than 2,300,000 letters and packages were diverted. An unknown, much-smaller number were opened, copied, resealed, and put back into the postal system. If the Agency found the item to be suspicious, a file was opened on the individual.[4] Did this mean that if you jokingly addressed your college chum in Moscow, Idaho, as "comrade" you were in the filing system of the Central Intelligence Agency? CIA Director Richard Helms conceded that the project had been illegal.

The CIA project CHAOS, starting in 1967, focused on antiwar and civil rights organizations as well as radicals and communists. More than 100 groups were targeted, including the Women's Strike for Peace, the American Friends Service Committee, Clergy and Laymen Concerned About Vietnam, the Nation of Islam, and the Youth International Party.[5] Some 10,000 files were opened on individuals within the United States. Under the Agency's professed concern for people having communist ties or suspicious foreign contacts, files were opened on Supreme Court Justice William O. Douglas, Senator Edward V. Long, and authors John Steinbeck and Edward Albee.

Broad and overzealous domestic spying is not a relic of the 1960s and 1970s. With new technologies come new potentials for abuse. In February 2000, a European Parliament Commission issued a report on Project Echelon, run by the CIA and the National Security Agency (NSA) in concert with intelligence agencies from Great Britain, Canada, Australia, and New Zealand.[6] This monitoring system is ground- and satellite-based. Its advertised purpose is to intercept communications of "suspected terrorists, drug traffickers, and money launderers." It scoops up a billion messages every hour in the United States and Europe—private telephones, fax machines, and e-mails. The Europeans are concerned that the system will be misused to engage in political spying and industrial espionage. Some Europeans charge that this had already occurred, alleging that U.S. companies have had an unfair advantage in bidding for contracts.

In response to these charges and concerns, a U.S. spokesperson insisted that Echelon be used exclusively for "national security" purposes. Testifying before Congress, CIA Director George Tenant assured, "Our targets are foreign." The NSA also claimed that Echelon was not a "big brother" operation: average citizens were not being spied upon. One of the researchers at the National Security Archives in Washington, D.C., where they obtained documents on the project via FOIA, opined that Echelon had a "potential for abuse both in areas of privacy and economic espionage."[7]

In 1988 the FBI was embarrassed when its library-spying program was "outed." It involved asking librarians to watch for, and report on, suspicious persons (defined by their behavior in the stacks or the titles they selected).[8] The Bureau was especially interested in communist bloc students, visitors, and diplomats. Said one FBI spokesperson: "We don't have enough personnel to keep track of everyone who comes into the country with an intelligence-gathering mission, and therefore public awareness is important."

Journalist Natalie Robbins interviewed FBI Director William Sessions concerning the "program":

ROBBINS: It seems that you are trying to turn librarians—the caretakers of our writers—into informants. What's really behind your seeking librarians' help? It's sort of a desperate move.

SESSIONS: I should not characterize it as a desperate move. I would think that it would be a logical move; that is, a move that should be understood very clearly by the American public and by any person who is aware of it. It is my understanding, therefore, for several years now—maybe as many as ten years—we have sought the assistance of librarians in connection with specialized libraries where there are people who come to gather technical research. Believe it! That these are places where foreign, hostile intelligence persons seek both to gather information and to recruit people who will be their agents in this country.[9]

While an "ordinary" citizen can become the subject of a file in an indiscriminate fishing expedition by a federal agency, most never do. For the vast majority of citizens, their files reflect only their routine interactions with government: student loans, passports, income taxes. In contrast, people who are politically active or have public notoriety (or both), or who know such people, are far more likely candidates for a dossier. It also depends where on the political spectrum such activities lie. Being active in fundraising for the Girl Scouts of America, or being the neighbor of a famous but apolitical TV chef are likely to be file-free experiences. Working with the nuclear-freeze movement, being a member of the Peace and Freedom Party, or having a close friend who once joined the Communist Party or the Black Panthers is a different matter. You do not have to be *very* famous or *very* connected in order to be a subject of interest.

Even so, what is there to worry about? If you have done nothing wrong, so what if an agency decides to hold some paper on you as part of its mandated function? The problem is that no matter how exemplary you are, a file can still create a problem for you. The more files, and the more extensive they are, the bigger the risk.

Files can contain errors: a computer glitch expunges your Veterans Administration check, an FBI criminal investigation gets a wrong name—yours. Lest anyone need reminding of bureaucracy's capacity to foul up, data systems can make the most whopping errors. Consider this one: In June 2000 the Pentagon "revised" the death toll of U.S. troops during the Korean War. It turns out that from 1953 to 2000 the number of estimated personnel killed was exaggerated by 17,000 (54,246 instead of 36,940). A "bureaucrat" had mistakenly added "noncombat deaths" to the military count. While this person was described as the "primary culprit," no military source caught the error for forty-three years, as it appeared ad infinitum in history books and Pentagon calculations.[10]

There are also inaccuracies that are not simply erroneous but malicious. A neighbor who has always hated your dog tells a credit investigator you frequently stagger from your car to your house. An FBI informant who has a grudge against you reports that you consort with dangerous revolutionaries.

Inaccurate or uncorroborated entries are difficult to detect and repair. They can result in harmful consequences for the subject, ranging from inconvenience or embarrassment to loss of employment and criminal investigation. The paranoid mentalities that have gripped certain agencies at certain times only exacerbate the problems created by indiscriminate spying and false accusations. The CIA perceived that the tamest of civil rights groups (the Congress of Racial Equality—CORE) was a direct "threat" to it. J. Edgar Hoover's obsession with communism impacted thousands of innocent citizens. Army Intelligence believed that the Civil Rights Movement of the 1960s constituted a dangerous and revolutionary emergency that had to be countered with Green Beret snipers and overflights by the U-2 spy plane.[11]

To discover files about you and to try to remedy any mistakes, *the* legal instrument is the Privacy Act of 1974. Its purpose is to give individuals access to their own records.[12] It had three main goals:[13]

• Access to your files (within the limits of its exemptions);
• The right to correct or amend a file if it is in error, incomplete, or irrelevant to legitimate governmental purposes; and
• The specific right to sue government for violations of the act.

The Privacy Act also limits how agencies can gather and circulate data. It requires that, to the fullest extent possible, data on you be gathered directly from you, not from informants or other files. The act forbids collecting data on how people exercise their First Amendment rights (freedom of speech, press, religion, and assembly). Courts have generally interpreted this provision as prohibiting agencies from snooping on the media, scholars, authors, or researchers as they perform their professional functions.

If you are lawfully holding a sign that urges the United States to end the trade embargo of Cuba, you are not supposed to be reported on. There are two legal exceptions: the person consents to surveillance (which makes little sense), or the agency has a legitimate law enforcement purpose. Thus, if you are regarded as a potential pro-Cuban terrorist, your First Amendment activities can be reported on.

The Privacy Act also restricts the circulation of files among agencies. A legitimate reason must exist, as opposed to the previous situation in which agencies could trade dossiers any time they wanted to—for political reasons, for fishing expeditions, for any other whim. But this law is helpless to prevent abuses that occur beyond federal agencies. What if there were a national intelligence organization that kept files on people, shared them at will, but was private, beyond the act's protection? Such an entity existed from 1956 until well into the early 1980s. Its name was the Law Enforcement Intelligence Unit (LEIU). Its activities are both instructive and chilling.[14]

LEIU was founded in 1956 at a secret meeting called by Captain James E. Hamilton, head of the Los Angeles Police Department's intelligence squad. The founding membership consisted of police and sheriff's departments from seven Western states. By 1975 (the year after the Privacy Act was passed), LEIU boasted 225 members—219 law enforcement agencies across the United States and 6 in Canada. The purpose was to create a national intelligence apparat that would be controlled by state and local departments, free from dependence on the FBI (or any other federal agency).

LEIU was organized in four "zones" (regions of the United States). Each had its own administrative structure that reported to a national chairman, vice chairman, and governing board. Member departments conducted investigations for themselves or other LEIU members, swapped data at will, and traded undercover operatives. When a member department's undercover officer had his cover blown, he would be geographically relocated to another member department where he could get a fresh start undercover. All of this occurred without federal participation or oversight. LEIU did, however, take federal money: Law Enforcement Assistance Act funds kept its computers running until 1977, under the falsely advertised purpose that it was a data system on organized crime.[15] Generous infusions of state funds also poured in.

The organization's spokesmen consistently claimed to the press and congressional committees that its purpose was to fight organized crime and that its files were exclusively on those targets.[16] This would later be disproved by LEIU's own documents, which revealed a fixation with political spying on any people deemed suspect, regardless of their disconnection from organized crime.

George O'Toole, a former CIA surveillance expert who provided a detailed portrait of LEIU, describes it as "a combination fraternal organization and intelligence agency."[17] To join, a law enforcement organization needed to apply: it had to have three sponsors among existing members and undergo a background check (of the organization and of the individual officers who would be conducting LEIU business). All member organizations were notified of the application and voted on it.

One policeman told O'Toole:

> LEIU meetings are mostly social affairs, but you build up lasting friendships when you go out and have a few drinks with an old boy. Then when he calls you up you know who you're talking to because you looked him in the eye just last week—some guy four states away. It's the closeness of the damn thing that I liked. It's just real good.[18]

These allegiances were forged beyond the purview of not only the feds but also governors, mayors, state legislatures, county and city managers, police commissions, and city councils.

Whereas everyone knew of the CIA and FBI, LEIU was so secretive that members regularly denied its existence. Some police higher-ups were not aware of it; nor were some of the leading attorneys specializing in privacy and civil liberties, both of which LEIU profoundly affected.[19] The organization's cover was partially blown in 1975 when the Houston (Texas) Police Department pulled out after allegedly receiving requests from other LEIU members to spy on Houston residents who had no criminal connections. One California department allegedly asked Houston to target a local businessman who was purchasing a chain of grocery stores out West: his finances, associates, family, and sex life.

While continuing to collect federal funds under the pretext of combating the Mafia, LEIU secretly pursued its real mission. As Frank Donner described in *The Age of Surveillance*, "information about dissidents was regularly exchanged at regional meetings, which also hosted speakers on subversion and foundation funding of radical groups. . . . Using a law enforcement cover, LEIU units have continued to collect files on dissenters and radicals. . . ."[20]

In a 1978 court-ordered release of Chicago Police Department intelligence files, dossiers circulated to and from LEIU were made public. The emphasis on ideologically driven political spying was manifest. LEIU "subject cards" had headlines for each individual being surveilled:[21]

- "Has assisted in organizing many radical groups and publications in Southern U.S."
- ". . . active in organizing marches and moratoriums."
- "Sells and distributes subversive literature."

- "Member, Black Panther Party."
- "Admitted active Muslim."
- "... recognized leader in peace movement."
- "Marxist scholar."

At a 1963 meeting, Lieutenant Frank Heimoski, Chicago Police intelligence division, proudly described LEIU's work:

> Subversive infiltrations of city employment has *[sic]* always been a concern of ours. The accumulation of records throughout the years has served to bar many suspect applicants seeking city employment and— in a number of instances—uncovered others already appointed.[22]

The Privacy Act aimed to stop witch-hunts by law enforcement and intelligence agencies. It forbade the indiscriminate collection and circulation of files, also the reporting on citizens who were merely exercising their rights of free speech and assembly. Yet LEIU did all of this, in secret. Any member of the clandestine brotherhood could get someone's file. Any member could get one started simply by filling out a handy form and sending it to the regional office for approval.[23] Congress had been concerned that federal agencies were sometimes acting above the law. LEIU *was* outside the law: FOIA, the Privacy Acts, and parallel state statutes.

In addition to being the two most revolutionary statutes for the public's right to know, the Privacy Act and Freedom of Information Act are intimately related legally, while also manifesting major differences. Both laws allow people to access records. FOIA allows "any person" to make a request. The Privacy Act grants request rights only to U.S. citizens or permanent resident aliens who are legally admitted. FOIA can be used to request any federal record on any topic that is not exempted. The Privacy Act is limited to agency records that are in a "system of records" and that relate to an individual who can be identified by name (or by other personal identifiers). The Privacy Act is more narrowly focused. FOIA can access data that is outside of "a system of records," data that is filed under other subjects besides a person's name—organizations, events, programs, and projects. The Privacy Act does not require an electronic search for information; FOIA does. Most experts advise that when seeking information about yourself, both statutes should be invoked in order to achieve a maximum search.

Files on other living persons will usually be withheld under the Privacy Act. If the third party waives their right to withholding, disclosure occurs. If an agency decides that the "public interest" in disclosure outweighs personal privacy, it can release a third-party file. However, the agency is legally required to withhold anything that constitutes "a clearly unwarranted invasion of privacy."[24] Corporations and other organizations have no rights to privacy. However, if the organization is sufficiently small so that individuals can be identified and related to specific information, the government can withhold data.

Dead people have no privacy rights (although, if release would cause anguish to surviving family or friends, agencies can withhold). This is why we know so much about deceased celebrities. A successful lawsuit for damages from an agency release of salacious gossip, or from the publication of it, is less of a threat. Relatives have a far heavier burden of proof concerning harm than does the subject of the file. Released documents become public sources whether printed by the *National Review* or the *National Enquirer.*

As with FOIA, the Privacy Act is easy to use; easier, in some ways. A short form letter will suffice (see appendix B). Agencies require varying degrees of proof of your identity. For some, a copy of a driver's license is acceptable; the FBI requires a notarized signature. Providing your name, address, and social security number is standard. The requester states that their *bona fides* are true "under penalty of perjury."

The burden of defining your subject in order to get an effective search is much less onerous than with FOIA. Still, there are ways of helping the agency find the data: providing nicknames, organizations to which you belonged, events that you participated in (political demonstrations), publications that you authored, geographic areas that relate to your activities (so that the appropriate field offices can be queried).

As previously described, under the Privacy Act (unlike FOIA), agencies can only charge for duplicating documents, not for finding them. The act does not require a response within a given time, although federal guidelines suggest ten working days. There is no legally required internal appeal process as with FOIA, but most agencies provide one. If you end up in court, the Privacy Act allows for the recovery of damages and attorney's fees if you can prove that the agency's file had "an adverse effect" on you.

The Privacy Act, like FOIA, has legally defined exemptions for withholding, even if the information *is* about you: files involving civil litigation, certain law enforcement and CIA files, certain files of security-cleared federal employees, presidential protection (Secret Service), legally required "statistical records," employment and promotion files (for the civil service, the armed forces, federal contractors), protection of national security, and confidential sources. The latter protection is one of the most crucial for agencies. Without it, informants would not provide information on such matters as organized crime figures, security clearance checks, people potentially threatening to the president, and cost overruns of federal contracts.

The protection of such sources has been a continuing issue of law and public policy. Agencies must protect their sources from embarrassment, confrontation, or reprisal caused by the people they report on. As J. Edgar Hoover put it in 1957, "To identify that [high level] informant would be to destroy the information for our subsequent work. It would very likely imperil the informant's life."[25]

On the other side of the argument are the due-process rights of the accused: the "right of confrontation," as it has been called. How can someone effectively defend themselves against charges that they are disloyal to the government of the United States or are drug users if they are not privy to the source of the allegation? Personnel review boards, disciplinary committees, and the courts have generally supported non-disclosure. Civil libertarians argue that an informant's story should be tested by cross-examination and investigation by the accused. Otherwise, mistaken or malicious reports can destroy careers.[26] This debate continues.

In spite of the possible nondisclosure, the Privacy Act does have a provision for correcting inaccuracies or incomplete entries. The requester writes to the agency that released the file and details the desired changes. The agency has ten working days to decide. It must inform the petitioner if further "proof" of the veracity of the requested revisions is needed. If this attempt fails, the person can go to federal court (the law requires the agency to inform requesters of this right). The agency has the advantage of knowing what is allegedly behind the entry at issue.

Factual errors (date of birth, years of employment) are easily corrected. Reports of communist affiliation or alcohol abuse are more difficult to refute. The percentage of successful corrections is unknown.

Let us now examine the files of some of the more prominent figures of recent decades. They are instructive—and hopefully interesting—at several levels. Most of these people are known to most of us in one way or another (TV, history books, music). The files of Marilyn Monroe and Martin Luther King, Jr., are in the public domain after being released to requesters. They provide windows into the process of surveillance and reporting by the FBI and CIA. In contrast, the author cannot obtain or discuss your file or those of his colleagues. I can write about my own files, as sparse or bland as they might be, without fear of suing myself (although, if my files were as rich with gossip as some of these celebrities, my wife could probably make a legal case for having suffered anguish).

While the people discussed here received attention from the agencies that was commensurate with their fame, two points are relevant. First, individuals of equal or greater notoriety did not receive such attention, and the level of surveillance was unjustified in terms of threat to national security. Second, one need not be a celebrity to have documents withheld on grounds of "national security" even when there is little or no justification. The rich and famous *are* different in terms of the attention they command. But the issues of privacy and secrecy that attend their files are the same ones that have existed for tens of thousands of ordinary Americans throughout our recent history. The simple fact is that the perceived magnitude of the issues, and the storyline, are enhanced by public stature. The scale may be different, but the problems are the same as those confronted by many "ordinary" citizens who find themselves on political turf of heightened concern to federal agencies, the White House, or the Pentagon.

The files of the people discussed here show a continuum of agency motives for targeting them: The FBI seemed pruriently curious about Marilyn Monroe, especially her relationships with John and Robert Kennedy. But the Bureau sought to destroy Martin Luther King, and to stop John Lennon's antiwar activities by deporting him. CIA paranoia was manifested over entertainer Harry Belafonte's role in the Civil

Rights Movement. The FBI fawned over J. Edgar Hoover's great friend Cardinal Richard J. Cushing.

In 2000 the *Boston Globe* used FOIA to obtain 802 pages of FBI documents on Cushing and published excerpts.[27] Hoover first met the stern, gravel-voiced Boston prelate in 1952 at a testimonial dinner for him (also attended by then-Congressman John F. Kennedy). The Bureau maintained a close relationship with Cushing throughout the 1950s and 1960s. The cardinal was not only a powerful church leader but stridently anticommunist—characteristics that endeared him to Director Hoover.

Documents show that the Bureau provided logistical assistance to the cardinal, at taxpayers' expense. Agents met him at airports during his travels here and abroad and served as his chauffeurs. A Cushing thank-you note to Hoover read: "You are one in a million. Your men certainly gave us the royal treatment wherever we went." The Bureau also gave the cardinal material for his anticommunist speeches. Hoover even provided him with a confidential memo on the political situation in communist-controlled Hungary.

Documents gush that Cushing is a "warm," "close," "valued" friend of Hoover. This meant that he was on a highly selective list for the director's "special correspondence." Unlike the hundreds of "BUFILES" (bureau files) that reported on people's communist contacts and subversive activities, this one described Cushing's travels, awards, celebrations, and health (asthma, shingles, ulcers, a kidney tumor—conditions kept from the press and public).

In 1954 Cushing was given a clean political bill of health by the Bureau: "There is no derogatory information regarding this individual," an agent wrote to Hoover. In 802 pages, there never was. In stark contrast, malicious gossip was the stock-in-trade for the Bureau's Martin Luther King file.

As friends, Cushing and Hoover exchanged editorial suggestions. The director gave advice on the cardinal's "catechism" on communism. Cushing suggested that a Bureau-distributed poster be changed to include the phrase: "America—this nation under God—pray, pray, pray."

The two men socialized when Cushing came to Washington, D.C. He spoke at the FBI academy's graduation. The cardinal frequently visited the Boston field office, which served as his pipeline to the director. He praised and quoted Hoover at every opportunity. "In these parts," he wrote the director, "if I quote J. Edgar Hoover it's just like quoting the Pope." The public praise was dutifully reported back to Hoover by agents covering the cardinal's speeches. Cushing warned Hoover of a "smear campaign" against him and pledged, "Our loyalty and fidelity to God and country requires that we stand behind you." He wrote asking the Bureau for material to use in rebutting attacks against Hoover. Professor Athan Theoharis, a historian who has conducted extensive research on the FBI, observed of the Cushing file: "Clearly this was an attempt to influence public opinion through a respected Catholic leader with a following in the public."[28]

Their mutual admiration and anticommunist zeal glossed over one of their major differences—the Kennedys. Cushing was very close to the family, presiding over its triumphs and tragedies as a spiritual confidant. Hoover detested both brothers and was engaged in a bitter power struggle with the president and the attorney general. In December of 1960, according to the file, Cushing assured Hoover that Robert Kennedy would not be appointed attorney general. When he turned out to be wrong, he wrote Hoover pledging public support if there was any attempt to fire him, which is precisely what the Kennedy brothers had in mind. Hoover responded with a disingenuous note denying any conflict with Robert Kennedy. Politics *does* make for strange bedfellows— the Kennedy brothers' worst political enemy and their best clerical friend.

The Cushing file ends tersely "Please delete the name Richard Cardinal Cushing from the list of SAC [special agent in charge] of the Boston office as he is deceased (Nov. 6, 1970)." Hoover died in office in 1972.

During many of the same years that Hoover's FBI was fawning over its political ally, the cardinal, it was persecuting its self-proclaimed arch enemy, Dr. Martin Luther King, Jr.[29] Hoover detested King personally and politically and used the full power of the Bureau in a protracted attempt to bring him down. Hoover falsely believed—or pretended to— that King was communist-influenced, if not controlled, despite his own agents' advice to the contrary. Hoover was clearly obsessed: "King is no good anyway," he scribbled, describing the Nobel-Prize-winning leader as "a tomcat with obsessive, degenerate urges."

The Bureau's surveillance was total. Offices and hotel rooms were bugged, agents tailed King, an informant was recruited within his organization. From 1965 until his assassination in 1968, the FBI spies within the Southern Christian Leadership Conference (SCLC) "soon eclipsed the wire taps on SCLC offices as the most valuable source of information on King," according to Professor David Garrow.[30]

Documents released from Bureau files show that it sought the "desired result" of "neutralizing King as an effective Negro leader," by painting him as "an immoral opportunist." According to one memo, the campaign against him would use "disgruntled acquaintances," "aggressive newsmen," and "colored agents." As Assistant Director William Sullivan put it, it must "be revealed to the people of this country and to his Negro followers as being [sic] what he actually is—a fraud, a demagogue and moral scoundrel." Sullivan predicted King's political demise if the campaign against him were "handled properly."

There was nothing proper about the Bureau's unconstitutional, dirty-tricks campaign. Hoover compiled alleged audiotapes of parties in King's hotel room. "They will destroy the burrhead," he joyously announced. In January 1965, the audio collage was mailed to King's home in Atlanta. His wife opened it. The accompanying, unsigned note read: "King, there is only one thing left for you to do. You know what it is. . . . You are done. There is but one way out for you. You better take it before your filthy, abnormal, fraudulent self is bared to the nation." Later, a Bureau bug captured King's reaction: "They're out to break me," he said.

The FBI peddled its allegations of King's communism and womanizing to the media and to various organizations and political institutions. When Hoover learned that King was to receive an honorary degree from Marquette University, he dispatched an agent who successfully talked them out of it. The agent got a cash award for his good work. Assistant Director Sullivan made a presentation to the National Council of Churches on King's "personal conduct."[31] Hoover tried to block King's 1965 Nobel Prize by having scandalous allegations fed to various officials (at the State Department, U.S. Information Agency, and United Nations). *New York Times* reporter John Herbers recalled that "a special agent . . . told me about these things they had on King. He was holding the tapes out for me in case I wanted to hear them. I thought they were off base."[32]

In April 1967, there was speculation that Dr. King might run for president on an antiwar platform with Dr. Benjamin Spock as his running mate. FBI wiretaps kept the Johnson White House informed. In a low point of the Bureau's antidemocratic behavior, FBI headquarters requested that field officers submit plans for "countermeasures" against a King/Spock ticket.[33]

Hoover's office sent a memo to the Johnson White House describing King as "an instrument in the hands of subversive forces seeking to undermine our nation."[34] Vice President Walter Mondale summed up the Bureau's campaign against its domestic archenemy: "The way Martin Luther King was hounded and harassed is a disgrace to every American."[35]

Meanwhile, the CIA, whose mission was to keep track of communist spies and hostile intelligence agencies around the world, had identified another domestic threat—singer/actor/political activist Harry Belafonte.[36] The Agency's gossipy reports falsely accused Belafonte of being a communist, worried that he was attaining a leadership position in the Civil Rights Movement (because of his friendship with King), and cataloged unsubstantiated assertions about virtually every aspect of his private life. These documents were not released until 1994. One is entitled, "Major 'Black Power' and Militant Personalities." It describes Belafonte's political activities: an antiwar march in New York City in 1967, signing an antiwar petition, "advising" the government of Ghana, and associating with King adviser Stanley Levenson (also accused of being a communist).

Another 1965 report based on "confidential" informant(s) focuses on his personal life and travels. It asserts that the communists have financial control over him. A "Secret," "eyes only" report from 1965 identifies Belafonte as a "leader of first magnitude," on a par with King, "who has been established clearly as a close and intimate friend of King and whose left-wing background is also known." King "is moving in a way that is indicative that he is being controlled by the Peking-line communists, possibly or probably through Belafonte, from whom there is some information that would indicate that he is a Maoist."

The tracking of Belafonte by the world's most powerful espionage agency was so relentless as to extend to television. A February 9, 1968, memo from the CIA's Cecil Tighe to the Chief of "Security Research Staff" relays:

——— [source deleted] viewed Belafonte's emceeing of the Johnny Carson show last night. ——— said that Sidney Poitier and Livingston Wingate, at the prompting of Belafonte, went into a lengthy discussion of how Martin Luther King obtained his money some years ago. According to ——— Belafonte is setting the stage for a future discussion of this matter when King appears tonight on the show.

After King's death, the fears reported to the Agency escalated. "——— received word from a reliable source that Belafonte, who is under Peking discipline, has now been instructed to move in to the home of Martin Luther King's widow in Atlanta," where he "will remain until several days after the funeral." The paranoid view of U.S. politics reached new heights in an "eyes only" report on Belafonte's sinister power:

——— suggests that television on Tuesday will disclose that Belafonte and Robert Kennedy will be in the forefront during funeral services [for King]. According to ———, Belafonte has sufficient information of a blackmail nature on Bobby Kennedy that will result in Kennedy reacting as a puppet to Peking direction in the coming presidential nominating campaign.

One cannot help but wonder what the CIA's Chief of the Security Research Staff did with this information. One report on Belafonte is signed by CIA higher-up Morse Allen, who says that the information comes from "a confidential informant who has provided reliable and valuable information [in the past]." Allen headed the Agency's BLUEBIRD project in the early 1950s, which pursued techniques of brainwashing and mind control.[37] He went on to serve the CIA by routing out alleged communists within the federal government. Allen's memo is sent not only to the "Chief, Security Research Staff," but also to the "Chief, Liaison and Exploitation Branch/SRS [Security Research Staff]." The reader of the document is left to ponder what the *exploitation* branch does and who or what it exploits.

The FBI collected dossiers on the rich and famous as if it were Robin Leach or the editors of *People* magazine: Frank Sinatra, Mickey Mantle, Ezra Pound, the Duke and Duchess of Windsor, folksinger Phil Ochs (429 pages), Albert Einstein (1,500 pages), more than 150 authors (including William Faulkner, Norman Mailer, Sinclair Lewis, and James Baldwin), and columnist Walter Lippman.

The policy was to surveil "writers, lecturers, newsmen and others in the mass media field" who "might influence others against the national interest or are likely to furnish financial aid to subversive elements."[38] This included such luminaries as columnists Peter Arnet and Joseph Alsop, folksinger Pete Seeger, conductor Leonard Bernstein, and labor leaders Cesar Chavez and Walter Reuther. Even Supreme Court justices were not exempt. FBI documents released in 1997–98 reveal that, on July 20, 1967, there was a three-page memorandum from the head of the FBI's Washington field office, Joseph Purvis, to Cartha DeLoach (the Bureau's number-three man) regarding "possible homosexual activities on the part of Justice Abe Fortis."[39]

The file of comedian Groucho Marx was obtained by University of California history professor Jon Wiener.[40] Several pages were withheld because of "national defense or foreign policy." The dossier began in 1953 when a confidential informant told the Bureau that Marx was a member of the communist party (he was a prominent member of Hollywood's liberal community).

Marx got caught up in the politics of McCarthyism—the sordid campaign to intimidate people into naming names of alleged communists—which divided Hollywood in the early 1950s. The bandleader for his hit TV show, "You Bet Your Life," Jerry Fielding, was accused of being a communist by the House Un-American Activities Committee (HUAC). Fielding claimed that the committee pressured him to name Marx as a "fellow traveler."

Marx's Bureau file contained newspaper clippings dating back to the 1930s when he voiced political views that seemed pro-communist. He joined the Committee for the First Amendment that opposed HUAC. It included Frank Sinatra, Humphrey Bogart, and Lauren Bacall. Marx's file was replete with letters from irate viewers who objected to his politically charged one-liners. One letter complained that when a TV guest told host Groucho that the guest was a pugilist and a bootlegger, Marx quipped, "You mean you were a bootlegger for the FBI." Such comments were bound to get the Bureau's attention and arouse its ire.

The FBI targeted political leaders, as well as celebrities, when their views on issues were suspect. Henry Wallace served as vice president under Franklin D. Roosevelt and secretary of commerce under President Truman; he ran for president in 1948 on the Progressive Party ticket. His 500-page Bureau file was obtained through FOIA by the *Des Moines Register* in 1983.[41] It reveals that agents tapped his phone, opened his mail, and interviewed his closest associates beginning in 1943 and continuing into his vice presidency. The Bureau's assumption was that this national political figure's leftist views made him a candidate for membership in pro-Soviet organizations (his candidacy for vice president and president notwithstanding).

Numerous authors and researchers have used FOIA to obtain FBI documents on Marilyn Monroe. Many pages are blacked out with a national security exemption. One former agent described her file as "voluminous."[42] Yet author Anthony Summers was given only thirteen out of a scant thirty pages found (and these were heavily censored). The Bureau met with Summers and his attorney, James Lesar. It told them that the withholding related to the actress's travels in Mexico, where she saw a man long suspected of being a communist. Even the Los Angeles District Attorney's Office was denied access to these particular documents. We have only the Bureau's word on what they relate to. In addition to the file, whether voluminous or strikingly thin, Hoover had another display of Marilyn's persona—an original print of her nude calendar hung in his home.[43]

The Bureau's surveillance of Monroe was complex. Her liaisons with both John and Robert Kennedy, while they were president and attorney general, respectively, were a central element of Hoover's motive. Agents cataloged Robert Kennedy's visits to Monroe's apartment in Los Angeles. This meant that Hoover was surveilling his titular boss, the attorney general of the United States. One memo describes Kennedy as arriving at her home driving a Cadillac convertible.[44] Marilyn reportedly "spent time with Robert Kennedy at Peter Lawford's home."

One released document states that the star discussed "the morality of atomic testing" with Robert Kennedy.[45] The withheld "national security" documents may contain more about her policy discussions with the two most powerful leaders in the country.

Hoover's vendetta against the Kennedy brothers and their plans to remove the legendary director from office made Marilyn Monroe not just another celebrity caught in the Bureau's sights but a key element in a power struggle. Her discussion of "atomic testing" and her travels to Mexico may be considered national security matters to be withheld from the public, but this file must be, or *have been,* extremely sensitive in terms of domestic politics. This actress was allegedly having affairs with a married president and a married attorney general, and the FBI Director was fighting for his job with every dirty trick in his playbook.

Professor Jon Wiener was writing a book on deceased Beatle John Lennon when he got the Bureau's file through FOIA in 1981.[46] Two hundred eighty-one pages were found in the search; a staggering 199 were withheld from release.[47] Disclosed documents were heavily blacked out (one entire page had nothing but Lennon's name) for reasons of "national security." With the help of the American Civil Liberties Union, Professor Wiener went to federal court to overturn the withholding. Fourteen years later, as the case moved to the U.S. Supreme Court, the Bureau gave Wiener a victory and agreed to settle—$204,000 in court and attorney's fees and all but ten pages of the file. Why was the FBI so determined to keep these secrets?

John Lennon's file started in 1971 when he became very active in opposing the Vietnam War. As with Harry Belafonte and the CIA, Bureau agents tracked their targets by watching television programs. A 1972 memo reports in detail on Lennon's appearance as cohost of *The Mike Douglas Show.* The paranoia-plagued Nixon White House learned that the musician was planning on organizing a national concert tour that would include Bob Dylan. It would fuse the power of rock music with antiwar politics and coincide with the presidential election of 1972. Lennon would urge audiences to register to vote and vote against the war. This was the first election in history in which eighteen-year-olds could vote.[48] The White House got the point: it wouldn't be Nixon that this potential horde of young rockers would vote for.

Senator Strom Thurmond wrote to Attorney General John Mitchell suggesting that deporting the singer back to England "would be a strategy *[sic]* counter measure." The Nixon administration's campaign to "neutralize" the music legend became a central topic of his BUFILE.[49] The Immigration and Naturalization Service began deportation proceedings in 1971.

Recall that the Privacy Act of 1974 specifically forbids compiling a file on someone who is exercising their first amendment rights—free speech and freedom of assembly. Previously there had been no specific prohibition of this practice. Lennon had no terrorist connections or criminal involvements. He was simply an enormously popular music icon who had decided to oppose the Nixon administration's Vietnam policies. The Bureau needed a hook: even they felt compelled to create a pretense that targeting Lennon was not an act of political revenge emanating from the White House.

Lennon did associate with political activists such as Jerry Rubin, who had been convicted of conspiracy to disrupt the Democratic National Convention of 1972. But the Bureau's assertion that this made Lennon a legitimate law enforcement target rings hollow.[50] The FBI's professed concern for national security was actually a reflection of *in*security concerning antiwar politics.

One document in the file was totally censored when originally released to Professor Wiener. The Bureau went all the way to the Supreme Court to preserve the blackout, and lost: it has nothing to do with foreign countries or international politics. Instead, it blew the cover on the Bureau's pretext for its Lennon file. The FBI had argued both publicly and in court (during Wiener's legal challenge) that its investigation was based on information that Lennon planned to participate in violent, disruptive demonstrations at the Republican National Convention in Miami (1972). The restored document asserts just the opposite. It states that Lennon had said he would go to Miami to demonstrate "if they are peaceful."[51] There was no evidence to contradict this report.

One released document from the New York field office to FBI headquarters reports that Lennon was

> reportedly a "heavy user of narcotics known as downers." This information should be emphasized to local law Enforcement Agencies covering MIREP [Republican National Convention in Miami], with regards to subject being arrested *if at all possible* [emphasis added]

on possession of narcotics charge. . . . INS [Immigration and Natural-ization Service] has stressed to Bureau that if Lennon were to be arrested in U.S. for possession of narcotics he would become more likely to be immediately deportable.[52]

A letter from Hoover to Nixon's chief of staff H. R. Haldeman, dated April 25, 1972, was entirely blacked out because of "national security."[53] When all but a few lines were finally restored, the text is shown to report on Lennon's possible deportation and on possible disruption of the Republican convention. This document shows that the targeting of Lennon was a matter that received attention at the highest levels of government, and that the restored portions had been improperly withheld on the pretense of "national security."

A handwritten note by a special agent on a 1972 memo sums up the FBI's file on John Lennon. It reads, "All extremists should be consid-ered dangerous." The political judgment inherent in this maxim is *who is an extremist?*

In July 2000 I conducted a kind of experiment with FOIA and the Privacy Act. In a series of highly detailed requests, I asked the FBI, CIA, and Secret Service for documents on myself. I'm no John Lennon, but I am an author. In FBI and CIA files, I had come across several memos relating to authors. In these memos, both agencies had taken the time to refute criticisms or to consider approaching "friendly" authors to write books about them. For example, a 1969 FBI memo from Assistant Direc-tor Cartha DeLoach to Clyde Tolson (one of Hoover's closest confidants) proposes:

> Now that Ray [King's alleged assassin James Earl Ray] has been con-victed and is serving a 99-year sentence, I would like to suggest that the Director allow us to choose a friendly, capable author, or the *Reader's Digest,* and proceed with a book based on this case.
>
> A carefully written factual book would do much to preserve the true history of this case. While it will not dispel or put down future rumors, it would certainly help to have a book of this nature on college and high school library shelves so that the future would be protected.
>
> If the Director approves, we have in mind considering cooperating in the preparation of a book with either the *Reader's Digest* or author

Gerald Frank. The *Reader's Digest* would assign one of their staff writers or contract the preparation of a book out to an established author. Gerald Frank is a well-known author whose most recent book is *The Boston Strangler.* Frank is already working on a book on the Ray case and has asked the Bureau's cooperation in the preparation of the book on a number of occasions. We have nothing derogatory on him in our files, and our relationship with him has been excellent. His publisher is Doubleday.

A 1967 CIA "dispatch from headquarters to chiefs, certain stations and bases" is titled "Countering Criticisms of Warren Report." It lamented the recent wave of books and articles suggesting a conspiracy in President Kennedy's assassination and even charging that the CIA was somehow involved. The dispatch described these publications as a threat to "the whole reputation of the American Government." It then went on to "provide material for countering and discrediting the claims of the conspiracy theorists" (by getting book reviews and feature articles published).[54]

Four of my books were potential subjects of interest for one or both of these agencies. One was on Lee Harvey Oswald's possible relationship with the CIA; one focused heavily on FBI and CIA surveillance of Martin Luther King, Jr.; a third was the first in-depth organizational profile of the U.S. Secret Service by someone who had not worked for the agency.[55] The latter work was both praising and critical of the Service. The fourth assessed the Bureau's investigation of the assassination of Robert F. Kennedy.

My request letter referenced my life and my work: book titles; geographic areas where I wrote, worked, and researched; personal descriptors. One of the first responses was from the CIA, erroneously limiting my request to a search under FOIA. I had specifically asked for a search under both FOIA and the Privacy Act—as one is advised to do by the experts. It took five weeks and two rounds of correspondence to fix this problem.

To my surprise—if not disappointment—all three agencies turned up little (the FBI) or nothing (the CIA and Secret Service). There was not one scrap of paper pertaining to my books. As the CIA put it, "No records were found responsive to your request regarding yourself."

The lone exception was the FBI's discovery of my 1985 correspondence asking for clarification of its RFK assassination document referring to "bullet holes" at the crime scene—bullet holes that would prove a second gun was fired. Some of the Bureau's notations on my letter were interesting. A handwritten entry at the top said, "Research matters." At the bottom were six blackouts "to protect the initials of FBI employees who saw the letter." I wondered why the letter was so internally popular at the Bureau and what the initialers were being "protected" from.

There was also an internal Bureau "Note" at the bottom of my letter: "Professor Melanson is the subject of BUFILE 190-37477. In association with Gregory Stone (190-10565), Professor Melanson has previously requested and received FBI materials relating to the RFK assassination." In 1974 Congress forbade agencies from opening a file simply because someone made a FOIA request. If the author's "BUFILE" is solely about FOIA and the release of the RFK files, it is illegal. If it contains other items, I should be so advised, even if they are withheld (I am legally entitled to know the number of pages and the reason for withholding).

The Bureau also found a letter I had written to the head of the Boston field office in 1973. I requested that a representative come to my university to speak to my political science class, "Public Policy in America." I suggested eight possible dates. A handwritten notation reads: "Talked to his secretary in his absence. Heavy schedule until first of year. Maybe can do after that. Send us another letter."

It is striking that this obscure item surfaced while there are no documents pertaining to my books or my numerous media appearances discussing the Bureau's secrecy policies and its investigations of the political assassinations of the 1960s. Also surprising was that no records appeared from the 1989 federal court case in which Greg Stone and I attempted to stop the Bureau's deletions of agents' names from the RFK assassination file. In short, it was difficult to believe they had conducted an adequate search for records.

In October 2000, I appealed on the grounds that the search was inadequate. I cited the voluminous documents from the 1989 court case, the four letters (two from me, two to me) regarding ballistics in the

RFK case that were not found in the search, and the reference to my "BUFILE" as demonstrating the inadequacy of the search.

Five months later (March 13, 2001), I received a decision from Richard L. Huff, co-director of the Justice Department's Office of Information and Privacy:

> After careful consideration of your appeal, I have decided to affirm the FBI's action on your request. The FBI informed you that it could locate no records responsive to your request. It has been determined that the FBI's response is correct because the FBI found no new records responsive to your request. I apologize for any confusion caused by the FBI's use of "no records" when it meant "no new records."

Now I was *really* confused. "New" to whom? It would all be new to me, since they found only two letters dating from 1973 and 1985. What of the four other letters that I had exchanged with the Director's office concerning ballistics in the Robert Kennedy assassination? Were these 1985–88 items *old?* Was not the Bureau's inability to find them evidence of an inadequate search?

Huff also informed me that,

> [a]lthough there are no new records, you are mentioned briefly in several Headquarters main files entitled Freedom of Information— Privacy acts and are the subject of one Headquarters main file entitled Litigation Files. Litigation files routinely are not processed in response to a FOIA request because they contain correspondence and court documents, material that is typically already in the possession of the requestor.

Here the Bureau is rewriting FOIA law behind the scenes for its own convenience. This means that if you are involved in a court case relating to the FBI, it will "routinely" not search there because it has made the assumption that you "typically" have everything that pertains to you. I agree that the *typical* requester with a good filing system would be likely to have his or her material from the case, but what about Bureau documents that refer to the requester but were not generated by the requester and not introduced into the court record (that is, what internal memos or rebuttal affidavits not submitted to the court refer to me and my submissions as a coplaintiff)? The latter should not be assumed by the Bureau to be a null set: it knows better. Notice also that the requester is not told of this policy unless the search is directly challenged in an appeal and the litigation is specifically mentioned. Huff also asserted that my BUFILE number, referred to in an FBI "note" on my 1985 letter, was "one of the FOIA files mentioned above [in Huff's letter]."

The decision did little to assuage my concern that, with all of my myriad, high-profile writings and involvements, the search that produced only two pieces of correspondence was inadequate. Federal court was not an option for me in this case. Proving that there was an inadequate search would be difficult, and there is no guarantee that anything fruitful (such as FBI memos about my books) would ever surface. Perhaps the Bureau routinely does not search *author* files because they assume that, "typically," authors retain copies of their own books. I was, however, mildly tempted to compel the Bureau to discuss in open court its intriguing distinction between old and "new" records—but only mildly.

The request for one's files is simple. Obtaining the existing information is not. Once the requester leaves the straightforward realm of Medicaid and small-business loans and enters the turf of confidential sources, national security, and law enforcement, disclosure is a different process. In the latter areas, agency filing systems are complicated, secretive, and prone to cover-ups. While the legal process is the same for everyone, the political process is not. The composition and disposition of files on *you* depend very much on who *you* are.

CHAPTER 4

Blackouts

[The CIA] would agree with historian David Hackett Fisher that history is not what happened but what the surviving evidence says happened. If you can hide the evidence and keep the secrets, then you can write the history.

—Thomas Powers, *The Man Who Kept the Secrets: Richard Helms and the CIA*[1]

There are three levels at which information is withheld: deletions of selected documents, refusal to release an entire file, and noninclusion of certain data in the disclosure process. In the latter case, information is lost, destroyed, or hidden (segregated so that it is "off the books" regarding public disclosure). Legally, recall that there are nine exemptions by which agencies can justify keeping secrets—privacy and national security being foremost. As the documents in appendix A illustrate, there is a continuum of blackouts via deletions: a word or words on a page, the withholding of entire documents (be it one page or twenty), or the withholding of an entire file (whether 50 pages or 5,000).

Then there are the preemptive blackouts: files hidden away in secret systems and/or secret locations—never to be accessed by anyone using the mainstream system. These data often pertain to agency activities so politically sensitive that they are purposefully unaccounted for in the central records system. Sometimes such exclusions are legal—the CIA's "operational files." Sometimes no legal authorization exists. Files are sometimes removed or destroyed to execute a cover-up, or to hide information from "outsiders" (whether they be the public, the media, oversight bodies, or distrusted agency higher-ups).

Another time-honored tactic to prevent records from being disclosed, or leaked, is to avoid generating any. Some offices and working groups have, at times, refused to create a record that might be accessible to the media and the public, while simultaneously refusing to talk apart from the non-record. This dramatically reduces leaks and criticisms.

In the early months of George W. Bush's presidency, his Energy Task Force took such a tack. This working group was hardly a private entity or an informal discussion group. It included the cabinet secretaries of energy, interior, transportation, agriculture, commerce, and treasury; the heads of the Environmental Protection Agency (EPA), the Federal Emergency Management Agency (FEMA); as well as the president's deputy chief of staff, intergovernmental affairs advisor, and budget director. Vice President Dick Cheney served as chair. The task was to produce a report recommending policies to reduce the imbalance between energy consumption and energy supply. This consensual goal was nevertheless politically volatile. It involved such hot-button issues as drilling for oil in the government-protected wilderness of Alaska and the Rocky Mountains, building new nuclear power plants (and relicensing old ones), building new oil refineries and pipelines, creating more power grids, and increasing the production and use of coal.

Attempting to operate without media scrutiny and apart from the heat of policy debate and political conflict, the panel created a shroud of secrecy. According to press reports, at the start of each meeting a member or members would request that the session be off the record. No documents were shared or circulated among participants, thereby drastically reducing the potential for leaks.[2] Members consistently refused to talk to the media and, if they did, they refused to discuss policy. Vice President Cheney would not meet with the heads of prominent environmental and energy groups seeking input, but he did have a series of sit-downs with industry representatives.

A telephone query from a reporter to a panel member was intercepted by an EPA spokesman, who asserted: "I'm sorry. We're not going to discuss process."[3] He then insisted that his name not be attached to his no-comment comment. A Treasury Department official went further, stating that: "There really isn't anything to talk about."[4] Critics felt otherwise, wanting to talk both process and substance before the panel made its recommendations without public discussion or outside input.

Some "black holes" of governmental secrecy are blacker than others. While contemporaneous information is more likely to be regarded as sensitive by secret keepers, this is not always the case. The Assassination Records Review Board, appointed by President Clinton to oversee the release of millions of pages of documents relating to President Kennedy's assassination, confronted an intense maze of secrecy even more than three decades after the event. Some of it was legitimate; some, not. The subjects included the Secret Service's cover-up of its terrible performance, the CIA's anti-Castro operatives and assets, CIA-Mafia assassination plots against Castro, and Lee Harvey Oswald's possible ties to the CIA, FBI, and Naval Intelligence.

Whether deletions are from current or ancient documents, agencies must provide justification. This takes the form of a number or letter that references one of the nine FOIA exemptions. In the author's experience, agencies only identify the reason if the deletion is large (a paragraph or page). Words and sentences are often removed without providing a coded reference.

Imagine the broad discretion possessed by tens of thousands of secret keepers and the pressure placed upon them as they wielded their black marker pens. The vague definitions of privacy and national security must be operationalized through a substantive reading of the document. Names of confidential sources must be deleted every time they appear in a 500-page file. The telephone numbers and addresses of witnesses in an FBI murder case must be expunged to protect their privacy. A paragraph in a Navy document must be purged because it refers to communications codes that could still be operational. (One result of this mindset is a twenty-four-page CIA document on Dr. Martin Luther King, Jr., that has twenty blank pages.)

If a name, code, address, or formula is not excised, the secret keeper may have committed a costly error. Depending on the type and significance of the information, some dire possibilities can arise: a deep-cover agent is exposed and assassinated, a corporation loses the secret formula for its best-selling tranquilizer, or ship-to-ship Navy communications in the North Atlantic are compromised.

In an age of automated, computerized information processes, the procedure for reviewing potentially secret documents is an anachronism. Someone has to read and delete—a task that is both tedious and demanding. I have sometimes tried to imagine what it is like being a secret keeper armed with a black marker. Reading thousands of pages on a topic that holds little or no familiarity, that may hold little or no substantive allure for the reader, must be punishing. There is no quiz, much less a final exam. Even so, this does not allow for the kind of rapid skimming or cursory attention that requesters can indulge in when they receive the documents. As soporific as a file might be, a qualified, security-cleared employee must go over it line by line.

Moreover, deletions are supposed to be conscious, substantive decisions that apply policies and laws. They are not supposed to be random acts reflecting boredom or frustration. Privacy is much more straightforward than national security for the employee to identify. Telephone numbers, names of former spouses, and references to medical conditions are readily apparent. In contrast, when is an item a threat to the security of the nation? Ideally, decision makers are required to envision the consequences of releasing the information. However, these consequences do not appear in black and white on the page in front of them. They must make a decision as to whether the potential damage outweighs the public interest in disclosure. What *public?* What *interest?* Standards, guidelines, and precedents do exist (both government-wide and agency-specific). But these must be applied in substantive contexts that vary significantly among topics, historical eras, and filing-system organization at a given point in time. If done knowledgeably and conscientiously, processing documents for public disclosure is a highly demanding job.

Occasionally documents can reveal snapshots of the mentality or competence of the secret keepers. The identity of a mysterious figure in the assassination of Dr. Martin Luther King, Jr., was accidentally disclosed by the FBI. One undeleted reference to the name, within dozens of deletions on dozens of pages, was all it took. Another Bureau file centered on a suspect (not James Earl Ray) detained at the King crime scene. His military service was completely deleted from all documents. Yet the names, addresses, and phone numbers of his employers, family, and associates remained, in clear violation of his rights to privacy.

The FBI has been ultra-sensitive about cases from the Hoover era, especially the assassination of Dr. Martin Luther King, Jr. (in part because of Director Hoover's unconstitutional vendetta seeking to destroy King personally and politically). This is manifested in blackouts. When alleged assassin James Earl Ray faced trial, he was represented by noted attorney Percy Foreman. But Foreman's role was ripe with controversy and conflict of interest. The super-lawyer signed a book deal while representing Ray.[5] The contract was contingent on there not being a trial, so that the real story of "who was James Earl Ray" would not be preemptively vetted by the media. Foreman advised Ray to plead guilty and avoid a trial, even though the case against his client was highly circumstantial and fraught with reasonable doubts. Ray did as his lawyer instructed.

FBI case documents relating to Foreman are among the most heavily deleted in the massive MURKIN file (short for murder of King). One document that refers to the plea bargain has twenty-three lines fully expunged. Other pages on Foreman are so blacked out that only his name and less than ten words remain.

A rare opportunity to see what the secret keepers deleted arose in the FBI's Robert Kennedy assassination file. Newly released documents arrived at the University of Massachusetts' RFK Assassination Archive in deleted form. A year earlier, 100 pages of this same file were accidentally released with no censorship by the Los Angeles District Attorney's (LADA) office. While processing the DA's file, someone in that office had failed to notice that, for some witnesses, their FBI interview was stapled to their DA's interview. A cardinal rule of public disclosure holds that an agency never releases documents originating with another agency before obtaining its permission. Yet this procedure was not followed: undeleted Bureau pages were placed in the California State Archives at Laguna Niguel, literally under the cover of the DA's documents relating to the same witness. This was quite an error. The FBI documents were clearly marked. Someone had failed even to skim the pages prior to release.

As a result of this error, I could now compare the full FBI text to the deleted LADA documents on the same witness, and also compare the FBI to itself. This was a rare opportunity to see what was being withheld. Beyond addresses and telephone numbers—deletions required by the Privacy Act—a clear pattern emerged.

A comparative analysis of the three sets of documents (LADA, deleted FBI, undeleted FBI) reveals that the DA's office conducted twelve of what I would term *deletions of substance* (relevant or potentially important information not related to privacy). The Bureau performed nine. Both agencies targeted the same substantive references for blackout 78 percent of the time. By far the most censored topic (six for the DA, five for the FBI) were witness accounts of seeing a suspicious woman (blond, attractive, wearing a polka-dot dress). She was allegedly seen with Sirhan in a variety of locations at the Ambassador Hotel crime scene the night of the assassination—including just before the shooting. She was also seen fleeing the hotel with another man. This woman was never found.

Other substantive deletions were not conspiratorial in implication, except for four references to a man in a suit (not Sirhan) acting suspiciously at the crime scene and fleeing just after the gunfire. Clearly, the redactors were sensitive to the fact that, if there were an accomplice, there could not be a lone assassin as both the FBI and the District Attorney's office had concluded.

In a strange twist of the clandestine mentality, the CIA attempted to black out its blackouts. My 1984 request for Dr. Martin Luther King, Jr.'s, file produced 134 pages that were heavily deleted. One twenty-four-page memo (dated March 7, 1968, one month before his assassination) was almost totally blacked out except for an occasional heading such as: "addresses," "foreign travel," "contacts." On the deleted pages and paragraphs there appeared letters: A through G. These seemed to be coded references to the reasons for withholding. But they were not the references to FOIA exemptions that I had seen in other federal files. I had no idea what "A" meant. National security? Privacy?

I wrote to the CIA's Information and Privacy Coordinator asking for an explanation. His response was, "As a matter of policy, this Agency does not provide such information to FOI requestors." I replied that under the law I was entitled to know the specific reasons. Two months later, I received a bizarre letter: "We are unable to locate the corresponding definitions." The CIA was telling me that it was clueless as to why it refused me information. Did the letters once have meaning for the secret keeper, but it was lost? Or was he or she just playing around with the alphabet? I sent two more letters protesting the illegality of the Agency's posture and threatened to "take appropriate administrative and legal action." Miraculously, the CIA's next "search" discovered the definitions.

"A" was the most frequently used reason. The Agency had sought to create the impression that its King file was cursory, derived from secondary sources (such as press reports) and dealt almost exclusively with his foreign travels as a world political figure. The CIA had publicly denied that it surveilled Dr. King during his civil rights and antiwar activities. "A" was revealed to be protection of "Intelligence Sources and Methods." Newspaper clippings on foreign travels do not qualify for such a withholding. Data gathered from informants, electronic surveillance, and the activities of CIA agents *do* qualify.

A brief encounter with blackout Canadian-style occurred in 1984. Dr. King's alleged killer, James Earl Ray, had fled to Toronto immediately after the shooting. Although he was being hunted by the Royal Canadian Mounted Police (RCMP) and the Toronto police, he eluded authorities for weeks. Canadian investigators whom I interviewed were convinced that Ray had been given assistance in Canada (money, possibly help in getting a passport), which would mean a conspiracy. I decided to query the RCMP for documents.

In response to my March 1984 inquiry, the Toronto office of the RCMP responded that it had no documents or data on the King case. I was referred to RCMP headquarters in Ottawa, where Public Affairs Officer John Lehman told me that, if I would put my request in writing, RCMP would review its case file and I could obtain copies of documents that were not classified. Two months after submitting my request, I was told that it had been forwarded to the RCMP's immigration and passport branch, because it was that office that had done most of the work on the case. I was assured that this constituted neither buck-passing nor resistance, but was simply a matter of getting the request to the correct office.

One week later, however, I received a surprisingly negative response from RCMP's Privacy and Access to Information Coordinator, P. E. J. Banning. The letter, and a follow-up call, made it clear that the promised disclosure had, for whatever reason, been squelched by rigid secrecy: all data on the King case was inaccessible.

Banning's first response was that only Canadian citizens could have access to government records. Fair enough. This presented no problem since I had contacts in the Toronto press who had offered to help. The real problem was the way in which Banning's office interpreted the Canadian privacy act. He stated that, under Canadian law, any material even distantly relevant to an individual was considered to be part of the individual's personal file and could only be accessed by the person in question. Therefore, Banning asserted, RCMP files on the case were dispersed within the personal files of individuals, and the residual material was negligible. As Banning described it: "Ninety-nine percent of a file of this kind is personal. All that would be releasable are newspaper clippings."

Banning's interpretation might have been subject to challenge in the Canadian courts, by a Canadian citizen acting on my behalf, but this would be an expensive, lengthy process. I consulted Professor Peter Dale Scott, a former Canadian diplomat and respected author who had considerable expertise in the area of governmental secrecy. Scott was not at all surprised by RCMP's response, observing that the Canadian government in general and RCMP in particular are not accustomed to public disclosure. Scott views Canadian freedom-of-information policy as being narrower and more rigid than in the United States, but more open than in Great Britain, where the Official Secrets Act has drastically curtailed public disclosure.

I retreated to simply trying to discover if the Ray/King case was still open; or, if not, on what date RCMP had officially closed it. I put the question in writing. Banning responded that RCMP refused to confirm "whether or not any investigations we may have regarding Mr. Ray are active or closed." Thus my Canadian inquiries produced nothing.

Deletions based on privacy are inconsistent both among and within agencies. The CIA regularly fails to delete the worst gossip and innuendo about the targets of its surveillance. These unverified assertions about people's personal lives should be considered matters impinging on rights of privacy. For example, a 1965 document based on "conversations with ——" (a deleted confidential source) contains allegations about the personal life of an identified celebrity who was prominent in the Civil Rights Movement: he "is having a great deal of trouble with this girl [his daughter] being delinquent and other problems." His wife is described as "a communist," "a notorious lesbian" who has had "a great many affairs." His first wife was "probably communist approved." He is "about to lose a large personal fortune" and is "losing his shirt." This same document also references the sex lives of actor Sidney Poitier, singer/actress Diane Carol, and Dr. King.

In its 1986 release of 32,000 pages on the assassination of Robert F. Kennedy, the FBI deleted the 1968 phone numbers, home addresses, and employers. This was done in order to protect the privacy of witnesses and other interviewees. In 1985 the Los Angeles Police Commission staff processed the Los Angeles Police Department's (LAPD) 1,500-page "Summary Report" on the case (analogous to the Warren Commission Report). They deleted the name of every source or witness on grounds of "privacy." This included dozens of people who had testified at trial or were interviewed by the media. It also included public figures: comedian Milton Berle, Olympic champion Rafer Johnson, football star Rosie Greer, and Jesse Unruh, the speaker of the California Assembly who had been a candidate for governor. After our working group protested this overzealous deletion to the Los Angeles Police Commission, the names were restored.

The FBI had released the names of thousands of witnesses and interviewees in its voluminous files on the assassinations of President Kennedy, Dr. Martin Luther King, Jr., and Robert Kennedy. Yet, in a file on a relatively obscure case, the Bureau would delete the name of every interviewee, citing FOIA's privacy exemption.

In 1973 there was a fire at the U.S. Military Personnel Records Center in St. Louis.[6] The facility held records on 56 million veterans. Most files were stored in cardboard boxes. The fire broke out just after midnight on the sixth floor. Firemen poured huge amounts of water into the building, creating further damage. The destruction was massive. An untold number of files were "irreplaceable," according to center officials. As described by J. D. Kilgore, Assistant Director for Military Records with the General Services Administration:

> Approximately 17.5 million of the 22 million folders stored on the sixth floor of the building were destroyed. About 85 percent of the records destroyed were those of veterans discharged from the Army between 1912 and 1959. The remainder belonged to Air Force veterans discharged between 1947 and 1963 whose surnames begin with I through Z. . . . Duplicate copies of those files lost in the fire do not exist.[7]

Among the lost files were those of numerous atomic veterans: military personnel who were exposed to radiation during U.S. testing of nuclear weapons. Many such veterans believed that their subsequent medical problems stemmed from military-ordered radiation exposure. Some were attempting to obtain financial compensation. The government had refused and disclaimed responsibility. Some veterans believed that a government that could deny responsibility—and, in some cases, deny that there was any exposure whatsoever—might deny them the chance to prove their case by "disappearing" their records. In fact, government documents accidentally released in 1983 would prove that there was a disregard for the safety of troops, an overexposure to radiation, and an ensuing cover-up.

The conspiracy theory of the St. Louis fire was fueled by suspicions about its origin. The *New York Times* reported that "agents of the Federal Bureau of Investigation were looking into the possibility of arson. One center employee said small fires that apparently were the work of arsonists had been found and extinguished in recent weeks."[8] In 1984, history professor Barton Hacker, who published an officially commissioned history of atomic testing, wrote to a researcher that he had been "told" that the fire "is regarded as arson."[9]

Since I was involved with atomic veterans groups seeking public disclosure, I requested the Bureau's file on the fire, hoping to shed light on the arson issue. Three hundred twenty-eight pages were found during the search. Two hundred ninety were released. Thirty-eight pages were deemed *totally* unreleasable because of "national security." This seemed curious since my request did not involve any military records, only documents concerning the investigation of a fire at a domestic, civilian facility.

The Bureau's elevated standard of privacy atypically withheld the names of every interviewee. This made the case very difficult, if not impossible, to follow: "—— reported to —— that —— had indicated extensive damage in section 5." The file did not resolve the issue of arson.

A similar loss of military records involved chemical weapons logs kept by the United States during the Gulf War. As with the atomic veterans' experience, many Gulf veterans believed that their postservice illnesses had been caused by exposure to Iraq's arsenal of chemical warfare devices. The Pentagon insisted that no such weapons were used by the enemy or otherwise released. Some veterans groups alleged a cover-up.

The circumstances of these logs' disappearance heightened their suspicions. First the Pentagon revealed that logs from a key eight-day period of possible exposure were missing. (During this period in March 1991, in the immediate aftermath of the fighting, Army demolition teams had blown up Iraqi storage facilities thought to contain chemical weapons.) Following the admission of the missing eight days came the Pentagon's disclosure that more than three-fourths of the logs for the entire war were "missing."[10]

According to the military's investigative report on the disappearance, a computer virus inadvertently brought into military headquarters in the Gulf *may* have caused half of the destruction (an officer had brought in some computer games that might have caused the infection). But the report also raised even more questions by describing the disappearance of all backup records. Two sets of the data on disk and one hard copy "appeared" to have been taken from a safe at the U.S. Central Command headquarters in Florida during an office "reorganization." Yet a third disk copy and a second hard copy also disappeared from a safe at the Aberdeen Proving Ground in Maryland. Regarding these disparate geographic disappearances, Matt Puglisi, director of Gulf War issues for the American Legion, stated that, while he could understand bureaucratic mistakes, "there's certainly the appearance of a cover-up. . . ."[11]

The FBI has another blackout practice: its released files typically provide no conclusion or overall evaluations of the case, only the raw information. This was true of the St. Louis military records fire. It was also true of the 32,000 pages on its investigation of the RFK assassination (as well as in six other case files that I have read). The Bureau simply does not state its findings. I could never decide whether such crucial analyses were never put in writing or were never put in the files. Did Sirhan Sirhan act alone? Did his gun (as opposed to other weapons present) kill Kennedy?

Agents almost never offer observations concerning the credibility or veracity of witnesses whose accounts they summarize. They dutifully synopsize what was said. Their reports are characterized by misspellings and faint typewriter ribbons. But they do not say what they think. One running joke is that FBI Director J. Edgar Hoover, ever the control freak, required agents to use worn typewriter ribbons so that requesters' eyes would be punished.

The Bureau's abstention from conclusions was a factor in the evidence issues of the RFK assassination. With a maximum of eight bullets from Sirhan's gun otherwise accounted for, any bullets in the wooden doorframe behind Kennedy would be second-gun bullets. Everyone, including LAPD, agreed with this. The question was whether holes found in the wood were bullet holes. In its released file, the FBI had captioned its photos of the doorframe "bullet holes," but offered no conclusions about a second gun.

In 1985 I wrote to FBI Director William Webster inquiring about this key area of evidence. Assistant Director William Baker responded that "neither the photographic log nor the photographs were ever purported to be a ballistics report." The descriptions were written "for the convenience of the photographic team in recording information." One would think that randomly captioning photographs would be a problem for the world's most sophisticated law enforcement agency. If the "team" labeled the holes as "rodent craters," would the evidentiary significance be the same?

I asked the Bureau to clarify its procedures for cataloging evidence. Baker replied, "The results of the FBI's crime-scene examination concerning that assassination were furnished to the Office of the District Attorney in Los Angeles and to the Los Angeles Police Department. . . .

It was the responsibility of the FBI to assist that agency however possible, not to draw conclusions from the investigation the LAPD conducted." The Bureau's "assistance" must have been lacking if it reached no conclusions about whether the crime scene was riddled with bullet holes or the doorframe simply had a distressed motif.

One highly authoritative source refuted Assistant Director Baker's backpedaling about conclusions. Retired Agent Amadee O. Richards had served as "case supervisor." His name was writ large in the released file. During our interview (June 4, 1986), he said emphatically, three times, that the FBI conducted a "parallel investigation" and an "independent" evaluation of the evidence. It reached its "own conclusions," he asserted. If so, these conclusions are not to be found in the released file.

Among the released documents was a 1977 letter to the Bureau from the chief administrative officer of Los Angeles County, Harry L. Hufford. He wrote:

> If more bullets were fired within the pantry [Ambassador Hotel crime scene] than Sirhan Sirhan's gun was capable of holding, we should certainly find out who else was firing. If, in fact, the FBI has no evidence that the questioned holes were bullet holes, we should know that so that the air may be cleared.

There was no response from the Bureau in its released file.

The FBI would elevate the privacy exemption to new heights in its RFK assassination file. The witnesses' names were disclosed, but the name of every FBI agent who worked the case was expunged in order to protect their rights. Only the names of Director Hoover and case supervisor Amadee O. Richards remained.

The "national security" exemption is applied with equal, if not more, inconsistency than the privacy exemption. Its meaning is more nebulous and complex. Pentagon officers have far broader and richer definitions of these terms than do Department of Commerce employees. One FBI secret keeper might decide that anything referencing a foreign country is national security. Another might hold a stricter definition that applies only to information useful to our foes.

Destruction of records is another form of censorship. These blackouts can be purposeful (a form of preemptive censorship), or accidental. Army Intelligence once had a file on Lee Harvey Oswald. In 1977 it told the

House of Representatives Select Committee on Assassinations that the file was "routinely destroyed" during a periodic purge of records. One can't help but be curious about the mentality of the army person who trashed the file marked "Lee Harvey Oswald." There is a government policy to preserve documents of "historical significance." A stamp exists for marking such documents. Was the army's record custodian so estranged from our country's history that the name bore no significance?

In 1973 CIA Director Richard Helms ordered the destruction of the records of MKULTRA, the agency's massive research into mind control using drugs, hypnosis, and other tools. This purge of records helped to save the agency from being directly accountable for its experiments on an untold number of unwitting human subjects, whose minds and lives were turned upside down by the agency's "mad scientists" operating under a cloak of secrecy. In 1957 a report on MKULTRA by the CIA's inspector general candidly stated the agency must take "precautions . . . not only to protect operations from exposure to enemy forces but also to conceal these activities from the American public in general. The knowledge that the agency is engaging in *unethical and illicit activities* [emphasis added] would have serious consequences in political and diplomatic circles."[12]

In the two decades of total secrecy (1968–88) that shrouded the Los Angeles Police Department's investigation into Robert Kennedy's assassination, much of the case record was "lost" or destroyed. LAPD would explain that it could not save everything, as if the missing data were superfluous and deserved to be tossed. However, a suspicious pattern emerged: missing or destroyed items related to issues of possible conspiracy; material successfully preserved was often tangential, if not irrelevant, to the official conclusions.[13]

Among the items lost or destroyed prior to public disclosure were:

- 2,400 photographs (which were not inventoried as to substance or significance);
- ceiling tiles and wood from a doorframe, removed from the crime scene (items central to the controversy over second-gun bullets);
- a test gun used for ballistics comparisons with the alleged murder weapon;

- photos confiscated by police which, according to photographer Scott Enyart, captured the actual shooting; and
- documents (quantity and substance unknown) burned in a hospital incinerator one month into the investigation.

In contrast, LAPD managed to perfectly preserve the following: biographical sketches and pictures of every officer who worked the case, newspaper clippings from around the nation, a log of the source and substance of every incoming phone call (no matter how frivolous), expense and overtime records for all personnel, a log of every automotive mishap involving official vehicles, and a complete roster of Kennedy campaign workers in the Los Angeles area.

In 1975 the CIA confronted a blackout in its own files. There was intense pressure from Congress and the press for the agency to root out and confess to its transgressions: mind-control experiments, foreign assassination plots, development of chemical and biological weapons. In the latter area, the agency discovered project NAOMI. Begun sometime in the late 1960s, this highly sensitive and secretive operation involved the production of deadly toxins and the development of "delivery systems." The CIA was attempting to discover what NAOMI had produced and how it was used.

An internal directive had ordered that "all past activities that might now be considered questionable be brought to the attention of agency management."[14] NAOMI was brought to management's attention by a CIA employee who was (according to an agency document) "not directly associated with the project." The office of the agency director decided that "this activity required further investigation."

A 1967 project approval memo listed the agency's goals: "maintenance of a stockpile of incapacitating and lethal agents in readiness for operational use," development of "disseminating systems for operational readiness," and, specifically, creation of a "nondiscernable microbioinoculator" (a James Bond–type of poison-dart gun that "cannot be identified structurally or easily detected in a detailed autopsy"). This dart, fired from a silent launcher, would penetrate the victim's clothing, go into the skin, then dissolve without a trace. The target would not be aware he or she had been struck. The CIA worked with the army in developing a

"small, hand-held dart launcher." Other delivery devices included atta-
ché cases, fountain pens, cigarette lighters, head bolts of automobile
engines, and lightbulbs—all designed to blow deadly toxins at the
victims.

By the late 1960s, the CIA had produced "a stockpile of some 15–20
different BW [biological weapons] agents and toxins. . . ." These included
shellfish toxin, tuberculosis, snake venom, clostridium botulism (deadly
food poisoning), and anthrax, as well as agents causing paralytic shellfish poisoning, "valley fever," encephalitis, and intestinal flu.

The nation's premier spy agency learned of its foray into this deadly
realm from one employee, then from two other officers who were "aware
of the project." The CIA began to search its own records for clues. Deputy
Director Thomas Karamessines dutifully reported that the Agency was
stymied by its own culture of secrecy: "Difficulties were immediately
encountered," he wrote in a 1975 memo, "because the project cryptonyms
[code words] could not be identified. . . . Almost no written records were
kept. . . . Only a very limited documentation of activities took place. . . .
No records on such things as material control, receipt, delivery, destruction, etc. can be found. . . . No documents relating to any possible operational use of the material have been found." Karamessines concludes
that these files "are quite different from those normally maintained in
the course of a typical CIA R&D [research and development] project."
Perhaps the atypically sensitive endeavor of creating undetectable murder weapons required atypical secrecy that did not lend itself to paper
trails.

One "cause for concern" was the Agency's discovery that "several
people" involved in NAOMI had also been involved in "specific assassination plans." With no operational records, it was anybody's guess whether
the toxins were used in assassinations.

What became of the lethal "stockpile"? The CIA had stored it at the
army's weapons laboratory at Fort Detrick, Maryland. After several
unsuccessful inquiries, the Agency telephoned a retired army officer who
had worked at the lab. He informed them that all of the deadly shellfish
toxin "might not have been destroyed." Following his lead, the Agency
found some of the toxin in a freezer in "a disordered storage facility" at

the fort. Karamessines wondered how the toxin could have languished there for years, "without anyone being aware of it." There were "no requirements for the use of the freezer in the intervening years"—a walkin homicide dispensary? "Several" containers were discovered, as were "two individual doses in tablet form." This find precipitated "a complete inventory. . . . A large number of dangerous chemicals or drugs of various types was *[sic]* found." And what of the material *not* found?

This is but one example of the general problem of maintaining accountability, oversight, and control of activities designed to be cloaked in secrecy and deception. Since its creation in 1947, the Central Intelligence Agency has engaged in an untold number of covert projects and activities—thousands of them.[15] It was CIA inspector General Lyman Kirkpatrick who described the ideal covert operation as one that would remain secret "from inception to eternity."[16]

Covert projects include a broad spectrum of activities ranging from radio broadcasts to mind-control experiments, to assassinations and bloody coups d'état. Oversight has been spotty, at best. At times Congress did not know of, much less approve, certain activities. It discovered them only after the fact. Sometimes presidents did not know; at least, not fully. The media and the public have even less knowledge.

The issues of ethics, policy, and accountability regarding covert action remain unresolved. Should the United States attempt to assassinate foreign leaders? Should the CIA secretly create political parties or armies in various countries, in order to manipulate political or military outcomes? Should the CIA protect or help alleged war criminals or drug lords who are useful to U.S. interests as defined by the CIA? Policy decisions costing millions of dollars and affecting millions of lives are often made within the black holes of Agency secrecy, where the State Department, the Pentagon, and presidential advisers are excluded from the policymaking process. The CIA's covert creation of "fronts" has included everything from detective agencies to airlines, banks, and militias. Wise and Ross have termed this the "invisible government," the hidden machinery that makes and carries out policy but is immune to the checks, balances, and controls of the visible government.[17]

The number of CIA covert operations is high but unknown. Like the shellfish toxin, there is no overt record of what happened when and where. Wise and Ross pointed out:

> CIA officials have insisted that the majority of these operations have been successful. However, there have been a large number of known failures. There is only one logical conclusion if one is to accept the CIA's claim of a high percentage of success: the total number of secret operations has been much greater than is supposed even in knowledgeable circles.[18]

Congressional oversight increased markedly in the 1970s after revelations of CIA misconduct. But it is still a huge arena of secret activity that defies normal accountability. The covert operations budget has grown to hundreds of millions of dollars per year—perhaps as much as $700 million. As far back as 1975, Congress reported that, between 1961 and 1975, the CIA had conducted "more than 900 major covert activities," and thousands of "smaller" ones.[19] Some of the known *major* ones are indeed that. In Vietnam under project Phoenix, the agency oversaw the assassination of an estimated 20,000 to 40,000 people who were targeted as enemy supporters in villages throughout South Vietnam. The South Vietnamese government claimed 40,000; the CIA reported more than 20,000 recorded deaths.[20]

How many covert operations have there been from 1975 to 1990, from 1991 to the present? What were the "major" ones? Who knows the answers: The President's National Security Council? The Senate Intelligence Committee? The CIA Inspector General's Office? None of the above?

The CIA's covert action is not the only arena in which secrecy precludes effective processes of policymaking and oversight. From the 1980s to the present, Congress has grappled with the Pentagon's "black budget." Billions of dollars (estimated to be more than $30 billion per year) are spent on secret weapons and research, about which Congress is given very little information in closed committee sessions.[21] Even then, secret keepers tend to limit the information to headlines rather than detailed specifics. Stealth aircraft, silent submarines, new tactical missiles: the black budget is so secretive that data on their development and specific cost are limited to "special access required" under the so-called "black umbrella."

How can Congress rationally and efficiently allocate funds if it does not know the particulars of what they are being spent on and why? There are two views. Pentagon spokesman Fred Hoffman insisted that "Congress is fully informed on so-called black budget programs." Congressman Les Aspen of the House Armed Services Committee disagreed: "It is simply bad public policy to hide increasing amounts of government spending." Congressman John Dingle of Michigan went further, charging that the lack of oversight had led to "mischarging, overcharging, and outright illegal activities."[22] Congress improved its oversight during the 1990s. But the black umbrella remains a blackout within the fiscal appropriations process.

In 1994, for example, there was the quintessential case of the pitfalls of secret money. In an upscale area of Chantilly, Virginia (thirty miles from Washington, D.C.), a sprawling, state-of-the-art office complex was under construction. Fairfax County officials thought that it was being built by Rockwell International, a major defense contractor. To their surprise and chagrin, they discovered that the $3.5 million per year that the county government had expected to collect in taxes was in jeopardy because this was not a private-sector construction project at all: it was the new headquarters for a super-secret federal agency, the National Reconnaissance Office (NRO), which handles the deployment, tracking, and analysis of spy satellite photography.

This budget item was so black that neither the Clinton White House nor Congress knew that $310 million was being spent. Administration budget chief Alice Rivlin told the press, "The president didn't know about this." That such a big-ticket item could be a complete surprise to both the executive and legislative branches of government raises serious questions about the degree of oversight being exercised in the development of black-budget weapons projects.[23]

Another variant of the informational blackout is the segregation of files to hide questionable or illegal activities. Former LA police detective Mike Rothmiller blew the whistle on the department's Organized Crime Intelligence Division (OCID). It kept secret files on its unconstitutional, illegal activities of surveillance and harassment.[24] The division spied on fellow cops, celebrities, politicians, and activists. According to Rothmiller, harassment of minorities was also a primary activity.

He left LAPD in 1983 after working in OCID. "Unbeknownst to both friends and enemies," he asserted, "LAPD maintained secret, Stalin-esque dossiers, some of them kept in privately rented storage units; there were files on virtually every mover and shaker in Southern California." Rothmiller had access to these files at OCID headquarters. There, a "wall" of file cabinets was filled with index cards bearing the names of public figures, with a few organized crime figures thrown in. The real "organized crime" was that organized by OCID against innocent civilians. It was not about criminal activity, Rothmiller observed, but about enhancing LAPD's power.[25] Gossip about the rich, famous, and powerful was OCID's coin of the realm—it dealt with sex, money, and political activities.

According to Rothmiller, OCID had a file on Robert Kennedy, cross-referenced with Marilyn Monroe. The file on RFK's assassination allegedly admitted that there were second-gun bullets involved. The dossier on former Governor Jerry Brown seemed obsessed with proving that he was gay. It was unable to do so, even though it reflected eavesdropping on his apartment and car phone. Actor Rock Hudson's gay trysts were chronicled. An enormous file on Frank Sinatra and his "Rat Pack" friends included descriptions of their club performances. Lakers owner Dr. Jerry Bus was the subject of a dossier, as was Elvis Presley.

OCID developed an elaborate system for hiding its illegal trove of often-sensational tidbits. No "outsiders" could penetrate it, whether they be reporters, members of the Police Commission, or officers from other units. The file cabinets full of index cards contained as many as forty cards on some famous subjects. Each card cited twenty or so intelligence reports on the person. Especially explosive items could be "disappeared" by removing the index card that described them. Pulling the card made such reports impossible to find among thousands of pages, claimed Rothmiller. The items were then effectively beyond the reach of a subpoena. The most secret of these "CFs" (confidential files) were kept in public storage. There was one rental for each of the twenty-six letters of the alphabet. Documents were stored under the name of the OCID officer who paid cash for the rental (from an untraceable slush fund). The rental locations were changed yearly to further insulate them from discovery by the Southern California American Civil Liberties Union— which was in hot legal pursuit of LAPD's surveillance files.

Rothmiller recalled a conversation between two OCID officers as they moved files to private storage: "The one thing I dread is the day an ACLU attorney gets into these files. That would be the day the entire lid is blown off the police department."

His colleague gestured toward the departing files and responded, "They don't exist. They're *not* files." When agencies go to such lengths to conceal their records, it usually takes an accidental event or a whistle blower to expose them.

A similar super-secret filing system was created by FBI Director J. Edgar Hoover. His personal files on celebrities, politicians, and activists were analogous to OCID's, but for purposes of political power rather than legitimate law enforcement. One of the director's closest colleagues, Assistant Director William Sullivan, described him as "a master blackmailer." Former Secretary of State Dean Rusk observed:

> Hoover passed along gossip to the president he served, and that practice would raise questions in a president's mind. What did Hoover know about him? In theoretical terms that put Hoover in the position of a veiled blackmailer.[26]

Journalist Anthony Summers investigated the fate of Hoover's secret files.[27] Summers recounts that "one prominent senator was terrorized into inaction [against Hoover] by reading his own file." This was a typical Hoover ploy: showing the subject what you have on them to keep them in line. No president could fire Hoover. He had compromising information on each one: Kennedy's trysts with mob consort Judith Campbell, Nixon's potential scandal involving a woman.

While Hoover's secret files were known to exist, no one seemed to know where they were kept. Clearly, no FOIA request would come anywhere near them. When the legendary law officer died in 1972 at the age of 77, he was still director. In response to his demise, G. Gordon Liddy, a former FBI agent and Nixon's specialist in political sabotage, phoned the White House and warned: "You've got to get those files. They're a source of enormous power. You don't have much time. There's going to be a race on."[28]

When the undertakers reached Hoover's home to take his body, William Reburn recalled what he encountered: "There were men in suits, fifteen or eighteen of them swarming all over the place, going through everything he had . . . like they were looking for something. . . . They were methodical."[29]

But Summers discovered from a Hoover neighbor that someone had apparently gotten there before this crew. Two men removed something long and heavy, wrapped in a blanket. The files never surfaced, much to the relief of many of the most celebrated and powerful figures in the nation. But there was always the worry that they might appear. Perhaps someone destroyed them; perhaps they were stored in a secret location known only to Hoover.

Concerted blackouts can be eliminated, even if it takes nearly forty years. Such is the case with government reports on the ill-fated Bay of Pigs invasion. This watershed debacle of CIA covert operations had a profound impact on foreign policy, defense policy, and the intelligence community—for decades. On April 17, 1961, a Cuban exile army of approximately 1,500 men put ashore on the south coast of Cuba at the Bay of Pigs. The invasion force had been trained and armed by the CIA, some of whose case officers waded in with the exiles.

The CIA's ultra-secretive plan called for the exiles to establish a beachhead, then expand their ground sufficiently to claim the establishment of a provisional government. According to the Agency, this would precipitate a widespread, indigenous uprising against Castro. He would be removed from power. This, despite the fact that the invaders numbered 1,500 and Castro's troops exceeded 200,000.[30] The effort was a catastrophic failure. The exiles floundered in the bay's muddy marshes. Castro's well-prepared forces sank the attacker's supply ships, depriving them of ammunition. Exile casualties were high; 1,000 were hauled off to Cuban prisons.

President John F. Kennedy publicly accepted full responsibility for the failure of the plan that he had inherited from the Eisenhower administration. Privately, Kennedy blamed the CIA and felt betrayed by it.[31] Director Allen Dulles had encouraged the president to believe that there would be a popular insurrection against Castro, even though the Agency's own intelligence reports deemed this highly improbable, if not impossible. Contrary to Kennedy's explicit order, CIA officers had participated in the fighting. The president retaliated by firing the legendary Dulles and threatening "to splinter the CIA into a thousand pieces and scatter it to the winds."[32] Kennedy's brother Robert, the attorney general, was placed in charge of anti-Castro operations.

With all of this controversy and intrigue surrounding the most embarrassing known failure of U.S. covert action, journalists and researchers eagerly pursued documents relating to the affair. Two major reports were known to exist: one compiled by the CIA itself; a second by an outside commission. The commission was appointed by President Kennedy and headed by General Maxwell Taylor. Robert Kennedy was also a member. The "Taylor Report" was so ultra-secret that it was blacked out not only from the public but also from most of officialdom. It was classified as "secret," "eyes only," and "ultra-sensitive."[33] It was considered so sensitive that General Taylor had it hand-delivered to each of the Joint Chiefs of Staff—sequentially. The messenger was General David W. Gray. He was present in each of the chief's offices, directly monitoring their reading of the report and making sure that none of the nation's top commanders took any notes.[34] Original notes on the operation made by participating officials had been shredded per order of General Lyman L. Lemnitzer.

Heavily deleted excerpts from the report were released under FOIA in 1977 and in 1986. The full volume was locked away in the JFK presidential library. In 1996 it was requested by the JFK Assassination Records Review Board, a civilian commission appointed by President Clinton to oversee the release of records relating to the assassination. The board had independent legal powers of review and disclosure that superceded FOIA. Even so, the highly volatile Taylor Report had to be separately reviewed by the CIA, the Defense Department Intelligence Agency, the Joint Chiefs of Staff, the National Security Council, the State Department, and the National Security Agency. While this was guaranteed to be a slow process, observers were chagrined that three years later there was still no disclosure, and the records review board's statutory life had expired.

The National Security Archive, a Washington, D.C.-based public interest entity, had long sought the Taylor Report. In 1999 its queries concerning release were met with an astonishing response. The Pentagon claimed that the report had simply been "lost" (the ultimate blackout). The archive immediately rerequested release: this time, under the policy of mandatory classification review established by the White House. Not only was the item rediscovered, but it was processed for release in near-record time (in major part due to the coordinating efforts of the National Archives and Records Administration). All of the government entities involved processed the report expeditiously (the dated "Declass" stamps on the cover page documented their speed).

In May 2000 the Taylor Report was finally out. Many of the deletions in the previously released excerpts were restored. The damning indictment of secret policymaking gone awry was now part of the historical record. The report concluded:

> Top level direction was given through ad hoc meetings of senior officials without consideration of operational plans in writing and no arrangement for recording conclusions and decisions reached.[35]

CIA icon Allen Dulles was quoted as renouncing paramilitary covert actions:

> I'm first to recognize that I don't think that the CIA should run paramilitary operations of the type in Cuba, and possibly not the type run in ———. The Cuban operation had a very serious effect on all our work. I believe there should be a new set up. I think we should limit ourselves more to secret intelligence collection and operations of the non-military [kind].[36]

Dulles' sweeping, candid advice was not heeded by the Agency in the decades to come, especially in Southeast Asia.

The disclosure of the Taylor Report followed the 1998 release of the CIA's internal assessment, obtained by the National Security Archive. It had been written in 1961 by the Agency's inspector general, Lyman Kirkpatrick. It, too, was brutally critical of the planning and execution of the Bay of Pigs fiasco. *Newsweek* reporter Evan Thomas called it "the most frank and honest government document ever written."[37] Former director Dulles had viewed it as a "hatchet job."[38] CIA Officer Richard Bissell, the invasion's chief architect, crafted a rebuttal appendix to Kirkpatrick's report.

As with similar documents, the Agency never intended to make this public. Author Peter Wyden wrote in 1979, "Kirkpatrick and his inspectors interviewed some three hundred CIA men who worked on the Cuban project. His report, never declassified and probably buried forever, was devastating."[39] Nearly four decades after the landmark historical event, the U.S. government's self-assessments, so crucial to covert policymaking and agency accountability, were finally circulated beyond the official elite that produced them, thanks to the National Security Archive and others who waited out the delays and the game of lost and found.

The origins and levels of blackouts vary. Yet all affect *what the surviving evidence says happened.* All diminish the public's right to know. Some are legally justified; others involve blackmail or cover-up—the darker side of the secrecy system.

CHAPTER 5

Front Lines

I consider FOIA to be perhaps the most important innovation in democratic theory since the Constitution.

—Attorney James H. Lesar, 2000

The public's right to know is a collective, system-wide facet of U.S. democracy. Even so, individuals can have a very significant impact on the boundary between secrecy and disclosure. The extraordinary involvements and groundbreaking efforts of the five people presented here have expanded public knowledge of government far beyond the substance of the specific records they obtained. These individuals—two lawyers, a professor, a researcher/activist, and a federal judge—have pushed the envelope of public disclosure. They did so in very different settings: federal court, living room meetings, and via a presidential appointment. The impact of their efforts is not distantly historical but contemporary. All contributed energy and personal/professional resources to their lengthy participation in the secrecy wars. The arenas in which they worked were fraught with conflict and often controversy. While the substance of the information being pursued differed, the problems in dealing with government agencies were very similar.

This is by no means a random sample or a top-five list. Thousands of people have labored extensively in the public disclosure process and many have had a measurable, positive impact. This is a group whose tenacity and skill I admire. I count three of them as professional colleagues; two are mentioned in the acknowledgments as being role models for my own activities. To varying degrees, their work has been a mixture of success and failure in the pursuit of classified information. Their involvements go far beyond the very brief profiles presented here. The purpose is not to chronicle their efforts but to give readers some sense of who is on the frontlines of public disclosure and what they have done.

DANIEL S. ALCORN

Attorney Daniel S. Alcorn is a leading national expert in FOIA law.[1] He began his practice after graduating from the University of Virginia School of Law. It was in 1985 that he first became professionally active in FOIA law, due in large measure to his association with two attorneys who were working on disclosure issues relating to U.S. political assassinations—Bernard Fensterwald and James H. Lesar.

Alcorn's most illustrious victory came in a 1997 court case. As the counsel for the National Association of Criminal Defense Lawyers, he successfully compelled the Justice Department to release a U.S. government Inspector General's report on the FBI's crime laboratory (*National Association of Criminal Defense Lawyers v. U.S. Department of Justice*). The report documented misconduct and errors in processing and analyzing evidence by the nation's most-used, most prestigious forensic facility. The laboratory's errors were numerous and major.

The FBI and the Justice Department fought doggedly against disclosure, which Alcorn describes as "impacting the entire criminal justice system." Because of the release of the report, evidentiary findings by law enforcement agencies in literally thousands of cases across the nation were challenged—as were the courtroom verdicts. There were shocking revelations of manipulation and mishandling of evidence, from ballistics to fibers to DNA. The ensuing political firestorm resulted in Alcorn being called to testify before the House of Representatives Judiciary Committee in May 1997.

"We got more information through FOIA [the report and more than 53,000 related documents] than the Judiciary Committee was getting from executive agencies," says Alcorn. "We had more rights: Congress faces executive privilege [as grounds for withholding]; we do not." Through his use of FOIA in court, Alcorn was better informed than the congressional oversight committee regarding the forensic scandal in the Bureau. "*We* were leading them," he observes incredulously. Congress obtained the report "privately" from the Justice Department. Alcorn vetted the entire report and accompanying documentation for the public and media to digest. The political reaction was therefore much more intense.

This case also established a crucial precedent for FOIA litigators. Alcorn convinced the court not only to award attorney's fees but to do so on an "interim" basis. This stopped the government from "stalling for years," as Alcorn describes it, preventing the more than $300,000 owed him from being withheld until the end of litigation. This means that FOIA lawyers may not be as financially pressured and disadvantaged when combating their taxpayer-paid counterparts. "The reason few people do this [FOIA law] is because they can't make any money," Alcorn says.

In another area of law, he is nationally recognized by the community of criminal defense attorneys as having pioneered an important new realm of FOIA law that significantly expands the defendant's rights to a fair trial. His breakthrough came in what he describes as "a high-profile, white-collar criminal case." He asserts, "Discovery [of prosecution evidence by the defense] is very limited in criminal cases, shockingly so to many people." He used a FOIA suit as an adjunct to the trial's discovery process. If the prosecution does not provide the defense with whatever information it has that is potentially exculpatory or strategically important, a separate FOIA suit can compel the evidence into the public domain. If significant evidence was improperly withheld from the defendant and this is revealed through FOIA, there are strong grounds for the appeal of any conviction, and prosecutors could face sanctions for misconduct. Alcorn is quick to add the qualifier that this in no way replaces discovery. But this new legal avenue "places some check on government to be forthcoming with evidence during a trial, because a second court may find out that they violated the defendant's rights." Alcorn states, without braggadocio, that this is "a powerful legal weapon" in the hands of defense attorneys. He has given numerous lectures and seminars on the topic.

The potential importance of this FOIA innovation was dramatized in a Cambridge, Massachusetts, superior courtroom on January 5, 2001.[2] Peter Limone, a reputed mob associate, was released from prison after serving thirty-three years (four on death row). He was convicted in 1965 for the murder of Edward "Teddy" Deegan.

Sometimes, as in this case, documents alone can prove innocence. A Justice Department task force probing FBI abuses and illegalities in its use of organized crime informants stumbled upon 1965 reports that exposed the fraudulent nature of Limone's conviction. The information had been withheld from the defense during the original trial and subsequent appeals. Bureau reports concluded that organized crime figure Vincent J. "Jimmy the Bear" Flemmi had planned Deegan's murder, and that Limone was not involved. Flemmi and his brother were FBI informants. The key witness against Limone was another organized crime figure who was also Flemmi's best friend. FBI informants told their handlers the identities of the three men who participated in the crime, excluding Limone.

The FBI agents suppressed evidence of innocence, presumably to protect the then-informants, the Flemmi brothers. Moreover, the documents revealed that agents had advance knowledge of the impending hit on Deegan and did nothing to prevent it. Clearly, if FOIA had been available at the original trial, or had been used in the following years (to search for information not given to the defense in the discovery process), Limone might have been saved decades of false incarceration orchestrated and covered up by those sworn to uphold the law.

Dan Alcorn becomes even more animated when he talks about the impediments to public disclosure than when discussing his successes—roadblocks such as delays, destruction, legal exemptions, and lack of resources. "Government has unlimited resources, essentially," he complains. "Individuals do not. . . . The FBI, CIA, and NSA [National Security Agency] attempt to avoid responding to requests."

In one of his cases, the FBI claimed that a four-year backlog prevented a response to the requester. Alcorn argued that Congress had appropriated additional funds in 1997 to reduce the logjam. He used the Bureau's own data to show that the actual backlog was months, not years. The judge split the difference, accepting a two-year backlog as valid.

Regarding the wholesale legal exemption of the CIA's "operational files" from FOIA, he asserts, "The entire government should be subject to FOIA. Not to do so is antidemocratic."

Alcorn cites a 1968 statute that forbids the destruction of records having legal, historical, or research value. The problem, he says, is that the Records Retention law is unenforced: "I keep running into illegal destruction; evidence of truth illegally destroyed. It is disturbing and very illegal. It is the ultimate roadblock to the public right to know." He predicts that this will be a recurring problem in the coming years because of the absence of enforcement. He also strongly favors increasing the agencies' resources: "They claim to have no money—appropriate money to make the system actually work."

Overall, Dan Alcorn is mildly optimistic but highly critical of the freedom-of-information process. He foresees an increasing use of FOIA by the public and the media. Yet he cautions that the next decade will be crucial in determining "how far the system is willing to go in the public right to know." He views the federal government as "quite frightened by FOIA. It's the law and they often choose not to obey it. They actually said in court that to live up to its provisions would ruin the functioning of government. We are unfunded individuals, and the U.S. government feels threatened by us because of the information we seek."

SANDRA MARLOW

Sandra Marlow never planned to chase government records for twenty years.[3] After getting a Master's of Fine Arts degree from the University of California-Davis and doing a lot of bronze casting, she obtained a Master's of Library Science degree. She then organized a library at Bridgewater State Prison in Massachusetts and an archive at a greater-Boston medical facility. These were the only "records" she cared about until 1977 when her father was stricken with a rare form of leukemia. He had been a colonel in the air force and was exposed to radiation in 1948 when he measured contamination onboard ships that were present at a nuclear blast. He was exposed again in 1955 when he attended an atomic test in the Nevada desert. In 1955 he wrote an illustrated letter home describing the test and the mushroom cloud. His daughter looked to government not to care for him or compensate him, but simply to "find out what happened to him," she recalls, "to understand."

This was the start of her odyssey in seeking government information relating to atomic veterans. She would devote an estimated accumulative total of three years of time in the ensuing decades to pursuing data from the air force, Pentagon, Department of Energy, Nuclear Regulatory Commission, and dozens of private collections and institutional archives. She would also testify before Congress and share her discoveries. Although her energy and persistence were high, her success rate was low. All government agencies were equally unresponsive. She estimates that she was unsuccessful 65 to 70 percent of the time. Marlow was confronting the stone wall of nuclear secrecy in the cold war era.

"For twenty years of my life I've been trying to understand what went on, what happened. It has been a huge trauma." Although she had "lots of help" from atomic veterans organizations and veterans' families, as well as friends and colleagues, she still regards it as a lonely enterprise. Except for some assistance from a handful of congressmen (most notably, Representative Gerry Studds and Senator Edward Kennedy, both of Massachusetts) and a couple of small grants, she was largely on her own, using her time, money, and psychological capital.

"I was naive starting out," she admits. Marlow thought that a simple request for her father's military records would help her to understand the cause of the inoperable cancer that claimed his life. Instead, the air force provided very scant documentation of his service. It responded that he was never on a contaminated ship and that his exposure to radiation had been no more severe than that of a single X-ray. The air force also asserted that there was no data to the contrary.

Insulted and perplexed by the government's rejection of her father's account of his atomic service, she pressed on. "How stupid does the government think a citizen could be?" she asks bitterly. But the government provided nothing more than its undocumented denials. The letter that Marlow's father had written home described the intense, radioactive contamination onboard the ships he was working. Another veteran had written home describing his fly-through of the mushroom cloud during the same test that her father witnessed. Documents relating to this fly-through were still classified when last requested in 1997.

Marlow began networking with atomic veterans groups and with families. She was very surprised at the large number of veterans and the extensiveness of the testing. In mailings, coffee klatches, and conferences, veterans began to piece together information on their nuclear experiences that their government continued to deny them. Letters, newspaper clippings, and personal accounts helped to bring more clarity to veterans' atomic-related service and their radiation exposures. Even the government's rejection letters were sometimes helpful, Marlow recounts. Thus, even with FOIA and the Privacy Act in place, veterans and families turned to each other to try to navigate through the blackout of nuclear secrecy.

Marlow describes the disclosure process for atomic veterans' records as a "plague of deceit." Government would refuse to release a person's records and insist that they had no radiation exposure, sometimes denying that the veteran was ever at a nuclear test. If there was documentation of being present, government would assert that exposure was absolutely minimal to the point of insignificance. The requesters compared government's stock responses: "no exposure," "very little radiation."

That individuals could not get their own records shocked and disturbed Marlow. But government's consistent, often absolute, refusal was fueled by more than keeping nuclear weapons secrets in a cold war. The financial claims spawned by the deaths and diseases incurred by veterans could conceivably cost billions. The public image of nuclear safety, both civilian and military, would suffer a crippling blow because of the negative publicity. Public trust in government would be severely eroded by the admission that decades of cover-up and deceit had victimized patriotic servicemen.

One veteran requested his records relating to a 1952 H-bomb test in the Pacific during which he was exposed to radiation. The results of his own blood test, conducted by the military during his exposure, were withheld from him—designated "top secret." As previously described, a 1973 fire at the government records facility in St. Louis destroyed an estimated 17.5 million folders containing veterans' service records.

There was no backup or duplication for the lost files. The conflagration was of suspicious origin—arson was never ruled out, according to FBI records. Untold thousands of atomic veterans were deprived of proof of their radiation exposure. Marlow and many of her associates remain highly suspicious, if not convinced, that the fire was government's preemptive blackout, designed to prevent the medical claims of atomic vets. In a 1987 FOIA suit, the National Association of Radiation Survivors and its pro bono attorneys were told in court that the Veterans Administration had "destroyed" the military records of some atomic veterans. The VA was fined $115,000 by the court, but no sanctions or criminal charges were levied against individuals involved in the destruction. Congressman Don Edwards called the VA's conduct "simply unconscionable."[4] The agency had destroyed the very documents that the suit was seeking. "[T]he VA appears to believe that it is a law unto itself," Edwards fumed. But the government was able to preserve some files, according to Marlow: "The Defense Nuclear Agency kept better track of my correspondence than I did."

While she does not regret her protracted and costly efforts to pursue vital information relating to tens of thousands of veterans, the experience has been negative in terms of her perceptions of government. "They *still* have not acknowledged atomic veterans' problems," she protests. "The more we asked, the more delaying tactics and evasiveness. They withheld information that could have helped us both psychologically and medically. It's up to them [veterans] to prove where they were. We don't want compensation so much as truth. The psychological damage to veterans by secrecy has been enormous."

JAMES H. LESAR

Washington, D.C., attorney James H. Lesar has been involved with FOIA longer and more extensively than anyone who has come to the author's attention.[5] He began during his first year out of the University of Wisconsin Law School in 1970. FOIA cases have accounted for 90 percent of his workload since 1975. As far as he knows, Lesar is "the only attorney in the country whose practice is full-time FOIA." At first his cases focused on the release of records relating to political assassinations (President Kennedy, Dr. King). He represented author/researcher Harold

Weisberg in a suit against the FBI for release of the results of spectrographic tests (ballistics) in the president's murder. He served as counsel for James Earl Ray, the alleged assassin of Dr. King, from 1970 to 1975. In so doing, he launched numerous FOIA requests and legal actions in pursuit of exculpatory evidence for his client. Lesar subsequently broadened his client base to include celebrated author James Baldwin, a Canadian newspaper, labor organizations, and political activists. It was Lesar who discovered in federal court the Clinton administration's secret deal with the FBI to exempt it from the executive order mandating the release of twenty-five-year-old records.

One of his steady clients has been British investigative journalist Anthony Summers. Lesar has worked intensively to get secret documents relating to four of Summers' book subjects: the JFK assassination, Marilyn Monroe, J. Edgar Hoover, and Richard Nixon. Over the years, the FOIA requests, negotiation sessions, and court battles have produced some of the most revelatory documents relating to these historical icons and events. Jim also represented Greg Stone and me, pro bono, in our FOIA request to the FBI seeking its Robert F. Kennedy assassination file and in the subsequent, unsuccessful lawsuit to compel the Bureau to release the names of agents who investigated the case.

Lesar's largest volume victory produced 700,000 pages of FBI documents on the JFK assassination for researcher Mark Allen; his smallest, a thin file for Professor Gerald McKnight of Hood College. Lesar has dealt primarily with the FBI and CIA. In the process, he has seen and heard it all, FOIA-wise. He obtained J. Edgar Hoover's telephone logs for Summers as well as the director's "official and confidential" files. He heard the Bureau argue in court that there was "no public interest" in reading Hoover's secret files. The judge read them and found them more than a bit interesting. The Bureau once deleted the name of a notorious KGB agent to protect his rights to privacy.

Lesar's lifelong professional involvement in the secrecy arena has made him critical but not embittered. He realizes, perhaps better than anyone does, the formidable advantages held by government agencies every time he goes up against them. "Some agencies are difficult and intractable to deal with," he observes, "the attitude of their personnel and how they treat, or mistreat, the law." In addition, "Government understands its filing systems; requesters do not. Unless you have a lawyer, you will get a standard, boilerplate response out of government, and most people won't know how to counter them."

The biggest disadvantage, with which Lesar struggles daily, is the David and Goliath nature of the legal process: "Government has staying power. Its lawyers, in a sense, work for free. They also have boilerplate affidavits and delaying tactics—all designed to drive up the cost of litigation. They want to make it as difficult as possible so you won't do it again: they want to punish you."

The major "punishment" is financial compensation, or lack thereof. "This is not a lucrative career," he asserts without lament. "You have to be committed [to the law]." Lesar takes cases wholly or partly on contingency, hoping to be awarded attorney's fees if he prevails in court. But it is "difficult, if not impossible, to make a living that way." FOIA attorneys are awarded what Congress has mandated as "reasonable fees." Lesar thinks it unreasonable that he is paid in "historic dollars rather than current dollars." He points out that normally in civil litigation attorneys are awarded the "going rate." FOIA suits often drag on for years. An attorney fortunate enough to be compensated for a case argued in 1994 may obtain fees in 2001 with no interest and no adjustment for inflation. Thus lawyers may get $250 an hour when their current going rate is $350. In contrast, government attorneys are salaried in current dollars with inflation escalators and merit raises. Lesar's compensation is either nonexistent, years late, or undervalued. "I had to settle one case because of dire financial circumstances," he recalls. "You can't really say that it is made up for by getting the money later. It's a very tough life. I don't recommend it."

When asked about what reforms he would like to see, he ceases to bemoan finances. His first priority would be a new law that more effectively preserves and discloses historical records than do FOIA's inadequate provisions. At present, Lesar contends, historical records are far too secretive—classified unnecessarily.

With all the inherent difficulties and inequities in his chosen field, Jim Lesar still maintains the sense of commitment, even idealism, that propelled him to be, arguably, the nation's most productive and pioneering FOIA litigator. He views FOIA as having grown stronger in recent years: not because of anything Congress has done but because of judicial decisions that have significantly expanded the public right to know (he never mentions his prominent role in this development).

"As critical as I am of the American FOIA," says Lesar, "the fact remains that the U.S. is far ahead of the world in this field. There is a decent FOIA in Canada but the rest pales in comparison. I consider FOIA to be perhaps the most important innovation in democratic theory since the Constitution."

JON WIENER

Jon Wiener has been a professor of history at the University of California-Irvine since 1984.[6] He received his Ph.D. from Harvard in 1972 and has published three books, an edited volume, and twenty-seven scholarly articles. He is also a contributing editor to *The Nation* magazine, for which he writes on politics and secrecy issues.

His involvement with public disclosure began as it did for millions of Americans: in the late 1970s, he requested his own file from the FBI. He had been politically active in the antiwar movement and was a member of Students for a Democratic Society (SDS), one of the Bureau's primary target groups in the 1960s. His assumption that he would be the subject of a file proved correct. Wiener would also have his first encounter with government withholding of information. Of the forty pages unearthed in the Bureau's search, two-thirds of the documents were unreleasable on the grounds of protecting "confidential sources and methods." He was taken aback by what he terms the "massive withholding" of his personal file.

In 1981 Professor Wiener used FOIA in his research into Beatle John Lennon's deportation case (and the politics surrounding it). The U.S. government had sought to deport the rock star during his activism against the Vietnam War. Wiener had read Professor David Garrow's book *The FBI and Martin Luther King, Jr.* (Penguin Books, 1983). He was impressed that Bureau files on King contained more detailed information than any other source. He wondered whether the same would be true of Lennon. Armed with a "how to" booklet from the American Civil Liberties Union, Wiener launched what he describes as "a shot in the dark to see if they had anything."

He requested Lennon's files from three agencies: the FBI, CIA, and Immigration and Naturalization Service (INS). The contrast in what he terms "immense differences among agency responses" was striking. He described the INS as "wonderful." It provided a box of documents containing legal briefs and transcripts of Lennon's deportation hearings, plus hundreds of letters that the agency had received from the artist's fans. "Almost nothing was blanked out," Wiener reports. In contrast, the CIA was, in Wiener's view, largely unresponsive (as he had predicted). He was given a mere four pages that were heavily deleted. The agency claimed to have nothing more on this international figure who had networked with leftist groups and individuals and had actively opposed the Vietnam War.

As for the FBI, Wiener expected to encounter some resistance. He observes: "The Bureau is still very protective of the records of its excesses in the Hoover era—abuses of power." Thus Wiener "knew it would be a long process, but I was thinking months, not years." Fourteen years later, he was before the U.S. Supreme Court where he was victorious in pursuit of the documents.

As reported previously, withholding of documents in the original release of Lennon's file was staggering even by Bureau standards. Two hundred eighty-one pages were found in the search; 199 were deemed unreleasable. Wiener appealed the decision within the Justice Department and lost. Two years after his original request, he was seeking legal help in order to take the FBI to court. After being turned down by dozens of lawyers and organizations, the American Civil Liberties Union took his case. Wiener notes the high cost of litigation, beyond the reach of average citizens.

The struggle for release consumed his time sporadically: "A lot of time once in a while," as he describes it. "When a brief was due or there was a court date, I would work extensively with the lawyers. There were periods of years when nothing happened." Ultimately, the Supreme Court compelled the Bureau to release all but ten pages and awarded Wiener $204,000 in attorneys' fees.

As for the Bureau's Lennon file, Wiener observes, "It confirmed my suspicion that this was political surveillance rather than legitimate law enforcement of any immigration law. There was nothing of the criminal violations [Lennon's] claimed by the Nixon administration." Professor Wiener has also obtained FBI files on comedian Groucho Marx, poet Allen Ginsberg, and actor Humphrey Bogart. The Marx file was more interesting than the professor had imagined, especially regarding Marx's alleged communist sympathies. But there were also several hundred pages dealing with a copyright infringement investigation, a criminal case involving the Marx brothers, which was of no interest to Wiener. He found Allen Ginsberg's file notable in that the FBI seemed to be trying hard to stereotype the poet's eclectic politics into the Bureau's cookie-cutter mold of pro-communism. Wiener noticed the "sameness" reflected in the Bureau's perception of these vastly disparate public figures.

As for the overall disclosure process, Wiener contends, "The law is pretty good. It is the administration of the law that is the problem—resistance, delays, ritual invoking of national security." He also faults the superficiality of agency processing of documents for release: "They don't really check to see who is dead or whose identity they are protecting." As with others who use FOIA extensively, he views delay as a major obstacle. "Time is on their side," he complains. "The strategy is just *delay*. Unless you have a couple of years to spend, you're not going to get anything useful. . . . It's a discouraging process."

Even so, Wiener sees an increasing use of FOIA beyond what he refers to as the "community" of scholars and journalists who use it extensively in their work. He observes that more college students, both graduate and undergraduate, are using the law. He views the FBI's website, offering previously disclosed, frequently requested files online, as an important development in broadening the public's access.

In terms of reforms, high on Wiener's list is getting "more personnel in FOIA offices in order to do the processing." He would also like to see a change of attitude in the secrecy culture of the FBI concerning what he regards as their "overprotectiveness" of information from the Hoover era.

Wiener's number-one priority is to restore the Carter administration policy of balancing the public interest for disclosure against the need for

secrecy. This mandated balancing in processing documents was eliminated altogether by a Reagan executive order. Despite a concerted
lobbying effort by pro-disclosure interests, President Clinton failed to
restore the Carter policy. Instead, his executive order made the weighing
of public interest versus secrecy an option for agencies, not a requirement (which, according to Wiener, means that agencies ignore it).

"We're still behind where we were in the Carter era," Jon Wiener concludes. "There was a giant setback in the Reagan era and we have never
recovered. The balance is very much on the side of secrecy."

JOHN TUNHEIM

In 1992, facing intense public pressure, Congress passed landmark legislation in the public's right to know: the JFK Records Act (see case
study in chapter 6). It mandated the presidential appointment of a five-
member board to oversee release of all records relating to the assassination of President Kennedy. The Assassination Records Review Board
(ARRB) was given extraordinary power. Under a broad definition of what
constituted a "record," the board itself would decide which documents
should be released, not the agencies. In a reverse of the FOIA process, it
was the agency that had to appeal the board's decision to release information (as disappointed requesters have to do under FOIA). Agency
appeals seeking to overturn a board decision went directly to the president. ARRB would eventually oversee the release of approximately four
and a half million pages of documents.

John Tunheim, now a federal district court judge, is a graduate of
the University of Minnesota Law School.[7] His four-year tenure as chair
of the ARRB came when he was serving as chief deputy attorney general for the state of Minnesota (a position he held for nine and a half
years). He had extensive experience with that state's public disclosure
statute but had what he describes as "minimal exposure" to FOIA or
federal disclosure issues. In fact, he had not even heard of the JFK
Records Act when he received a phone call from the American Bar Association informing him that his was one of the names the ABA would
nominate for possible appointment to the board.

Tunheim's impressions of the ARRB's life and times are vivid and
insightful. The board got off to a very rocky start: delays in presidential

appointment of its members and budget problems with Congress. "There were real hindrances at the beginning of the process," he recalls. "It was difficult to get up and moving." The law required that the board's staff not be federal employees and that they undergo the security clearance process before having access to secret documents. This meant that the clearance process had to start from square one, preventing the board from going to work for several months. The tight security for the board's Washington, D.C., offices was not a hindrance, Tunheim reports. Ultimately there was "good security" for the board's sensitive mission.

At the outset there was considerable confusion, and resistance, on the part of the agencies. Tunheim remembers a meeting with CIA officials in which they said, essentially: "We can't tell you why documents must be withheld, but you're going to have to trust us. It relates to ongoing operations." The law required the board to weigh the potential harm from release against the public interest in disclosure. The ARRB took a firm stand, says Tunheim, informing the agency that "unless we know what you are talking about, then how can we weigh harm if we don't know what harm is?" Tunheim recalls a CIA official turning to an agency lawyer and mouthing, "Can they do that?" The attorney nodded affirmatively.

"At first it was terribly difficult for the CIA to understand the process," Tunheim recalls. And the National Security Agency seemed to be in "culture shock" concerning the reality of civilian hegemony in the disclosure process. The Secret Service failed to assign sufficient resources to their JFK disclosure task. The Service also took the position that documents relating to presidential protection that had been made public by the National Archives decades ago should now be classified and withheld. The board rejected this idea. The CIA's blanket position was that the identity of *any* source was sacrosanct and had to be protected, no matter how many decades had passed or whether the informant was dead or alive. Again, says Tunheim, the ARRB exercised its legally mandated clout, announcing a firm policy: "If the source is dead it [documents] gets released; if alive, there must be proof of harm. . . . Hiding behind dead people is not fair in a subject of this magnitude."

The ARRB's mandate was to pursue all records—not just federal files but privately held material as well. To the surprise of the board, the media seemed at times as resistant as the CIA regarding the protection of confidential sources. Tunheim is openly critical of the fourth estate's intractability at "protecting deceased sources thirty-seven years after the information was obtained."

Congress had specifically required that the State Department assist the board in obtaining assassination-related files from foreign governments. For example, Lee Harvey Oswald had defected to the Soviet Union and lived there for more than two years. The KGB was thought to have rich and voluminous files on the pre-assassination ex-Marine. To the board's chagrin, according to Tunheim, "the State Department failed to provide the necessary assistance. We criticized them, justifiably so, in our final report." As a result of the department's inaction, Tunheim regards the release of Soviet files to be "an incomplete project."

Regarding their right to appeal board decisions to the president, agencies varied. The CIA did not launch a single appeal. The FBI took a different tack: it initiated a flurry of appeals at the outset. To the board's chair it seemed "almost as if they were challenging our authority." The appeals were a drain on the board's staff: a legal brief had to be prepared for each case and sent to the president.

Tunheim was summoned to the White House for a meeting with FBI Director Louis J. Freeh and presidential counsel Judge Abner Mikva. President Clinton had promised the ARRB that he would support its decisions if it carefully followed the law. Now the Bureau put this commitment to the test. Mikva expressed the White House's concern about the growing number of appeals. He also asserted that Congress had given the board very specific authority such that the president was not inclined to overrule them. Tunheim perceives that this "sent a message" to the FBI: "Pick the cases [appeals] carefully. Don't just appeal every decision you don't like." Tunheim felt fully supported by the president, who never overturned a board decision to release documents. One can only imagine the shock waves throughout the culture of secrecy when the president's backing of the board was understood. The ARRB was *indeed* in charge of disclosure. After the White House meeting, the FBI withdrew its pending appeals. Tunheim saw a change in the Bureau's attitude. "I'm not sure they liked it," he observes, "but they cooperated."

According to Tunheim, once the process was established, there was a striking change in the board's relationship with the agencies. "We had a very good working relationship with the FBI after that [the White House meeting]." The agencies, which at first viewed the board as "a terrible nuisance that would harm national security," eventually came to view it as a partner and even as a "helpful resource" (in bringing about the release of older records that, in the perception of some agency personnel, should have been released years ago, if not decades). Even the "culture-shocked" National Security Agency came to view the board as helpful, Tunheim says, as did the Secret Service. One key element of this positive evolution: "We knew their filing systems as well as they did; sometimes, better."

Tunheim also witnessed a phenomenon unexpected by those who view the culture of secrecy as a monolith of antidisclosure ideology. He dealt with people at the CIA who were "strong pro-release people." He notes that, as this author has described, the existing system is biased toward having employees classify and overclassify documents. The harm or embarrassment that might ensue from a release could result in an employee being ostracized, demoted, or fired. Little or no enforceable punishment exists for erring on the side of secrecy. But in the case of the ARRB, here was an independent board that could not be fired. This liberated the secret keepers from the specter of sanctions. It "immunized" them, as Tunheim describes it, allowing them to "unload" troves of documents that they had wanted to release for a long time. "It was perfect for them," he observes. "Many of them really believe in the public right to know."

As for the possible future of this unprecedented process, Tunheim believes "the model is pretty good. I wouldn't tinker with it much." He believes that it works extremely well for defined groups of records but not as a system-wide disclosure process. When I asked him if atomic-veterans' records and records on experimentation with human subjects would be too broad or would fit within his parameters, he was confident that both areas could be effectively served by an ARRB-type process.

Tunheim's tinkering would involve avoiding some of the major pitfalls and obstacles that his board encountered. Because it took so long to get up and running with a staff in place, deadlines for agency disclosures to the board had already passed before the board was functional. Moreover, its eventual definition of what constituted "records" as defined in its policies turned out to be much broader than some agencies had assumed, requiring them to go back and search and compile all over again. This wasted resources and caused further delays. Tunheim suggests that future boards be given a three-year lifespan but that they have a full year to get everything in place, *before* the three-year clock starts ticking.

Usually the head of any organizational entity will take the position that more human resources are (were) needed to do the job. Judge Tunheim is an exception: the staff of twenty-five was "just right." But he is definite about changing its composition and its occupational status. The JFK Records Act forbade any federal employees from serving as staff. This, Tunheim believes, was ill advised. Having some staffers be on loan from key federal agencies would speed up the disclosure process, especially at the crucial early stages. He favors a mix of federal employees, academics, legal practitioners, and archivists, all of whom would take "sabbaticals" from the jobs that they will return to. The ARRB suffered in its final year because some staffers left to take permanent positions in the face of impending unemployment when the board was dissolved.

Congress gave the board subpoena power, but only if it was exercised through the Justice Department. Tunheim would give this power directly to the board. The Justice Department's procedures and policies created "roadblocks" to an effective subpoena power, he asserts (a power that he says the board used "judiciously and well"). He cites the department's refusal to subpoena records from media organizations as a prime example of the problem.

Finally, he would remove what he regards as one of the major impediments to disclosure: "the other-agency equity rule." Law enforcement and intelligence agencies almost universally refuse to release information that came from another agency, unless the latter approves of the disclosure by signing off on it. Obtaining these third-party permissions was a painfully slow process. Tunheim suggests that the other agencies be given no more than thirty days to respond, after which the information would be automatically disclosed.

Foreign agencies present a special problem. They are even more resistant to release of their data and often exist in political systems that have given them absolute power over their files (or where FOIA-type statutes are weak or nonexistent). Foreign agencies almost always say no to disclosure. Tunheim recalls the case of the Swiss Federal Police, who had a file on Lee Harvey Oswald. The response to a broad request had been a resounding "no." Tunheim did an end run, meeting with the Swiss ambassador to the United States to explain the historical import of the file. "Of course that should be released," said the ambassador. This is indeed a circuitous process for disclosure.

The questions regarding Tunheim's role in this historically unique experience in public disclosure are not whether it was successful or important: the six million pages ultimately released with no known harm to national security has answered that. The real question is whether Judge John Tunheim will go down in history as one of only two or three such board chairs in the entire span of public disclosure in the United States.

Despite the diverse backgrounds, historical topics, and arenas of these five pioneers in public disclosure, there is considerable overlap in their experiences. All were refused information based on agency assertions that national security would be harmed. In general, these allegations of "harm" ranged from incorrect, to exaggerated, to invented. All five people had to grapple with the blurred boundaries between legitimate secret keeping and cover-ups designed to avoid embarrassment and/or accountability: the atomic veteran whose own blood test was withheld from him; the CIA's plea to the ARRB to "take their word" about harm; and the politicization of law enforcement by a White House seeking to deport John Lennon. All five people labored in a rich political context that heavily influenced the disclosure process—conspiracy-versus-lone-assassin ideologues, the erosion of public confidence in nuclear power, and the surveillance of Dr. Martin Luther King, Jr., and the Civil Rights Movement. Another theme is the records that got away: the media files on the JFK assassination that were refused to Tunheim's board, the 1973 fire that destroyed the service records of millions of veterans, and withheld FBI documents on Marilyn Monroe and John Lennon.

All five of these people have invested not weeks or months but years, if not decades, in pursuing the public right to know as defined by their various clients, causes, and roles. Financial sacrifice has been the norm in these involvements rather than the exception. Then there is the success, always a relative concept except in super bowls and presidential elections. By any measure, these five individuals have been successful in expanding the freedom-of-information process, their "failures" notwithstanding. Sometimes success can be measured in millions of pages; sometimes dozens. Sometimes it is measured in the legal/administrative precedents that will expand access for others, or in the release of information that will empower or improve their lives. Clearly, the impact of this small group of people on the public's right to know is a lasting one, as is true of hundreds of others whose stories do not appear here. If voter participation is the lifeblood of democracy, the pursuit of information from government is the lifeblood of the public's right to know.

It should also be noted that the front lines of disclosure are worked by organizations as well as individual requesters acting primarily on their own. For example, the National Security Archives in Washington, D.C., a private institution, has led the successful fight for release of thousands of pages of key documents in various areas of foreign policy, human rights, and national defense. The Coalition on Political Assassinations has launched FOIA requests and lawsuits and has assisted the ARRB. The Assassination Archives and Research Center, a private entity also located in the nation's capital, has actively pursued records concerning political assassinations and related topics, both domestic and foreign.

CHAPTER 6

Secrecy Wars

The fact is that the primary function of governmental secrecy in our time has not been to protect the nation against external enemies, but to deny the American people information essential to the functioning of democracy, to the Congress information essential to the functioning of the legislative branch and—at times—to the President himself information which he should have to conduct his office.

—Historian Henry Steele Commanger, 1976[1]

In addition to FOIA and the Privacy Act, a series of legal/political campaigns have been launched to release massive files or key records. These campaigns played out in various courtrooms, hearing rooms, the media, and behind-the-scenes negotiations. What sets these cases apart from most individual requests is that they involve a prolonged back-and-forth that can go on for years. Agency resistance and pressure from pro-disclosure interests are intense: *wars* are fought over the public's right to know. They differ markedly in terms of political turf, numbers of participants and, most important, outcomes.

The long campaign to obtain release of the Los Angeles Police Department's (LAPD) file on the assassination of Robert F. Kennedy was successful. It involved Kennedy associates, Hollywood luminaries, politicians, and concerned citizens opposing LAPD's staunch secrecy and the daunting persona of its chief, Daryl Gates. In contrast, the effort to free Congress's Martin Luther King assassination file has gone on for over two decades, without success. Sometimes, political pressure is exerted to try to move the legal process of disclosure forward or to overcome agency resistance. At other times, politics is the process: the issue of disclosure is fought in the political arena, and the legal/administrative dimensions play a secondary role.

LAPD CONFIDENTIAL

In 1984 when I became active in the Robert F. Kennedy assassination case, not a single file had been released from any agency: the FBI, CIA, LAPD, and Los Angeles District Attorney—all files were sealed. The centerpiece of disclosure was LAPD's 50,000-page file. In 1968 the murder of a presidential candidate was not a federal crime. It was in response to RFK's assassination that it was made a federal crime and that Secret Service protection was given to presidential candidates. In 1968 this assassination was technically a "local" crime. LAPD had jurisdiction in the investigation; its case file was considered the primary case record. The problem was, LAPD had no intention of releasing it. The federal statutes (FOIA, Privacy Act) did not apply to state/local documents. The California Public Records Law exempted law enforcement files from public disclosure. There was no legal right to LAPD's file—only a political one, if it could be realized.

A group led by Greg Stone and Paul Schrade geared up for obtaining the files. Stone had worked for the late Congressman Allard Lowenstein in his efforts to achieve disclosure and resolution to the case's unresolved issues. Schrade was a friend of Robert Kennedy and a political supporter (as a union leader). He was seriously wounded when RFK was killed. I weighed in with the fledgling RFK Assassination Archive at what was then Southeastern Massachusetts University. This facility started with thirty boxes of material from a private collection—the Castellano/Nelson collection, assembled by the Los Angeles–based Kennedy Assassination Truth Committee. Actor Mike Farrell, of *MASH* and *Providence* fame, was a founding member of the group.

The university archive was politically important to the campaign. It helped with the media as well as with politicians. An archive served to demonstrate academic interest in the records, manifesting an intent to preserve them and make them publicly available. It also relieved requesters of the burden of appearing selfish or greedy (driven by advancing their pet theories or making "bucks from books"). Congressmen, editors, and academics who were not comfortable supporting disclosure to Stone/Schrade/Melanson felt at ease writing the Los Angeles Police Commission on behalf of a university archive. The archival hook provided a political safe haven. It also seemed to help that the archive was located in Massachusetts, as if this were some logical extension of the Kennedy legacy (which it was not and never pretended to be).

The archival presence also removed the disclosure issue from the politics of conspiracy. Archives are neutral; they do not hold theories. The debate between LAPD and its critics over whether there was a conspiracy had embroiled the disclosure issue: released files will prove conspiracy; there's no need to release them because there was no conspiracy; and so on.

This separation of issues was manifested in a *Los Angeles Herald* editorial of March 6, 1986, entitled "A Call for Public Disclosure." It read:

> We have no quarrels with the way the LAPD handled the investigation or with the follow-up by the Police Commission. The investigators, however, have yet to fulfill the promise they made in 1969 to release the complete file on the Sirhan probe.

Letters of support flowed to the Los Angeles Police Commission (the elected board that oversaw the department)—Congressman Barney Frank, Frank Mankiewicz (the powerful Washington lobbyist who had been Kennedy's press secretary and who announced his death), Henry Guazda, archivist at the Kennedy Presidential Library in Boston. In his 1984 letter to the Los Angeles Police Commission, Arthur Schlesinger, Jr., adviser to John and Robert Kennedy and noted historian, intoned:

> There would seem no reason why, seventeen years after this tragic event, this information should be withheld. The material is of undisputed historical significance. . . . Every consideration of scholarly and national interest calls for disclosure of all information relating to Robert Kennedy's death.

I had informed the Kennedy family of the disclosure efforts. The only response was a brief letter from Massachusetts Congressman Joseph

Kennedy, Robert Kennedy's son, stating that he "hoped having all the information in one place would be beneficial." That is the closest to a Kennedy endorsement that we got. Paul Schrade, who was a friend of the family, kept them informed at every stage of the process through Melody Miller, Senator Ted Kennedy's chief of staff. To my knowledge, the Kennedy family never used its formidable political clout in Los Angeles to oppose release of the files. This was very important to the political equation. If they had stated publicly or let it be known privately that the release would merely replay old traumas and serve no useful purpose, our political task would have been considerably more difficult.

LAPD's political position of nondisclosure was eroding. Many documents relating to the other two assassinations of the 1960s (President Kennedy and Dr. King) had been made public. Even the much-maligned Warren Report had been released the year after the president's death. In contrast, not only had LAPD refused to open its files, but it also refused to release its 1,500-page *Summary Report* (analogous to the *Warren Commission Report*). The Los Angeles District Attorney's Office had released a couple of hundred pages and more were on the way. This breaking rank increased the pressure on LAPD. Why was the department so obstinate when precedent, public opinion, and history argued strongly for disclosure? What were they trying to hide? Why couldn't people see the case record and decide for themselves if the crime was solved?

Chief Daryl Gates would not budge from his position, stated June 26, 1984, in a letter to my colleague Greg Stone:

> . . . [P]lease be advised that criminal investigations are confidential. In addition, the Superior Court has ordered that the Department's files on that investigation remain confidential. Therefore, it is not possible to furnish you with information from those files.

The California Superior Court *had* refused release in 1975. But this was not the same thing as ordering that the files remain sealed in perpetuity. CBS News and Paul Schrade brought suit to force disclosure. The crux of their case centered on the 1970 book *Special Unit Senator,* written by Assistant Chief Robert Houghton and Theodore Taylor (a civilian writer).[2] Houghton had headed the department's assassination investigation and, in his book, proceeded to tell the inside story. In the absence of released files or reports, this book *was* the public record. CBS and Schrade claimed that during the writing Taylor had been given access to the files, which constituted prior disclosure to a member of the public. Thus the files must now be disclosed to the plaintiffs as well.

City attorneys weighed in with an array of sworn affidavits from police officials, rebutting the plaintiffs' claim: Retired Chief Edward Davis and Acting Chief Jack G. Collins provided statements, as did Houghton himself. To their knowledge, they said, the Robert Kennedy case file had been under lock and key. Access was limited to a strict need-to-know basis.

Houghton's affidavit asserted:

> I did write a book with the assistance of Theodore Taylor. I had no recollection of having shown the ten-volume *Summary [Report]* to Taylor, but I did show Taylor some items and some material from LAPD files. Much of the material I showed Taylor was material used in the trial of Sirhan, or held by the district attorney. . . . At no time did Taylor ever come to Parker Center [LAPD headquarters] and go into the police investigative files.

The court had been mistaken in accepting LAPD's version of Taylor's role. Being more enterprising than CBS's lawyers, I tracked Taylor down in 1986 at his seaside home in scenic Laguna Niguel, California. Ironically, Taylor was just across town from a branch of the California State Archives where the first release of records from the district attorney's office now resided. He described how he had come into possession of LAPD files. In a two-hour, tape-recorded conversation, Taylor related that he had picked up tapes and documents and transported them to his home, while the investigation was still ongoing. "My car was parked outside of Parker Center and I kept loading this crap in there. I don't know, the guy helped me with a cart; he had a big cart. And I thought, Jesus Christ, what really do I have here?" He laughed.

Taylor drove the files to his home and stored them in an office in his garage: there wasn't room in his study. I asked him how complete his access was.

TAYLOR: I had access to some papers that I shouldn't have had access to. . .

MELANSON: In what sense, since they were giving you most everything? What do you mean, "you shouldn't have"?

TAYLOR: Well now, these papers were not involved, did not come from LAPD. They were FBI . . . Central Intelligence [CIA]. He [Houghton] said, "For Chrissakes, you know, you're looking at 'em and I'll give 'em to you for forty-eight hours and then you get 'em back up here and don't copy anything down from 'em."

MELANSON: That's an example of how much he turned over?

TAYLOR: He just turned over everything he had.

It would seem that "the best of" Chief Houghton's knowledge to the court had been none too accurate.

LAPD's *Summary Report* was released in 1986—the full file in 1988. But it was not easy. Gates put up strong resistance. The police also maintained a strong presence at pro-disclosure headquarters—the adjoining North Hollywood apartments of Greg Stone and Floyd Nelson. Gate's department was notorious for spying on its enemies, real and imagined.[3] By LAPD's own admission, the RFK case was a major litmus test of its credibility.

Stone and Nelson's neighbors were surprised by the sudden, comforting presence of L.A.'s finest. The marked cars would circle the neighborhood several times a day. The unmarked vehicles with plainclothes personnel just sat. Some residents reasoned that this conspicuously increased presence was due to the fact that our group seemed "important" (because we wore suits) and were doing police-related business (which was true).

The acrimonious flavor of the battle for disclosure is captured by a February 12, 1986, incident in which I requested to speak before the Los Angeles Police Commission. The process had bogged down, nothing had been made public, and promised deadlines had been passed. It was no secret that I was going to be critical: I had expressed my displeasure in several letters and telephone calls. But I wanted to voice my criticisms publicly in the hopes of putting pressure on LAPD and the police commission.

The afternoon before my scheduled appearance, I returned to my hotel to find a message to call Commander Mathew Hunt of LAPD. I was impressed with the department's resourcefulness, since I was not in the habit of providing it with my local address when I arrived in town. Only my wife and Floyd Nelson knew where I was staying, or so I thought.

I telephoned Hunt at 5:30 P.M. The assistant to Chief Gates informed me that I could not appear before the police commission the next day. He explained that he had been "going through" the statutes and had discovered that my appearance would violate the law: it would constitute an illegal change of agenda. I informed Hunt that I *was* on the agenda and that I would appear no matter how many technicalities he unearthed. He replied that when Police Commission President Robert Talcott learned of the "error," he would change his mind about my appearance.

The next morning, Greg Stone, Paul Schrade, and I went to the offices of the Southern California American Civil Liberties Union seeking help. Attorney Joan Howarth agreed to accompany us to the hearing. She and her colleague Katherine Leslie asked what statute Hunt had quoted. I replied that it was something called the "Brown Act." The attorneys found this ironic: it was the California open meeting law.

At police headquarters, outside the police commission's offices, the ACLU attorneys, Schrade, Stone, and I confronted commission President Talcott, several LAPD officers assigned to the commission, and a representative from the city attorney's office. As Hunt predicted, Talcott had changed his mind about my appearing before the commission. After a highly charged exchange, Talcott offered to listen to us in executive session. We rejected the proposal on the principle that a discussion of public disclosure should not be held in secret. Moreover, without the press, the police commission would feel no pressure to respond.

We were finally given permission to speak in public. But the victory was rendered hollow by the skillful maneuvering of the Los Angeles law enforcement authorities. Inside the hearing room, Talcott announced that the police commission would recess from the meeting to discuss another matter, and the audience would be called back when business resumed. Press and spectators scurried for the exits, under the mistaken impression that either nothing would be happening or they weren't supposed to be there. We vainly attempted to woo the press back but most got away, chatting with commission staff as they departed down the long corridor. Our protests played to a largely empty house.

In 1985 Police Chief Gates was asked by the press when the file might be released. He responded, "At a future date certain." When pressed further he replied, "Sometime in the nineties." He almost got his wish. During the various police commission hearings from 1984 to 1986, Chief Gates pulled out all the red herrings. He argued that "there are still people living that I think would be harmed, seriously harmed [by release]."[4] He did not explain *who* or *how*. At another point, he referred to "documents on Marilyn Monroe." This was calculated to put a chill in those close to the RFK legacy, implying that the alleged scandalous liaison between the actress and the then–attorney general may turn up in the files. There was nothing on Ms. Monroe in the released file. Gates referred to "national security" as a reason for withholding, but did not elaborate.

Years later, in his 1992 book, *Chief: My Life in the LAPD,* Gates decided to take credit for the disclosure he had so vehemently opposed:

> By now, everyone was demanding to see our files. Personally, I had no objection to opening them up. The problem was, the files contained information given to us on a confidential basis. We had all kinds of information from people who were around the senator, what they were doing, and who they were with, *private* information. I didn't think we had any right to disregard a confidential relationship. This only added more fuel to the conspiracy theories. "If the police weren't hiding something, they'd let us into that file. So they're hiding something, they know there's a conspiracy, and that's why they won't give us that file."
>
> Finally, I got so sick of this, I recommended the files be placed in the hands of our archivist, pointed out what we thought was confidential and let him worry what to do about it.[5]

Police Commissioner Samuel Williams picked up on the theme of potential scandal. "Can you tell me," he asked me pointedly at a hearing, "that if someone was staying as a guest in the hotel [the Ambassador Hotel, where RFK was shot] that night, and no one knew they were there, that information would *not* come out?"

I responded, "In past disclosures, at both state and federal level, rights to privacy have been protected by those agencies conducting the disclosure." "Specifically," Williams demanded, "would that *not* come out?" "It may or may not," I conceded. "There is no fixed standard."

To keep the pressure on for timely disclosure and minimum censorship, we talked with any media who would listen. Paul Schrade and I took to the airwaves in Los Angeles, San Francisco, Boston, and New York. If the *NBC Evening News* didn't call, we would do *People Are Talking* in San Francisco. If *60 Minutes* showed no interest, I would do *Geraldo* and *Entertainment Tonight*.

By the twentieth anniversary of Robert Kennedy's death, the public disclosure situation had been completely reversed—from total secrecy to largely uncensored release. LAPD's file was finally taken from the department by Mayor Tom Bradley's office. A committee of civilians was appointed, and they voted to ship the files to the California State Archives in Sacramento for processing. There, archivist John Burns and his staff released everything but autopsy photographs and criminal records—no more excessive redactions by LAPD and police commission staff.

In 1988, in addition to police files, the public record now included the District Attorney's Office files, FBI files, and the 10,000-page trial transcript. The latter had to be taken from its inaccessible storage in a courthouse basement and transported by armored car to a copying facility. The duplicates were then housed at the University of Massachusetts archive and in Greg Stone's apartment, publicly accessible for the first time. Disclosure was as complete as it could be, with one major exception.

AGENTS OUT OF PLACE

The FBI's 32,000-page file was arriving at the University of Massachusetts in batches of 1,500 to 2,200 pages. It was exciting to receive these hefty packets of previously unreleased documents—to be the first to read them. Some of the substantive deletions (of paragraphs or sentences) for reasons of privacy, confidentiality, and national security were disappointingly extensive. But at least the censorship was sporadic: very few entire pages and no entire documents were withheld. There was one huge exception—agents' names. The name of every agent was deleted from every document, except for Director Hoover and case supervisor Amadee O. Richards. This had not been done with the Bureau's files on the assassinations of President Kennedy and Dr. King.

Unresolved issues in the case were raised by these very documents: the possibility of too many bullets for Sirhan's gun, Sirhan seeming out of position to have inflicted the fatal wound (there was no released film or photo of the assassination), a possible female conspirator. Without agents' names, it was impossible to learn who worked on what. Who took the photos marked "bullet holes"? Who labeled them? Who interviewed the witnesses who alleged that Sirhan had a female accomplice? How could the Bureau's performance and conclusion be effectively scrutinized by the media and scholars without names? How could the FBI be held accountable?

The agents named in the files were working in their professional capacity at taxpayer expense. A witness who just happened to go to the hotel with his girlfriend to glimpse Kennedy and a busboy who happened to be in the kitchen when Kennedy was shot had their names revealed. The names of LAPD officers were provided in their released file. In fact, the Bureau's previous, minimal release in this same case file (3,200 pages in 1975) did not delete agents' names.

Our attorneys Larry Teeter and James Lesar immediately wrote the Bureau's chief FOIA/Privacy Officer, Emil P. Moschella, and asked that the deletion stop and the names be restored. They cited numerous Bureau case files in which names were included. The Bureau refused our request. Protecting agents' "right to privacy" outweighed "historical research," Moschella replied.

This made little sense. The names of more than 100 special agents who worked the RFK case were already in the public record via books, media reports, and previously released documents. What these deletions were "protecting" was not privacy but who did what in the Bureau's investigation. We knew that Special Agents William Bailey and Alfred Greiner were at the crime scene. We wanted to know what they did there and what they saw or concluded. Asking an interviewee to comment on or explain documents is difficult if you do not know which of the 32,000 pages applies to them.

Retired Agent Bailey decided to share his RFK case experience with the media and several authors (including this one). His account is provocative because he claims to have seen what would definitely be second-gun bullets. Says Bailey:

> As I toured the pantry area I noticed in the wood doorframe, a center divider between two swinging doors, two bullet holes. I've inspected quite a few crime scenes in my day. These were clearly bullet holes: the wood around them was freshly broken away and I could see the base of a bullet in each one.[6]

Retired agent Greiner declined to be interviewed by anyone, including myself, despite repeated requests. That was his right and he exercised it. If I or anyone else were to become too intrusive in pursuing agents, legal remedies were available to them. The idea that preemptive censorship was needed in order to protect an elevated concept of privacy was a radical position. It seemed that the Bureau simply did not want its agents queried about issues of evidence: the same issues that the Director's Office had refused to address despite several outside requests during the late 1970s and 1980s.

The FBI made a counteroffer to Stone and me to avoid litigation. They would restore agents' names to any particular context in which we could prove that it had been previously disclosed. If we could provide a document or clipping showing that an agent conducted a certain interview, the name would be provided in that particular document. We declined this less-than-generous offer to give us what we already had (and to turn us into research drones for the Bureau's RFK file). We were concerned with the principles of public disclosure and agency accountability more than the names, as valuable as they were. In a show of legal strength, we sent a list of more than 100 agents whose names had been previously disclosed in one way or another. The Bureau refused to budge.

Again, as we had done when the FBI had stubbornly refused to grant us a fee waiver, we went political. Five congressmen wrote letters to FBI Director William Webster urging that the names not be deleted. Two, Barney Frank of Massachusetts and Don Edwards of California, were members of the House Judiciary Committee that oversaw the Bureau. Edwards chaired its Subcommittee on Civil and Constitutional Rights.

He was also a golfing chum of the director's and a close political acquaintance of Paul Schrade. My confidence soared. His forceful endorsement of our position in his January 17, 1986 letter to Director Webster read:

> I urge release of these names. In order for Prof. Melanson to evaluate these materials and fill out the historical record of this event, it is important for him to know who were the agents involved so he can seek to interview them. (The individuals, of course, can always decline to be interviewed.)
>
> The public and scholarly interest in the Kennedy assassination seems to me clearly to outweigh whatever privacy interest there might be in maintaining the anonymity of law enforcement officers who were acting in their official capacities, unless there are special considerations such as protecting the identity of an undercover agent.

Despite Congressman Edwards' "warmest regards," Webster refused. He responded to all five representatives with essentially the same letter:

> The identities of remaining FBI and other law enforcement personnel are being withheld as disclosure would constitute an unwarranted invasion of their privacy. . . . Public identification could conceivably subject them to harassment or annoyance in the conduct of their official duties and in their private lives.

We went to federal court: *Stone and Melanson v. the Federal Bureau of Investigation* (no. 90-5065, D.C. Cir. Ct.). Much of the time between 1987 and 1989 was spent on motions and countermotions for "summary judgment." Both sides asked for postponements due to calendar exigencies.

I was confident about the development of our case. We garnered twenty-three supporting affidavits of high quality and stature. What impressed me most was that several came from former law enforcement people: ex-FBI Agents William Turner and William Bailey; Joseph L. Jacobson, former Assistant District Attorney of Kings County, Brooklyn, New York; and Quinlin J. Shae, formerly the Justice Department's FOIA/Privacy appeals officer. There were noted scholars and authors who had done work on the Bureau and its files (including Professor David Garrow, author of *The FBI and Martin Luther King, Jr.,* Penguin

Books, 1983). Steven Weinberg, Executive Director of Investigative Reporters and Editors (then the only national association of its kind), also provided an affidavit.

There were three main themes of our case: the overriding public interest in disclosure, the numerous precedents and their absence of harm to the agents involved, and the Bureau's history of inconsistent, politically motivated disclosure decisions (that is, "friendly" authors seemed always to get names). As Lesar's brief argued:

> Don Whitehead's *The FBI Story* (Random House, 1956), includes the names of many operational FBI personnel, sometimes accompanied by birthdates or other personal data. In the Foreword to the book, FBI Director Hoover wrote: "My one regret has been that the author did not have the space to call the full roll of loyal men and women who have contributed so much to the achievement of the FBI."

The Bureau did not produce a single affidavit supporting its blanket assertion of potential harm—not one agent alleging harassment or personal discomfort. The arguments and case precedents seemed heavily in our favor.

In January 1989, Judge Charles Ritchey proved my optimism unfounded by ruling in favor of the Bureau. Judge Ritchey concluded that agents involved in the RFK case "have a legitimate interest in preserving the secrecy of matters that conceivably could subject them to annoyance or harassment in either their official or private lives." Even worse for public disclosure, Ritchey opined that agents' privacy rights were actually *increased* with the passage of time:

> Thus, the agents' status as public officials does not rob them of their privacy rights, especially in light of the lengthy period of time that has elapsed. Senator Kennedy was assassinated over twenty years ago, and the parties agree that many of the FBI agents who participated in the RFK investigation have long since retired. Whether they have retired, moved on to another profession, or continue to serve their state or Nation as law enforcement officials, these agents have earned the right to be "left alone" unless an important public interest outweighs that right.

So this was the price that the historical record paid for no one telling the Bureau how to find its trove of RFK documents until 1985. If we had somehow obtained release in 1969, we would have more of a right to have the names provided? A three-judge federal appeals court unanimously upheld Judge Ritchey's decision. The U.S. Supreme Court, the next step, did not seem like a viable option.

For a time, my ego recoiled at the dozens of court documents that referred to the case as *Stone et al. v. the FBI*. It wouldn't require much more ink to include the single "et al.'s" name. After the decision, however, I was no longer concerned: like the Bureau's retired agents, I enjoyed my anonymity.

OLIVER'S TWIST

By far the greatest windfall of important federal documents relating to a particular subject came between 1994 and 1998. It was accomplished outside FOIA and the Privacy Act. It was entirely political, and it deserves to be called a war. From 1976 to 1979, the Congress's House Select Committee on Assassinations (HSCA) spent two and a half years reinvestigating the cases of President Kennedy and Dr. King. It concluded:

> That on the basis of the evidence available . . . President John F. Kennedy was probably assassinated as a result of a conspiracy. . . . The committee believes that on the basis of circumstantial evidence available to it, that there is likelihood that James Earl Ray assassinated Dr. Martin Luther King, Jr., as a result of a conspiracy.[7]

HSCA was created because of increasing public skepticism regarding the lone-assassin conclusions and a climate of distrust fueled by governmental secrecy and suspicions of cover-up. The Warren Commission had intended to seal its records for seventy-five years and release only its report and twenty-six volumes of exhibits.

In the wake of this legacy of secrecy and distrust, HSCA proclaimed at its inception: "It is essential not only that persons be able to judge the performance of executive agencies, but that they are able to judge the committee's performance as well."[8] Two years later, however, HSCA reneged. After issuing its final report, it engaged in one of the most spectacular rejections of the public's right to know manifested in recent decades. Instead of opening its records, Committee Chairman Louis Stokes (Dem., Ohio) and Chief Counsel G. Robert Blakey arranged to seal them for fifty years (a slight improvement over the Warren Commission's attempted seventy-five years).[9] All the committee's documents, transcripts, and investigative reports were declared "congressional material" and locked away until 2039.

The magnitude of the secrecy was staggering—an estimated 600,000 pages of documents on the King case and several hundred thousand more on the president's assassination. Congress had already exempted itself from FOIA in 1966. Thus the committee's secrecy vault was beyond any legal access—totally sealed. To compound the withholding, Chairman Stokes requested that the agencies declare their relevant documents to be congressional materials also, rather than agency records. The FBI and CIA were ecstatic to comply: this meant that these documents were then beyond the reach of FOIA, which *did* apply to these agencies. Thus the congressional vault became a safe haven for the two agencies that seemed to critics to have the most to cover up regarding their performance and activities in these two assassinations.

The seal also meant that scholars and journalists could not independently evaluate the committee's performance or the validity of its conclusions based on the primary source records. Chief Counsel Blakey's response to critics was: "I'll rest on the historians' judgment fifty years from now when everything becomes available."[10] However, not everyone wanted to wait. Author/researcher Harold Weisberg charged: "What Stokes has done is arrange it so that the mechanisms by which people can correct the errors of government don't apply to Congress. He's arranged his own private cover-up."[11] Blakey, then a professor at Notre Dame, retorted: "He [Weisberg] can kiss my ass. And you can quote me on that."[12]

The next decade saw more failed efforts to liberate the files. Special legislation from Congress was required, and such groups as ACCESS, the Assassination Archives and Research Center, and the Committee for an Open Archives (all Washington, D.C.–based) tried to generate public support. In spite of the energetic efforts of a host of people too numerous to mention here, the necessary bill died in committee (was never reported out for a vote). The 1983 version of the bill was even endorsed by five former members of HSCA, to no avail (Representatives Stuart McKinney, Robert W. Edgar, Harold S. Sawyer, Walter E. Fauntroy, and Harold E. Ford).

The problem was that pro-disclosure groups were unable to create enough public pressure to overcome congressional inertia, despite all the public lectures and media appearances and the "Free the Files" bumper stickers. On the other side, Blakey and Stokes used their power and entrée as people who *knew* the files, who helped create them. When someone from the antisecrecy lobby put on a good suit and visited their congressperson, they got a polite response. When insiders Blakey and Stokes said, from authority, that the files contained no bombshells, were not worth the money to process, and that confidential sources had to be protected, congressmen listened attentively.

Blakey wrote a letter to House members strongly opposing the bill to release the records. In one interview, he argued that confidentiality had been promised to witnesses and sources and could not be breached. He also cited "intense privacy interests" that made disclosure unworkable and inappropriate.[13] These were the same arguments Chief Daryl Gates had used against releasing the RFK files.

What Blakey failed to remind Congress was that thousands of pages of documents on these same two cases (JFK, MLK) had been processed and released under FOIA—documents from the same agencies (the FBI, CIA, and Secret Service). Protection of privacy and confidentiality are built into FOIA's legal exemptions. HSCA records could be processed in the same way. Blakey was arguing for a return to the bad old days of pre-FOIA when agencies could simply assert a claim without proof and conduct blanket withholding.

Over the protests of the assassination research community and a few supportive legislators who intoned the "aura of mistrust and skepticism" created by congressional secrecy and the overriding "national interest" in release, Blakey continued his theme: "Of course history should judge what we do; but in the normal cause of events, when it doesn't touch so much on individuals."[14] Release, he asserted, "is not worth the money it would take to do it . . . the gain would be marginal, marginal to nothing."

The gain to Blakey's historical reputation was indeed marginal. But Congress had spent more than $6 million generating the files. The price of history and governmental accountability may have been high in the dollars needed for disclosure, but the political cost of citizen alienation and mistrust was much higher.

If quotes from Thomas Jefferson and bumper stickers didn't work, Hollywood did. In 1992 Oliver Stone released his highly publicized and controversial film, *JFK*. Its grand conspiracy and cover-up theories blamed virtually every element of the military-industrial complex for President Kennedy's assassination. Hundreds of thousands of movie-goers emerged from theaters blurry-eyed and mind-boggled after the three-hour onslaught of mayhem and intrigue.

Stone was savagely criticized. On the television show *This Week,* George Will observed that the movie represented "the clearest expression of violent hatred of the United States government." Cokie Roberts immediately agreed: "Absolutely right. You are right." Sam Donaldson also concurred; "You're exactly correct."[15] CBS anchor Dan Rather termed the film, "an outright rewrite of history."[16] Stone was accused of polluting the minds of America's youth by turning them against their government with his cinematic bag of distortions. His every "inaccuracy" was seized upon by the media (including two that were accurate). In defense of the film, I told audiences that, while I sharply disagreed with the accuracy of some of its portrayals, it *was* only fiction. It made audiences think. The Warren Report had a lower score on accuracy (given what we know today), and it comprised the official conclusions of our political and law enforcement institutions.

While the portrayal of New Orleans District Attorney Jim Garrison as a flawless patriot was a stretch and the grassy knoll was so crowded with conspirators that they almost ran into each other, there was one indisputably accurate revelation. Amid the final credits was the statement: "A Congressional investigation from 1976–79 found a 'probable conspiracy' in the assassination of John F. Kennedy and recommended the Justice Department investigate further. The files of the House Select Committee on Assassinations are locked away until the year 2039." And then: "What is past is prologue."

Public reaction was intense. Congress was bombarded with letters, faxes, and phone calls. The disclosure issue had been given a celluloid push into the political mainstream. Moviegoers would not abide governmental secrecy. In 1992 Congress passed the JFK Records Act which sought release of all government files relating to the assassination. Behind the scenes, Stone kept pressing for disclosure with some staff and other resources even after the movie screens went dark.

The JFK Records Act deserves to be called revolutionary in its intent. It not only aimed to open agency vaults but also to take the secret keepers out of their dominant role as the processors of disclosure. A five-member review board appointed by the president would decide what should be released. If agencies disagreed, they could appeal directly to the president. The legal-administrative tables had been turned. Unlike FOIA, agency outsiders were now the gatekeepers of secrecy, and agencies, like FOIA requesters, had the right to appeal. Moreover, the new mandate stated that documents should be released "unless public disclosure would be so harmful that it outweighs the public interest."

This is an extraordinary model for the public's right to know. The review board was mandated to have access to all records. Nothing was to be withheld from them. They were given the keys to the vaults, but only an agency knew how the locks worked.

The political battle did not end with passage of the JFK Records Act: it entered a new phase. Agencies conducted rearguard actions to stymie the process. They, too, had friends in Congress, the media, and the White House. They weren't about to turn their secrets over to strangers without a struggle. The recently formed Coalition on Political Assassinations (COPA), a Washington, D.C.–based group pursuing disclosure of files and reopening of the cases, worked to protect the board from its enemies and help it do its job.

Potential appointees were nominated by professional associations (archivists, historians, and lawyers). President George Bush failed to appoint the board before he left office. When he took his White House papers back to Texas to be housed in his presidential library, he took the nomination papers with him. The names had to be renominated to President Clinton. The incoming administration was notoriously disorganized and tardy in making key appointments—including attorney general. Although Congress had required that the panel be appointed by January 1993, Clinton took nearly a full year. Senate confirmation of appointees took still longer.[17] The board was not operational until April 1994, a year and a half after the JFK Records Act was passed. Congress extended the board's life until 1998. A $1.3 million budget was appropriated, and an executive director, David Marwell, and a staff of twenty-five were put in place.

Its work was difficult. Member Anna K. Nelson was surprised to hear the CIA and FBI argue that the information from more than three decades ago was as sensitive as that gathered three days ago.[18] Both agencies asserted a blanket protection for all sources, no matter how long ago or how low level, or whether they were dead or alive. Nelson wrote that the agencies seemed to expect the board to accept their generic justifications for withholding.[19] Board members were appalled at the agencies' "seemingly irrational obsession" with protecting sources. The CIA was especially effusive in its dire predictions concerning the release of its secrets: "Governments would fall," said Nelson, "allies would be lost, and cooperation with other intelligence agencies would come to an end. . . . The accidental release of one word or phrase will not only kill countless people but also send the country to its knees."[20]

Nelson also recalled the many problems the board encountered. They waited for documents in their secured offices and conference rooms (doors opened only with key cards and numerical codes). CIA and FBI "briefings" to the board were gloom-and-doom entreaties to uphold the original classifications made by the agencies. The board's staff had to receive security clearance—more delay. Even with all the precautions, the agencies would provide only a single copy of each document and would not allow the board to make copies—a logistical nightmare for a group potentially working with voluminous files. The only agency to comply with the congressionally mandated deadlines for submitting documents was the National Archives.[21]

COPA Executive Secretary John Judge, who worked extensively to monitor the process, observed, "They [the board] picked their battles very carefully in the early days. The president sat on a lot of agency appeals [urging withholding], and the agencies capitulated. The president wanted the board and agencies to work it out."[22]

Besides political support, the most knowledgeable of assassination researchers provided invaluable assistance. Some of them had researched agency files for many years and/or used FOIA to obtain documents. They had insights into what files to look for, where and how they might be found, how released documents provided clues to other documents, and, yes, how agencies hid things. Such expertise helped the board cope with agencies who could not be counted on to be thorough in their searches and forthcoming with their files—agencies who at best sought to avoid the disclosure process; at worst, to sabotage it.

The board held regional hearings at which such researchers testified. I was asked to provide information regarding possible files on Oswald held by U.S. intelligence agencies.[23] His complex involvement as a security-cleared marine, a defector to the Soviet Union, and a participant in Cuban politics in the United States offered rich possibilities. Outside the March 23, 1995, hearing, I talked extensively with reporter Doris Sue Wong of the *Boston Globe*. I explained the uniqueness of this disclosure process, its impact on the public's right to know, and the possible extent and significance of unreleased files.

The next day I was appalled to pick up the *Boston Globe* and read her trivializing account of the event: "JFK Panel Hears from Conspiracy Buffs." Although conspiracy theories abound, the entire hearing had focused on what files the board might find and release. No one tried to settle the *Who killed JFK?* question. This incident made it clear how difficult the board's political life would be: when a prestigious, big city newspaper cannot understand the importance of the public disclosure process before its eyes and chooses to marginalize the event as a forum for conspiracy buffs, the board had a major image problem.

The Assassination Records Review Board did not obtain all of the government records relating to this historic event. For example, the Secret Service destroyed its files on two of President Kennedy's trips in the months before the assassination (to Miami and Chicago), trips that involved assassination plots. They did so *after* the JFK Records Act was passed. This clear violation of the law was asserted by the Service to be "routine destruction." Nor did the board process for release all that it obtained. Agencies still hold secrets behind their deletions and in documents or files squirreled away beyond the reach of disclosure laws. Even so, consider this result. From the Warren Report until 1994, released federal records numbered in the hundreds of thousands of pages. From 1994 to 1998, the review board oversaw the disclosure of approximately four and a half million pages (more than anyone has been able to read).

An estimated one and a half million more were released after the board's statutory life ended—a total of six million pages.

This plethora of information will probably not "solve" the case. But it will clarify its key issues: Oswald's relationships with intelligence agencies, Secret Service failures in presidential protection, manipulations of the Warren Commission by Hoover's FBI. Our history will also be enriched measurably by knowing more about Cuba and Castro, JFK and Vietnam, CIA covert operations, and more. The public's right to know has been strengthened by both the substance and the process of this disclosure.

THE BLACK CAUCUS'S POLITICAL BLACKOUT

In stark contrast to the JFK records, the HSCA's 600,000 pages of documents on the King case remain sealed. The film was *JFK,* not *MLK:* the film spawned the JFK Records Act, which said nothing about the King documents. The JFK files are infinitely larger and broader than the King files. There can be no doubt, however, as to the historical and criminal justice value of the King files. They contain documents that would help resolve the major questions of conspiracy and of agency activities before, during, and after the assassination. Having read related files and having talked with lawyers for the late James Earl Ray, as well as with HSCA investigators, I discovered leads that were not pursued by the committee. Its investigation had been flawed by its preoccupation with attempting to prove that James Earl Ray's brothers, John and Jerry, were coconspirators, as well as its inability to understand the scope and intensity of CIA and FBI activities focusing on Dr. King and the Civil Rights Movement.

There appeared to be an excellent opportunity to achieve disclosure. On the coattails of the JFK release, who was going to argue for continued secrecy in the King case without being politically ineffective, or politically incorrect? Was it that King was not a president? Was it that disclosure was too expensive (we had just spent a bundle on JFK files)? Was it that the millions of pages already released should be "enough"? Many politicians and journalists were already aware that the issues and controversies in the King case were just as compelling as in JFK's, only not as widely known to the public.

With COPA leaders and others, I joined the campaign to release the files, giving talks at colleges, universities, and other public forums and making TV and radio appearances (especially around the King holiday and the anniversary of the assassination). One of my points was, "Do we need to wait until Oliver Stone makes an *MLK* movie?" Actually, in the first few years after *JFK,* I had several conversations with Eric Hamburg, an executive in Stone's Ixtlan production company. A film dealing with King's assassination went from exploratory discussion to the back burner. Apparently, we would have to rely on politics rather than cinema to free these files.

There did seem to be progress. In a 1995 appearance on CNN's *Both Sides Now* hosted by Rev. Jesse Jackson, there was encouragement not only from Jackson and Walter Fauntroy (a former member of HSCA), but from an unlikely source—G. Robert Blakey. As planned off-air with Jackson, the disclosure issue was raised. Blakey rendered a tepid endorsement while issuing the qualifiers that Ray had acted alone and that my book on the King case was "garbage."

From 1995 to 1997, it appeared that political support within the Afro-American community was increasing. I talked to a half dozen mostly black audiences at colleges and cultural events and saturated the black-oriented media. The Black Caucus of the Ohio state legislature offered a resolution of support. Jackson and Fauntroy gave supportive responses when asked questions. Afro-American citizens contacted the Congressional Black Caucus. It seemed that we were getting close. One floor speech from a John Conyers or a Kweisi Mfume or a Maxine Waters and the vault would again be opened.

It never happened. It probably never will. Disclosure will likely occur at Professor Blakey's preferred date of 2039. Pro-disclosure advocates misread the political equation. Despite all the rhetoric about the public's right to know, agency accountability, and the truth about King's death, some powerful (albeit quieter) voices of those concerned with Dr. King's legacy may have spoken. They may see a different balance. For some, the risk of another round of scurrilous gossip from federal files (of the kind created and used by J. Edgar Hoover) is not worth the marginal gain of enhancing the truth about King's killing. John Judge, executive secretary for the Coalition on Political Assassinations, told the author: "They [Congressional Black Caucus] had a problem with release. They didn't want dirt to come out."

While I know enough about HSCA files from leaks, discussions with committee staff, and footnotes to the locked documents to be able to say that potentially scandalous material is quite probably absent, no one can guarantee it. I would argue that the worst of this smear was unleashed in the 1960s, and that the public and media have a better understanding that agencies lied about King and, in the FBI's case, tried to destroy him. Yet it is too easy to envision some of the media picking out the one document in 600,000 pages where an unknown informant talks about hotel rooms. This is the scare tactic used by Chief Gates in referencing Marilyn Monroe and was Los Angeles Police Commissioner Samuel Williams's worry about hotel trysts being revealed. Those working for continued secrecy who have also seen the files can always report, exaggerate, or conjure up such specters. This would explain why our grassroots campaign never left the statehouse lawns, never got to the U.S. Capitol.

INTELLIGENCE LOST

A legal tug-of-war over other King assassination documents continues. On March 21, 1993, the Memphis *Commercial Appeal* published the findings of its eighteen-month investigation into the presence of Army Intelligence units in Memphis at the time of the shooting. Written by Steve Thomkins, the piece analyzed documents obtained under FOIA.[24] It revealed that Army Intelligence was indeed present, that it worked closely with the FBI, that it surveilled King, and that Green Berets were dispatched to Memphis and other cities to scout riot-control routes and sniper perches.

These files showed that yet another intelligence organization was added to the Memphis surveillance mix, a conclusion reached not by conspiracy theorizing but by examining federal documents. A Memphis police intelligence squad and "federal agents" (as one police report describes) were around the Lorraine Motel when King was killed there. The federal agents were most likely FBI. There has been speculation (based on CIA files) that the CIA was also present. Now comes evidence that Army Intelligence was on the scene as well, potentially with its

own cameras, bugs, and agents. One document had an intriguing reference to a surveillance van parked outside the Lorraine Motel.

On behalf of COPA, Washington, D.C., attorney Dan Alcorn sent a
1997 request letter to the Pentagon for "any and all records relating to
any surveillance of Dr. Martin Luther King, Jr. during March or April
1968." Exhibits accompanied the letter from sources showing an Army
Intelligence presence in Memphis at the time of the assassination.

The Pentagon responded that it had no photos or documents—not
one. In the intervening years, Alcorn continued to pursue possible files
via written exchanges and court petitions and appearances. In another
FOIA case, Army Intelligence told a requester that it could find no documents relating to his subject. Eight years later, it found 3,000 pages;
obviously, its searches are suspect.

This is the same agency that "routinely" destroyed its file on Lee
Harvey Oswald sometime in the 1970s. Alcorn laments that there is no
enforcement of the 1968 statute that forbids agencies from destroying
any file that is of "historical," "legal," or "research" importance and,
therefore, no penalty for destruction. A host of reasons exist why a file
on King would have historical and research value. Moreover, as Alcorn
pointed out in his brief, up until the death of alleged assassin James
Earl Ray in 1998, his lawyers had initiated a series of legal actions to
which a crime-scene surveillance file would be exceedingly relevant.

Despite all this, the army's response was that any files on King, if
they existed, would have been destroyed in the 1970s (along with all
other files on individuals) in the agency's massive purge of documents. If
not destroyed, anything that still existed was allegedly given to the
National Archives for preservation and processing. The army was asserting that it kept or had nothing on King. The National Archives informed
Alcorn that it had no army subject file on King. It did, however, find and
declassify one army document on King, in response to Alcorn's request.

The fifty-page, single-spaced "After-Action Report" is a summary of
Army Intelligence activities in Memphis from March 28 to April 12,
1968. It shows that the 111th military intelligence unit was in Memphis, as the documents obtained by the Memphis *Commercial Appeal*
indicated. Twelve to sixteen army personnel were there, planning response capabilities for the "civil disorder" associated with King's visit

and with the local strike by garbage workers. This was done as part of project "LANTERN SPIKE," the army's 1960s effort to surveil and quell civil unrest.

The report states that the army coordinated its activities with the FBI and "shared all information." It further says that the Bureau informed them that King was departing Memphis on April 5 via Eastern Airlines. The amount of detail in this summary certainly indicates that either the army surveilled King or it received data from other agencies or both.

The only way to find out would be to see the original items on which this lengthy document was based. There must have been primary-source reports covering this period. They were probably extensive, considering the length of the summary. The King assassination entry reads:

> 1803 hours. Dr. King was fatally wounded by shots fired from a high-powered rifle with telescopic sights, while he (King) was on the balcony of the Lorraine Motel. The assailant, a white male, sped on foot to an automobile, eluded police crusiers [sic] and escaped without leaving any apparent clues to his identity.

Where did this data come from and what specifics are contained in the original reports on which this "after-action" summary was based? All intelligence and law enforcement summaries vary in their accuracy and scope. Another item states: "2300 hours. Ellis TATE, age 50, was observed behind a liquor store with a rifle in his hands. Police ordered him to drop the weapon. He fired at Patrolman E. T. TREADWAY and Police officers returned fire, wounding TATE several times." This is clearly based on something more substantive than a headline. The National Archives responded that "any such files would remain with the army." The army claims that they do not so remain (they were destroyed or given to the Archives). Why did the agency provide the Archives with a summary but destroy or fail to provide the originals?

In 2000 a federal district court judge rejected Alcorn's argument that the army was failing to disclose its records *(Coalition on Political Assassinations v. United States Department of Defense)*. The government introduced a complex, highly detailed affidavit from Russell A. Nichols, the army's chief FOIA/Privacy officer. He defended the quality of the search for records, citing various indices, records storage and retrieval processes, and army regulations. The defendant's lead counsel, U.S. attorney Wilma A. Lewis (working with two assistant U.S. attorneys) asserted:

> Plaintiff, however, makes no attempt to show that the search performed was not responsible. . . . Mr. Nichols explains that there is no way to reconstruct what records may have existed such a long time ago, whether they were destroyed, and, if so, how the destruction was authorized.

Proving that the army could have, should have, or did keep better track of its files was an uphill battle for Alcorn. He points out that, under federal law, judges are required "to assume government actions are proper unless it is proved otherwise."[25] He appealed the decision in federal appeals court, asking it to reject the agency's plea of ignorance and require that it be held accountable for the disposition of its files on King. The government moved for a summary judgment dismissal of Alcorn's case but it was denied.

Oral arguments and written briefs were scheduled to go to the three-judge appeals court in May 2001. There were two positive developments for Alcorn's case. Author Douglas Valentine produced Army Intelligence "unit records" relating to personnel assignments in Memphis at the time of Dr. King's assassination. The documents had allegedly been furnished to a Memphis reporter by the Pentagon's Center for Military History, via the army's public affairs office. This release occurred in 1997 when the FOIA request by COPA was met with the response that nothing could be found. A second indication of the army's failure to search adequately came in the Justice Department's 2000 report on new evidentiary developments in the King case. It stated that officials had analyzed Pentagon documents relating to King's presence in Memphis, some of which were classified. The government argued that such "new" information could not be introduced by Alcorn at the appeals stage, and that COPA should launch a new FOIA request for the "new" documents. Given that there were eighteen months of nonresponse to COPA's original request, Alcorn was disinclined to start over. The government also argued that COPA could not prove that the documents it has never seen are responsive to its FOIA request—another legal catch-22 erected by the U.S. attorneys.

Despite COPA's new discoveries about the existence of documents, it lost the case. On May 25, 2001 the appeals court ruled that the government had "satisfied its obligation under the FOIA to search for records responsive to the appellate's request"; further, that COPA "had not offered any evidence rebutting the adequacy of the search." The only legal options remaining for the plaintiff were to file for a rehearing before the appeals court or to go to the Supreme Court. Alcorn considered the chances for success exceedingly slim. This legal battle was at an end.

UNSOLVED HISTORY

One of the more high-impact battles for public disclosure was spearheaded by the National Security Archive in Washington, D.C., which describes itself as a public interest research center. The campaign culminated in the November 2000 release of 50,000 pages of formerly secret documents on Chile. These records were at the core of a cluster of intense political/historical issues regarding the role of the U.S. government in the violent 1973 coup that toppled socialist president Salvador Allende and installed the military dictatorship of General Augusto Pinochet. Unresolved issues also existed concerning CIA accountability for its actions, the Pinochet regime's massive human rights violations, and the 1976 assassination of Chilean dissident Orlando Letelier in Washington, D.C. The complex legal process of bringing the aged and infirm General Pinochet to trial in Chile for his alleged crimes began to unfold as the documents were released.

The Central intelligence Agency had steadfastly denied, then minimized, its role in the overthrow of an elected president and its support of Pinochet and his brutal, secret police apparat, which "disappeared" and otherwise murdered thousands of Chileans. In 1973 CIA Director Richard Helms testified before Senator Frank Church's Senate Intelligence Committee (known as the Church Committee). Under oath, Helms denied that the Agency had provided direct assistance to any candidates in the Chilean presidential election or that it had participated in the ousting of Allende (who either killed himself or was assassinated during the coup).[26] As Helms' chronicler Thomas Powers observed:

> CIA people are cynical in most ways, but their belief in secrets is almost metaphysical. In their bones they believe they know the answer to that ancient paradox of epistemology that asks: If a tree falls in the forest without witness, is there any sound? The CIA would say no.[27]

In 1976 Helms was charged with violating a federal statute that required witnesses to testify "fully and completely" before Congress.[28] He pleaded *nolo contendere* on two misdemeanor counts. Clearly, the National Security Archive was in a fight for disclosure on one of the CIA's most sensitive and protected turfs.

Peter Kornbluh, a senior analyst at the archive and the head of its Chilean Documentation Project, led the effort. The archive credited the Clinton administration's national security staff, particularly William Leary who coordinated the disclosure process, with being the primary force for the release (via the White House's Chilean Declassification Project).[29] The final declassification had been delayed for two months while behind-the-scenes politics played out. Under the archive's watchful eye and with the White House's pressure on the Agency, hundreds of CIA intelligence records were made public over its strong opposition. Had it not been for the archive's determination and energy and the commitment of the Clinton administration, the veil of secrecy would, no doubt, have remained. The archive also praised unnamed State Department officials who manifested "a strong commitment to using declassified U.S. documents to advance the cause of human rights abroad and the American public's right to know at home."[30]

This momentous release consisted of documents from the CIA, the White House, and the departments of Justice and Defense (1,600 "documents" totaling 50,000 pages). Included were 700 controversial CIA documents that the Agency's Directorate of Operations had refused to release under FOIA. Some 800 other CIA records were also made public. The release contained information on CIA covert operations in Chile from 1968 to 1975—operations designed to destabilize the elected government and bolster the Pinochet dictatorship. Kornbluh asserted that the information would "provide evidence for a verdict of history on U.S.

intervention in Chile as well as for potential courtroom verdicts against those who committed atrocities during the Pinochet dictatorship."[31]

Among the key revelations were some that undeniably refuted official claims of U.S. noninvolvement in the extensive violence in Chile:

- Records relating to the 1976 assassination of former Chilean ambassador to the U.S. Orlando Letelier, who also served as Allende's foreign minister, and Ms. Ronni Moffitt. A car bomb exploded in downtown Washington, D.C. Only the driver, Ms. Moffitt's husband, survived. The Justice Department had previously withheld these documents, claiming that they contained evidence relevant to General Pinochet's personal involvement in this infamous act of terrorism. For the first time, documents linked Pinochet to two Chilean intelligence agents implicated in the assassination by the U.S. investigation. A CIA report describes the Chilean government's efforts to obstruct the U.S. probe.
- Minutes of meetings of the "40 committee," the elite, interagency group chaired by National Security Advisor Henry Kissinger. It coordinated the effort to prevent Allende's election, with plans for "drastic action" designed to "shock" the Chilean political system into blocking his ascent to power.
- Documents from meetings of the National Security Council and the cabinet, chaired by President Richard Nixon. One expresses a commitment to "do everything we can to bring Allende down."
- CIA memos on the 1970 assassination of Chilean General Rene Schneider, including one that assesses the Agency's susceptibility to charges that it was involved in the plot. The document is heavily censored.
- Other documents reveal the U.S. government's policy of refusing to pressure the Pinochet regime to curb its human rights violations; requests to the CIA for training and equipment for the Chilean secret police; information on Operation Condor (planned assassinations abroad).
- CIA summaries describing meetings and lunches (hosted by the Agency's deputy director) with Chilean Manuel Contreras, who in 1979 was facing extradition to Chile for alleged human rights and criminal violations.

- FBI and Drug Enforcement Agency records relating to the case of U.S. citizen Frank Teruggi, who was allegedly executed by Chilean military after the coup.

Peter Kornbluh concluded: "With these documents the history of the U.S. role in Chile and the Pinochet dictatorship can be written." The disclosure, he asserted, was "a victory for openness over the impunity of secrecy."[32] Even so, few victories are total. The archive claims that records directly implicating Pinochet in his regime's atrocities remain classified. In addition, many of the released CIA documents were heavily deleted. As Kornbluh observed, "CIA censors continue to dictate what Chileans and Americans alike can know about this shameful history." He pledged that the National Security Archive would continue to press for full disclosure via all the legal means available.

The secrecy wars continue in various arenas—nuclear-testing records, human rights abuses, CIA mind-control research, and National Aeronautics and Space Administration cost overruns. Yet for tens of thousands of requesters there is a relatively simple "back-and-forth," but no war. An exchange of letters takes place with the agency, perhaps an appeal; and, for a few, a court case. But these requests do not involve dozens or even hundreds of people and numerous organizations. Instead, they are usually made by individuals in the solitude of their homes or offices.

In contrast, the secrecy wars involve not only people and/or groups but also numerous written exchanges, legal actions, media coverage (however sparse), and political activity. The wars usually go on within or around the legal/administrative frameworks, but sometimes they supersede it (as in the JFK records case). Political opinions and positions become polarized; for example, the CIA asserts that if the Records Review Board forces disclosure, the nation will collapse; some critics then accuse the Agency of covering up a conspiracy to assassinate President Kennedy. The intensity, scope, and duration of these kinds of disclosure cases set them apart from the norm.

In these conflicts, one side or the other is not routed in such a fashion that it cannot regroup to fight another day. In that sense, at least, the conflicts are separate: a group such as the National Association of

Atomic Veterans can lose one battle and go on to win another. But there is also a cumulative effect. Each major success or failure by disclosure advocates or secret keepers reverberates beyond the particular context—legally, administratively, and politically. The legal precedent in *Stone et al. v. the FBI* can be used by other agencies to delete the names of their employees in order to protect privacy. The results of the JFK Records Act prove that carefully selected citizens can administer a mammoth disclosure without getting people killed or wrecking an agency. The ramifications of these cases are partly why they are so intense. Both sides realize that the outcomes will impact the public's right to know far beyond the substance of the records at stake.

CHAPTER 7

Leaks from the Vault

For when everything is classified, then nothing is classified,
and the system becomes one to be disregarded by the cynical
or the careless, and to be manipulated by those intent on self-
protection or self-promotion.

—Supreme Court Justice Potter Stuart,
concurring opinion in the
Pentagon Papers case, 1971

The governmental secrecy system is designed to be tightly sealed: locked vaults at the CIA, the State Department, the Pentagon; documents marked "eyes only," "need-to-know basis," and "top secret." Despite all the document classification policies, the highly trained secret keepers and the security technology, secrets leak out. It is, after all, a system run by humans, by men and women of vastly different training and ideology. There are attack leaks, friendly leaks, and leaks that happen simply by accident.

Perhaps the most famous attack leak was the "Pentagon Papers" in 1971. Daniel Ellsberg, a former department of defense official, was an analyst at the Rand Corporation—a large and prestigious think tank that had contracted with the military and intelligence agencies to analyze and strategize for the Vietnam War. To expose government falsehoods and misrepresentations, Ellsberg smuggled out the "papers": a series of top-secret memos, documents, and intelligence reports (totaling seven thousand pages) describing U.S. policies and decisions regarding Vietnam. He leaked the material to the *New York Times* and the *Washington Post*.

It was Ellsberg who, at Rand, was assigned the task of compiling the history of U.S. involvement in Vietnam, overt and covert. His leak was devastating to official credibility. Among other revelations, the papers showed that the United States had not been drawn unwillingly into the conflict as was widely assumed. The Gulf of Tonkin Resolution, passed by Congress to widen U.S. military involvement, was drafted months before the alleged attack on U.S. naval vessels—the event that supposedly precipitated the resolution. It was also revealed that President Lyndon Johnson had been committing infantry to Vietnam while telling the public that there were no long-range plans for military action. The "papers" had a profound impact on official credibility and on the raging debate over the war.

The Nixon administration sought to prevent publication by the *Times* and the *Post*. It did obtain temporary injunctions. But on June 30, 1971, the U.S. Supreme Court ruled in favor of publication, stating: "These documents may have serious impact, but there is no basis for sanctioning a previous restraint [by a lower court] on the press."[1]

Ellsberg was indicted on several counts relating to the leak. A federal court dismissed all charges in 1973, because a Nixon White House team known as "the plumbers" had broken into the office of Ellsberg's psychiatrist looking for information to discredit him. The plumbers were too late to stop the leak and too unconstitutional to stop Ellsberg.

Friendly leaks are common. A State Department official concerned about the direction of our policy in the Middle East phones a contact at the *New York Times* and gives the reporter a "heads-up" on a policy shift. A deputy director at CIA leaks limited information on domestic spying to a CIA-friendly journalist, hoping for a less-negative spin than might result from upcoming congressional hearings. An official in the Drug Enforcement Administration asks CBS News to shelve a story that might expose undercover operatives, in return for an inside scoop on the latest efforts to stop the flow of drugs at the Mexican border.

Another variant of the leaking or release of classified information is the privileged access of insiders. For some untold number of them in an untold number of cases, the sealing of records does not apply. A most bizarre instance occurred in March of 2001.

Richard V. Allen had served as President Reagan's national security advisor when the president was seriously wounded by would-be assassin John W. Hinkley in 1981. Twenty years later, Allen published a riveting memoir of the behind-the-scenes deliberations in the White House situation room in the immediate wake of the shooting ("The Day Reagan Was Shot," *Atlantic Monthly,* April 2001). He used transcribed excerpts of the high-level deliberations that came from an audiotape of the session, which was described as "being made public for the first time, twenty years after the event."[2]

In an interview with National Public Radio, Allen was asked why the public had not heard this tape previously and why he was vetting it now. Incredibly, his response indicated he seemed to be inventing his own, personalized FOIA policies: "Well, I think a twenty-year interval is a perfectly respectable one." When asked if he had submitted the tape to the FBI or CIA for clearance he replied, "In twenty years, I think we've long passed technologically any threats to national security."[3] This is a quite liberal standard, considering that these same agencies have refused to release records twice as old on grounds of national security.

While the circumstances of Allen's possession of the tape and the legal issues involved remain murky, this much is known: A strict, pro-secrecy national security directive signed by President Reagan sought to prevent leaks of classified information. Mr. Allen apparently ignored the secrecy policy of the administration in which he served. Moreover, while there is no known record of governmental declassification of the tape (and while it was admittedly not censored by the CIA or FBI), it *has* been redacted (without explanation concerning FOIA withholding exemptions, as required by law). Did Allen himself decide what to excise? In his present status as a civilian, he has no legitimate authority either to declassify or classify information. Moreover, legal penalties exist for civilian and military personnel who remove classified information.

It is also clear that the tape does not fall into the category of "personal uncirculated records" (diaries, for example), which federal employees may take with them when they leave government employment. The tape was of a government in crisis. Discussions concerning everything from military readiness, to the possession of nuclear warhead codes, to the line of presidential succession were hardly personal to Allen. Insider access to the vaults sealed to others can distort history (with self-serving, selective releases) as well as circumvent the laws and policies of the secrecy system.

In addition, mistakes occur. Secret-keeping agencies are not a monolithic entity whose policies, priorities, and personnel are in lockstep, all reading from the same manual on how to keep secrets. Keeping secrets is just one function of these agencies. Even within the guidelines of the federal classification system and the relevant laws, each agency must decide for itself how important this function is. They all want to protect their secrets; they all want more personnel on line, in the trenches; they all want comfortable offices and pleasant dining facilities. How much money will be spent to keep secrets? What will be the caliber of the personnel? What investments of physical plant and technical support systems will be made? How strict, and strictly enforced, will the agency's policies be?

If an agency wants to train secret keepers in the substance and sensitivity of the documents they process, as does the CIA, it requires more investment. Resources are always scarce, or are at least viewed as such by the competing offices and departments within a bureaucracy. If an agency wants to economize, it can use lower-level personnel armed with agency manuals and black marker pens. However, this personnel may have little or no clue about the substance and significance of the papers in front of them.

In late 1985 to early 1986, at Los Angeles Police headquarters, senior officers who are knowledgeable about their department's 1968 investigation of the assassination of Senator Robert F. Kennedy sit in a room with younger colleagues and police commission staff. They pore over the 50,000-page investigative file, wielding black markers. They delete "sensitive" information that would allegedly compromise rights to privacy or police methods and sources. They could be doing other jobs; some could be out on the street solving or preventing crimes. But these documents, and the case they represent, constitute a high priority for LAPD. The department views its performance in this case as a litmus test of its credibility, and has so stated.

Across town at the headquarters of the Los Angeles District Attorney's Office, files on the same case are being processed. Some of the investigators and lawyers who actually worked on the case in one era or another are present. In the basement sits a solitary intern. He is in his third year at the UCLA law school, knows virtually nothing about the RFK case or its issues and controversies, is not familiar with the DA's filing system, and works without supervision. His instructions are simple: do not release "other agency" documents (LAPD, FBI) and do not release autopsy photos or the photos or phone numbers of witnesses. In the summer of 1985, my colleagues Greg Stone and David Cross were actually allowed into the basement *while* the file was being processed. They even brought their own equipment for duplicating audiotapes and film as soon as they were cleared for release—hands-on, instant access.

In 1985, after months of negotiation with Assistant District Attorney Sheldon Brown, and some political pressure (previously described), the RFK files were scheduled for release. This was a major breakthrough for both the RFK case and the public's right to know. While the intern labored over boxes and file cabinets in the basement of LADA headquarters, an event occurred in the Van Nuys branch office that would dramatically change the record of the RFK assassination. In July 1985, an assistant district attorney who was searching for a file on another case came across a large cardboard box labeled "Sirhan Case." He was aware that the files were being processed for release downtown, so he had the box sent over to headquarters in an official car. The box went directly to the basement.

Among the personnel on the floors above was William R. Burnett, who had been the DA's chief investigator on the RFK case for fifteen years. As I would later hear in Burnett's own words (on a released audiotape): "I've been on this case since 1970. I'm still on it. It's a career case; it'll never go away. Every time something pops up on it, it always falls back in my lap."

In 1970–71, when a small group of Los Angeles citizens (including actor Mike Farrell) formed the Kennedy Assassination Truth Committee, Burnett had visited several of their homes. He was fishing for information on what the group was doing, under the pretext of investigating mishandling of case records by the LADA's evidence custodian (about which group members had no relevant knowledge).

On May 29, 1985, after I had just returned from Los Angeles where I was attempting to get the files released, Burnett phoned me at home.

His pretext this time was that he needed to determine if then South-eastern Massachusetts University (now University of Massachusetts-Dartmouth) was a public or private institution. This, Burnett asserted "would affect disclosure of the files."

Answering that question took thirty seconds. The rest of the half-hour consisted of a soft but thorough debriefing by Burnett: "Will you reopen the case?" (as if my professional powers were omnipotent). "Are the Kennedys at all involved in this?" "Is someone writing a book that you know of?"

Just days earlier, I had given Assistant District Attorney Sheldon Brown a priority list of what should be processed and disclosed first. I compiled the list from the footnotes of a 1977 reinvestigative report (the Kranz Report) issued by the DA's office. Brown gave the list to Burnett. None of the items I requested were produced by Burnett and brought down to the basement for rush processing. It is unclear whether Burnett could not find the items because they were in another office or had copies of them and ignored my list. Nonetheless, most of the items did find their way there, when the magic box arrived from the Van Nuys closet. In this box were items that an unknown party or parties in the DA's office had segregated from the main case file and banished to the boondocks. It was a treasure trove of evidence conflicting with the official conclusions—evidence strongly suggesting conspiracy.

The intern released all of it, as Burnett walked the floors above. In the basement, Burnett's voice could be heard on a 1977 tape of a telephone conversation with ex-FBI Agent William Bailey. Bailey confirmed that he and another agent had definitely seen second-gun bullet holes at the Ambassador Hotel crime scene. Convicted assassin Sirhan Sirhan's gun held only eight bullets and he could not reload. All eight were accounted for in other locations at the crime scene. Bailey saw the ninth and tenth bullets in a wooden doorframe located behind Kennedy.

On a screen in the basement flickered two poorly filmed, official reen-actments of the crime, made in 1969 and 1977. Freed from their long sup-pression, both challenged the official explanation of the shooting. The witness reenactments showed that it was impossible for Sirhan to have gotten in position to inflict point-blank wounds from behind Kennedy.

Burnett had been instrumental in arranging the 1977 film. He had mistakenly believed that a key witness in the reenactment would place Sirhan's gun point blank, in order to be consistent with the autopsy and powder burn tests which showed that the fatal bullet was fired from a gun held at "contact" to one inch away from the senator's head. Instead, she placed the gun three to five feet away, graphically emphasizing the difficulty of Sirhan's bullets having inflicted Kennedy's wounds (the problem is compounded by the absence of a ballistic match between the Kennedy bullets and Sirhan's weapon).

Now it was all out of the closet: tapes and transcripts of witnesses who alleged that there was a female accomplice with Sirhan, a second gun wielded by someone other than Sirhan, too many bullets for one gun. One batch of tapes captures Burnett collaborating with a former prison associate of Sirhan's. In exchange for dropping pending charges, the former inmate is attempting to entrap Sirhan's family into a plot of his own invention. The convict's improbable yarn was that Sirhan was plotting (from prison) a plutonium heist to provide Libya's Gaddafi with the atom bomb.

Had Burnett or others visited the basement during the two days the box was inventoried, the public record of the Robert F. Kennedy assassination may well have been sparser. Whoever labeled the box should have scrawled: "Sirhan case: conspiracy."

The DA's office's accidental gifts of public records had actually begun a year earlier. It is a cardinal principle that no federal, state, or local agency will release "other agency" documents without that agency's permission. The full-court political press for release of the files had not yet peaked. But there was progress. As a token response, the DA's office had shipped approximately one hundred pages of witness interviews to the California State Archives at Laguna Niguel. The public could access them, but the pages had been heavily redacted. Researchers Greg Stone, Floyd Nelson, and I were the first to obtain the batch (since I had inside foreknowledge of its arrival).

The FBI's 32,000-page RFK assassination file was still locked up in Washington, D.C., except for a minor release of 3,000 pages in 1976. In 1986–87 the Bureau's file was released directly to the University of

Massachusetts-Dartmouth's Robert F. Kennedy Assassination Archive, under FOIA. The file was significantly censored.

As described previously, the palm-tree-encircled seaside state archives building held nearly 100 pages of totally uncensored FBI documents. The LADA's personnel, whoever they were, had committed a serious error: Stapled to each redacted witness-interview summary written by the DA's office was the undeleted text of the Bureau's summary for the same witness. That this could happen illustrates why most agencies fear the disclosure process. Human error can result in painful breaches of security and confidentiality, or in just plain embarrassment. Even so, it is difficult to imagine the spaced-out mentality in which someone energetically wielding a blackout marker fails to notice the attached FBI summary.

Throughout most of the 1980s, I was involved with the Center for Atomic Radiation Studies (CARS) in Boston and served on its board of directors from 1984 to 1988. CARS' mission was to gather and collate information on atomic testing and to assist individual atomic veterans. During U.S. nuclear testing conducted in the 1940s and 1950s, tens of thousands of U.S. military personnel were exposed to radiation, whether marching through ground zero after an explosion in the Nevada desert or watching from a ship in the South Pacific. Over the ensuing decades, many atomic veterans developed cancers, leukemias, tumors, and other disorders that they, and numerous medical experts, attributed to radiation exposure. CARS physicians concluded that the incidents and patterns of these diseases strongly indicated that they were, in fact, caused by exposure to atomic testing. They asserted this to the press and the federal government.

But the Department of Defense and the Atomic Energy Commission claimed that there was no connection: exposed personnel had been properly monitored for radiation levels and protected by safety procedures that prevented overexposure. Thus, government took no financial responsibility for the hundreds of millions of dollars in medical bills—past, present, and future. The litigations for wrongful deaths would stretch for decades if overexposure could be proven.

In many cases, atomic veterans' military records were classified by the government or were conveniently missing. As previously described, millions of records had been destroyed by a 1973 fire in a government records facility in St. Louis. Investigators believed the fire to be of suspicious origin. These veterans could not prove that they were exposed at all, much less overexposed. Politically, the admission that our military had savaged its own troops with excess radiation would be catastrophic. The nuclear establishment's credibility was on the line. As an official in the Reagan administration stated in 1981, an admission of overexposure would "be seriously damaging to every aspect of the Department of Defense's nuclear weapons and nuclear propulsion programs," as well as raising questions about "the use of radioactive substances in medical diagnosis and treatment."[4]

In the summer of 1983, a huge crack developed in the government's stone wall regarding nuclear testing. In 1982 the widow of Army Colonel Stafford Warren had donated his papers to the University of California at Los Angeles. Warren had served as a medical adviser on the Manhattan Project (which developed the first atomic bomb). Later, he was the radiological safety officer for the 1946 nuclear tests at Bikini Atoll in the South Pacific. His papers, which had been classified "Top Secret" and "Secret," were discovered by atomic veteran Anthony Guarisco. The National Association of Atomic Veterans rushed more than 100 pages of key documents to this author, who hastily produced the exposé, "The Human Guinea Pigs at Bikini" (*The Nation,* July 9–16, 1983).

The documents contained graphic and damning evidence of the overexposure of U.S. military personnel. Dubbed "Operation Crossroads," two atom bombs were detonated in a Bikini lagoon on July 1 and July 25, 1946. As part of the test, eighty-four unmanned "target ships" laden with test animals, instruments, and experimental setups were anchored at ground zero. Another 100 "nontarget" ships, anchored farther away, hosted some 42,000 persons—military personnel, scientists, doctors, and civilian contractors.

After the blasts, the Navy's ghost fleet was transformed into a floating labyrinth of radioactive hellholes. Military personnel would labor in them for weeks, retrieving vital data and "cleaning up" contamination. The Warren papers reveal that military commanders knew of the dangers to troops in advance. They also knew that the men were overexposed during the "cleanup" but continued with it anyway. This most damning indictment of the military's nuclear safety program is in its own words: "On some target ships, possibly within 1,000 yards of detonation, boarding-inspection may be dangerous for weeks." The military task force was in such a state of eager anticipation of the data that men were sent aboard the radioactive fleet three days after the blasts.

Conditions for the cleanup crews were horrendous. Ventilation systems aboard the vessels were "heavily contaminated." "Thick layers of dry dust," that were "heavily contaminated with fusion products" lurked below decks. Even stripping the ships of their paint was not effective. Some measures of contamination actually *increased* during the messy and invasive cleanup attempts. Colonel Warren warned his Joint Task Force Commander: "Contamination of personnel, clothing, hands and even food can be demonstrated readily in every ship in the JTF-I [Joint Task Force-1] in increasing amounts day by day." He suggested postponing the work until adequate safeguards could be implemented and "proper radiological equipment be brought in." The cleanup efforts continued, uninterrupted.

Individual exposure-monitoring badges were acknowledged to have been both maxed-out and inadequate. The men worked long hours day after day to the point of exhaustion. Some even slept at the sites overnight, wallowing in the contamination. Specially trained "monitoring personnel" (on-line safety officers) were scarce, due to a nationwide shortage in their ranks. Many workers had no expert safety supervision and little idea of where the most acute dangers lay. They sometimes toiled without protective gloves; they did not know how to properly dispose of their contaminated clothing. Warren summed up the tragic bottom line of safety at Bikini: "Without special equipment and the properly trained personnel to measure each site for alpha emitters (and very few qualified personnel are available in the U.S.) no one can say any place is safe for any given length of time."

The overexposed, underprotected servicemen took their radiation overdoses home, where many would experience excruciating, often terminal, medical conditions. They had been ordered to risk their lives in a cleanup operation that failed, except for the retrieval of singed goat carcasses and instruments. Six months after the tests, Warren received a "Top Secret" Navy analysis of the cleanup. It recommended that thirty-two ships be sunk, "in order to remove any possible damages which might result to personnel working on them, or from their use as scrap metal."

That the military did not provide adequate nuclear safety for the men under its command is disconcerting enough. That it knew about the problem, continued to expose them, and covered up is far more difficult to accept.

Sometimes, leaks of "missing" or classified documents are designed to influence how history is written, or someone's place in it. Former law enforcement and intelligence officers often become frustrated with portrayals of the investigations or events in which they participated. They look for carefully selected opportunities to "set the record straight" by providing a file or a journal. The CIA is so conscious of this phenomenon that it established a program to deal with it. Retirees of a certain rank are given private cubicles at headquarters in Langley, Virginia, and a stipend. They commute to the office and write their memoirs of Agency activities (and skullduggery). The only catch is that their writing remains under perpetual lock and key and can never be shown to anyone who does not possess the appropriate, elite security clearance.

When writing my book on the assassination of Dr. Martin Luther King, Jr., there was a shadowy figure (known only to a small group of researchers) in whom I had a keen interest. This Memphis police lieutenant was the former second-in-command of the Memphis Police Intelligence Unit at the time of the assassination. His footprints were all over some of the case's most intriguing avenues. The lieutenant was instrumental in the removal of a black police officer who was stationed across from the Lorraine Motel (where King was shot) the day of the shooting. He was the control for a police spy whose code name was "Max." "Max" was actually Officer Marrell McCullough, who infiltrated a radical black-activist group, the Invaders, and made contact with King's entourage. McCullough was the first person to Dr. King's side after the shot rang out, bending down and apparently checking for life signs.[5] He later went to work for the CIA.

In addition to reporting McCullough's intelligence data to the FBI, the lieutenant reported extensively to the Bureau concerning King's activities in Memphis. He served as liaison between his department and the local FBI office, and boasted that he could "walk in" to J. Edgar Hoover's office in Washington.[6] The lieutenant had such close ties with the Bureau that his boss, Jewell Ray, locked documents in his desk for fear the lieutenant would routinely turn them over to William Lawrence at the local Bureau office (Ray felt the FBI was refusing to reciprocate regarding shared information).

In November of 1985, I phoned the now-retired lieutenant and asked for an interview. He responded, "I don't talk over the phone 'cause I don't know who I'm talking to." He asked that I send him some bona fides. My 1984 book on the U.S. Secret Service (*The Politics of Protection: The U.S. Secret Service in the Terrorist Age,* Praeger, 1984) is the perfect calling card for retired spooks and detectives: scholarly, fair, sympathetic; in essence, an objective, outside account that portrayed the Service in a mostly positive light. It almost always worked, and this subject was no exception, or so I thought.

In January 1986, I traveled to Memphis to conduct numerous interviews. I phoned the lieutenant and he suggested we meet at TGI Friday's restaurant in Overton Square. After two lemonades and a beer, I returned to my hotel, surmising that the lieutenant had decided to surreptitiously check me out first. Now, hopefully, we could get down to business.

I phoned again. Without apology, he said he had forgotten. He proposed that we meet early that afternoon at a local park. Again, he failed to show. Now I was annoyed: were *two* screenings really necessary, or was he going to stall indefinitely?

At five o'clock, the lieutenant (an imposing figure) came to my hotel room unannounced. The interview went well, but it was clearly I who was being interviewed. His first revelation was that he worked as a bouncer in a local nightclub, not for the money but to "keep fit."

Finally, after I asked a few questions about the King case, he began to talk about intelligence gathering. He went on to describe a 140-page report entitled "Civil Disorders, Memphis, Tennessee, February 12–April 16, 1968," which I would ultimately track down in uncensored form. It was a detailed summary of all the intelligence data gathered by the Memphis police before, during, and after the assassination. The last forty pages consisted of more than 400 endnotes to other documents and reports from which the summary had been compiled. They were quite tantalizing: "399: Richmond and Reditt report 4/4/68 [the day of the assassination] RE: Surveillance of Martin Luther King."

The backup files cited in the notes had allegedly been destroyed in 1976. The Memphis American Civil Liberties Union (ACLU) had launched successful legal action to obtain police intelligence files on King and others. ACLU lawyers, armed with a court order, arrived at police headquarters fifteen minutes too late: the documents had just perished in an "accidental" fire. The lieutenant blithely told me that these files resided in his basement. When I could not contain my excitement about accessing them, he responded with a wry smile: "But maybe I'm wrong about that. Maybe I'm mistaken."

The retired policeman's basement aside, the 140-page report would turn out to be a tremendous find. It had allegedly been seen only by an elite group of Memphis police and officials. The report had been subpoenaed by the House of Representatives Select Committee on Assassinations (1976–78), which reinvestigated King's killing. But the congressional copy was sealed with the rest of the committee's documents on its King investigation—until the year 2039.

The report described extensive surveillance of virtually everything and everyone around King at the time of the assassination (including the crime scene). Contrary to all official conclusions, police spies reported that "federal agents" were seen outside the Lorraine Motel shortly before the shooting. The report provided hundreds of individual names as well as the titles of reports and documents concerning who in the intelligence community knew what—a veritable blueprint for reinvestigation of possible intelligence agency involvement in the crime. The latter was a main focus of the House Select Committee on Assassinations.

I wondered why the congressional committee had not maximized the use of this document. The House Committee's final report and thirteen companion volumes contained brief excerpts from the Memphis Police Department (MPD) document, but it was not treated as the mother lode of intelligence data that it was. A comparison of my copy of the full MPD report to the congressional excerpts made it abundantly clear what had happened: Congress had been given a censored, falsified version.

The congressional excerpts had no footnotes. Forty pages of rich resources appeared to be missing. As the lieutenant said, "The footnotes tell all." Since the entire report was organized chronologically, by day and by time of day, it was easy to detect missing items. There were some missing items for each day that the committee had excerpted in its final report (April 1–5). For April 3, six items on surveillance of black activists are missing from the congressional chronology, as are twelve items on April 4. Most of the latter related to police activities at the crime scene immediately after the shooting. The MPD report concerning the presence of "federal agents" was absent, as were any references to Max (police undercover spy Marrell McCullough).

The congressional copy had been doctored to focus more on racial violence and civil disorders rather than on the assassination itself. And the violence was escalated by the editor(s). A surveillance report on a peaceful meeting at a church now reported "talk of firebombs and burning"; this was not contained in the original document. A new report of "16 incidents of vandalism" appears on April 4 in Congress's version. Incidents of disorder were inflated, sometimes doubled.

In 1989 when making their documentary "Who Killed Martin Luther King?" (which aired September 27, 1989 on BBC television), British producers John Edginton and John Sargeant agreed that the issue of forgery should be raised. Former chairman of the House Select Committee on Assassinations, Louis Stokes (Dem., Ohio) was asked by Edginton: "Would it surprise you if a document supplied to your committee by the Memphis Police Department had been in any way sanitized or doctored?"

"It would surprise me," Stokes replied, "because I'm not aware of any document given our committee by the Memphis Police that was sanitized or doctored."

Congressman Stokes looked a bit surprised. Still, his only reaction was mild discomfort with the TV camera, not concern as to whether his committee had been deceived by the Memphis Police.

Although the former Memphis police intelligence officer who met with me was purposefully leaking information, the FBI had done so accidentally in 1984. One of the unresolved issues in the King case involved the so-called "fat man." Alleged assassin James Earl Ray fled to Toronto after the shooting. There the world's most wanted fugitive had a visitor, described by Ray's landlady as a fat man. He handed Ray an envelope. Toronto police later found the man and cleared the incident as the innocent returning of a lost letter written under Ray's alias, George Raymond Sneyd. The visitor was simply a Good Samaritan.

Many reporters were highly skeptical of this explanation, suspecting that the man might have been a courier. Ray's escape ticket to London had languished at a local travel agency for a week. Why would the target of what was described as "the greatest manhunt in law enforcement history" not flee when informed that his ticket and passport were ready? Perhaps because he did not have the money. Within hours of receiving the letter-sized envelope with only a name typed on the front (according to the landlady), Ray collected his traveling papers. Moreover, Ray was a squirrelly fugitive who insisted that meals be left outside the door and would not emerge to take phone calls. Yet, when informed by the landlady that he had "a visitor," he went downstairs to meet the fat man without hesitation. The Canadian media energetically pursued the story without success. Authorities refused to identify the alleged Samaritan and the media could not find him. No U.S. law enforcement officers talked to him.

At the FBI reading room in 1984, I had reviewed the sixteen pages of documents relating to the incident—documents contained in the Bureau's voluminous MURKIN file (short for murder of King). The fat man's identity was deleted from every page (two or three times per page), with a single exception: the name leaped out, undeleted. Imagine the Bureau redactor blacking out the name page after page. He or she looks up at the clock, or yawns or sips coffee. The place on the page is lost; the name is missed.

While researching the case in Toronto, I pursued the long shot that the man might still be in the area. Public record searches failed to turn up *anyone* with this surname, much less the fat man. Since FBI documents are often replete with misspellings, I excluded the letter "u" from the three-syllable name. This produced not only three candidates but the right man.

In a rundown suburb of Toronto containing large dogs and small houses, I delivered my carefully prepared opening line to the tall, heavy-set man who had just entered his driveway. "I am a professor of political science and I'm interviewing persons like yourself who had interesting encounters sixteen years ago."

His face confirmed his identity even before he spoke. And he was panicked. "How did you find me?" he demanded. "What's going on with the case? I told them all I know."

The fat man's brief narrative would prove this last statement wrong. Visibly upset, he pleaded for continued anonymity. He then made a series of vague but dark references: His life was now in danger. There were "gangsters" behind Ray. "They'll kill anyone." There was "big money" involved in the assassination. He claimed that the letter he found proved that Ray had help fleeing from Canada to Portugal. When I attempted to press him for details and broached the apparent conflict between the innocence of the Good Samaritan story and running afoul of men who would kill him, he terminated the conversation: "That's all I'll say." His distress seemed genuine. Unless there exists an international cartel of bad Samaritans that kills the finders of lost letters, there would seem to be much more to the fat man's story than emerged in 1968. But neither the FBI, nor the House Assassinations Committee, nor the Justice Department knows what it is. To this day he has never been interviewed by U.S. authorities. Shortly after a redactor's error put me in his front yard, the fat man departed the Toronto area for Western Canada.

In 1983, using the Freedom of Information Act, I obtained 362 pages of previously classified documents from the CIA. If this was not a leak or a huge mistake, then it was certainly a New Year's gift. The CIA is perhaps the stingiest, most tenacious secret-keeping organization in the U.S. government. It uses every available tactic, both legitimate and nonlegitimate, to disclose as little as possible about its sources, methods, operations, agents, and friends (nonagency "assets").

Every provision of FOIA is used to maximum advantage, sometimes by ignoring it. The Agency will break the law with long delays, implicitly challenging the requester to go to the expense and delay of taking it to federal court. The costs of searching for documents, born by the requester, are often inflated in an attempt to render them prohibitive. I have received documents that were entirely deleted: page after page was completely blank except for the document number and a letter (A through E) indicating the reason for withholding (national security, privacy, and so on). The CIA has stonewalled congressional committees and presidential commissions, claiming loss, destruction, or inability to "find" files. Recall that it has hidden its documents relating to its illegal, domestic surveillance of Martin Luther King, Jr., in its "Western Hemisphere file," which contains records on its eight assassination attempts against Cuban President Fidel Castro. There, no one—whether a college professor or a congressional committee—could retrieve the documents in a request concerning King. All of this was told to the author by a retired CIA agent whose bona fides had been established by *60 Minutes* and who participated in the surveillance of Dr. King.

These allegations explained my astonishment at being handed the documentation for a major national exposé ("The CIA's Secret Ties to Local Police," *The Nation,* March 26, 1983). The pages were largely undeleted and even contained the names of police higher-ups in various cities. The story would be carried by fifty-one print, television, and radio outlets, including the *New York Times,* the *Washington Post,* and National Public Radio. Congressmen were contacted for comment. The Agency suffered an embarrassing vetting of one of its most secret and sensitive domestic programs. All because the secret keepers failed to perform as usual.

Before describing the revelations, it is necessary to set the context of illegality and cover-up. As mentioned earlier, the CIA's 1947 charter bars it from domestic security involvements and forbids the exercise of any "police, subpoena or law enforcement powers, or internal security functions."

In 1972 the *New York Times* and several members of Congress got wind of CIA links to city police departments. Assistant CIA Director Angus Theurmer told the *Times* that only a few New York Police Department (NYPD) personnel had been given "briefings" on hijacking, terrorism, drug trafficking, and "similar courtesies."[7] In a 1972 memorandum, Theurmer boasted to his Agency colleagues: "I low-keyed the whole thing, saying there was no 'program.' . . . I said the matter was of such an occasional nature that no one kept records. I, therefore, couldn't tell them what other cities were involved" (something that the released file would belie).

The Agency offered "guidance" to NYPD to admit very little. An internal CIA memo to Director William Colby urges, "if pressed, to respond with minimal information." Congressional inquiries got the same low-key, minimal responses. Although the Agency did tell then-Congressman Ed Koch (Dem., N.Y.) that about fifty officers from a dozen cities had been "briefed" from 1970 to 1972.

In contrast, the released documents depict a broad range of clandestine activities in which both police and CIA evade oversight and, sometimes, the Constitution. Police from big city departments were more than briefed: they were trained in concealing "bugs" and hidden cameras, tapping telephones, creating disguises, deactivating alarm systems, and breaking and entering. "Hands-on" field exercises were conducted in the Washington, D.C., area, which was turned into a covert laboratory for practicing the above skills (it would be interesting to know how the targets were selected). As in any self-respecting academy, there was a final exam: each trainee had to successfully execute a "break and enter."

The Agency was very generous to its law enforcement friends. It lavished them with golf, fishing, and hunting opportunities (weapons provided by the host). Trainees could cook their own top-cut steaks. "Get acquainted" parties were long, and the liquor flowed. Air transportation, limousines, and suites at the Washington Hilton were included; gifts were dispensed. CIA field offices at home and abroad treated vacationing police higher-ups to rental cars and free lodging at CIA "safe houses." (One document admits, however, that police chiefs in several unnamed cities could not receive such largess. They were not apprised of the working relationship between their departmental intelligence unit and the CIA.)

These perquisites paled in comparison to the sophisticated equipment police were given. Items not only came free, but were unaccounted for by local departments or by the civilian commissions that oversaw them. The James Bond world of the CIA's technical services lab and photo lab was opened to these officers. Agency safe houses were made available for police business (and possibly pleasure). Dispensed items included: forged ID's, decoders, transmitters, "beacons," explosive detection kits, polygraph equipment, "document destruction devices," lamps with concealed eavesdropping devices, miniature spy cameras, radio-equipped vehicles, mine detectors, tear gas, gas masks, flak jackets, grenades, and exotic ammunition.

Although the quantities of these gifts are not specified (nor is their use), the documents name forty-four city and county police organizations as receiving some form of assistance. Trained by the best, armed with state-of-the-art devices and technology, police intelligence units were poised to operate like their big brother, the CIA. What covert operations and activities did they conduct? The Agency candidly admits that items were provided on a "no questions asked" basis for "operational missions" by police. The question arises as to whether police superiors who were ignorant of the Agency's role in their department were also ignorant of some of the "operational missions."

The Agency's friends in law enforcement generously reciprocated. A 1975 document entitled "Relationship with Police" touts that the CIA will request police help in "resolving certain personal problems of [CIA] employees"—employees who are either victims or arrestees. The latter raises the chilling possibility that police contacts may elevate certain CIA personnel above the law. Another document refers to a break-in conducted jointly by police and CIA agents to retrieve files in which the Agency had an interest. Neither party had obtained a search warrant.

One memorandum describes a clearly illegal breach of the Agency's charter. In May 1971, "eighteen to twenty police identification credentials were obtained from the Metropolitan Police Dept. in Washington, D.C. . . . " During an unspecified number of antiwar demonstrations in the nation's capital between 1968 and 1971, the CIA loaned cars and drivers to police and set up "command posts" for police at CIA headquarters. CIA Director of the Office of Security, Howard Osborn, summed it up best:

> Some aspects of Agency support to police operations have served to greatly enhance our working relationship and to secure, in return, police commitment to activities and operations, which might otherwise have the department's negative response.

Subsequent to the exposure of the CIA-police file, the Agency tightened up its vault. At least two researchers made FOIA requests for the same, and related, documents that I had received. They were told that no relevant documents could be found. The 362 pages released to me had disappeared at Langley, but not from my safe.

In 1984, as previously described, President Reagan issued an executive order. Among several changes restricting the flow of information to the public was one that allowed federal agencies to *recall* previously released documents, if the agency believed that they should not have been released. I waited nervously for a recall letter, wrestling with the question of whether I would return *all* of the copies I had made (for safekeeping of this unique and controversial find). I heard nothing. Perhaps the damage had been done and the Agency was not inclined to have the national media revisit the issue over a recall of the documents.

Most of these previously described instances involved only one researcher. It is almost certain that an untold number of other people who have pursued documents—lawyers, authors, journalists, activists, and curious citizens—have had similar experiences. No wonder the secret keepers so dread anything capable of expanding the leakage: the Freedom of Information Act, the Privacy Act, and legally mandated declassification schedules. If these would be repealed and not replaced, agencies would have nothing to fear beyond the disloyalty of their own employees. Keeping the vault sealed would be infinitely easier.

CHAPTER 8

Reasonable Reforms

"Secrecy is essential in the affairs of state."

—Cardinal de Richelieu

The solution to the problem of secrecy in government does not lie in the simple expedient of abolishing executive authority to withhold information. This will not be done and should not be done; for the withholding of information has its legitimate uses even in the service of constitutional rights. . . . It is the abuse of authority that must be controlled. Failing this, scientific advance will suffer, the public will be forced to exist on the sugar-water of the public relations man, and important aspects of public policy will go unresolved by Congress, the press, and the electorate.[1]

—Richard P. Longaker, "On the Nature of Governmental Secrecy," 1961

In the four decades since Longaker's challenge, we have created nearly 200 statutes that affect secrecy, including FOIA and the Privacy Act. We have seen the secrecy system grow to a previously unimagined scope and size. We have continued to struggle at balancing that system with our democratic ideals. For all the previous reforms, the freedom-of-information process needs to be strengthened in ways that will not cripple legitimate governmental secret keeping.

Before considering some specific proposals for moderate change (proposals that would increase access and preserve secrecy), some perspective is in order—both from within our political system and outside it (for example, Great Britain). Reforming the secrecy/disclosure system and dealing with its problems is not a high-visibility issue. Nor is it a widespread public concern on a par with the economy, crime, drugs, world peace, terrorism, and health care. Even though the level of public information impacts all of these, the connection is rarely made even by journalists and academics who work directly with the power of information. But this does not mean that we can afford a runaway secrecy system and a diminished right to know for the public. This condition can only have a negative impact on our democracy and our lives within it. The extreme posturing of secret keepers who preach doom at any increase in public access and of agency critics who see nothing but criminality and cover-up behind the secrecy cloak will not suffice as an informed discussion of what needs to be done.

The experience of our sister democracy is instructive. Great Britain is now going through a political backlash against the severe restriction of its public's right to know—the Official Secrets Act of 1989. This strict law makes it a seriously punishable crime to leak, receive, or in any way transmit or expose information that the government has classified. This is absolute. There is no weighing the balance between public benefit from disclosure and what harm the information might cause.

Recall the Pentagon Papers case. The U.S. Supreme Court ruled that, even though the documents on Vietnam were classified and had been spirited away by a security-cleared employee, Daniel Ellsberg, the *New York Times* and the *Washington Post* could publish them. The information was judged to be more politically embarrassing to government than harmful to national security. Under the British Official Secrets Act, there would be no such decision. Because the material was classified, it could not be published. Ellsberg and anyone at the *Times* or *Post* who handled the secrets would have, ipso facto, committed an illegal act. Recently (July 2000), Scotland Yard warned that Internet service providers who *unwittingly* publish classified information would be prosecuted.[2]

Britain's informational straightjacket has long been criticized as too inflexible and antidemocratic. The act is enforced unevenly but has had a negative effect on agency accountability, citizen knowledge, policy debate, and media coverage.[3] The act is written to preclude consideration of public interest and of most mitigating circumstances (including the absence of harmful intent by the persons involved). This tight noose of secrecy, combined with the penalties, shuts out these considerations. Unlike the United States' FOIA, the burden of proof is not on the British government, which has been largely relieved of it. Moreover, FOIA is not a criminal statute, whereas people convicted of violating the British law are "punishable by imprisonment for a term not to exceed fourteen years."

Consider the tight, if not draconian, language of the Official Secrets Act.[4] The following could be categorized "guilty until proven innocent":

> If any sketch, plan, model, article, note, document or information relating to or used in any prohibited place [virtually any site related to national defense], or anything in such a place, or any secret official code word or password is made, obtained, collected, recorded, published or communicated by any person other than a person acting under lawful authority, it shall be deemed to have been made, obtained, collected, recorded, published or communicated for a purpose prejudicial to the safety or interests of the State unless the contrary is proved.

Also guilty are individuals in the media who receive leaks:

> Every person who receives any secret official code word, password, sketch, plan, model, article, note, document or information, knowing, or having reasonable ground to believe, at the time he receives it, that the code word, password, sketch plan, model, article, note, document or information is communicated to him in contravention of this Act, is guilty of an offence under this Act, unless he proves that the communication to him of the code word, password, sketch, plan, model, article, note, document or information was contrary to his desire.

The following broadens the "big chill" effect:

> Every person who attempts to commit any offence under this Act, or solicits, incites or endeavors to persuade another person to commit an offence under this Act, or aids or abets and does any act preparatory to the commission of an offence under this Act, is guilty of an offence under this Act and liable to the same punishment, and to be proceeded against in the same manner as if he had committed the offence.

Great Britain has no counterpart to our FOIA. But the passage of such a law is a serious proposal backed by Prime Minister Tony Blair.

As one would expect, the political battle has been long and intense; the stakes are perceived as high. Blair stated in 1996, "FOI is not some isolated constitutional reform but a change that is absolutely fundamental to how we see politics developing in this country. . . . It is genuinely about changing the relationship of politics today."[5] Yet, as of this writing, FOIA-type legislation is still not law despite years of trying.

Proponents put out a 1997 "white paper proposal" for a British-style FOIA entitled: "Your Right to Know." This paper is the focus of the debate. The proposal is described by David Clark, its principal author, as one of the most radical, pro-disclosure proposals in the world:

> [I]f fully implemented it would transform this country from one of the most closed democracies to one of the most open. . . . Unnecessary secrecy in government leads to arrogance in government and defective decision making.[6]

The white paper does seem somewhat more user-friendly and pro-disclosure than the United States' FOIA. There is a greater burden imposed on agencies to justify withholding, and public access to information seems broader. The "seems" and "somewhat" reflect the fact that this is not yet law. If and when it is, there will be political/legal/administrative infighting to determine how much access the law will actually provide. For example, British Home Secretary Jack Straw has objected to the white paper's position that agencies can withhold only if disclosure would cause "*substantial* harm" rather than "harm" (a familiar debate).[7] The final wording will result from the usual amendments and revisions. After passage, a second round of politics will begin.

Proponents of the law are very aware that agency compliance is crucial. They have quoted the Australian FOI reform commission:

> The culture of an agency and the understanding and acceptance of the philosophy of FOI by individual officers can play a significant part in whether the Act achieves its objectives. [Senior managers] can seriously hinder the success of the Act.[8]

In October of 2000, there was a dramatic development that is predicted to significantly weaken the Official Secrets Act. For the first time in its history, Great Britain formally adopted a bill of rights similar to the one found in the U.S. Constitution. Since free speech is now guaranteed, legal analysts predict that this will result in challenges to the constitutionality of the act's severe restrictions.[9]

Within the United States, there have been periodic suggestions by members of Congress or the executive branch that something akin to the Official Secrets Act should be adopted here. This has usually been in response to a disclosure that has, in fact, threatened federal agents or sensitive negotiations, or has embarrassed government. The British "solution" of stifling the public's right to know by locking the vaults and throwing away the keys is surely not the answer, however conflict-ridden and error-prone our disclosure process might be. Even the British increasingly seem to perceive this. In addition to the white paper mentioned previously, there has been a campaign to scrap the Official Secrets Act and replace it with a narrower law that would apply only to secrets that would cause "serious damage," as opposed to every secret.[10]

In the United States, "mini–Official Secrets Acts" for specific areas have been proposed periodically. In June 2000, Republican Senator Richard Shelby of Alabama, chair of the Senate Intelligence Committee, was the main sponsor of a bill that would stop the media from obtaining secrets: disclosing classified information of *any* kind to the media would be a felony punishable by up to three years in prison, for both leaker and recipient.[11] Attorney General Janet Reno criticized the bill as too broad. The Clinton administration wanted the punishment to apply only in the case of "highly classified" information that discloses intelligence sources and methods, or that places lives in jeopardy. Reno urged that the law concentrate on the leakers, not the media.[12] The CIA had asked for such a bill, claiming that leaks had cost the lives of agents and the loss of sophisticated spying technology. Defense Secretary William Cohen told the Center for Strategical and International Studies that his biggest disappointment during his four-year tenure was the constant leaks of top-secret information to Washington newspapers.[13]

Despite these frustrations, President Clinton vetoed the bill on November 4, 2000, stating that the "badly flawed provision" might "chill legitimate activities that are at the heart of democracy."[14] The administration was particularly concerned that whistle blowers would be silenced. Attorney General Janet Reno stated that the difficulty was not in the scope of punishment but in finding the leakers. The *Boston Globe* noted that "the only leak prosecution in recent memory occurred in 1985, when a Navy researcher was prosecuted for leaking a satellite photo of a Soviet Navy ship under construction to the publication *Jane's Fighting Ships.*"[15] Four news organizations had lobbied the White House to veto the bill because of a perceived threat to freedom of the press—CNN, the *Washington Post,* the *New York Times,* and the Newspaper Association of America. In retort, Representative Peter Goss, chair of the House Intelligence Committee, asserted that the law was "narrowly crafted to protect the rights that all Americans hold dear."[16]

Such proposed laws raise complex questions. Consider the case of Professor Theodore Postal of the Massachusetts Institute of Technology. He challenged Pentagon reports on the accuracy of the patriot missile used during the Gulf War, disputing its highly touted accuracy. Later (June 2000) he challenged the scientific feasibility of the Clinton administration's proposed missile defense system (a variant of the "Star Wars" proposal put forth by the Reagan administration).[17]

On both occasions, Professor Postal was visited by officers of the Pentagon's Defense Secrecy Service who accused him of using and vetting classified information. He claimed that he had not. Postal also alleged that the officers tried to show him documents marked secret, to prove that he *was* divulging classified data, but that he refused to look. Under the statute proposed by Senator Shelby, would both Postal and any media he talked to be charged with a crime, based on the government's claim that secrets were involved? What about Pentagon whistle blowers who inform the media of cost overruns or fraud on secret weapons projects?

No one can propose expanding a governmental function without an eventual discussion (and debate) over cost. Usually this is defined in dollar amounts. Most of the following proposals will cost additional tax dollars, no doubt. But this does not make them "too" expensive or cost-ineffective, and it should not preclude their consideration.

There are costs—some hidden, some bottom line—for everything the government does or does not do. Not putting enough funds into the Environmental Protection Agency's toxic cleanup program can produce harm ("cost")—both environmental and human. Not adequately funding our secrecy/disclosure system, and thereby rendering it ineffective, has enormous cost: the quality of scientific research, the ideals of democracy, the accuracy of history (as discussed at the beginning of this work).

The cost of leaking a secret and getting an undercover law officer killed is immediately discernable. The cost of losing, destroying, or sealing off the record of what government did or did not do, and how it decided and acted, is huge, but it is less immediate and less vivid. This cost is measured in political, cultural, and intellectual capital as well as financial. The dollar costs of excessive secrecy include waste, duplication, overspending, fraud, bad decision making, and nonperformance. More indirect costs such as historical ignorance, unconstitutional actions by agencies, erosion of public trust, and slowed progress developing solutions for medical and environmental problems creep up at a slower pace. Secrecy's role in these outcomes often goes unmeasured, if not unnoticed. On the spending side, increased money for offices, computers, and—most unpopular of all—bureaucrats is needed. What the investments proposed here might produce in increasing the effectiveness of the secrecy/disclosure system is more difficult to calculate. But it is real nevertheless.

Money is, of course, relative. As Senator Everett Dirkson once quipped, "A billion here, a billion there, pretty soon it adds up to real money." We have spent hundreds of millions of dollars for ineffective social programs, for mind-control research that was allegedly never applied, and for foreign aid to regimes that history now vilifies. In a very real sense, funds effectively targeted and efficiently used for improving the secrecy system are an investment in national security.

Not all such investments involve weapons, troops, and strategic bases. At times it has been asserted by members of Congress and the executive branch that a strong economy bolsters national security, as does increasing Secret Service resources for protection of our leaders. If secrecy/disclosure can be improved, the nation will be stronger and more secure in every dimension, from public trust in government to better foreign policymaking. Excessive secrecy and cover-ups have most often been cloaked in "national security." In reality, illegitimate secrecy, advertised as protecting the United States from its enemies, has created a profound national insecurity within our democratic system.

The following proposals do not require a massive rearrangement of fiscal resources, nor should they require new revenues. They are incremental increases in keeping with the political style of budgeting in the United States. "Incrementalism" does not abide radical reallocations (whether increases or decreases).[18]

A sufficient level of resources, rationally allocated and cost-benefit–monitored, is necessary for any governmental function. Proponents of the British FOI have criticized the proposed law (white paper) for not recognizing this reality. As one critic put it, "It is an aspirational white paper in which the staffing and resource implications are never mentioned; but without adequate resources FOI risks becoming a hollow shell."[19] As federal policy changes go, the following reforms require modest expenditures, with one exception.

CHANGES IN FEDERAL POLICY
VIA LAW OR EXECUTIVE ORDER

Classification Levels. All records held by all agencies should be classified at the lowest level possible while still honoring the reason for their secrecy. Information comes in grades of sensitivity and importance—from none to some to super. The classification process must more adequately reflect these distinctions. The easy way out is for secret keepers to whack their *top secret* stamp and be done with it. This quick fix may relieve the secret keeper of making an error in the opposite direction, and it may protect the agency from embarrassment or accountability (at least in the short run), but the long-term costs are unacceptable.

Indiscriminate overclassification undermines the public's right to know by creating an artificial cover over the entire process. This cover makes disclosure slower and more difficult. It is also a major contributor to the creation of petrified mountains of paper that remain sealed for decades. These have a cumulatively inhibiting effect on future disclosure by clogging the process. All of this results, in part, when secret keepers fail to exercise sufficient discretionary judgment when originally handling a document. The practice of overclassification is akin to marking every storage box in your attic: "Save: Do Not Discard" for a period of thirty years, then being overwhelmed to the point of immobilization at clean-out time.

Standards for Release. Withholding should be exercised for information that *would significantly* cause harm, not that *could* cause harm. Since information *is* power, presumably most secrets could conceivably cause harm in some imagined scenario. But this lax standard has the same consequences as classifying at the highest level: it encourages agencies to be indiscriminately broad in their refusals to release.

It is the very essence of the culture of secrecy to want to make almost everything a secret and never let it out, a preference motivated by fear of the consequences or by principle. The first two reforms discussed above attempt to curb this tendency of agencies to overcompensate at both ends of the secrecy/disclosure process. The present secrecy-prone standards encourage indiscriminate processing that significantly constricts the flow of public information.

Clarifying the "Public Interest" Standard. There needs to be a detailed, government-wide statement of what constitutes public interest, drawing upon the clear intent of the laws (in presenting recommendations here, any references to "FOIA" or "laws" are intended to include the Privacy Act as well, but for readability it is not specifically named in every context). Presently we have some officials asserting that the public interest should not be considered in deciding disclosure. There are also some agency personnel whose definitions of "public interest" are so narrow as to be patronizing if not irresponsible. It cannot be precisely defined, but a clearer set of guidelines will enable secret keepers to balance public and agency interests more judiciously. The definitions of "national security," "rights of privacy," and "harm" are vague. These are supposed to be balanced against a concept (public interest) that is the vaguest of all in a process dominated by ill-defined concepts. If given more specificity, "public interest" will receive more appropriate consideration in the disclosure process.

Agency Resources and Accountability. Congress must earmark increased funding in each agency budget for administering public disclosure: personnel, computers, and office space. Allocations should be commensurate with the number of requests typically received and the volume of records held. Additional resources will also be required to implement the first two recommendations, which require more demanding decision making for both classification and disclosure. Such resources should be at a level that would reduce the unwieldy backlog of requests at the FBI, CIA, State Department, and Defense Department, and that would also enable agencies to comply with President Clinton's executive order regarding the processing of twenty-five-year-old national security records.

Increased funding has been recommended here in lieu of fines or penalties to be levied on agencies for excessive delays or noncompliance with disclosure orders. It has been suggested that agencies should pay incremental fines to requesters for delays: a base amount for violating the twenty-day response rule, escalating fines for the ensuing months or years. This would not improve the quality of the process, only its speed (if it did indeed work).

Through the annual budget process, Congress can monitor how these increases were spent (as with any other appropriation). In addition, each agency should report to its congressional oversight committee annually concerning requests, backlog problems, number of withholdings, fee waiver decisions, and so on. The General Services Administration (GSA), Congress's fiscal watchdog, should assess the government-wide performance concerning disclosure on a semiannual basis. This review can also compare and contrast agencies to highlight particular problems that need addressing (by reallocating or increasing resources or by changing agency policy).

Legal Penalties for Destruction or Malicious Withholding. Current statutes regarding destruction of records or the sabotaging of disclosure are vague, usually unenforced, and are often codicils to other statutes. A specific law is needed that clearly sets forth prohibitions and penalties.

Any documents of historical or legal value should be preserved. Guidelines are needed as to what kinds of materials the statute is protecting. There can be no precise definitions, and legal guidelines are more easily developed than historical ones. But some focus and substance must be provided or the law will be impossible to implement.

This is not an attempt to turn federal bureaucrats into paralegals or archivists. The secret keepers need something to work with regarding these laudable but vague goals of preservation. Such a statute would encourage agency personnel to be cognizant of history and legality. In the darkest scenario, it might help to curb politically motivated cover-ups that seek to avoid accountability. Again, in fairness to those over-worked, politically pressured employees, why should they risk sanctions in the workplace (formal or informal) by making a historical disclosure "mistake"? A concrete and understood legal context for the decisions concerning what to do with records is important for those making the decisions. It requires more time and skill to make accurate judgments, as opposed to tossing paper into a shredder or burn bag. In this sense, this change is linked to lower-level classification and to providing a positive definition of public interest: it expands the base of informa-tion that might be released, and sharpens the decision-making process within the agencies.

In addition to legally mandated preservation, this statute should address attempts to evade disclosure laws by the purposeful destruc-tion or hiding of documents. Such cover-ups of embarrassments, mis-takes, and illegalities cannot be tolerated. It is hoped that this statute will serve as a deterrent. A stiffer penalty should be levied for these cases than for the lazy or incompetent processor who disposes of a piece of U.S. history without malicious intent. In all realms, our legal code struggles to make such distinctions, such as manslaughter versus murder.

Diverting CIA files on the surveillance—and who knows what else—of Dr. Martin Luther King, Jr., to the Western Hemisphere file (Castro/Cuba/assassination plots) is a case in point. This was nothing more than an effort (and a successful one at that) to evade the consequences of activities that were politically embarrassing, illegal, or both.

Similarly, there was FBI Director J. Edgar Hoover's tactic for avoid-ing accountability for his bureau. To cover activities that were ques-tionable, if not illegal, Hoover did more than seek to hold a potential blackmail file on all who might criticize or sanction him: he engaged in the wholesale diversion and destruction of documents. His "Do Not File" order became a clandestine part of the Bureau's records system for excluding sensitive material. "Do Not File" documents were purged annually.[20]

A New Sunset Law / Disclosure Process. This is the most costly and far-reaching of the proposals. A sunset law would require that all records be automatically declassified after twenty years (this somewhat follows the 1997 recommendation of Senator Daniel Patrick Moynihan's Commission on Protecting and Reducing Governmental Secrecy, although they recommended ten years). Reclassification could be done only if "demonstrable harm" would occur upon release. This provision would require a considerable increase in resources, but it is essential to the improvement of the system.

Records that are "sunsetted out" would automatically go to the National Archives. Senator Moynihan's commission proposed a "declassification center" within the archives. Information could still be withheld under the existing statutory exemptions (although technically the archives processing would not be under FOIA or the Privacy Act). Archivists, like their agency counterparts, could destroy records that have no legal or historical value. Thus, in this proposal, nonagency personnel would do the processing and make the final decisions. Agencies would retain direct control over the disposition of their more recent records (fewer than two decades old).

This proposal provides a beneficial two-track system for release. Agencies have shown an inability (or unwillingness) to process massive backlogs. Also, as in the case of the CIA's interaction with the Assassination Records Review Board, some agencies seem disinclined to part with old secrets and have difficulty treating them differently from newer ones (or distinguishing trivial ones from significant ones).

For this new role, the archives will need considerable additional resources. In 1993 Acting Director Trudy Peterson complained that the processing of State Department records from the 1960s, which had been recently delivered, would take nineteen years. "This is intolerable," she wrote the White House. "Documents from the World War I era still remain classified [at the archives]."[21]

Interim Fees for FOIA Attorneys. Current law must be amended to require courts to pay the "reasonable fees" (that go to lawyers who win FOIA cases) on an "interim" basis rather than at the end of a multiyear legal struggle. Congress provided for compensation precisely because it recognized that this was necessary for requesters to be able to challenge the government in court. Government has often undermined this provision by creating legal delays, which drive up the cost of the legal process and discourage private practice lawyers from taking FOIA cases. Being paid some of the fees at, say, the two-year mark rather than the five-year mark would also help to assuage the loss of revenue that comes from being paid in "historic dollars" (fee schedules at the time litigation was initiated) rather than current dollars (fee schedules as of when the litigation is over). Putting this provision in the act would render it universal, rather than something that happens only occasionally at the discretion of the court.

PRIVACY ACT REFORMS

No Release of Gossip and Innuendo. The act requires that information that invades privacy or causes harm *can* be withheld, even in the case of deceased people (if it would be so harmful to survivors that this outweighs public interest). In this requester's experience, the provision is not sufficiently adhered to by the FBI and CIA. The policy needs to be clarified and reinforced to prevent the dissemination of derogatory information that is typically speculative, hearsay, and proffered by informants of unknown identity and reliability. Whether the agencies are being neglectful or spiteful, this problem exists.

For example, the CIA released documents during the 1990s that relate to leaders of the civil rights and antiwar movements and to people involved in radical politics, many of whom were, and are, still alive. Included in the papers are items regarding their sexual preferences and partners, finances, alleged drug use, mental state, and the character and political persuasion of their associates and family.

In another instance, the FBI released documents on a witness/suspect in the King assassination. His military serial number and activities are consistently expunged from the pages concerning him. The phone numbers and addresses of his ex-wives and his employment history remain. So also do observations of his mental state: he allegedly cried during one interview and said that he needed psychiatric help.

These types of violations have occurred in both agencies over a broad span of years and in different files. It is not an aberration of one processor, file, or agency. These two agencies are tenacious to a fault in protecting the identities of all informants no matter what year or level they operated in. But these unproven, possibly malicious, or self-serving allegations (often hearsay) too frequently get past the redactors.

Informing Individuals of Their Files. At present, people find out if there is a file on them by asking (via FOIA and Privacy). Most often the agency will tell them if there is, although there are some loopholes. Yet tens of millions of citizens never ask the question. And many of them do have files that they do not suspect exist. The Privacy Act is not as widely known to the public as it should be, and its usage is minimal. To some, it seems irrelevant (since they have done nothing wrong); to others, intimidating; to some, almost subversive. Massive numbers of people are not exercising their legal rights to protect their privacy.

Agencies should be required to provide a brief notice when creating or holding a file on someone. Agencies are supposed to tell individuals if they ask, but the disengagement of the vast majority of the population reduces the positive impact intended at the act's passage. Mandatory notification would not cost the agency much in time or money. It would increase the burden on its disclosure process, creating more requesters. However, it would strengthen two of the law's provisions in very positive and significant ways.

1. *The right of rebuttal.* The act provides that if people discover that their file contains errors, false statements, incomplete entries or irrelevancies, they can petition the agency for the appropriate correction(s). Should the agency refuse, individuals have the right to enter a statement in their file expressing their disagreement. This cannot be done if people are unaware of the file. Being informed of its existence will serve to reduce the negative impact of errors and falsehoods, as more people pursue their right of rebuttal.

2. *First Amendment, antisurveillance right.* The law forbids reporting on individuals who are simply exercising their First Amendment rights (such as freedoms of speech and assembly), unless they or their actions fall under a particular statute or are the subject of "authorized law enforcement activity." The worst surveillance excesses of law enforcement and intelligence agencies, which the act was created to prevent, involved indiscriminate reporting on nonviolent civil rights and antiwar groups, as well as writers and other celebrities who did nothing more than avail themselves of the Bill of Rights. These "projects" included the CIA's CHAOS and MERRIMAC, the FBI's COINTELPRO, and Army Intelligence's GARDEN PLOT and LANTERN SPIKE. Thousands of Americans never knew there were files on them.

The requirement that agencies inform individuals of the existence of files would help to curb any impulse to surveil and report on lawful political activities purely on speculation. This provision would also curb an even worse impulse—pursuing "enemies lists" or other politically motivated spy or agent provocateur activities. Knowing about a file and requesting it, individuals could (if familiar with their rights) see for themselves whether there seemed to be a legitimate governmental purpose behind it. If they thought there was none, they could take action.

USING THE MODEL OF
THE ASSASSINATION RECORDS REVIEW BOARD

The Assassination Records Review Board was a highly successful and novel experiment in public disclosure. A citizen panel appointed by the president oversaw the release of 4.5 million pages of documents relating to the assassination of President Kennedy. The panel was given full legal access to all agency records. It was the panel that decided whether to withhold or release, subject only to an agency appeal directly to the president. Never before has a citizen board been so completely responsible for deciding on so many documents from so many agencies.

This model should be employed, with minor modifications, in other subject areas as well—areas in which:

1. There is a historic, long-running subject, encompassing both old and new records over a period of many years or decades. As previously described, agencies have too much difficulty letting go of old information.
2. The topic is politically sensitive or contentious (agencies are caught up in a political clash).
3. There is a large volume of records.
4. The regular disclosure process is not working, in terms of timeframe, reasonable release, or both (that is, too slow, too much secrecy).

Such subject areas include, but are by no means limited to, the following: the radiation exposure of U.S. troops during atomic testing, human rights controversies in which U.S. agencies are alleged to be complicitous (El Salvador, Chile, Guatemala), the policies and conduct of the Vietnam War, nuclear safety (plants, projects, waste disposal—both military and civilian), unidentified flying objects (a topic in which secrecy has fueled substantive suspicion and distrust of government), and experimental testing of unwitting human subjects by U.S. military and intelligence agencies.

Only a few changes are needed to strengthen the prototype, based upon the experience of the Assassination Records Review Board (ARRB) from 1994 to 1998. Such boards should have a fixed, four-year term. The clock should begin ticking only when the board has been appointed and is operational (with staff and resources ready to go). The more-than-a-year's delay in presidential appointment of the ARRB necessitated a congressional extension of the term. This distracted the board and weakened its political position at the outset. Such boards should not have to fight political battles for their continued existence or in order to claim their rightful term.

In the complex, controversial areas in which these entities would operate, four years is by no means excessive. The process is a slow one, characterized by massive files and varying degrees of agency resistance. Historically, panels with short life spans (two years) are subject to the brunt of agency delaying tactics designed to wait out the outsiders until they go away. Congress's House Select Committee on Assassinations had this problem during its chaotic two-year life span. Having to both defend its existence and pursue its money severely distracted the committee. Secret keepers in certain agencies sat back and watched the clock. In one case, an agency sent the wrong expert to testify, then delayed sending the right one. In other cases, records systems were searched at a snail's pace, or the committee was told, "Your document is in the mail." While no fixed-term body can ever be immune from foot-dragging by the agencies, four years renders delaying tactics more difficult to execute.

The boards need a staff component of lawyers who are expert regarding disclosure laws and the secrecy system, particularly the policies of the agencies being dealt with. This knowledge will provide crucial support for the citizen panel, some or many of whom will lack such expertise. In addition, although the boards have no judicial or oversight powers, their work will undoubtedly involve the legal issues of records disposition. The statute proposed earlier concerning the destruction and hiding of records will not be enforced by these boards, but the problem will quite probably come to their attention. If so, such instances would be referred to the Justice Department for handling. This capacity for legal discovery of malfeasance will also help to prevent new abuses during a board's tenure.

In the ARRB setup, agencies seeking to appeal the board's decision to disclose went directly to the president. This is cumbersome and unproductive. If two or more boards functioned simultaneously, this procedure could result in long delays in decision making by an already overburdened White House. It could also create a new political game among the board, the agencies, and the president's office.

A more administratively efficient, and slightly less political, procedure would have agency appeals going before a presidential panel that was drawn from different sectors (retired judiciary and law practice, archives, academe, and federal bureaucracy). A precedent exists: President Clinton created a panel to decide on appeals in his "mandatory declassification review" process (a process separate from FOIA). Appeals from requesters who are denied by agencies are handled by the president's interagency appeals panel. The proposal here is for agency appeals of review board decisions to go before a panel composed of appointees who are not currently working for the agencies.

FOIA REFORMS

Fair Use of Vaughn Motions. As mentioned in chapter 2, this motion is made in federal court by requesters who are challenging a government decision. If the court grants the motion, the agency must provide an "index" of every item withheld, along with a legal justification for it. This is essential to plaintiffs' ability to make their case effectively. Plaintiffs are already disadvantaged by not knowing the specific substance of the information they seek. It is essential that they at least know its title or headline and why it is being withheld. Otherwise, a meaningful challenge of the agency's claims becomes even more difficult, and the courtroom process is all the more inequitable in the government's favor.

Courts often do not grant Vaughn motions until after plaintiffs have presented their complaint and the government has responded. Instead, FOIA should be amended to require agencies to produce this index before the case goes to court. The information in the index is the same no matter when it is provided. This is not a matter of secret keeping but of judicial fairness regarding timing.

Equitable Fee Waivers. The existing policy should be broadened to be commensurate with the goal of *public* disclosure. Present criteria inappropriately inhibit the flow of information. The Justice Department guidelines to agencies are tied too closely to "government operations," or "understanding of government." FOIA was not intended to be limited to civics lessons in how government works. Anything that the government does or does not do is relevant to the increased knowledge of a democratic citizenry.

Free public access should not be limited to that which government defines as its important or relevant activities. The policy that requesters can only get a waiver if they ask for records that are judged "significant" or "contributing" to understanding government is patronizing. Essentially, it allows agencies to decide which documents are important. Seemingly insignificant disclosures to three journalists may have a synergy that would be of great significance once the information was released and collated.

The singling out for fee waivers of educational, scientific, and research institutions, as well as the requesters who are affiliated with them, is not only narrow but elitist. Under current law, to obtain a waiver, the individual's research must *not* be individual in nature, but instead be "a scholarly research goal of the institution." Yet some of the most important public disclosures that have profoundly and positively affected agency accountability and policy debates have been obtained by people unaffiliated with such institutions, or by researchers whose projects and goals were not part of some collective institutional enterprise.

It is not certain that the organizations specified for waivers under the existing policy (or the individuals doing projects within them) will disseminate released information to the public. Documents could be used to "understand" government or serve a collective research goal without ever being made available to the public, as opposed to elite members of it or to private institutions.

The standard for granting fee waivers must be public access and dissemination: Can the requester show that the information will be available to the public in a noncommercial manner? In contrast, we now have a public's right to know that is semipublic and semiprivatized, whereby certain information, as defined by the government, is provided free to elite requesters.

Current policy rejects the cumulative nature of the information process in science, history, and politics. Documents that are disseminated through publication or other means, or are made available in libraries or other knowledge centers that conduct no research, have a domino effect. They provided a rich database from which independent scholars, journalists, citizens, and political groups (none of which is an "institution") have produced discoveries and discourses that have significantly enlightened society. While it is true that under existing guidelines media-based requesters get some preference for being able to disseminate,[22] this should not be limited to working journalists. Freelance authors, curious citizens, and unemployed academics should get the same treatment. Thus, the requester's ability to make the information public should be the main criterion, not a footnote.

Training for Upper-Level FOIA / Privacy Administrators. This idea comes from the Australian FOI Law Reform Commission, which recognized that "agency culture" and the attitudes of "senior management" are crucial to the success of disclosure. It recommended training sessions for agency personnel to enhance their understanding of the goals, law, and process of freedom of information. Why not? The federal government already does this for employee motivation, sexual harassment, and how to retire; we can surely do it for the public's right to know.

The need for training records custodians was graphically illustrated by a class assignment of my course, "Public Policy in America," taught at the University of Massachusetts-Dartmouth in the fall of 2000. Eighteen students were given the assignment of using the Massachusetts Public Records Law (described in chapter 1, note 6), which is perhaps the most user-friendly, pro-disclosure statute in the nation (far more liberal than the federal Freedom of Information Act). Students were required to select a subject or issue for which it could be reasonably assumed that a state or local agency would have some records: for example, a decision by a city planning board, a decision on a town curfew, violent crime statistics for the university, state highway department decisions on road repairs, the salaries of administrators at the university, state health department records on the West Nile virus, municipal court data on numbers of probation cases, and records relating to local police investigation of an alleged satanic cult.

Armed with "A Guide to Massachusetts Public Records Law" (a clear and simple step-by-step "how to" pamphlet), students made their requests and followed them through with the help of their professor. They then wrote up the answers to my fifteen questions on how their experience compared with the provisions of the state law and with the broad rights of access that it provided. The law had existed for more than three decades and the state produced "A Guide for Records Custodians" informing them of their responsibilities to requesters. Despite this, the range of responses from custodians and their ignorance of the law (or unwillingness to follow it) were startling. Some examples of the inappropriate or illegal responses:

- The requester must meet with the agency's lawyer to determine if the request is legal. *This is not only intimidating to an undergraduate but is outside the law, since the attorney is not the custodian.*
- The requester must put the request in writing. *The law provides for oral requests. Written requests are the option of the requester, not the agency.*
- A student was told that if he obtained a letter from his professor, then the custodian could process the request. *This response is illegal.*
- A requester asking for records concerning a controversial local ordinance was given only a copy of the ordinance and told there were no records, documents, or transcripts relating to the decision to pass the ordinance. *This cannot be possible, given the way in which municipal governments operate.*
- The requester must pay $40 for twenty-one pages. *There was no search fee (the records were found instantly), and the law mandates charges of twenty cents a page.*
- A university clerk told one student that she was not entitled to the administrative salary list because she was not twenty-one years old. *This is the clerk's fertile imagination—the act has no age requirement.*

- A requester was told that a trip to Boston and an in-person interview about the request were necessary. *Neither of these requirements is legal.*
- A requester was informed that it would take at least a month for the custodians to respond. *The law gives them ten working days.*

Clearly, a well-intentioned statute and a manual on how to comply with it do not ensure the public's right to know.

No Blanket Exemptions. It must be admitted that undoing the CIA and FBI's hard-won political victories is extremely unlikely. But as a matter of principle and consistent policy, Congress and the president should not create exemptions for large categories of records, placing them beyond FOIA (as with the CIA's "operational files" and the FBI's dispensation from President Clinton's executive order on older records). These decisions express a lack of confidence in the disclosure process, feeding on agency distrust.

While agencies can be predicted to lobby for such privileges, Congress and the White House should not give in. (However, since Congress already exempted itself from FOIA, my argument may well be falling on two sets of deaf ears—the agencies' and Congress's.) The CIA's exemption is exceedingly broad, as is the FBI's exclusion of older records. In both cases, a major portion of the records system has been placed beyond the public disclosure process.

CONCLUSION

"It is time for a new way of thinking about secrecy," said Senator Moynihan's commission.[23] The foregoing changes would help to create a healthier balance between secrecy and disclosure; any one of them would improve the current procedures. With the noted exception of the sunset law/archives proposal, none is radically pricey. These proposals merely tinker with a system in need of repair. They do not impair legitimate secret keeping, although some agencies or officers would undoubtedly think otherwise. Under these revisions, competent, well-resourced secret keepers could still preserve privacy, national security, and law enforcement functions. Indeed, they would be in a better position to administer the public disclosure process effectively.

With these proposed changes, the vaults would not be as tightly, arbitrarily sealed. The culture of secrecy would experience a malaise. But agency accountability would grow. Illegitimate secrecy (and the misfeasance, illegality, and cover-ups that go with it) would be reduced. The republic would not crumble. The public's right to know would finally be elevated to an equitable status vis-à-vis governmental secrecy, and democratic ideals would be better realized.

Secrecy Sampler: Selected Documents from Law Enforcement and Intelligence Files

APRIL 4, 1968(Thursday)

At 9:40AM April 4, 1968 Memphis Police Department received information through Intelligence Sources that the Ku Klux Klan would not come to Memphis 4/4/68 for fear that they might be blamed for anything which might happen, and any Klansman in Memphis on 4/4/68 was here without the approval of the Klan officials. 342)

At 1:45PM April 4, 1968 there was a rumor abroad that Stokeley Carmichael had arrived in Memphis but this was not verified. 343)

At approx. 3:30PM Intelligence information was received that there was a plot abroad to kill Detective E. E. Redditt. He had been called at the Fire House, where he was maintaining surveillance on the activities of Martin LUTHER KING, and his party, at 12:45PM by a Female Colored, who indicated that she knew he was there, and said his spying was an offense against his people. After receiving this information Detective Redditt was removed from his post at the Fire Station for his own safety, and Ptlmn. W. B. Richmond remained at the Firestation keeping Surveillance on the Lorraine Motel and DR. KING''S party. 344)

Mr. Frank C. Holloman relates that on April 4, 1968 he, and Chief H. E. Lux, and Chief J. C. Macdonald, were in Federal Court, where they testified in connection with the injunction that the City was seeking. ANDREW YOUNG, and others testified for the Southern Christian Leadership Conference. At 4PM the Court took the case under advisement, and a temporary restraining order was issued against MARTIN LUTHER KING and the Southern Christian Leadership Conference.

At 5PM a confidential report from outside Memphis arrived advising that R. A. M. (Revolutionary Action Movement) had plans to assassinate Detective E. E. Redditt, who had been active throughout the strike providing the Police Department with Intelligence Information and a security plan was laid out for him. 345)

Detective Redditt's report for 4/4/68 indicates from 10;30AM on there was considerable activity at the Lorraine Motel, and almost continuous meetings between, S. C. L. C.(Southern Christian Leadership Conference) officials, local C. O. M. E. (Community on the Move for Equality) officials and the local black activists known as the Invaders. Of this latter group, JOHN HENRY FERGUSON, THEODORE MANUAL, CHARLES CABBAGE, JOHN B. SMITH, MILTON MACK and others were observed coming and going from Room

- 66 -

Page from secret Memphis Police Department intelligence report. This 140-page document was leaked to the author. It describes events surrounding the April 4, 1968, assassination of Dr. Martin Luther King, Jr. A sanitized version was given to the House Select Committee on Assassinations (1978): the congressional version had some items taken out of the chronology and others edited or added. It was also missing forty pages of footnotes. The committee's copy remains sealed until 2039 along with the rest of its King assassination files. To the author's knowledge, this is the only full copy to leave the possession of the Memphis Police inner circle.

Prep: S.A. Stern/aw/3-13-64
cc: Mr. Willens
     Mr. Stern
     Files

PC 6
P PL
GA 1

March 13, 1964

MEMORANDUM OF CONFERENCE

At 3:00 P.M. on Wednesday, March 11, representatives of the Department of the Treasury and of the Commission met to consider Secretary Dillon's letter of January 28, 1964, to the Chairman, and his response of February 28, 1964.

Present for the Commission - Chairman Warren, General Counsel Rankin, Messrs. Willens and Stern; for the Treasury - Chief Rowley of Secret Service and Robert Carswell, Special Assistant to Secretary Dillon.

Chairman Warren explained that he had two basic problems:

a. The Commission is unwilling to agree in advance to any limitation upon its prerogative of suggesting any change in arrangements for Presidential protection which it may consider desirable. Of course, the Commission has no interest in publishing in its report any information which might in any way suggest opportunities to a possible assailant. However, the danger of this happening should be eliminated by restricting the information which the Commission obtains about particular protection matters (see point b. below). The Chairman felt that the Commission would itself have to determine what could properly be covered in its report, without being subject to veto by the agency involved, or by the President.*

----

*The question of an ultimate determination by the President whether information should appear in the report arose because of a suggestion made at an earlier meeting, on March 6, 1964, when Messrs. Rankin, Willens, and Stern met with Mr. Carswell and General Counsel of the Treasury Belin. At that conference, a possible solution was discussed which would involve notice by the Commission to the Agency originating information concerning Presidential protection that the Commission intended to treat this information in its public report, an opportunity by the agency involved to attempt to dissuade the Commission from doing so because of security, and an opportunity to seek Presidential review of any disagreement.

This March 13, 1964, memorandum of a meeting between representatives of the Warren Commission and the U.S. Secret Service focused on their discussion of secrecy. The Service sought assurances that its protective methods and procedures would not be publicized. The Warren Commission rejected the Secret Service's desire to censor the commission's final report in order to protect its secrets.

RMM:ej

Destroy
not used
9-12 64

M E M O R A N D U M

STAFF

To : ~~Wesley J. Liebeler~~   June 17, 1964

FROM   :   Richard M. Mosk

SUBJECT :   Oswald's Reading

The following is a list of books that Oswald checked out
of the New Orleans Library (*Secret Service Control No.564, C.d.87*)

CARD SHOWS RETURN DATE	TITLE	AUTHOR	DATE WOULD HAVE BEEN CHECKED OUT
10/3/63	"Goldfinger"	IAN FLEMING	9/19/63
7/8/63	"Thunderball"	"	6/24/63
10/3/63	"Moonraker"	"	9/19/63
9/5/63	"From Russia With Love"	"	8/22/63
10/3/63	"Ape And Essence"	ALDOUS HUXLEY	9/19/63
10/3/63	"Brave New World"	"	9/19/63
9/5/63	"The Sixth Galaxy Reader"	H. L. GOLD	8/22/63
9/5/63	"Portals of Tomorrow"	AUGUST DERLETH	8/22/63
8/13/63	"Mind Partner"	Edited by H. L. GOLD	7/30/63

A Warren Commission memo on Lee Harvey Oswald's reading habits
the summer before the assassination of President Kennedy bears the
handwritten note: "*Destroy,* not used 9-12-64." It survived to indicate
Oswald's penchant for James Bond novels, including *From Russia With
Love* (Oswald had defected to the Soviet Union in 1959 and lived there
until June 1962).

AFFIDAVIT OF RICHARD HELMS

STATE OF VIRGINIA)
                 : ss.
COUNTY OF FAIRFAX)

       RICHARD HELMS, being duly sworn, deposes and says that he is the
Deputy Director for Plans of the Central Intelligence Agency, and that
based on his personal knowledge of the affairs of the Central Intelligence
Agency and on detailed inquiries of those officers and employees within his
supervision who would have knowledge about any relationship Lee Harvey
Oswald may have had with that Agency, he certifies that:

              Lee Harvey Oswald was not an agent, employee, or
informant of the Central Intelligence Agency;

              the Agency never contacted him, interviewed him,
talked with him, or received or solicited any reports or
information from him, or communicated with him, directly
or indirectly, in any other manner;

              the Agency never furnished him any funds or money,
or compensated him, directly or indirectly, in any fashion;
and

             Lee Harvey Oswald was never associated or connected,
directly or indirectly, in any way whatsoever with the Agency.

                                                  (L.S.)
                            —————————————————
                                 RICHARD HELMS

       Subscribed and sworn to this _____ day of _____,
1964, before me, a Notary Public in and for the State of Virginia, by the
said RICHARD HELMS, who is personally known to me and he duly
acknowledged to me the execution of the foregoing instrument.

                                —————————————————
                                   Notary Public

                                   My commission expires _____

(Seal)

This affidavit by then–Deputy CIA Director Richard Helms swore that
Oswald had no contact with the CIA prior to the president's assassination. A cover page reads, "Never sent to commission—unsigned,
undated and never used." The Agency was anxious to convince the Warren Commission that it had no relationship to the alleged assassin. The
issue prompted a 1975 meeting between CIA Director William Colby
and Dan Rather and Les Midgley of CBS News.

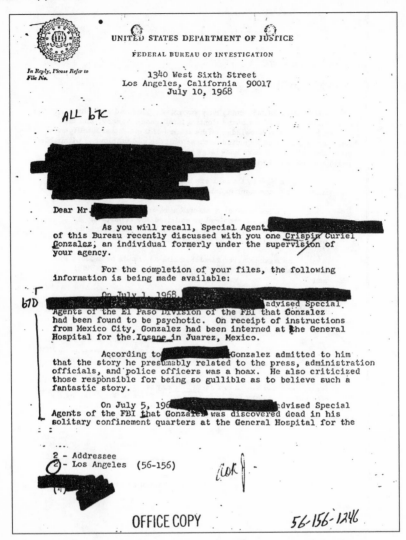

This FBI document from the Bureau's Robert Kennedy assassination file concerns the apparent suicide of an acquaintance of convicted assassin Sirhan Sirhan. The document is deleted to protect the source and the name of an FBI agent (line one). In a typical example of inconsistent censoring, the name of the agent who wrote it (Wesley Grapp) remains, as does information of a personal nature about the deceased.

Insane in Juarez, Mexico at 7:45 p.m., July 4, 1968. Gonzalez
had apparently put together a rope from the mattress material
located in his room which he used to hang himself and was
subsequently discovered by an attendant of the hospital.

The cooperation previously extended by you to this
Bureau is greatly appreciated and I trust that the foregoing will
suffice for your file.

Very truly yours,

WESLEY G. GRAPP
Special Agent in Charge

- 2 -

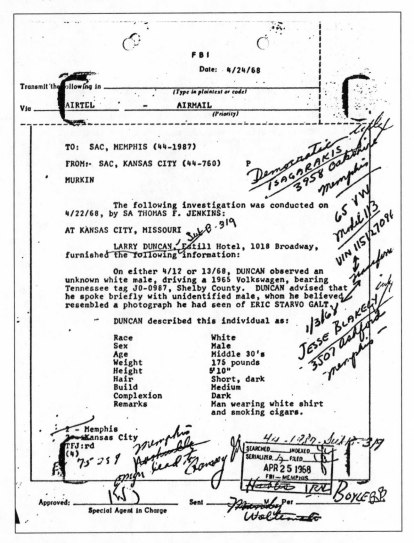

In contrast to the FBI's censorship of agent names from its RFK assassination file, many documents in its King assassination file were released totally uncensored. This document not only gives the names of the source and the investigating agent, it also includes all the margin notes and routing references. The latter were deleted from the bureau's RFK file when it was released.

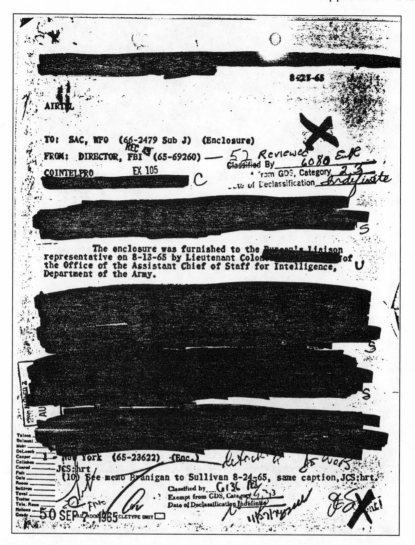

This 1965 FBI memo involves its infamous COINTELPRO program of domestic spying and disruption of civil rights and antiwar groups. The only remaining substantive reference tells us that the deleted data was furnished by Army Intelligence. Ward Churchill and Jim VanderWall, *The Cointelpro Papers* (Boston: South End Press, 1990).

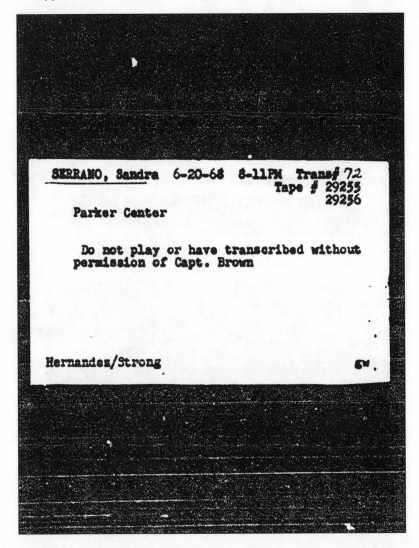

SERRANO, Sandra 6-20-68 8-11PM Trans# 72
                                    Tape # 29255
                                           29256

Parker Center

   Do not play or have transcribed without
permission of Capt. Brown

Hernandez/Strong   SW.

This note in the LAPD file on the Robert Kennedy assassination embargoed the interview record of witness Sandra Serrano, who claimed to see Sirhan Sirhan in the company of a woman suspected of being an accomplice. The reason for the sensitivity on LAPD's part became clear when the tape and transcript of Serrano's interview were released by the California State Archives in 1988: she had clearly been browbeaten by the interviewing officer in a successful attempt to force her to recant her account.

Excerpts: Sandra Serrano Polygraph/Interview Session

June 20, 1968, 9:0.0 - 10:15 p.m. (approximate)

Operator/Interviewer - Sergeant Enrique Hernandez (LAPD)

POLYGRAPH TEST:

H: Did you make up the story about seeing the girl in the
     polka dot dress?

S: No. (...)

H: Have you ever smoked a marijuana cigarette?

S: No. (pp. 16-17)

H: ...I do want to talk to you like a brother. Look, I presume,
     I don't know what religion you are, I'm Catholic. (...)
     You know that for some reason this was made up. (...) I
     think you owe it to Senator Kennedy, the late Senator Ken-
     ned, to come forth, be a woman about this. If he, and you
     don't know and I don't know whether he's a witness right
     now in this room watching what we're doing in here. Don't
     shame his death by keeping this thing up. I have compassion
     for you. I want to know why, I want to know why you did what
     you did. This is a very serious thing.

S: (starts) I seen those people!

H: No, no, no, no Sandy. Remember what I told you about that
     you can't say you saw something when you didn't see it? (...)
     I can, I can explain this to the investigators where you don't
     even have to talk to them and they won't talk to you. I can
     do this. (...) I don't know if you've been sleeping well at
     night or not, I don't know this. But I know that, as you get
     older, one of these days you're gonna be a mother. You're
     gonna be a mother, you're gonna have kids, and you know that
     you can't live a life of shame, knowing what you're doing
     right now is wrong.

S: Well, I don't feel I'm doing anything wrong. (pp. 17-19)

H: ...after we leave this room, if you want to tell me <u>why</u> it
     is that you made up this story, I can assure you that nobody
     else will talk to you about anything. (...) But please, in
     the name of <u>Kennedy</u>... (...)

3 9

1 Uecker, and Kennedy at the time you heard the shooting?

2   A   No. I don't think so. There might

3 have been somebody to my right in front of me because we

4 were very congested. I don't remember if there was anybody

5 closely behind me, you know, if they were six inches, six

6 feet. I really don't know.

7   Q   You drew your revolver?

8   A   After I got up off the floor.

9   Q   Did you ever fire a shot?

10   A   No.

11 BY MR. TRAPP:

12   Q   Did you unload the weapon when you

13 got back home that night?

14   A   No. I keep it up in the closet

15 loaded all the time. Actually, the weapon, when I am not

16 using it for a part time moonlight job, is at the house

17 for my wife, you know, when she's home alone.

18   Q   Did you clean it sometime later?

19   A   Ah --

20   Q   Days later, months later, weeks

21 later?

22   A   I had only fired the gun one time

23 after I had bought it.

24   I say one time, I shot about twenty

25 five rounds with a friend of mine on the Sheriff's Depart-

26 ment. We went up to the San Fernando Shooting Range, you

The controversy regarding other guns (besides Sirhan Sirhan's) being fired at the scene of Senator Kennedy's assassination came up in this 1971 interview that was sealed by Los Angeles authorities for nearly two decades.

-21-

Execution of Operational Crisis-Management Procedures

No Secret Service Special Agent or Uniformed Division
Officer had been posted at George Washington Hospital on March
30, 1981. Immediately upon learning that the President had
been taken to this hospital, Acting Special Agent in Charge
Andrew Berger of the Washington field office sent one supervisor (Assistant to the Special Agent in Charge Pat Miller) and
a small group of Special Agents to the hospital. When it
arrived at the hospital, the Presidential motorcade radioed a
request for more manpower; within a few minutes, Berger sent
another Special Agent followed at approximately 3:00 p.m. by a
small group of additional Special Agents.

Information prepared later by the Washington field office
suggests that some other agents may have gone on their own or
been sent over during this period, but between 3:00 p.m. and
5:00 p.m., no additional agents were requested by Pat Miller,
and none were sent spontaneously by Berger. Throughout these
hours, Berger recalls receiving no communications from the
Presidential detail concerning the situation at the hospital,
and recalls no significant communications from headquarters
concerning manpower needs. A reserve of Special Agents was
gathered in the Washington field office conference room, and
was parcelled out on other assignments during the course of the
afternoon.

Most of the attention of supervisory Washington field
office personnel was directed to the arrangements concerning
the custody of Hinckley; the transmittal of information derived
from Hinckley's personal effects (the first significant intelligence accumulated to help determine the nature and extent of
the crisis) to the Command/Control Center at headquarters and
to the appropriate field offices; and coordination with other
protective details in the Washington, D.C., area.

In the meantime, Gerald Bechtle, acting as Assistant
Director of Protective Operations, sent instructions to the
Washington Hilton to hold the original security contingent at
the hotel in order to execute his understanding of the "interim
federal presence" requirements of the April 23, 1979 memorandum. That memorandum actually assigned the responsibility
for maintaining that presence to the first intelligence team on
the scene and did not, at least in its express terms, require
that the intelligence team keep other Special Agents there.

Just after 4:00 p.m., Bechtle directed the Uniformed
Division to send as many officers as possible to the hospital.

In a rare moment of candor and openness, the U.S. Treasury Department's Office of the General Counsel issued a report entitled "Management Review on the Performance of the U.S. Department of the Treasury
in connection with the March 30, 1981 Assassination Attempt on President Ronald Reagan." The 101-page analysis discussed every procedure,
goal, and action regarding Secret Service's failure to protect the president. The level of specificity concerning how agents go about their work
has not been seen before or since. This is the kind of report that the
Secret Service usually attempts to classify because it reveals "operations
and methods" (including the names and duties of all agents involved).

-22-

Then, a little after 5:00 p.m., Bechtle received a call from Miller at the hospital asking for a substantial number of Special Agents. This call had been diverted from the Washington field office because Miller could not get through on the telephone lines. Miller was anticipating the President's removal from surgery, and he expected to need additional manpower to station in a couple of additional areas of the hospital. In response, Bechtle had the Office of Training at headquarters queried to see if Special Agents could be located in the in-service training classes that were being conducted in downtown Washington.

During the first hour and a half the Office of Investigations received no requests for help from the Presidential detail at the hospital, or from Bechtle in Protective Operations, from whom they would have expected any requests to come. Assistant Director Burke recalls calling Berger at the Washington field office around 6:00 p.m. to ask whether Inspection should provide manpower to the hospital, and that Berger said no.

While additional small numbers of Special Agents were sent to the hospital site during the afternoon, it does not appear that supervisory Secret Service agents away from the hospital had any specific information concerning the number of Secret Service personnel actually there or, except as noted above, attempted to increase manpower on the site during the first two hours or so.

In effect, headquarters crisis managers followed the implications of existing procedures and assumed that the Presidential detail personnel on site, and the Washington field office personnel sent there shortly afterward, would request whatever assistance was necessary. The requests they received from the hospital site were few, and took some period of time to fulfill; as a consequence, the number of Service personnel at the hospital did not reach a level substantially greater than the security that had been established at the Hilton prior to the shooting until late in the afternoon of March 30.

Office of Public Affairs: Crisis Response

Procedures

The Office of Public Affairs at Secret Service has no written procedures which prescribe how office functions are to

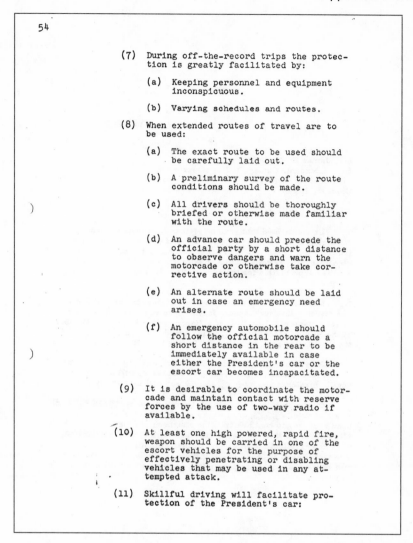

54

(7) During off-the-record trips the protection is greatly facilitated by:

   (a) Keeping personnel and equipment
        inconspicuous.

   (b) Varying schedules and routes.

(8) When extended routes of travel are to
be used:

   (a) The exact route to be used should
        be carefully laid out.

   (b) A preliminary survey of the route
        conditions should be made.

   (c) All drivers should be thoroughly
        briefed or otherwise made familiar
        with the route.

   (d) An advance car should precede the
        official party by a short distance
        to observe dangers and warn the
        motorcade or otherwise take cor-
        rective action.

   (e) An alternate route should be laid
        out in case an emergency need
        arises.

   (f) An emergency automobile should
        follow the official motorcade a
        short distance in the rear to be
        immediately available in case
        either the President's car or the
        escort car becomes incapacitated.

(9) It is desirable to coordinate the motorcade and maintain contact with reserve
forces by the use of two-way radio if
available.

(10) At least one high powered, rapid fire,
weapon should be carried in one of the
escort vehicles for the purpose of
effectively penetrating or disabling
vehicles that may be used in any attempted attack.

(11) Skillful driving will facilitate protection of the President's car:

So sensitive is the Secret Service that it argued before the Assassination
Records Review Board (in the 1990s) that its training manual and other
documents not be released with the JFK records. They took this position even though much of the material had already been cited in articles
and books (including the author's). It had also appeared in memoirs and
had been publicly available at the National Archives for decades. This
page from the 133-page, 1954 training manual instructs agents concerning protection of the presidential limousine.

169

17 AUG 1967.

Mr. James E. Conlisk
Superintendent, Chicago Police Department
1121 South State Street
Chicago, Illinois

Dear Mr. Conlisk:

    I am delighted that you can visit with us in early October. We feel that the bringing together of chief police administrators from the major metropolitan areas of the country in a relaxed environment will serve a mutual, useful purpose and enable us to express appreciation for the cooperation we have received through the years.

    Mr. Helms has a keen, personal interest in our meeting and has directed that such Agency facilities as you may require be put at your disposal. He will host a dinner in your honor on 6 October at the Headquarters Building. This would envision your arrival in the Washington area sometime during the late afternoon of 6 October.

    All travel arrangements to and from Washington, including hotel reservations for the evening of 6 October, will be made and details furnished you by ▮▮▮▮▮▮ who will accompany you.

    On the morning of 7 October we will move by ▮▮▮▮▮▮▮ to a classified ▮▮▮▮ area where a highly flexible program has been arranged to continue until the afternoon of 8 October. We have allowed liberal time for recreational activities, and our ▮▮▮▮▮ base has excellent facilities for fishing, swimming, and tennis. The facilities of ▮▮▮▮▮▮▮▮▮▮, including its outstanding golf course, are in close proximity to our area and will be available to you.

A 1967 letter from CIA Director of Security Howard Osborn to the superintendent of the Chicago Police Department illustrates the friendly, social nature of Agency programs for police.

I am sure that you are aware of the sensitivity of our ▮▮▮▮ base, and knowledge of your presence there will be confined to senior Agency officials and members of my immediate staff. During your visit you will be provided with communications facilities to your home and office, and our ▮▮▮▮▮▮▮ will be available to you for emergency travel requirements.

Howard J. Osborn
Director of Security

203

```
PROJECT        :

SUBJECT        : SURREPTITIOUS ENTRY PLANNING

TIME           : 10 Days

NUMBER STUDENTS: 6

OBJECTIVES     : To instruct the students in the theory,
methods and techniques of clandestine entry.

COURSE CONTENT : This course introduces the basic types
of locks, their construction and nomenclature, and their
weaknesses.   The student will fabricate a set of lock-
picking tools, and will learn how to employ them against
a variety of luggage, lever, wafer and pin-tumbler locks.
The course material will be presented via lecture and
demonstration.   The students will participate in practi-
cal work exercises.

                    A field exercise will be given at the
conclusion of the course.

COMMENT        : The course material will be directed
toward fulfilling the requirements' of the students.
```

SANITIZED COPY

The CIA course on surreptitious entry includes a final exam for police trainees—"a field exercise." The documents do not reveal the nature or location of this field work, but it must have involved a break-in of some kind, however real or simulated it might have been.

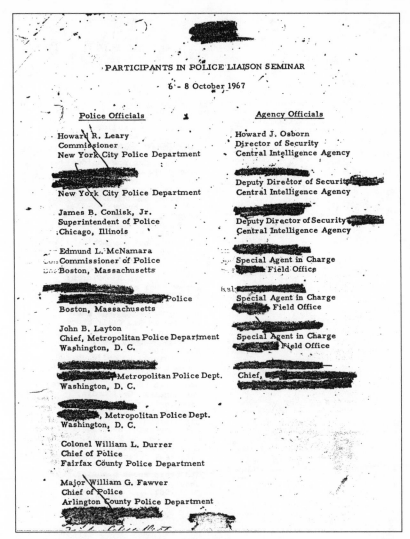

PARTICIPANTS IN POLICE LIAISON SEMINAR

6 - 8 October 1967

Police Officials	Agency Officials
Howard R. Leary Commissioner New York City Police Department	Howard J. Osborn Director of Security Central Intelligence Agency
▓▓▓▓▓▓▓▓▓▓▓▓ New York City Police Department	Deputy Director of Security ▓▓▓▓▓ Central Intelligence Agency
James B. Conlisk, Jr. Superintendent of Police Chicago, Illinois	Deputy Director of Security ▓▓▓▓ Central Intelligence Agency
Edmund L. McNamara Commissioner of Police Boston, Massachusetts	▓▓▓▓▓▓▓▓ Special Agent in Charge ▓▓▓▓ Field Office
▓▓▓▓▓▓▓▓▓▓▓ Police Boston, Massachusetts	▓▓▓▓▓▓▓▓▓ Special Agent in Charge ▓▓▓▓ Field Office
John B. Layton Chief, Metropolitan Police Department Washington, D. C.	Special Agent in Charge ▓▓▓▓ Field Office
▓▓▓▓▓▓▓ Metropolitan Police Dept. Washington, D. C.	Chief, ▓▓▓▓▓▓▓
▓▓▓▓▓, Metropolitan Police Dept. Washington, D. C.	
Colonel William L. Durrer Chief of Police Fairfax County Police Department	
Major William G. Fawver Chief of Police Arlington County Police Department	

In a strange series of selective deletions, some of the CIA's law enforcement friends are protected while the names of others are revealed. It would be interesting to know the rationale behind these seemingly inconsistent deletions.

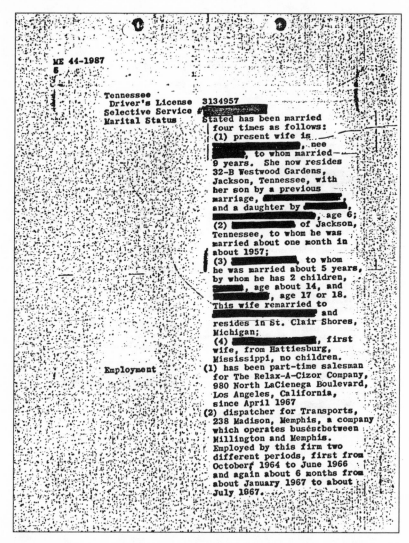

ME 44-1987
6

Tennessee
Driver's License 3134957
Selective Service #
Marital Status   Stated has been married
four times as follows:
(1) present wife is
, nee
, to whom married—
9 years. She now resides
32-B Westwood Gardens,
Jackson, Tennessee, with
her son by a previous
marriage,
and a daughter by ,
, age 6;
(2) of Jackson,
Tennessee, to whom he was
married about one month in
about 1957;
(3) , to whom
he was married about 5 years,
by whom he has 2 children,
, age about 14, and
, , age 17 or 18.
This wife remarried to
and
resides in St. Clair Shores,
Michigan;
(4) , first
wife, from Hattiesburg,
Mississippi, no children.
Employment   (1) has been part-time salesman
for The Relax-A-Cizor Company,
980 North LaCienega Boulevard,
Los Angeles, California,
since April 1967
(2) dispatcher for Transports,
238 Madison, Memphis, a company
which operates buses between
Millington and Memphis.
Employed by this firm two
different periods, first from
October 1964 to June 1966
and again about 6 months from
about January 1967 to about
July 1867.

This Bureau document provides undeleted, personal information about a man questioned at the scene of Dr. King's assassination. All military-related data are excised while other, more personal, data are left in. The first deletion (of his selective service number) was done by the FBI. The other deletions of the names of his spouses and children were done by the author.

```
                                    FEDERAL ... ...
                                    U.S. DEPT ... ...
                                    COMMUNICATIONS SECTION.
                                      JUN 1 1968
                                    .TELETYPE

FBI WASH DC                                    |

FBI MEMPHIS

849 AM URGENT 6-12-68 MCP


TO DIRECTOR AND BUFFALO
FROM MEMPHIS 44-1987   1  P


MURKIN.

     RE BUFFALO TEL EIGHT ELEVEN P.M., JUNE ELEVEN PAST.

     IT IS NOTED ████████████ IN INFORMATION FURNISHED

TORONTO PD EXPLAINED HE HAD USED PUBLIC PHONE BOOTH IN VICINITY

NINE SIX TWO DUNDAS STREET AND FOUND ENVELOPE THERE ADDRESSED

TO SNEYD AT DUNDAS ADDRESS.  REQUEST BUFFALO THROUGH LIASON

WITH TORONTO PD DETERMINE IF POSSIBLE LONG DISTANCE PHONE

CALLS THAT MAY HAVE EMANATED FROM PHONE BOOTH OF INTEREST.  STRONG

POSSIBLIITY EXISTS THAT SUBJECT MAY VERY WELL HAVE USED PHONE

BOOTH AND THIS MIGHT ACCOUNT FOR ENVELOPE BEING THERE.

CORRECTION  LINE 4, LAST WORD IS ADDRESSED.

     A & D.                      REC 88              4396

     P.  END                              JUN 13 1968


JTM

FBI WASH DC
 P    70 JUN 18 1968
```

Mr. Tolson ___
Mr. DeLoach ___
Mr. Mohr ___
Mr. Bishop ___
Mr. Casper ___
Mr. Callahan ___
Mr. Conrad ___
Mr. Felt ___
Mr. Gale ___
Mr. Rosen ___
Mr. Sullivan ___
Mr. Tavel ___
Mr. Trotter ___
Tele. Room ___
Miss Holmes ___
Miss Gandy ___

One FBI document failed to delete the name of the witness whose identity the Bureau was supposed to be protecting. I found him and interviewed him via this error. I have deleted his name.

of Government. While Mr. ████did not absolutely refuse to cooperate
with the Bureau, he made it obvious that only if there was a matter which
he felt was of interest directly to the Bureau locally, would he furnish
this type of information; otherwise, he would furnish it as he has done
previously or cease altogether. The writer attempted, more or less unsuc-
cessfully, to discuss jurisdiction with Mr.████ but Mr.████ maintained his position that the matter was not one of jurisdiction for the FBI
or any single Government agency, but was one that the Government, including
CIA, should be interested in; namely, the international Communist efforts
at corrupting and seizing the Negro Civil Rights Movement.

Mr.████ thoughts regarding a possible writing of a series of novels
aimed at improving the picture of CIA and defending this Government's actions
and the activities of the CIA in support of the Government.

4. During the long conversation, Mr.████introduced this subject by saying that he was sick and tired of the poor public picture that
was constantly being presented of the CIA by all sorts of writers, left-
wing and otherwise. He stated that Government agents were generally painted
as fools and idiots, and that the Headquarters activities obviously were
some sort of super government who acted solely on their own and often against
the interests of the United States. He stated that he had read a number of
books such as "The Invisible Government", and this type of reporting dis-
gusted him. He stated that he had in mind the writing of a series of novels,
using a CIA agent as hero, which would reflect decent, intelligent, and
courageous work on behalf of the United States. He stated that the James
Bond books by Fleming averaged 190-200 pages, and he felt that he could
write this type of a novel once or twice a year in addition to his serious
work as a novelist.

NOTE: Mr.████s latest novel is about to be published, and he was in
Washington for the American Booksellers Association Convention.

5. Mr.████stated he was certain that he could handle this type
of writing since he had demonstrated his capacity as a writer, but that he
might require certain technical assistance, particularly in terms of tradecraft and certain fundamental matters of which he had little knowledge. He
indicated that perhaps some support could be given him if it was agreed that
the idea of the novels had merit, and that support could take the shape of
area knowledge, tradecraft, terminology, and perhaps some operational
matters which were not sensitive or classified.

- 2 -

In a "secret, eyes only" memo to the chief of the Security Research Staff
in 1965, CIA Officer Morse Allen discusses a proposal for improving the
Agency's image through a series of novels. He then goes on to give an
update on the politics of J. Edgar Hoover's smear campaign against
Dr. King.

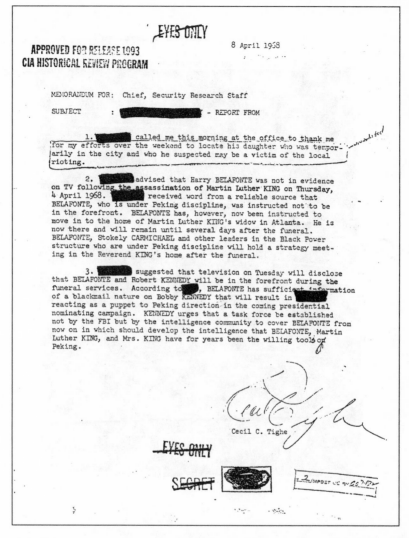

EYES ONLY

8 April 1968

MEMORANDUM FOR: Chief, Security Research Staff

SUBJECT   : ▮▮▮▮▮▮▮▮ - REPORT FROM

1. ▮▮▮▮▮ called me this morning at the office to thank me for my efforts over the weekend to locate his daughter who was temporarily in the city and who he suspected may be a victim of the local rioting.

2. ▮▮▮▮▮ advised that Harry BELAFONTE was not in evidence on TV following the assassination of Martin Luther KING on Thursday, 4 April 1968. ▮▮▮▮▮ received word from a reliable source that BELAFONTE, who is under Peking discipline, was instructed not to be in the forefront. BELAFONTE has, however, now been instructed to move in to the home of Martin Luther KING's widow in Atlanta. He is now there and will remain until several days after the funeral. BELAFONTE, Stokely CARMICHAEL and other leaders in the Black Power structure who are under Peking discipline will hold a strategy meeting in the Reverend KING's home after the funeral.

3. ▮▮▮▮▮ suggested that television on Tuesday will disclose that BELAFONTE and Robert KENNEDY will be in the forefront during the funeral services. According to ▮▮▮, BELAFONTE has sufficient information of a blackmail nature on Bobby KENNEDY that will result in ▮▮▮ reacting as a puppet to Peking direction in the coming presidential nominating campaign. KENNEDY urges that a task force be established not by the FBI but by the intelligence community to cover BELAFONTE from now on in which should develop the intelligence that BELAFONTE, Martin Luther KING, and Mrs. KING have for years been the willing tools of Peking.

Cecil C. Tighe

EYES ONLY

SECRET

A 1968 CIA memo reports on television coverage of Dr. King's funeral. It reveals the depth of the Agency's anticommunist paranoia: Senator Robert F. Kennedy, who had been criticized for his anticommunist zeal when working for Senator Joseph McCarthy's committee as a staff lawyer, was now a Peking communist puppet.

Pages 460 and 531 (deleted and restored versions) of LAPD's *Summary Report* on Robert Kennedy's assassination. When LAPD first released the report, it engaged in massive withholding. Almost all of the withheld files were ultimately restored by the California State Archives.

POSSIBLE ASSOCIATION WITH COMMUNISTS

On the day following the assassination of Robert Kennedy, information was received from a confidential and reliable source that a man named Walter S. Crowe, Jr. had been talking to people about his long-standing acquaintance with Sirhan Sirhan.

Crowe had told the informant that he had been with Sirhan a few weeks before the assassination and that the two had discussed Crowe's activities with the Communist Party. Walter Crowe subsequently told investigators that he feared that he might have influenced Sirhan's decision to kill Senator Kennedy because he attempted to interest Sirhan in the Communist movement.

The F.B.I. report of Crowe's remarks also described a 1961 Volkswagen sedan registered to Adel B. Sirhan, brother of Sirhan Sirhan, which was observed parked in the vicinity of Baces Hall, 1528 North Vermont, Los Angeles. The vehicle was observed on two occasions, December 5, 1963, and January 16, 1966, while meetings of the "Citizens Committee to Preserve American Freedoms" and the W.E.B. Du Bois Club were in progress at that location. The occupant of the venicle was not seen on either occasion.

A confidential source also reported that members of the Southern California District Communist Party were greatly concerned that an association between Sirhan and the Communist Party might be created. This fear apparently developed after

-460-

message. Several of those interviewed likened his approach to
that of a "confidence man."

His record would tend to support that description. Owen has
been involved in six fires beginning in 1939 in Castro Valley,
California. On several occasions he collected insurance settle-
ments from these fires. The cases occurred in: (1) Castro
Valley, 1939; (2) Crystal Lake Park, Oregon, 1945; (3) Dallas,
Texas, 1946; (4) Mount Washington, Kentucky, 1947; (5) Ellicott
City, Maryland, 1951; and (6) Tucson, Arizona, 1962.

Owen's $16,000 claim for the fire in Maryland was denied because
of fraud. A witness observed Owen moving personal effects out
of the house prior to the fire and then return them. Owen
subsequently collected $6,500 when the denial was appealed.

In 1963, Owen was arrested in Costa Mesa, California, on a
fugitive warrant from Tucson, Arizona, for arson with the intent
to defraud an insurance company. A church, Our Little Chapel,
which was owned by Owen was destroyed by fire on July 31, 1962,
in Tucson. The investigation by the Tucson Police Department
revealed that arson was the suspected cause of the fire. Owen
was subsequently convicted of three counts of arson and sentenced
to serve 8-10 years in prison. The decision was appealed and
reversed on June 27, 1966.

In addition to fire claims, Owen has been involved in sex
offenses over the years. In 1943, Jacqueline Banks, 16 years of
age, joined Owen's gospel camp in Milwaukee, Oregon. She had

-531-

SEĊRET

11 DEC 1967

MEMORANDUM FOR : Deputy Director for Support

SUBJECT : Threat to CIA by Some "Black Power" Elements

1. This memorandum is for information only.

2. The growing hostility expressed toward this Agency by some of the more volatile advocates of so-called "black power" presents this Agency with what might be a new threat to its operations abroad and its image in the United States.

3. In the past, denunciation of the Agency by a scattered few for the alleged Agency "assassination" of Patrice Lumumba and Malcolm X. Little might have been dismissed as natural fall-out from embittered followers of the two, seeking a publicly-recognizable scapegoat, and necessarily distorting the true facts behind the deaths to have them "prove" the case against the scapegoat. Presently, however, the growing militancy of "black power" disciples--with clear links to both Maoist and Moscow Communist ideologies--and similarly clear threats to counter this Agency's activities, necessitates placing the problem in an entirely new perspective.

4. The term "black power," despite its militant origins, has been accepted by some to describe the laudable efforts of economic "self-help" and "pride of race" efforts of many Negroes at the community and collegiate level. Indeed, some of those of sincere dedication to the orthodox civil rights movement have accepted the use of the term "black power" to describe their efforts. This presents the problem of separating these constructive efforts--and advocates--from those whose goal is the destruction of the legally constituted government of this Nation.

SECRET

A formerly "secret" memo from 1967 (released in 1993) reveals that the CIA feared that some "black power" groups were a serious threat to the Agency and the nation. The memo was written by Howard Osborne, director of security.

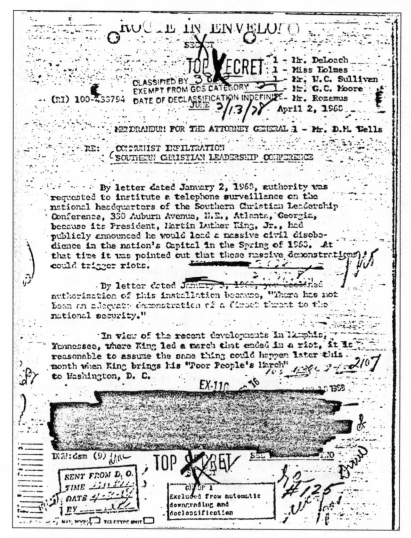

The FBI had requested a wiretap of Dr. King's headquarters in Atlanta based on the fact that his planned demonstrations for the spring of 1968 "could trigger riots." The Attorney General's office refused because: "There has not been an adequate demonstration of a direct threat to the national security." Because Dr. King's march in Memphis had ended in violence, the Bureau was restating its case for a tap. The Memphis disruptions may well have been created, at least in part, by Bureau-commissioned provocateurs.

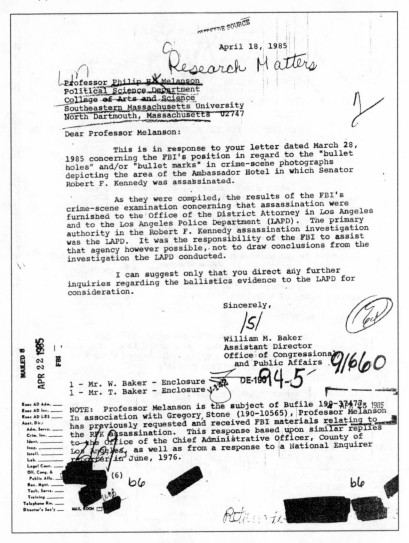

OUTSIDE SOURCE

Research Matters

April 18, 1985

Professor Philip H. Melanson
Political Science Department
College of Arts and Science
Southeastern Massachusetts University
North Dartmouth, Massachusetts 02747

Dear Professor Melanson:

This is in response to your letter dated March 28, 1985 concerning the FBI's position in regard to the "bullet holes" and/or "bullet marks" in crime-scene photographs depicting the area of the Ambassador Hotel in which Senator Robert F. Kennedy was assassinated.

As they were compiled, the results of the FBI's crime-scene examination concerning that assassination were furnished to the Office of the District Attorney in Los Angeles and to the Los Angeles Police Department (LAPD). The primary authority in the Robert F. Kennedy assassination investigation was the LAPD. It was the responsibility of the FBI to assist that agency however possible, not to draw conclusions from the investigation the LAPD conducted.

I can suggest only that you direct any further inquiries regarding the ballistics evidence to the LAPD for consideration.

Sincerely,

/s/

William M. Baker
Assistant Director
Office of Congressional
and Public Affairs

1 - Mr. W. Baker - Enclosure
1 - Mr. T. Baker - Enclosure

NOTE: Professor Melanson is the subject of Bufile 190-37477. In association with Gregory Stone (190-10565), Professor Melanson has previously requested and received FBI materials relating to the RFK assassination. This response based upon similar replies to the Office of the Chief Administrative Officer, County of Los Angeles, as well as from a response to a National Enquirer reporter in June, 1976.

(6)

"Note" on the FBI's 1985 letter to the author indicates that he was the subject of a Bureau file (BUFILE 190 37477). The file did not surface in his FOIA/Privacy request. (The four FBI documents on Lennon are from Jon Wiener, *Gimme Some Truth: The John Lennon FBI Files* [Berkeley: Univ. of California Press, 1999].)

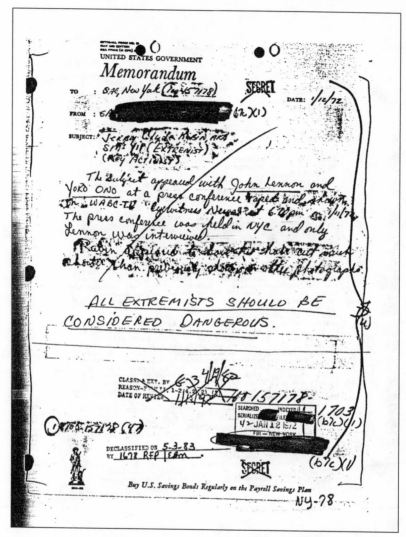

John Lennon's FBI file, requested by Professor Jon Wiener, contains
some provocative documents. A memo on Lennon's political philanthropy
was originally totally deleted of substance, until Wiener's successful
legal battle to restore it. In a rare handwritten notation of ideological fer-
vor, someone in the Bureau asserts, "All extremists should be considered
dangerous."

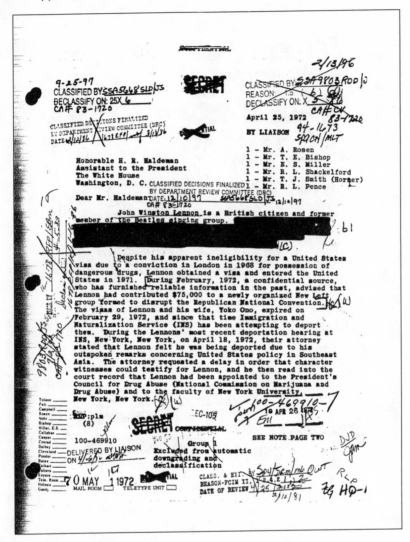

FBI memo from Director Hoover to H. R. Haldeman in the Nixon White House shows how high up the preoccupation with Lennon's politics went. As originally released to Professor Wiener, the body of this letter was totally blacked out. The restorations, forced by Wiener's court challenge, show that the Bureau's deletion was designed to cover up its politically motivated actions against Lennon.

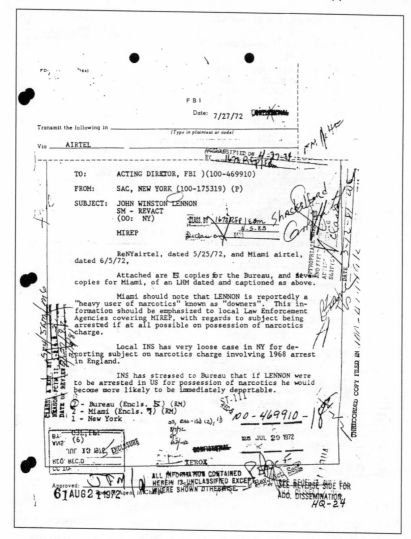

The Bureau's plot to deport Lennon was not above suggesting that he be arrested on drug charges based on unsourced allegations. This memo prescribes that he "be arrested if at all possible on possession of narcotics charge" by Miami authorities.

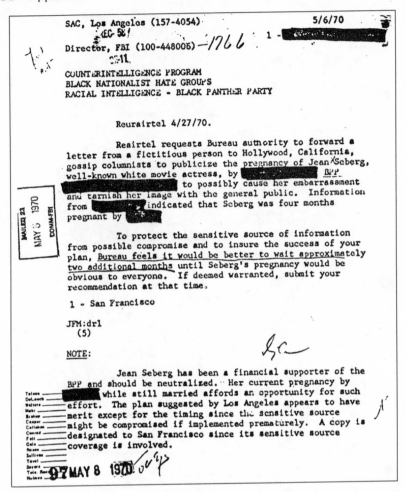

SAC, Los Angeles (157-4054)   5/6/70
    EC-5
Director, FBI (100-448006) —1766   1 -

COUNTERINTELLIGENCE PROGRAM
BLACK NATIONALIST HATE GROUPS
RACIAL INTELLIGENCE - BLACK PANTHER PARTY

            Reurairtel 4/27/70.

            Reairtel requests Bureau authority to forward a
letter from a fictitious person to Hollywood, California,
gossip columnists to publicize the pregnancy of Jean Seberg,
well-known white movie actress, by   BPP
████████████████ to possibly cause her embarrassment
and tarnish her image with the general public. Information
from ██████ indicated that Seberg was four months
pregnant by ███.

            To protect the sensitive source of information
from possible compromise and to insure the success of your
plan, Bureau feels it would be better to wait approximately
two additional months until Seberg's pregnancy would be
obvious to everyone. If deemed warranted, submit your
recommendation at that time.

    1 - San Francisco

    JFM:drl
      (5)

    NOTE:

            Jean Seberg has been a financial supporter of the
BPP and should be neutralized. Her current pregnancy by
██████████ while still married affords an opportunity for such
effort. The plan suggested by Los Angeles appears to have
merit except for the timing since the sensitive source
might be compromised if implemented prematurely. A copy is
designated to San Francisco since its sensitive source
coverage is involved.

The FBI's "counterintelligence program" (in this case, dirty tricks)
seeks to "neutralize" actress Jean Seberg because of her support for the
Black Panther Party. Churchill and VanderWall, *Cointelpro Papers*.

ROUTE IN ENVELOPE

SAC, St. Louis (157-5818)   2/28/69
         REC 44
Director, FBI (100-448006) —727   1 -
                                       1 - ▮▮▮▮▮▮▮
                                       1 -

COUNTERINTELLIGENCE PROGRAM
BLACK NATIONALIST - HATE GROUPS
RACIAL INTELLIGENCE
(BLACK LIBERATORS)

          Reurlet 2/14/69.

          St. Louis is authorized to send anonymous letter
set out in relet and Springfield is authorized to send the
second anonymous letter proposed in relet. Use commercially
purchased stationery and take the other precautions set out
to insure this cannot be traced to this Bureau.

          The Bureau feels there should be an interval between
the two letters of at least ten days. St. Louis should advise
Springfield of date second letter should be mailed.

          St. Louis and Springfield should advise the Bureau
of any results.

2 - Springfield

TJD:ckl
   (8)

NOTE:

          The Black Liberators are a black extremist group
in St. Louis ▮▮▮▮▮▮▮▮▮▮▮▮▮▮▮▮▮▮▮▮▮▮▮▮▮▮▮▮▮▮▮▮▮
▮▮▮▮▮▮ of the Student Nonviolent Coordinating Committee
(SNCC) for the Midwest. SNCC is also a black extremist
group. St. Louis recommends anonymous letters be sent ▮▮
and his wife regarding ▮▮▮▮▮▮▮▮extramarital activities.
▮▮▮▮▮▮The letters might cause Koen to spend more of
his time at home since ▮▮▮will know his wife is aware of
his activities. Since ▮▮▮and his wife are separated, the
letters cannot hurt the wife but might draw ▮▮▮back to
his wife.

          St. Louis also feels that the Black Liberators
will try to discover the writer within the organization
which will help neutralize new and potential members.
Since the letters are to be sent anonymously, there is no
possibility of embarrassment to the Bureau. St. Louis has
prepared the first anonymous letter using the penmanship and
grammar of the typical member of the Black Liberators.

          Based on data furnished by St. Louis, it appears this
separation is due to ▮▮▮▮organization work among black
extremists and not because of marital discord, however,
it is known ▮▮▮has had extramarital affairs.

Director Hoover's office authorizes the FBI's St. Louis field office to send poison-pen letters on "commercially purchased stationary [sic]" with "other precautions set out to insure this cannot be traced to this Bureau." Churchill and VanderWall, *Cointelpro Papers*.

Standard Form 509
Promulgated August 1948
By Bureau of the Budget
Circular A—32

CLINICAL RECORD	NARRATIVE SUMMARY	
DATE OF ADMISSION	DATE OF DISCHARGE	NUMBER OF DAYS HOSPITALIZED
Out- Patient		

(Sign and date at end of narrative)

6 March 54 ENTRY FOR MEDICAL RECORD PURPOSES:

Notes on patient examination and history.

#3-3-54: Exposed to radiation on Rongerik Island on 3-2-54. No official film badge readings available here. Estimate group generally exposed to about 40 R.

Slight upset stomach yesterday and today. Eyes are a little sore and burning. Has two small cuts on right hand and one on left hand which occured on day of fall-out (3-1-54) Has old laceration on right calf. No nausea, vomiting or diarrhea. Man ate supper, breakfast, juice and had lunch and a liberal amount of water on contaminated island prior to removal. Evacuated Rongerik approximately 1200 3-2-54

3-4-54: No symptoms other than a little tiredness. No nausea vomiting or diarrhea.

READING BEFORE DECONTAMINATION	READING AFTER FINISH WASH	READING	READING
~~XXXXX~~ 3-2-54	~~XXXXXXX~~ 3-2-54	3-3-54	3-4-54
250	10 Plus	10	2.5

CBC: 3-2-54
WBC - 12,000
RBC - 4.90
HEMO- 12.4
DIFF - NEUTRO 67, LYMPH 28, EOS 3, BANDS 2

DOWNGRADED TO
CONFIDENTIAL
SECRET
RESTRICTED DATA

(Use additional sheets of this form (Standard Form 502) if more space is required)

SIGNATURE OF PHYSICIAN	DATE	IDENTIFICATION NO.	ORGANIZATION
W. J. Hall, CDR MC USN	3-6-54	11231289	USAF

PATIENT'S LAST NAME—FIRST NAME—MIDDLE NAME | REGISTER NO. | WARD NO.

[redacted] A/1c

INFIRMARY, U S NAVAL STATION, NAVY 824
NAME OF HOSPITAL OR OTHER MEDICAL FACILITY

NARRATIVE SUMMARY
Standard Form 509

This Navy medical report of the examination of an atomic veteran had been classified "secret." He was exposed to radiation on Rongerik Island in the Pacific in 1954. Note that a key piece of data comparing "readings" before and after "decontamination" of radiation were excised by someone in the government before he received his own medical report. His name was deleted by the author.

Sample FOIA and Privacy Act Request Letters

Your address
Phone number
Date

Freedom of Information Office
Agency
Address

FOIA Request

Dear FOI Officer:

Pursuant to the federal Freedom of Information Act, 5 U.S.C. 552, I request access to and copies of **(subject description, see chapter 2).**

Optional: I would like to receive the information in electronic **(or microfiche)** format.

I agree to pay reasonable duplication fees for the processing of this request in an amount not to exceed $**(state amount).** However, please notify me prior to your incurring any expenses that exceed that amount.

Please waive any applicable fees. Release of this information is in the public interest because it will contribute significantly to public understanding of government operations and activities **(if applicable).**

If my request is denied in whole or part, I request that you justify all deletions by reference to the specific exemptions of the act. I also expect you to release all segregable portions of otherwise exempt material. I reserve my right to appeal your decision to withhold any information or to deny a waiver of fees.

Please provide expedited review of this request which concerns a matter of urgency **(if applicable, state reasons).** I certify that my statements concerning the need for expedited review are true and correct to the best of my knowledge and belief.

I look forward to your reply within 20 business days, as the statute requires.

Sincerely,

Your signature

PRIVACY ACT REQUEST LETTER

Your address
Phone number
Date

Privacy Act/FOI Act Office
Agency
Address

Privacy Act/FOI Act Request

Dear FOI/PA Officer:

Pursuant to both the Freedom of Information Act, 5 U.S.C. 552, and the Privacy Act, 5 U.S.C. 552a, I seek access to and copies of all records about me which you have in your possession.

To assist with your search for these records, I am providing the following additional information about myself: **full name, social security number, date and place of birth. Also list whatever additional personal data you wish, such as other names used, former places of residence, foreign travel, government and other employment, political activities, etc. Ask for a search of field offices geographically relevant to your experiences and activities.**

If you determine that any portions of these documents are exempt under either of these statutes, I will expect you to release the non-exempt portions to me as the law requires. I reserve the right to appeal any decision to withhold information.

I promise to pay reasonable fees incurred in the copying of these documents up to the amount of $**(amount)**. If the estimated fees are greater than that amount, please contact me by telephone before such expenses are incurred.

If you have any questions regarding this request, please contact me by telephone. Thank you for your assistance. I look forward to receiving your prompt reply.

Sincerely,

Your signature
(must have your
signature notarized for
most agencies).
phone number

APPENDIX C

Sample Vaughn Motion

SAMPLE VAUGHN MOTION

UNITED STATES DISTRICT COURT
FOR *(the District where you have filed)*

YOUR NAME,	)
Plaintiff,	)
v.	) Civil Action No. _____
AGENCY YOU ARE SUING,	)
Defendant.	)

PLAINTIFF'S MOTION TO COMPEL
PREPARATION OF A VAUGHN INDEX

Plaintiff (**your name**) moves this Court for an order requiring Defendant (**name of agency**) to provide within 30 days after services of the Complaint in this action, an itemized, indexed inventory of every agency record or portion thereof responsive to Plaintiff's request which Defendant asserts to be exempt from disclosure, accompanied by a detailed justification statement covering each refusal to release records or portions thereof in accordance with the indexing requirements of <u>Vaughn v. Rosen</u>, 484 F. 2d 820 (D.C. Cir. 1973), <u>cert. denied</u>, 415 U.S. 977 (1974).

Sincerely,

<u>Your signature</u>
Name
Address

Dated: (**date**)

NOTES

Introduction: SECRECY AND DEMOCRACY

1. Information Security Oversight Office, *1996 Report to the President* (Washington, D.C.: Information and Security Oversight Office, 1996), ii.
2. James Bamford, *The Puzzle Palace* (New York: Penguin Books, 1983), 92–93.
3. Commission on Protecting and Reducing Governmental Secrecy, *Report of the Commission on Protecting and Reducing Governmental Secrecy* (Washington, D.C.: U.S. Government Printing Office, 1997).
4. Nicholas Lemann, "Lawyers Take Advantage of Freedom of Information," *Washington Post,* July 1, 1980.
5. Guy Benvenisti, *The Politics of Expertise* (Berkeley, Calif.: Glendessary Press, 1972), 124–25.
6. Evan Thomas, "Bureaucratic Secrecy Reform," *Newsweek,* March 17, 1997, 8.
7. Thomas B. Ross and David Wise, *The Invisible Government* (New York: Dell, 1974), 299–300.
8. Quoted in Victor Marchetti and John D. Marks, *The CIA and the Cult of Intelligence* (New York: Dell, 1974), 165.
9. Marchetti and Marks, *CIA and the Cult of Intelligence,* 29.
10. Marchetti and Marks, *CIA and the Cult of Intelligence,* 122.
11. Morris P. Fiorina and Paul E. Peterson, *The New American Democracy* (Needham Heights, Mass.: Allyn and Bacon, 1998), 477.
12. Fiorina and Peterson, *New American Democracy,* quoting Francis E. Roark from "Executive Secrecy: Change and Continuity," in Roark, ed., *Bureaucratic Power in National Policy Makers* (Boston: Little Brown & Co., 1986), 536–37.

Chapter 1: YOUR RIGHT TO KNOW

1. Joseph Cayer and Louis F. Weschler, *Public Administration: Social Change and Adaptive Environment* (New York: St. Martin's Press, 1988), 54.
2. William E. Mullen, *Presidential Power and Politics* (New York: St. Martin's Press, 1976), 80–82.
3. Richard Gid Powers, in introduction to *Secrecy: The American Experience,* by Daniel Patrick Moynihan (New Haven: Yale University Press, 1998), 26.
4. Quoted in David Wise, *The Politics of Lying* (New York: Random House, 1973), 59–60.
5. From Ross Gelbspan, "Reagan Changes in Information Act Under Scrutiny," *Boston Globe,* June 13, 1986, 3.
6. Each state determines its public disclosure process. States vary greatly in their degree of public access. In my home state of Massachusetts, the Public Records Act is perhaps the most pro-disclosure, user-friendly law in the nation. Whether it be a town planning board or the state lottery commission, citizens have broad and speedy access. There are, however, twelve exemptions by which the state can withhold information.

   In Massachusetts, requests can be oral or written. The requester can show up without an appointment and ask for information. Unlike FOIA, where (as we shall see in chapter 2) you get only what you specifically ask for, with no help provided, the Massachusetts "records custodian . . . is expected to use his superior knowledge of the records in his custody to assist the requester in obtaining the desired information." Fees for searching and duplicating are very reasonable, and agencies are "encouraged" to waive them. Records are broadly defined. The Secretary of State's office has a Public Records Division that provides information, a hotline, and enforcement of requesters' rights.

   In sharp contrast to the federal law, disappointed requesters can immediately appeal *outside* the agency, without investing the time and money to go to court. Upon denying a request, the custodian is required by law to inform the requester that he or she can seek redress via the office of the Supervisor of Public Records. The latter acts promptly in having one of its lawyers or legal interns contact the agency and review the case. The mission of this office is to defend the requester's rights.

   The Public Records Supervisor's office can issue an order compelling release or a fee waiver. If the record keeper fails to comply, the Supervisor's Office refers the case to the State Attorney General's Office, which will seek enforcement of the requester's rights in court. Unlike FOIA, where individuals must pursue remedies on their own and at their own expense, Massachusetts provides free legal machinery that works on behalf of the requester at every stage of the process.

The state law is so liberal in its provisions that government could conceivably be slowed if not clogged by tens of thousands of requesters showing up on its doorstep, demanding documents. Yet the statute has not created an oppressive burden for the state bureaucracy. It has fairly low public visibility and is not widely used by average citizens (except my students). Massachusetts has elevated the public right to know far above the priorities of governmental agencies (Mass. Public Records Act, G.L.C 4, 57(26), described in "A Guide to the Massachusetts Public Records Law," Office of the Secretary of State, Public Records Division).

7. Nicholas Lemann, "Lawyers Take Advantage of Freedom of Information," *Washington Post,* Sept. 8, 1968, 5.
8. "Opening Up Those Secrets," *Time,* April 14, 1975, 28–29.
9. "Opening Secrets," 29.
10. "Opening Secrets," 28.
11. John Barron, "Two Laws That Undermine the Law," *Reader's Digest,* April 1980, 53, 57.
12. Leslie Harris, "How the Bush Team Wants to Make it a Crime to Reveal Nonsecrets," *Los Angeles Times,* April 27, 1989, 3.
13. Associated Press, "Secret Label May be Taken from Many Documents," *Boston Globe,* April 18, 1995, 6.
14. Federation of American Scientists, "Secrecy and Government Bulletin," no. 80 (September 1999).
15. George Lardner, Jr., "FBI Exempt from Order on Secrecy," *Washington Post,* July 19, 1998, A1.
16. CIA "Press Release," McLean, Va., October 2, 2000.
17. Tatsha Robertson, "JFK Library Releases 4,500 documents on Foreign Policy Topics," *Boston Globe,* August 24, 2000, A21.
18. Reporters Committee for Freedom of the Press, "How to Use the Federal FOIA Act," 8th ed., 9.
19. Professor Jon Wiener, interview with author, Univ. of California, Irvine, October 12, 2000.
20. Philip H. Melanson, *The Politics of Protection: The U.S. Secret Service in the Terrorist Age* (New York: Praeger, 1984), 109.
21. Mark Fritz, "CIA Opens Its Files on Third Reich Figures," *Boston Globe,* April 27, 2001, A2.
22. Mark Fritz, "Hitler Quirks Detailed in CIA Files," *Boston Globe,* April 28, 2001, 2.
23. Fritz, "CIA Opens Its Files," A2.
24. Fritz, "Hitler Quirks," 2.
25. Fritz, "CIA Opens Its Files," A2.
26. Lardner, "FBI Exempt from Order," A1.
27. Lardner, "FBI Exempt from Order," A1.

Chapter 2: THE USER-UNFRIENDLY LAW

1. The Reporters Committee for Freedom of the Press, "How to Use the Federal FOIA Act," Arlington, Virginia, 8th ed., 1998, 2.
2. Reporters Committee, "How To," 5.
3. These are discussed in William Klaber and Philip H. Melanson, *Shadow Play: The Untold Story of the Robert F. Kennedy Assassination* (New York: St. Martin's Press, 1997).
4. *Bureau of National Affairs v. Department of Justice,* 742 F. 2nd 1077 (Wash., D.C. Cir. Ct. 1983).
5. Philip H. Melanson, "The CIA's Secret Ties to Local Police," *The Nation,* March 26, 1983.
6. Reporters Committee, "How To," 6–7.
7. Department of Justice memo to all federal agency heads, "New FOI Fee Waiver Policy Guidance," issued by the Office of Legal Policy (April 2, 1987). These are the criteria that the Department issued to agencies: (a) the request focuses on "government operations and activities," (b) the release is likely to contribute to understanding of the above, (c) "public understanding" of the subject will result, (d) the increase in public understanding of operations and activities will be "significant," and (e) the requester has limited commercial interest in the release.
8. Reporters Committee, "How To," 6.
9. Athan G. Theoharis, ed., *A Culture of Secrecy* (Lawrence: Univ. Press of Kansas, 1998), 27.
10. CIA Information Act (Public Law 98-447, 98 Stat. 2009, 1984). This statute was the subject of much debate in Congress and in the press.
11. Reporters Committee, "How To," 11.
12. As discussed in Reporters Committee, "How To," 6: in 1989 the high court ruled that the public interest under FOIA was limited to information that told the public what government was doing (government operations and activities). Thus the privacy exemption applied to documents that did not reveal how government works *(Dept. Of Justice v. Reporters Committee for Freedom of the Press).* In 1996 Congress specifically rejected this ruling in its Electronic FOI Improvements Act, asserting that FOIA was intended to encompass "any" purpose—not just how government operates.
13. James X. Dempsey, "The CIA and Secrecy," in *The Culture of Secrecy,* ed. Athan Theoharis (Lawrence: Univ. of Kansas Press, 1998), 55–56; Robert M. Gates, *From the Shadows: The Ultimate Insider's Story of Five Presidents and How They Won the Cold War* (New York: Simon and Schuster, 1996), 19.
14. Morris P. Fiorina and Paul E. Peterson, *The New American Democracy* (Needham Heights, Mass.: Allyn and Bacon, 1998), 477.
15. Although it is primarily organized for working reporters, the Reporters Committee for Freedom of the Press does provide assistance to the public

in its booklet (cited above) and through its hotline advice; the committee's address and hotline number are:

> FOI Service Center
> c/o Reporters Committee for Freedom of the Press
> 1101 Wilson Boulevard, Suite 910
> Arlington, VA 22209
> (703) 807–2100

Two other organizations sometimes provide assistance or expertise on a limited basis, especially in more specialized cases: The American Civil Liberties Union (national headquarters in New York City), and the Center for National Security Studies, Washington, D.C.

The General Services Administration and the Department of Justice put out a detailed publication entitled: "Your Right to Federal Records: Questions and Answers on the Freedom of Information Act and the Privacy Act." It is available on the Internet at:

> http://www.pueblo.gsa.gov/cic_text/fed_prog/foia/foia.txt

Another source is the National Security Archive, which pursues disclosure of records relating to foreign and defense policy:

> The National Security Archive
> Gelman Library, Suite 701
> 2130 H Street, N.W.
> Washington, D.C. 20037
> Phone: (202) 944–7005
> Website: http://www.nsarchive.org/ *or*
>   http://www.gwu.edu/~nsarchiv/

There are numerous websites that have information about these laws and that suggest additional governmental and private organizations that provide information and/or assistance.

Chapter 3: DOCUMENTS ABOUT YOU

1. Anthony Summers, *Official and Confidential: The Secret Life of J. Edgar Hoover* (New York: Putnam's, 1993), 142.
2. Frank Donner, *The Age of Surveillance* (New York: Random House, 1981), 78–84.
3. Donner, *Age of Surveillance,* 147–78.
4. Donner, *Age of Surveillance,* 275.
5. Donner, *Age of Surveillance,* 270. Morton Halperin et al., *The Lawless State* (New York: Penguin Books, 1976), 136–43.
6. Charles Trueheart, "Electronic Eavesdropping Led by U.S. Has Europeans Up in Arms," *Boston Globe,* April 13, 2000, A23.
7. Tom Raum, "CIA, NSA Are Not Spying on Average Americans, Officials Testify," *Boston Globe,* April 13, 2000, A23.

8. Natalie Robbins, "The FBI's Invasion of Libraries," *The Nation,* April 9, 1988, 1.
9. Robbins, *FBI's Invasion,* 18.
10. "Pentagon Cuts Tally of Korean War Dead," *Boston Globe,* June 5, 2000, A12.
11. Morton Halperin et al., *The Lawless State* (New York: Penguin Books, 1976, 146 (Congress of Racial Equality); *Report to the President by the Commission on CIA Activities within the United States* (Rockefeller Commission) (New York: Manor Books, 1976), 153. Using FOIA, journalist Steve Tomkins obtained documents from Army Intelligence that attested to the presence of the U-2 and the Green Berets. The Privacy Act's purpose is to give individuals access to their own records.
12. "Privacy" is much broader than the problems discussed here. It relates to a wide range of constitutional, legal, and policy issues: video surveillance in the workplace, mandatory drug testing, law enforcement incursions into the home, private sexual practices, access to medical and educational records, Internet invasions, credit reports, school searches for drugs and guns, adoption information, zealous media attention, snooping by private detectives, telephone taps, and escalating technology (for example, night-vision scopes, satellite surveillance, parabolic microphones, miniature bugging devices, hidden cameras).

    Most analysts agree that in both the public and private sectors, the technology for gathering and circulating information on individuals has outstripped legal protections of privacy. The disagreements concern the size of this gap and what should be done to correct it. "Privacy" is a complex topic affected by hundreds of laws and policies. Some of the major statutes that attempt to regulate the gathering and use of information about people are:

    The Fair Credit Reporting Act of 1970
    The Educational Rights and Privacy Act of 1974
    The Video Privacy Protection Act of 1982
    The Employee Polygraph Protection Act of 1988
    The Cable Act (extending privacy rights to cable and to cellular phones)
    The Children's On Line Privacy Protection Act of 1998

    These and the hundreds of other laws are much like FOIA and the Privacy Act: they grapple with ever-changing issues in complicated arenas of law and politics. Each privacy statute has its strengths and weaknesses. Each attempts to broker the conflict between those entities that gather and use information and the individuals affected by these functions. For a survey of privacy issues and court cases, see Ellen Alderman and Caroline Kennedy, *The Right to Privacy* (New York: Knopf, 1995).

13. U.S. General Services Administration, "Your Right to Federal Records," November 1996, 7–12.

14. This account is taken from George O'Toole, *The Private Sector* (New York: Norton, 1978), 127–48; Donner, *Age of Surveillance,* 426–27.

15. "FBI Is Concerned About Crime Files," *Washington Post,* November 26, 1978, 7.

16. Bill Richards, "U.S. Funded Police Unit Spied on Activists, Documents Show," Washington Post, September 22, 1978, A24.

17. O'Toole, *Private Sector,* 128.

18. O'Toole, *Private Sector,* 135.

19. O'Toole, *Private Sector,* 128.

20. Donner, *Age of Surveillance,* 426.

21. Michigan Coalition to End Government Spying, "Proof of LEIU Political Focus" (newsletter), September 1978, 2.

22. Michigan Coalition, "Proof of LEIU," 2.

23. O'Toole, *Private Sector,* 131.

24. Reporters Committee for Freedom of the Press, "How to Use the Federal FOIA Act," 8th ed., 1998, 13.

25. *Report of the Commission on Governmental Secrecy* (Washington, D.C.: U.S. Government Printing Office, 1957), 57–58.

26. One of the earliest, most perceptive treatments of this issue was Robert B. McKay's "The Right of Confrontation," *Washington Law Quarterly,* 122 (1959): 146–60.

27. Michael Paulson, "Cushing, FBI Linked," *Boston Globe,* April 13, 2000, B1.

28. Paulson, "Cushing, FBI," B1.

29. See David Garrow, *The FBI and Martin Luther King, Jr.* (New York: Penguin Books, 1983); Philip H. Melanson, *The Martin Luther King Assassination* (New York: Shapolski, 1991), 2, 18–19; Summers, *Official and Confidential,* 352–61.

30. Garrow, *FBI and Martin Luther King,* 10–11.

31. Summers, *Official and Confidential,* 355.

32. Summers, *Official and Confidential,* 358.

33. Summers, *Official and Confidential,* 132.

34. Garrow, *FBI and Martin Luther King,* 182.

35. Summers, *Official and Confidential,* 349.

36. Sixty pages of CIA documents pertaining to its surveillance of the Civil Rights Movement during the 1960s were released in 1994 by President Clinton's Assassination Records Review Board, which was overseeing disclosure of files on President Kennedy's assassination. Belafonte was prominently featured in the documents, along with Dr. King. This was not the Belafonte CIA file, which has not, to the author's knowledge, been made public. The documents were provided to the author by attorney Dan Alcorn.

37. John Marks, *The Search for the Manchurian Candidate* (New York: McGraw-Hill, 1980), 23–26.

38. Athan G. Theoharis, ed., *A Culture of Secrecy* (Lawrence: Univ. Press of Kansas, 1998), introduction, 3.

39. Alan Charns and Peter Green, "Playing the Information Game: How it Took Thirteen Years and Two Lawsuits to Get J. Edgar Hoover's Secret Supreme Court Sex Files," in Theoharis, *Culture of Secrecy,* 103–104.

40. "Did FBI Take Groucho Seriously? You Bet Your Life," *Boston Globe,* October 13, 1998, A1.

41. "FBI Kept Watch on Henry Wallace," *New York Times,* September 6, 1983, A18, quoting documents originally obtained by the *Des Moines Register.*

42. Anthony Summers, *Goddess: The Secret Lives of Marilyn Monroe* (New York: Signet, 1985), 61.

43. Summers, *Goddess,* 181.

44. Summers, *Official and Confidential,* 299.

45. Summers, *Goddess,* 459.

46. Jon Wiener, *John Lennon and His Time* (New York: Random House, 1984).

47. Lori Moody, "Give History a Chance," Los Angeles *Daily News,* September 10, 1991, appearing in *The Providence Journal,* B1; Jon Wiener, *Gimme Some Truth: The John Lennon FBI Files* (Berkeley: Univ. of California Press, 1999).

48. Wiener, *Gimme Some Truth,* 2.

49. Wiener, *Gimme Some Truth,* 2.

50. Wiener, *Gimme Some Truth,* 3.

51. Wiener, *Gimme Some Truth,* 13.

52. Wiener, *Gimme Some Truth,* 289 (reprint of FBI document).

53. Wiener, *Gimme Some Truth,* 240–41 (reprints of censored and uncensored document).

54. Philip H. Melanson: *Spy Saga: Lee Harvey Oswald and U.S. Intelligence* (New York: Praeger, 1990), 143.

55. Melanson, *Spy Saga; The Martin Luther King Assassination* (New York: Shapolski, 1991); *The Politics of Protection: The U.S. Secret Service in the Terrorist Age* (New York: Praeger, 1984); *The Robert F. Kennedy Assassination, New Revelations on the Conspiracy and Cover-up, 1968–1991* (New York: Shapolski, 1991).

Chapter 4: BLACKOUTS

1. Thomas Powers, *The Man Who Kept the Secrets: Richard Helms and the CIA* (New York: Pocket Books, 1979), 382.

2. Dana Milbank and Eric Pianin, "Bush's Panel on Energy Works Off the Record," *Boston Globe* April 17, 2001, A2.

3. Milbank and Pianin, A2.
4. Milbank and Pianin, A2.
5. For an analysis of Foreman's role, see Howard Weisberg, *Martin Luther King: The Assassination* (New York: Carroll & Graff Publishers, 1969), 62–87, 93–120. The documents on Foreman were obtained by the author from the Assassination Archives and Research Center, Washington, D.C.
6. "Missouri Fire Ruins Data on Veterans," *New York Times,* July 13, 1973, 20.
7. J. D. Kilgore (Assistant Director for Military Records, General Services Administration), letter to researcher Sandra Marlow, January 16, 1978.
8. "Missouri Fire Ruins Data."
9. Professor Barton Hacker, letter to researcher Sandra Marlow, April 26, 1984.
10. "Pentagon Says Most Logs Missing on Gulf War Chemical Weapons," *Boston Globe,* February 28, 1997, A11.
11. "Pentagon Says Logs Missing," A11.
12. Athan G. Theoharis, ed., *A Culture of Secrecy* (Lawrence: Univ. Press of Kansas, 1998), 10–11.
13. Philip H. Melanson, *The Robert F. Kennedy Assassination: New Revelations on the Conspiracy and Cover-up, 1968–1991* (New York: Shapolski, 1991), 92–98.
14. Thomas H. Karamessines, "Summary Report on CIA Investigation of HKNAOMI." Deputy Director for Plans, declassified September 15, 1975.
15. Victor Marchetti and John D. Marks, *The CIA and the Cult of Intelligence* (New York: Dell, 1974), 44–73.
16. Powers, *Man Who Kept Secrets,* 82.
17. David Wise and Thomas B. Ross, *Invisible Government* (New York: Vintage Books, 1974), 1.
18. Wise and Ross, *Invisible Government,* 351.
19. U.S. Senate, Select Committee to Study Government Operations with Respect to Intelligence. *Final Report,* 1976 (known as the Church Committee Report), Section I.
20. Morton Halperin et al., *The Lawless State* (New York: Penguin Books, 1976), 46.
21. "Secret Pentagon Programs Questioned," *Boston Globe,* April 14, 1986, 5.
22. "Secret Pentagon Programs," 5.
23. Michael Kranish, "The Spy Satellite Complex: White Elephant or Cash Cow?" *Boston Globe,* August 14, 1994, 8.
24. Mike Rothmiller and Ivan G. Goldman, *L.A. Secret Police* (New York: Pocket Books, 1992). The documents were described and quoted by Rothmiller, but were not reproduced in his book. Thus, the descriptions of OCID files are his and not this author's.
25. Rothmiller and Goldman, *L.A. Secret Police,* 107–110.

26. Quoted in Anthony Summers, *Official and Confidential: The Secret Life of J. Edgar Hoover* (New York: Putnam's, 1993), 260.
27. Summers, *Official and Confidential,* 12.
28. Summers, *Official and Confidential,* 423.
29. Summers, *Official and Confidential,* 423.
30. Haynes Johnson, *Bay of Pigs* (New York: Norton, 1964); Anthony Summers, *Conspiracy* (New York: McGraw-Hill, 1980), 254–57.
31. Summers, *Conspiracy,* 254–57.
32. "The CIA: Policy Maker or Tool," *New York Times,* April 25, 1966, 1.
33. Peter Wyden, *Bay of Pigs: The Untold Story* (New York: Simon and Schuster, 1979), 30 (note).
34. Wyden, *Bay of Pigs,* 30 (note).
35. *Final Report to the Taylor Commission,* 1961 (Taylor Report), quoted in Wyden, *Bay of Pigs,* 317.
36. National Security Archive Electronic Briefing Book no. 29, "The Ultrasensitive Bay of Pigs," May 3, 2000. http://www.nsarchive.org/, 1.
37. Briefing Book no. 29, 2.
38. Wyden, *Bay of Pigs,* 322–24.
39. Wyden, *Bay of Pigs,* 322.

Chapter 5: FRONTLINES

1. The following section is based on a telephone interview of Daniel S. Alcorn by the author, September 5, 2000.
2. Ralph Ranalli, "Court Frees Limone after 33 Years in Prison, *Boston Globe,* January, 5, 2001, B3.
3. The following section is based on a telephone interview of Sandra Marlow by the author, September 10, 2000.
4. "House Panel Debates Probe of VA After Records Destroyed," Torrance, Calif., *News Sun Sentinel,* January 11, 1987, 2.
5. The following section is based on a telephone interview of James H. Lesar by the author, September 14, 2000.
6. The following section is based on a telephone interview of Jon Wiener by the author, October 12, 2000.
7. The following section is based on a telephone interview of John Tunheim by the author, November 6, 2000.

Chapter 6: SECRECY WARS

1. Henry Steele Commanger, "Intelligence: The Constitution Betrayed," *New York Review of Books,* September 30, 1976, 34. Quoted in John Newman, *Oswald and the CIA* (New York: Caroll & Graff, 1955), 432.

2. Robert Houghton and Theodore Taylor, *Special Unit Senator* (New York: Random House, 1970).

3. See Mike Rothmiller and Ivan G. Goldman, *L.A. Secret Police* (New York: Pocket Books, 1992).

4. David Freed, "Police Told to Disclose Summary of RFK Case," *Los Angeles Times,* July 31, 1985, 3.

5. Darryl Gates, *Chief: My Life in the LAPD* (New York: Bantam Books, 1992), 152.

6. William Klaber and Philip H. Melanson, *Shadow Play* (New York: St. Martin's Press, 1997), 82.

7. Report of the Select Committee on Assassinations, U.S. House of Representatives, *The Final Assassinations Report* (New York: Bantam, 1979), table of contents (I.C, Kennedy; II.B, King).

8. George Lardner, Jr., "Secrecy Shrouds Assassination Data," *Boston Globe,* May 27, 1981, 28.

9. Lardner, "Secrecy Shrouds."

10. Lardner, "Secrecy Shrouds."

11. Lardner, "Secrecy Shrouds."

12. Lardner, "Secrecy Shrouds."

13. Paul Hoch, ed., *Echoes of Conspiracy* (Berkeley, Calif.), 5, no. 4 (November 16, 1982): 1–2. (privately published newsletter).

14. Hoch, *Echoes of Conspiracy.*

15. *This Week,* ABC television, April 23, 1995.

16. Fairness and Accuracy in Media, newsletter/magazine *Extra* (New York), March 1992, 1; Rather, December 16, 1991.

17. Appointees were: chair, John R. Tunheim, a federal district judge in Minnesota; Professor Henry F. Graf, Columbia University historian; Professor Kermit L. Hall, Ohio State University (history and law); William Joyce, Princeton University archivist; and Professor Anna K. Nelson, a historian at George Washington University. During the board's tenure, I had the opportunity to interact with some of them at several lunches and meetings in my capacity as a member of the executive board of the Coalition on Political Assassinations. Their dedication and understanding of the problems they faced were notable.

18. Anna K. Nelson, "The John F. Kennedy Assassination Records Review Board," in Athan G. Theoharis, ed., *A Culture of Secrecy* (Lawrence: Univ. Press of Kansas, 1998), 224, 229; Tim Wiener, "A Blast at Secrecy in Kennedy Killing," *New York Times,* September 28, 1998; Jon Wiener, *Gimme Some Truth: The John Lennon FBI Files* (Berkeley: Univ. of California Press, 1999), 102–124.

19. Nelson, "Assassination Records," 224.

20. Nelson, "Assassination Records," 224.
21. Nelson, "Assassination Records," 215–20.
22. John Judge telephone discussion with researcher, July 10, 2000.
23. Philip H. Melanson, *Spy Saga: Lee Harvey Oswald and U.S. Intelligence* (New York: Praeger, 1990), based on documentary research into released files, some limited FOIA requests, and a review of the literature on U.S. intelligence agencies in the 1950s and 1960s.
24. See William Pepper, *Orders to Kill* (New York: Carroll & Graf, 1995), 304–305, 316–17, 338–39. Pepper interviewed Thomkins, who provided documents and analysis.
25. Dan Alcorn, telephone discussion with author, July 12, 2000.
26. Thomas Powers, *The Man Who Kept the Secrets: Richard Helms and the CIA* (New York: Pocket Books, 1979), 386.
27. Powers, *Man Who Kept Secrets,* 381–82. See also Franklin L. Ford, *Political Murder* (Cambridge, Mass.: Harvard University Press, 1985), 341, 379.
28. Powers, *Man Who Kept Secrets,* 388–89.
29. National Security Archive (NSA) press release, November 13, 2000, "Chile: 16,000 Secret U.S. Documents Declassified." http://www.nsarchive.org/
30. NSA press release, 2.
31. NSA press release, 3.
32. NSA press release, 3.

Chapter 7: LEAKS FROM THE VAULT
1. "The Pentagon Papers: The Supreme Court Decides" (excerpts from the court's opinion), in Philip H. Melanson, ed., *Knowledge, Politics and Public Policy* (Cambridge, Mass: Winthrop Publishers, 1973), 231.
2. *Secrecy News,* Federation of American Scientists, March 26, 2001.
3. *Secrecy News.*
4. Department of Defense General Counsel William H. Taft IV, letter to House of Representatives' Veterans Affairs Committee, September 4, 1981.
5. In the famous Lau photograph taken just after King was struck, Andrew Young, Ralph Abernathy, and Jesse Jackson are pointing across the street in the direction that they think the shot came from. McCullough, who for years was mistakenly referred to as "a King aid," is kneeling beside Dr. King.
6. Agent William Lawrence, the head of the Bureau's Memphis field office, had worked in Director Hoover's personal office in a supervisory capacity.
7. David Burnham, "14 City Police Got CIA Training," *New York Times,* December, 1972, 23.

Chapter 8: REASONABLE REFORMS
1. Richard P. Longaker, "On the Nature of Governmental Secrecy," reprinted from *The Presidency and Individual Liberties* (Ithaca, N.Y.: Cornell Univ.

Press, 1961), in *Knowledge, Politics, and Public Policy,* ed. Philip H. Melanson (Cambridge, Mass.: Winthrop, 1973).

2. John Lewell, "American Magazine Spreads M16 Secrets to Newsgroups," *Internet-News News Archives,* May 14, 1999, 6.

3. See T. S. Gopi Rethinaraj, "In the Comfort of Secrecy," *Bulletin of Atomic Scientists,* (November/December 1999). In India, their Official Secrets Act places information on the safety of nuclear power plants beyond public access. The data on the country's problem-plagued nuclear facilities is under the same secrecy cloak as its nuclear weapons program.

4. "Official Secrets Act," December 31, 1999, 3.

5. Campaign for Freedom of Information (Great Britain), "Secrets and Lies," August 18, 1998, 2.

6. Rick Snell and Helen Sheridan, "Developments in the United Kingdom White Paper—Your Right to Know," July 23, 2000.

7. Campaign for Freedom of Information, "Secrets and Lies," 2.

8. Snell and Sheridan, "Development," 2.

9. Sarah Lyle, "209 Years Later, the English Get an American-Style Bill of Rights," *New York Times,* October 1, 2000, A3.

10. Campaign for Freedom of Information, "United Kingdom—Developments," July 23, 2000.

11. Tom Raum, "Reno Criticizes Proposal on Classified Data," *Boston Globe,* June 15, 2000, 3.

12. "Reno Backs Criminal Penalties for Leaks," *Boston Globe,* June 19, 2000, 4.

13. Sue Plemming, "White House Weighs Measure to Punish Officials for Leaks," *Boston Globe,* November 1, 2000, A9.

14. Deb Richmann, "Clinton Vetoes Crackdown on Release of Classified Data," *Boston Globe,* November 5, 2000, A3.

15. Richmann, "Clinton Vetoes Crackdown."

16. Richmann, "Clinton Vetoes Crackdown."

17. David Abel, "Critic Accuses Pentagon of Trying to Silence Him," *Boston Globe,* June 24, 2000, 1.

18. In incremental budgeting, an agency's budget for last year becomes its "base" for the current year. The policy debate focuses on whether to increase or decrease the base, not on whether the base is justified. The latter is "zero-based budgeting" in which, rather than exclusively dealing with increments, the entire budget is reassessed from "ground zero." See James E. Anderson, *Public Policy Making* (Boston: Houghton Mifflin, 2000), 175–76.

19. Snell and Sheridan, "Developments," 2.

20. Morton Halperin et al., *The Lawless State* (New York: Penguin Books, 1976), 227.

21. Tim Weiner, "Clinton Acts to Unlock Long-Held Government Secrets from Archives," *New York Times,* May 5, 1993, 5.

22. Reporters Committee for Freedom of the Press, "How to Use the Federal FOIA Act," 8th ed., 1998.
23. Commission on Protecting and Reducing Governmental Secrecy, *Report of the Commission on Protecting and Reducing Governmental Secrecy* (Washington, D.C.: Government Printing Office, 1997), xxi.

    Moynihan's commission made six major recommendations:
    a. Information should remain classified for only ten years, unless an agency reclassifies it and specifically justifies the need for continued secrecy. All thirty-year-old secrets would be automatically declassified unless an agency can show that demonstrable harm would result.
    b. The president will establish procedures for classification and declassification.
    c. Information can only be classified when there is a demonstrated need to protect national security.
    d. In deciding whether to classify, an agency must weigh the benefits of public disclosure versus the needs for secrecy. If significant doubt exists regarding this balance, the data should be disclosed.
    e. There should be a national declassification center to oversee and implement public disclosure.
    f. There will be no authority for agencies to withhold information from Congress.

SELECTED BIBLIOGRAPHY

BOOKS

Adler, Allen, ed. *Litigation Under the Federal Open Government Laws.* Wye Mills, Md.: American Civil Liberties Union, 1997.

Alderman, Ellen, and Caroline Kennedy. *The Right to Privacy.* New York: Knopf, 1995.

Bamford, James. *The Puzzle Palace.* New York: Penguin Books, 1983.

Buitrago, Ann Marie, and Leon A. Immerman. *Are You Now or Have You Ever Been in the FBI Files?* New York: Grove Press, 1981.

Churchill, Ward, and Jim VanderWall. *The Cointelpro Papers.* Boston: South End Press, 1990.

Corson, William. *The Armies of Ignorance: The Rise of U.S. Intelligence Agencies.* New York: Dial Press, 1977.

Donner, Frank. *The Age of Surveillance.* New York: Random House, 1981.

Felt, Mark. *The FBI Pyramid: From the Inside.* New York: Putnam's, 1979.

Garrow, David. *The FBI and Martin Luther King, Jr.* New York: Penguin Books, 1983.

Halperin, Morton H., Jerry J. Berman, Robert L. Borosage, and Christine M. Marwick. *The Lawless State.* New York: Penguin Books, 1976.

Longaker, Richard P. *The Presidency and Individual Liberties.* Ithaca, N.Y.: Cornell University Press, 1961.

Marchetti, Victor, and John D. Marks. *The CIA and the Cult of Intelligence.* New York: Dell, 1974.

Melanson, Philip H. *The Martin Luther King Assassination,* New York: Shapolski, 1991.

———. *The Politics of Protection: The U.S. Secret Service in the Terrorist Age.* New York: Praeger, 1984.

————. *Spy Saga: Lee Harvey Oswald and U.S. Intelligence.* New York: Praeger, 1990.

————, ed. *Knowledge, Politics and Public Policy.* Cambridge, Mass.: Winthrop, 1973.

Mitgang, Herbert. *Dangerous Dossiers: Exposing the Secret War Against America's Greatest Authors.* New York: Ballantine, 1988.

Moynihan, Daniel Patrick. *Secrecy: The American Experience.* New Haven: Yale University Press, 1998.

Olmsted, Kathryn S. *Challenging the Secret Government: The Post-Watergate Investigations of the CIA and FBI.* Chapel Hill: Univ. of North Carolina Press, 1996.

O'Reilly, Kenneth. *Racial Matters: The FBI's Secret Files on Black Americans.* New York: Free Press, 1989.

O'Toole, George. *The Private Sector.* New York: Norton, 1978.

Pessen, Edward. *Losing Our Souls: The American Experience in the Cold War.* Chicago: Ivan R. Dee, 1993.

Powers, Thomas. *The Man Who Kept the Secrets: Richard Helms and the CIA.* New York: Pocket Books, 1979.

Ranelagh, John. *The Rise and Fall of the CIA.* New York: Simon and Schuster, 1986.

Robbins, Natalie. *Alien Ink: The FBI's War on Freedom of Expression.* New York: William Morrow, 1992.

Rositzke, Harry. *The CIA's Secret Operations.* New York: Reader's Digest Press, 1977.

Ross, Thomas B., and David Wise. *The Invisible Government.* New York: Dell, 1974.

Rothmiller, Mike, and Ivan G. Goldman. *L.A. Secret Police.* New York: Pocket Books, 1992.

Shills, Edward. *The Torment of Secrecy.* Glencoe, Ill.: Free Press, 1956.

Summers, Anthony. *Goddess: The Secret Lives of Marilyn Monroe.* New York: Signet, 1985.

————. *Official and Confidential: The Secret Life of J. Edgar Hoover.* New York: Putnam's, 1993.

Theoharis, Athan G. *The FBI: An Annotated Bibliography and Research Guide.* New York: Garland, 1994.

————. *From the Secret Files of J. Edgar Hoover.* Chicago: Ivan R. Dee, 1991.

————, ed. *A Culture of Secrecy.* Lawrence: Univ. Press of Kansas, 1998.

Walsh, Lawrence E. *Firewall: The Iran-Contra Conspiracy and Cover-Up.* New York: Norton, 1997.

Wiener, Jon. *Gimme Some Truth: The John Lennon FBI Files.* Berkeley: Univ. of California Press, 1999.

Wilson, James Q. *Bureaucracy: What Government Agencies Do and Why They Do It.* New York: Basic Books, 1989.

———. *The Investigators: Managing FBI and Narcotics Agents.* New York: Basic Books, 1978.

Wise, David. *The American Police State.* New York: Vintage Books, 1976.

———. *The Politics of Lying.* New York: Random House, 1973.

Wise, David, and Thomas B. Ross. *Invisible Government.* New York: Vintage Books, 1974.

ARTICLES

Abel, David. "Critic Accuses Pentagon of Trying to Silence Him." *Boston Globe,* June 24, 2000.

American Library Association. "Less Access to Less Information by and About the U.S. Government." Washington, D.C.: American Library Association, 1985.

Armstrong, Scott. "The War Over Secrecy: Democracy's Most Important Low Intensity Conflict." *A Culture of Secrecy,* edited by Athan G. Theoharis. Lawrence: Univ. Press of Kansas, 1998.

Associated Press. "Secret Label May Be Taken from Many Documents." *Boston Globe,* April 18, 1995, p. 6.

Barron, John. "Two Laws that Undermine the Law." *Reader's Digest* (April 1980), 53–60.

"Clinton Order Declassifies Millions of Records." *Los Angeles Times,* April 18, 1995.

"Did FBI Take Groucho Seriously? You Bet Your Life." *Boston Globe,* October 13, 1998.

Hall, Kermit L. "JFK's Assassination in an Age of Open Secrets," Bloomington, Ind.: Organization of American Historians, 1997.

Jehl, Douglas. "Clinton Revamps Policy on Secrecy of U.S. Documents." *New York Times,* April 18, 1995.

Jennings, Charles, and Lori Fena. "Privacy Under Siege." *Brill's Content,* May 2000.

Lardner, George, Jr. "FBI Exempt from Order on Secrecy." *Washington Post,* July 19, 1998, A1.

———. "Secrecy Shrouds Assassination Data," *Boston Globe,* May 27, 1981, 28.

Massachusetts Secretary of State. "A Guide to the Massachusetts Public Records Law." Boston: Secretary of State, 1997.

Maxwell, Bruce. "Computers Ease Transfer of Information—Except When Public Access to Government Files is Involved." *Common Cause Magazine,* September/October, 1989.

McKay, Robert B. "The Right of Confrontation." *Washington University Law Quarterly* 122 (1959).

McMasters, Paul, and Eleanor Randolph. "Is U.S. Keeping Too Many Secrets?" *Los Angeles Times,* May 17, 1997.

Melanson, Philip H. "The CIA's Secret Ties to Local Police." *The Nation,* March 26, 1983.

———. "The Human Guinea Pigs at Bikini." *The Nation,* July 9, 1983.

Nelson, Anna K. "The John F. Kennedy Assassination Records Review Board." In *A Culture of Secrecy,* edited by Athan G. Theoharis. Lawrence: Univ. Press of Kansas, 1998.

Paulson, Michael. "Cushing, FBI Linked." *Boston Globe,* April 13, 2000, B1.

"Pentagon Says Most Logs Missing on Gulf War Chemical Weapons." *Boston Globe,* February 28, 1997.

Raines, Howell. "Order Broadens Power to Withhold Information." Fort Worth *Star-Telegram,* April 3, 1982.

Raum, Tom. "CIA, NSA are Not Spying on Average Americans, Officials Testify." *Boston Globe,* April 13, 2000, A1.

Reporters Committee for Freedom of the Press. "How to Use the Federal FOIA Act," 8th ed., 1998.

Robbins, Natalie. "The FBI's Invasion of Libraries." *The Nation,* April 9, 1988.

Ryan, Michael. "Could Someone Steal Your Identity?" *Parade Magazine Sunday Boston Globe,* January 4, 1998.

Schnapper, M. B. "How Reagan Put Wraps on His Records." *Legal Times,* July 17, 1989.

"Things You Can Do [to protect privacy]." *Boston Globe,* September 8, 1993.

Thomas, Evan. "Bureaucratic Secrecy Reform." *Newsweek,* March 17, 1997.

Tye, Larry, and Marla Van Schuyver. "Technology Tests Privacy in the Workplace." *Boston Globe,* November 4, 1995.

U.S. General Services Administration. "Your Right to Know." Washington, D.C., 1996.

Wiener, Tim. "Bills Seek to Slash Number of U.S. Secrets." *New York Times,* March 3, 1994.

———. "A Blast at Secrecy in Kennedy Killing." *New York Times,* September 20, 1998.

Wicklein, John. "Foiled FOIA." *American Journalism Review* (April 1996).

GOVERNMENT REPORTS

Commission on Government Security. *Report of the Commission on Government Security.* Washington, D.C.: Government Printing Office, 1957.

Commission on Protecting and Reducing Governmental Secrecy. *Report of the Commission on Protecting and Reducing Governmental Secrecy.* Washington, D.C.: U.S. Government Printing Office, 1997.

House Committee on Government Operation. *Executive Classification of Information: Security Classification Problems Involving Exemption B1 of FOIA,* 1973.

Information Security Oversight Office, *1996 Report to the President.* Washington, D.C.: Information Security Oversight Office, 1996.

Office of the Press Secretary, White House Press Release, "Remarks by the President on the Fiftieth Anniversary of the CIA, September 16, 1997. http://www.whitehouse.gov/

Report to the President on CIA Activities within the United States (Rockefeller Commission Report). New York: Manor Books, 1976.

U.S. Department of Justice. "Overview of the Privacy Act of 1974." Washington, D.C.: Dept. of Justice, 1997.

U.S. Senate, Select Committee to Study Government Operations with Respect to Intelligence Activities. *Final Report.* (94th Cong. 2nd session), 1976 (known as the "Church Committee Report").

INDEX

ABOUT THE AUTHOR

Philip H. Melanson is a Chancellor Professor of Political Science at the University of Massachusetts-Dartmouth, where he serves as coordinator of the Robert F. Kennedy Assassination Archive (the world's largest collection on the subject) and served as chair of the Political Science Department for twelve years. He has written thirteen books and fourteen articles, most relating to political assassination and violence, governmental secrecy, law enforcement, and intelligence agencies.

Dr. Melanson is an internationally recognized expert in political violence and governmental secrecy. He has lectured widely to varied audiences: colleges and universities, law enforcement conferences, and military installations. He has been a consultant to television and movie productions in the United States, Canada, and Germany. Melanson served as an expert witness or consultant in three court cases involving the release of documents or their financial value.

He has appeared on numerous national television shows, documentaries, and news programs, and more than 100 radio shows, from local to international. His credits include: National Public Radio's *All Things Considered,* the *CBS Evening News, CNN News,* ABC's *Prime Time Live,* CNN's *Both Sides Now, Entertainment Tonight, Hard Copy, Inside Edition,* and BBC Channel 4 *Newsmakers.* His work has been the featured subject of three Associated Press wire stories.

In his roles as author, archival coordinator, and consultant, Dr. Melanson has made more than 100 requests to various agencies for documents and information using the Freedom of Information Act and the Privacy Act. These efforts resulted in the release of approximately 150,000 pages of material obtained over a period of nearly three decades.